COURAGE

BRAVERY

DETERMINATION

THE HARRY POTTER SERIES

In reading order:
Harry Potter and the Philosopher's Stone
Harry Potter and the Chamber of Secrets
Harry Potter and the Prisoner of Azkaban
Harry Potter and the Goblet of Fire
Harry Potter and the Order of the Phoenix
Harry Potter and the Half-Blood Prince
Harry Potter and the Deathly Hallows

Also available in Latin:
Harry Potter and the Philosopher's Stone
Harry Potter and the Chamber of Secrets

Also available in Welsh, Ancient Greek and Irish:
Harry Potter and the Philosopher's Stone

COMPANION VOLUMES

Fantastic Beasts and Where to Find Them
Quidditch Through the Ages
(Published in aid of Comic Relief and Lumos)

The Tales of Beedle the Bard
(Published in aid of Lumos)

The three companion volumes also available as:
The Hogwarts Library
(Published in aid of Comic Relief and Lumos)

ILLUSTRATED EDITIONS

Illustrated by Jim Kay
Harry Potter and the Philosopher's Stone
Harry Potter and the Chamber of Secrets
Harry Potter and the Prisoner of Azkaban

Illustrated by Olivia Lomenech Gill
Fantastic Beasts and Where to Find Them

J.K. ROWLING

Harry Potter

and the Chamber of Secrets

20TH ANNIVERSARY EDITION

BLOOMSBURY
CHILDREN'S BOOKS
LONDON OXFORD NEW YORK NEW DELHI SYDNEY

Bloomsbury Publishing, London, Oxford, New York, New Delhi and Sydney

First published in Great Britain in 1998 by Bloomsbury Publishing Plc
50 Bedford Square, London WC1B 3DP

www.bloomsbury.com

Bloomsbury is a registered trademark of Bloomsbury Publishing Plc

This edition published in 2018

A CIP catalogue record for this book is available from the British Library

Hardback ISBN 978 1 4088 9809 3
1 3 5 7 9 10 8 6 4 2

Paperback ISBN 978 1 4088 9810 9
1 3 5 7 9 10 8 6 4 2

FSC www.fsc.org
MIX
Paper from
responsible sources
FSC® C020471

Typeset by RefineCatch Limited, Bungay, Suffolk
Printed and bound in Great Britain by CPI Group (UK) Ltd, Croydon CR0 4YY

For Séan P. F. Harris,
getaway driver and foulweather friend

GODRIC
GRYFFINDOR

Contents

With house illustrations by Levi Pinfold

GRYFFINDOR

♦ AN INTRODUCTION ♦

'You might belong in Gryffindor,
Where dwell the brave at heart,
Their daring, nerve and chivalry
Set Gryffindors apart'
THE SORTING HAT

BUT FOR AN outstanding act of true Gryffindor daring, Harry Potter wouldn't have made it back to Hogwarts for his second year. Locked in his room by the Dursleys for ruining their dinner party, it looks as though he may be heading for a year spent eating cold soup and rattling the bars on his bedroom window.

In his midnight rescue mission Ron Weasley is ably assisted by his twin brothers, Fred and George. Not many young wizards would have the nerve to borrow their father's enchanted car and fly for miles through the night sky to find out what has happened to a friend.

Gryffindors may be accused at times of pointless heroics, but courage and determination are the key to achieving many things in life, and Fred and George Weasley certainly know how to get things done. Undeterred when they find Harry barricaded into his bedroom, they simply rip the bars off his window to liberate Harry, leaving Vernon Dursley apoplectic with fury.

The twins may infuriate their mother Molly Weasley with their high jinks but their rescue of Harry Potter is a moment to make all Gryffindors proud.

The late and great Sir Nicholas de Mimsy-Porpington, the Gryffindor house ghost, illustrates another characteristic Gryffindor trait: chivalry. In his extravagantly plumed hat, and neck ruff that conceals his dangerously wobbly half-severed neck, Nearly Headless Nick is always a model of courtesy.

His five hundredth Deathday Party provides another memorable Gryffindor moment. Nearly Headless Nick is delighted to welcome the famous Harry Potter to his party, hoping Harry will tell Sir Patrick Delaney-Podmore of the Headless Hunt how very impressive and frightening he is. But the Gryffindor Achilles heel is the tendency to show off, and Nick's efforts to impress are dashed when Sir Patrick guesses he asked Harry to big him up, and then starts a game of Head Hockey in the middle of Nick's speech.

The brave and daring Weasley brothers and chivalrous Nearly Headless Nick – all embody the spirit of Gryffindor. In a year when danger stalks the corridors of Hogwarts, the Gryffindor traits of courage and bravery are needed more than ever as Harry Potter and his friends seek to discover what lies hidden in the Chamber of Secrets.

HOGSMEADE
QUIDDITCH STADIUM
PRACTICE PITCH
BROOM SHED
HOGWARTS SCHOOL
of
WITCHCRAFT + WIZARDRY

FORBIDDEN FOREST
HAGRID'S CABIN
WHOMPING WILLOW
GREENHOUSES
HOGWARTS CASTLE
HOGSMEADE STATION

CHAPTER ONE

The Worst Birthday

Not for the first time, an argument had broken out over breakfast at number four, Privet Drive. Mr Vernon Dursley had been woken in the early hours of the morning by a loud, hooting noise from his nephew Harry's room.

'Third time this week!' he roared across the table. 'If you can't control that owl, it'll have to go!'

Harry tried, yet again, to explain.

'She's *bored*,' he said. 'She's used to flying around outside. If I could just let her out at night ...'

'Do I look stupid?' snarled Uncle Vernon, a bit of fried egg dangling from his bushy moustache. 'I know what'll happen if that owl's let out.'

He exchanged dark looks with his wife, Petunia.

Harry tried to argue back but his words were drowned by a long, loud belch from the Dursleys' son, Dudley.

'I want more bacon.'

'There's more in the frying pan, sweetums,' said Aunt Petunia, turning misty eyes on her massive son. 'We must feed you up while we've got the chance … I don't like the sound of that school food …'

'Nonsense, Petunia, I never went hungry when *I* was at Smeltings,' said Uncle Vernon heartily. 'Dudley gets enough, don't you, son?'

Dudley, who was so large his bottom drooped over either side of the kitchen chair, grinned and turned to Harry.

'Pass the frying pan.'

'You've forgotten the magic word,' said Harry irritably.

The effect of this simple sentence on the rest of the family was incredible: Dudley gasped and fell off his chair with a crash that shook the whole kitchen; Mrs Dursley gave a small scream and clapped her hands to her mouth; Mr Dursley jumped to his feet, veins throbbing in his temples.

'I meant "please"!' said Harry quickly. 'I didn't mean –'

'WHAT HAVE I TOLD YOU,' thundered his uncle, spraying spit over the table, 'ABOUT SAYING THE M WORD IN OUR HOUSE?'

'But I –'

'HOW DARE YOU THREATEN DUDLEY!' roared Uncle Vernon, pounding the table with his fist.

'I just –'

'I WARNED YOU! I WILL NOT TOLERATE MENTION OF YOUR ABNORMALITY UNDER THIS ROOF!'

Harry stared from his purple-faced uncle to his pale aunt, who was trying to heave Dudley to his feet.

'All right,' said Harry, *'all right ...'*

Uncle Vernon sat back down, breathing like a winded rhinoceros and watching Harry closely out of the corners of his small, sharp eyes.

Ever since Harry had come home for the summer holidays, Uncle Vernon had been treating him like a bomb that might go off at any moment, because Harry *wasn't* a normal boy. As a matter of fact, he was as not normal as it is possible to be.

Harry Potter was a wizard – a wizard fresh from his first year at Hogwarts School of Witchcraft and Wizardry. And if the Dursleys were unhappy to have him back for the holidays, it was nothing to how Harry felt.

He missed Hogwarts so much it was like having a constant stomach ache. He missed the castle, with its secret passageways and ghosts, his lessons (though perhaps not Snape, the Potions master), the post arriving by owl, eating banquets in the Great Hall, sleeping in his four-poster bed in the tower dormitory, visiting the gamekeeper, Hagrid, in his cabin in the grounds next to the Forbidden Forest and, especially, Quidditch, the most popular sport in the wizarding world (six tall goalposts, four flying balls and fourteen players on broomsticks).

All Harry's spellbooks, his wand, robes, cauldron and top-of-the-range Nimbus Two Thousand broomstick had been locked in a cupboard under the stairs by Uncle Vernon the instant Harry had come home. What did the Dursleys care if Harry lost his place in the house Quidditch team because he hadn't practised all summer? What was it to the Dursleys if

Harry went back to school without any of his homework done? The Dursleys were what wizards called Muggles (not a drop of magical blood in their veins) and as far as they were concerned, having a wizard in the family was a matter of deepest shame. Uncle Vernon had even padlocked Harry's owl, Hedwig, inside her cage, to stop her carrying messages to anyone in the wizarding world.

Harry looked nothing like the rest of the family. Uncle Vernon was large and neckless, with an enormous black moustache; Aunt Petunia was horse-faced and bony; Dudley was blond, pink and porky. Harry, on the other hand, was small and skinny, with brilliant green eyes and jet-black hair that was always untidy. He wore round glasses, and on his forehead was a thin, lightning-shaped scar.

It was this scar that made Harry so particularly unusual, even for a wizard. This scar was the only hint of Harry's very mysterious past, of the reason he had been left on the Dursleys' doorstep eleven years before.

At the age of one, Harry had somehow survived a curse from the greatest dark sorcerer of all time, Lord Voldemort, whose name most witches and wizards still feared to speak. Harry's parents had died in Voldemort's attack, but Harry had escaped with his lightning scar, and somehow – nobody understood why – Voldemort's powers had been destroyed the instant he had failed to kill Harry.

So Harry had been brought up by his dead mother's sister and her husband. He had spent ten years with the Dursleys, never understanding why he kept making odd things happen without meaning to, believing the Dursleys' story that he had got his scar in the car crash which had killed his parents.

And then, exactly a year ago, Hogwarts had written to Harry, and the whole story had come out. Harry had taken up his place at wizard school, where he and his scar were famous … but now the school year was over, and he was back with the Dursleys for the summer, back to being treated like a dog that had rolled in something smelly.

The Dursleys hadn't even remembered that today happened to be Harry's twelfth birthday. Of course, his hopes hadn't been high; they'd never given him a proper present, let alone a cake – but to ignore it completely …

At that moment, Uncle Vernon cleared his throat importantly and said, 'Now, as we all know, today is a very important day.'

Harry looked up, hardly daring to believe it.

'This could well be the day I make the biggest deal of my career,' said Uncle Vernon.

Harry went back to his toast. Of course, he thought bitterly, Uncle Vernon was talking about the stupid dinner party. He'd been talking of nothing else for a fortnight. Some rich builder and his wife were coming to dinner and Uncle Vernon was hoping to get a huge order from him (Uncle Vernon's company made drills).

'I think we should run through the schedule one more time,' said Uncle Vernon. 'We should all be in position at eight o'clock. Petunia, you will be –?'

'In the lounge,' said Aunt Petunia promptly, 'waiting to welcome them graciously to our home.'

'Good, good. And Dudley?'

'I'll be waiting to open the door.' Dudley put on a foul, simpering smile. 'May I take your coats, Mr and Mrs Mason?'

'They'll *love* him!' cried Aunt Petunia rapturously.

'Excellent, Dudley,' said Uncle Vernon. Then he rounded on Harry. 'And *you*?'

'I'll be in my bedroom, making no noise and pretending I'm not there,' said Harry tonelessly.

'Exactly,' said Uncle Vernon nastily. 'I will lead them into the lounge, introduce you, Petunia, and pour them drinks. At eight fifteen –'

'I'll announce dinner,' said Aunt Petunia.

'And Dudley, you'll say –'

'May I take you through to the dining room, Mrs Mason?' said Dudley, offering his fat arm to an invisible woman.

'My perfect little gentleman!' sniffed Aunt Petunia.

'And *you*?' said Uncle Vernon viciously to Harry.

'I'll be in my room, making no noise and pretending I'm not there,' said Harry dully.

'Precisely. Now, we should aim to get in a few good compliments at dinner. Petunia, any ideas?'

'Vernon tells me you're a *wonderful* golfer, Mr Mason … *Do* tell me where you bought your dress, Mrs Mason …'

'Perfect … Dudley?'

'How about: "We had to write an essay about our hero at school, Mr Mason, and *I* wrote about *you*."'

This was too much for both Aunt Petunia and Harry. Aunt Petunia burst into tears and hugged her son, while Harry ducked under the table so they wouldn't see him laughing.

'And you, boy?'

Harry fought to keep his face straight as he emerged.

'I'll be in my room, making no noise and pretending I'm not there,' he said.

'Too right you will,' said Uncle Vernon forcefully. 'The Masons don't know anything about you and it's going to stay that way. When dinner's over, you take Mrs Mason back to the lounge for coffee, Petunia, and I'll bring the subject round to drills. With any luck, I'll have the deal signed and sealed before the *News at Ten*. We'll be shopping for a holiday home in Majorca this time tomorrow.'

Harry couldn't feel too excited about this. He didn't think the Dursleys would like him any better in Majorca than they did in Privet Drive.

'Right – I'm off into town to pick up the dinner jackets for Dudley and me. And *you*,' he snarled at Harry, 'you stay out of your aunt's way while she's cleaning.'

Harry left through the back door. It was a brilliant, sunny day. He crossed the lawn, slumped down on the garden bench and sang under his breath, 'Happy birthday to me … happy birthday to me …'

No cards, no presents, and he would be spending the evening pretending not to exist. He gazed miserably into the hedge. He had never felt so lonely. More than anything else at Hogwarts, more even than playing Quidditch,

Harry missed his best friends, Ron Weasley and Hermione Granger. They, however, didn't seem to be missing him at all. Neither of them had written to him all summer, even though Ron had said he was going to ask Harry to come and stay.

Countless times, Harry had been on the point of unlocking Hedwig's cage by magic and sending her to Ron and Hermione with a letter, but it wasn't worth the risk. Underage wizards weren't allowed to use magic outside school. Harry hadn't told the Dursleys this; he knew it was only their terror that he might turn them all into dung beetles that stopped them locking *him* in the cupboard under the stairs with his wand and broomstick. For the first couple of weeks back, Harry had enjoyed muttering nonsense words under his breath and watching Dudley tearing out of the room as fast as his fat legs would carry him. But the long silence from Ron and Hermione had made Harry feel so cut off from the magical world that even taunting Dudley had lost its appeal – and now Ron and Hermione had forgotten his birthday.

What wouldn't he give now for a message from Hogwarts? From any witch or wizard? He'd almost be glad of a sight of his arch-enemy, Draco Malfoy, just to be sure it hadn't all been a dream …

Not that his whole year at Hogwarts had been fun. At the very end of last term, Harry had come face to face with none other than Lord Voldemort himself. Voldemort might be a ruin of his former self, but he was still terrifying, still cunning, still determined to regain power. Harry had slipped through Voldemort's clutches for a second time, but it had been a narrow escape, and even now, weeks later, Harry kept waking in the night, drenched in cold sweat, wondering where Voldemort was now, remembering his livid face, his wide, mad eyes …

Harry suddenly sat bolt upright on the garden bench. He had been staring absent-mindedly into the hedge – *and the hedge was staring back.* Two enormous green eyes had appeared among the leaves.

Harry jumped to his feet just as a jeering voice floated across the lawn.

'I know what day it is,' sang Dudley, waddling towards him.

The huge eyes blinked and vanished.

'What?' said Harry, not taking his eyes off the spot where they had been.

'I know what day it is,' Dudley repeated, coming right up to him.

'Well done,' said Harry. 'So you've finally learned the days of the week.'

'Today's your *birthday*,' sneered Dudley. 'How come you haven't got any cards? Haven't you even got friends at that freak place?'

'Better not let your mum hear you talking about my school,' said Harry coolly.

Dudley hitched up his trousers, which were slipping down his fat bottom.

'Why're you staring at the hedge?' he said suspiciously.

'I'm trying to decide what would be the best spell to set it on fire,' said Harry.

Dudley stumbled backwards at once, a look of panic on his fat face.

'You c-can't – Dad told you you're not to do m-magic – he said he'll chuck you out of the house – and you haven't got anywhere else to go – you haven't got any *friends* to take you –'

'Jiggery pokery!' said Harry in a fierce voice. 'Hocus pocus … squiggly wiggly …'

'MUUUUUUM!' howled Dudley, tripping over his feet as he dashed back towards the house. 'MUUUUM! He's doing you know what!'

Harry paid dearly for his moment of fun. As neither Dudley nor the hedge was in any way hurt, Aunt Petunia knew he hadn't really done magic, but he still had to duck as she aimed a heavy blow at his head with the soapy frying pan. Then she gave him work to do, with the promise he wouldn't eat again until he'd finished.

While Dudley lolled around watching and eating ice-creams, Harry cleaned the windows, washed the car, mowed the lawn, trimmed the flowerbeds, pruned and watered the roses and repainted the garden bench. The sun blazed overhead, burning the back of his neck. Harry knew he shouldn't have risen to Dudley's bait, but Dudley had said the very thing Harry had been thinking himself … maybe he *didn't* have any friends at Hogwarts …

'Wish they could see famous Harry Potter now,' he thought savagely, as he spread manure on the flowerbeds, his back aching, sweat running down his face.

It was half past seven in the evening when at last, exhausted, he heard Aunt Petunia calling him.

'Get in here! And walk on the newspaper!'

Harry moved gladly into the shade of the gleaming kitchen. On top of the fridge stood tonight's pudding: a huge mound of whipped cream and sugared violets. A joint of roast pork was sizzling in the oven.

'Eat quickly! The Masons will be here soon!' snapped Aunt Petunia, pointing to two slices of bread and a lump of cheese on the kitchen table. She was already wearing a salmon-pink cocktail dress.

Harry washed his hands and bolted down his pitiful supper. The moment he had finished, Aunt Petunia whisked away his plate. 'Upstairs! Hurry!'

As he passed the door to the living room, Harry caught a glimpse of Uncle Vernon and Dudley in bow-ties and dinner jackets. He had only just reached the upstairs landing when the doorbell rang and Uncle Vernon's furious face appeared at the foot of the stairs.

'Remember, boy – one sound …'

Harry crossed to his bedroom on tiptoe, slipped inside, closed the door and turned to collapse on his bed.

The trouble was, there was already someone sitting on it.

CHAPTER TWO

Dobby's Warning

Harry managed not to shout out, but it was a close thing. The little creature on the bed had large, bat-like ears and bulging green eyes the size of tennis balls. Harry knew instantly that this was what had been watching him out of the garden hedge that morning.

As they stared at each other, Harry heard Dudley's voice from the hall.

'May I take your coats, Mr and Mrs Mason?'

The creature slipped off the bed and bowed so low that the end of its long thin nose touched the carpet. Harry noticed that it was wearing what looked like an old pillowcase, with rips for arm and leg holes.

'Er – hello,' said Harry nervously.

'Harry Potter!' said the creature, in a high-pitched voice Harry was sure would carry down the stairs. 'So long has Dobby wanted to meet you, sir … Such an honour it is …'

'Th-thank you,' said Harry, edging along the wall and sinking into his desk chair, next to Hedwig, who was asleep in her large cage. He wanted to ask, 'What are you?' but thought it would sound too rude, so instead he said, 'Who are you?'

'Dobby, sir. Just Dobby. Dobby the house-elf,' said the creature.

'Oh – really?' said Harry. 'Er – I don't want to be rude or anything, but – this isn't a great time for me to have a house-elf in my bedroom.'

Aunt Petunia's high, false laugh sounded from the living room. The elf hung his head.

'Not that I'm not pleased to meet you,' said Harry quickly, 'but, er, is there any particular reason you're here?'

'Oh, yes, sir,' said Dobby earnestly. 'Dobby has come to tell you, sir … it is difficult, sir … Dobby wonders where to begin …'

'Sit down,' said Harry politely, pointing at the bed.

To his horror, the elf burst into tears – very noisy tears.

'S-sit down!' he wailed. *'Never … never ever …'*

Harry thought he heard the voices downstairs falter.

'I'm sorry,' he whispered, 'I didn't mean to offend you or anything.'

'Offend Dobby!' choked the elf. 'Dobby has *never* been asked to sit down by a wizard – like an *equal* –'

Harry, trying to say 'Shh!' and look comforting at the same time, ushered Dobby back onto the bed, where he sat hiccoughing, looking like a large and very ugly doll. At last he managed to control himself, and sat with his great eyes fixed on Harry in an expression of watery adoration.

'You can't have met many decent wizards,' said Harry, trying to cheer him up.

Dobby shook his head. Then, without warning, he leapt up and started banging his head furiously on the window, shouting, '*Bad* Dobby! *Bad* Dobby!'

'Don't – what are you doing?' Harry hissed, springing up and pulling Dobby back onto the bed. Hedwig had woken up with a particularly loud screech and was beating her wings wildly against the bars of her cage.

'Dobby had to punish himself, sir,' said the elf, who had gone slightly cross-eyed. 'Dobby almost spoke ill of his family, sir …'

'Your family?'

'The wizard family Dobby serves, sir … Dobby is a house-elf – bound to serve one house and one family for ever …'

'Do they know you're here?' asked Harry curiously.

Dobby shuddered.

'Oh no, sir, no … Dobby will have to punish himself most grievously for coming to see you, sir. Dobby will have to shut his ears in the oven door for this. If they ever knew, sir –'

'But won't they notice if you shut your ears in the oven door?'

'Dobby doubts it, sir. Dobby is always having to punish himself for something, sir. They lets Dobby get on with it, sir. Sometimes they reminds me to do extra punishments …'

'But why don't you leave? Escape?'

'A house-elf must be set free, sir. And the family will never set Dobby free … Dobby will serve the family until he dies, sir …'

Harry stared.

'And I thought I was hard-done-by staying here for another four weeks,' he said. 'This makes the Dursleys sound almost human. Can't anyone help you? Can't I?'

Almost at once, Harry wished he hadn't spoken. Dobby dissolved again into wails of gratitude.

'Please,' Harry whispered frantically, 'please be quiet. If the Dursleys hear anything, if they know you're here …'

'Harry Potter asks if he can help Dobby … Dobby has heard of your greatness, sir, but of your goodness, Dobby never knew …'

Harry, who was feeling distinctly hot in the face, said, 'Whatever you've heard about my greatness is a load of rubbish. I'm not even top of my year at Hogwarts, that's Hermione, she –'

But he stopped quickly, because thinking about Hermione was painful.

'Harry Potter is humble and modest,' said Dobby reverently, his orb-like eyes aglow. 'Harry Potter speaks not of his triumph over He Who Must Not Be Named.'

'Voldemort?' said Harry.

Dobby clapped his hands over his bat ears and moaned, 'Ah, speak not the name, sir! Speak not the name!'

'Sorry,' said Harry quickly. 'I know lots of people don't like it – my friend Ron …'

He stopped again. Thinking about Ron was painful, too.

Dobby leaned towards Harry, his eyes wide as headlamps.

'Dobby heard tell,' he said hoarsely, 'that Harry Potter met the Dark Lord for a second time, just weeks ago … that Harry Potter escaped *yet again.*'

Harry nodded and Dobby's eyes suddenly shone with tears.

'Ah, sir,' he gasped, dabbing his face with a corner of the grubby pillowcase he was wearing. 'Harry Potter is valiant and bold! He has braved so many dangers already! But Dobby has come to protect Harry Potter, to warn him, even if he *does* have to shut his ears in the oven door later … *Harry Potter must not go back to Hogwarts.*'

There was a silence broken only by the chink of knives and forks from downstairs and the distant rumble of Uncle Vernon's voice.

'W-what?' Harry stammered. 'But I've got to go back – term starts on September the first. It's all that's keeping me going. You don't know what it's like here. I don't *belong* here. I belong in your world – at Hogwarts.'

'No, no, no,' squeaked Dobby, shaking his head so hard his ears flapped. 'Harry Potter must stay where he is safe. He is too great, too good, to lose. If Harry Potter goes back to Hogwarts, he will be in mortal danger.'

'Why?' said Harry in surprise.

'There is a plot, Harry Potter. A plot to make most terrible things happen at Hogwarts School of Witchcraft and Wizardry this year,' whispered Dobby, suddenly trembling all over.

'Dobby has known it for months, sir. Harry Potter must not put himself in peril. He is too important, sir!'

'What terrible things?' said Harry at once. 'Who's plotting them?'

Dobby made a funny choking noise and then banged his head madly against the wall.

'All right!' cried Harry, grabbing the elf's arm to stop him. 'You can't say, I understand. But why are you warning *me*?' A sudden, unpleasant thought struck him. 'Hang on – this hasn't got anything to do with Vol– sorry – with You-Know-Who, has it? You could just shake or nod,' he added hastily, as Dobby's head tilted worryingly close to the wall again.

Slowly, Dobby shook his head.

'Not – not *He Who Must Not Be Named*, sir.'

But Dobby's eyes were wide and he seemed to be trying to give Harry a hint. Harry, however, was completely at sea.

'He hasn't got a brother, has he?'

Dobby shook his head, his eyes wider than ever.

'Well then, I can't think who else would have a chance of making horrible things happen at Hogwarts,' said Harry. 'I mean, there's Dumbledore, for one thing – you know who Dumbledore is, don't you?'

Dobby bowed his head.

'Albus Dumbledore is the greatest Headmaster Hogwarts has ever had. Dobby knows it, sir. Dobby has heard Dumbledore's powers rival those of He Who Must Not Be Named at the height of his strength. But, sir,' Dobby's voice dropped to an urgent whisper, 'there are powers Dumbledore doesn't … powers no decent wizard …'

And before Harry could stop him, Dobby bounded off the bed, seized Harry's desk lamp and started beating himself around the head with ear-splitting yelps.

A sudden silence fell downstairs. Two seconds later Harry, heart thudding madly, heard Uncle Vernon coming into the hall, calling, 'Dudley must have left his television on again, the little tyke!'

'Quick! In the wardrobe!' hissed Harry, stuffing Dobby in, shutting the door and flinging himself onto the bed just as the door handle turned.

'What – the – *devil* – are – you – doing?' said Uncle Vernon through gritted teeth, his face horribly close to Harry's. 'You've just ruined the punchline of my Japanese-golfer joke … one more sound and you'll wish you'd never been born, boy!'

He stomped flat-footed from the room.

Shaking, Harry let Dobby out of the wardrobe.

'See what it's like here?' he said. 'See why I've got to go back to Hogwarts? It's the only place I've got – well, I *think* I've got friends.'

'Friends who don't even *write* to Harry Potter?' said Dobby slyly.

'I expect they've just been – hang on,' said Harry, frowning. 'How do *you* know my friends haven't been writing to me?'

Dobby shuffled his feet.

'Harry Potter mustn't be angry with Dobby – Dobby did it for the best …'

'Have you been stopping my letters?'

'Dobby has them here, sir,' said the elf. Stepping nimbly out of Harry's reach, he pulled a thick wad of envelopes from the inside of the pillowcase he was wearing. Harry could make out Hermione's neat writing, Ron's untidy scrawl and even a scribble that looked as though it was from the Hogwarts gamekeeper, Hagrid.

Dobby blinked anxiously up at Harry.

'Harry Potter mustn't be angry … Dobby hoped … if Harry Potter thought his friends had forgotten him … Harry Potter might not want to go back to school, sir …'

Harry wasn't listening. He made a grab for the letters, but Dobby jumped out of reach.

'Harry Potter will have them, sir, if he gives Dobby his word that he will not return to Hogwarts. Ah, sir, this is a danger you must not face! Say you won't go back, sir!'

'No,' said Harry angrily. 'Give me my friends' letters!'

'Then Harry Potter leaves Dobby no choice,' said the elf sadly.

Before Harry could move, Dobby had darted to the bedroom door, pulled it open – and sprinted down the stairs.

Mouth dry, stomach lurching, Harry sprang after him, trying not to make a sound. He jumped the last six stairs, landing cat-like on the hall carpet, looking around for Dobby. From the dining room he heard Uncle Vernon saying, '… tell Petunia that very funny story about those American plumbers, Mr Mason, she's been dying to hear …'

Harry ran up the hall into the kitchen and felt his stomach disappear.

Aunt Petunia's masterpiece of a pudding, the mountain of cream and sugared violets, was floating up near the ceiling. On top of a cupboard in the corner crouched Dobby.

'No,' croaked Harry. 'Please ... they'll kill me ...'

'Harry Potter must say he's not going back to school –'

'Dobby ... please ...'

'Say it, sir ...'

'I can't!'

Dobby gave him a tragic look.

'Then Dobby must do it, sir, for Harry Potter's own good.'

The pudding fell to the floor with a heart-stopping crash. Cream splattered the windows and walls as the dish shattered. With a crack like a whip, Dobby vanished.

There were screams from the dining room and Uncle Vernon burst into the kitchen to find Harry, rigid with shock, covered from head to foot in Aunt Petunia's pudding.

At first, it looked as though Uncle Vernon would manage to gloss the whole thing over ('Just our nephew – very disturbed – meeting strangers upsets him, so we kept him upstairs ...') He shooed the shocked Masons back into the dining room, promised Harry he would flay him to within an inch of his life when the Masons had left, and handed him a mop. Aunt Petunia dug some ice-cream out of the freezer and Harry, still shaking, started scrubbing the kitchen clean.

Uncle Vernon might still have been able to make his deal – if it hadn't been for the owl.

Aunt Petunia was just handing round a box of after-dinner mints when a huge barn owl swooped through the dining room window, dropped a letter on Mrs Mason's head and swooped out again. Mrs Mason screamed like a banshee and ran from the house, shouting about lunatics. Mr Mason stayed just long enough to tell the Dursleys that his wife was mortally afraid of birds of all shapes and sizes, and to ask whether this was their idea of a joke.

Harry stood in the kitchen, clutching the mop for support as Uncle Vernon advanced on him, a demonic glint in his tiny eyes.

'Read it!' he hissed evilly, brandishing the letter the owl had delivered. 'Go on – read it!'

Harry took it. It did not contain birthday greetings.

Dear Mr Potter,

We have received intelligence that a Hover Charm was used at your place of residence this evening at twelve minutes past nine.

As you know, underage wizards are not permitted to perform spells outside school, and further spellwork on your part may lead to expulsion from said school (Decree for the Reasonable Restriction of Underage Sorcery, 1875, Paragraph C).

We would also ask you to remember that any magical activity which risks notice by members of the non-magical community (Muggles) is a

serious offence, under section 13 of the International Confederation of Warlocks' Statute of Secrecy.

Enjoy your holidays!

Yours sincerely,

Mafalda Hopkirk

Improper Use of Magic Office

Ministry of Magic

Harry looked up from the letter and gulped.

'You didn't tell us you weren't allowed to use magic outside school,' said Uncle Vernon, a mad gleam dancing in his eyes. 'Forgot to mention it … slipped your mind, I dare say …'

He was bearing down on Harry like a great bulldog, all his teeth bared. 'Well, I've got news for you, boy … I'm locking you up … you're never going back to that school … never … and if you try and magic yourself out – they'll expel you!'

And laughing like a maniac, he dragged Harry back upstairs.

Uncle Vernon was as bad as his word. The following morning, he paid a man to fit bars on Harry's window. He himself fitted the cat-flap in the bedroom door, so that small amounts of food could be pushed inside three times a day. They let Harry out to use the bathroom morning and evening. Otherwise, he was locked in his room around the clock.

* * *

Three days later, the Dursleys were showing no sign of relenting and Harry couldn't see any way out of his situation. He lay on his bed watching the sun sinking behind the bars on the window and wondered miserably what was going to happen to him.

What was the good of magicking himself out of his room if Hogwarts would expel him for doing it? Yet life at Privet Drive had reached an all-time low. Now the Dursleys knew they weren't going to wake up as fruitbats, he had lost his only weapon. Dobby might have saved Harry from horrible happenings at Hogwarts, but the way things were going, he'd probably starve to death anyway.

The cat-flap rattled and Aunt Petunia's hand appeared, pushing a bowl of tinned soup into the room. Harry, whose insides were aching with hunger, jumped off his bed and seized it. The soup was stone cold, but he drank half of it in one gulp. Then he crossed the room to Hedwig's cage and tipped the soggy vegetables at the bottom of the bowl into her empty food tray. She ruffled her feathers and gave him a look of deep disgust.

'It's no good turning your beak up at it, that's all we've got,' said Harry grimly.

He put the empty bowl back on the floor next to the cat-flap and lay back down on the bed, somehow even hungrier than he had been before the soup.

Supposing he was still alive in another four weeks, what would happen if he didn't turn up at Hogwarts? Would someone be sent to see why he hadn't come back? Would they be able to make the Dursleys let him go?

The room was growing dark. Exhausted, stomach rumbling, mind spinning over the same unanswerable questions, Harry fell into an uneasy sleep.

He dreamed that he was on show in a zoo, with a card reading 'Underage Wizard' attached to his cage. People goggled through the bars at him as he lay, starving and weak, on a bed of straw. He saw Dobby's face in the crowd and shouted out, asking for help, but Dobby called, 'Harry Potter is safe there, sir!' and vanished. Then the Dursleys appeared and Dudley rattled the bars of the cage, laughing at him.

'Stop it,' Harry muttered, as the rattling pounded in his sore head. 'Leave me alone … cut it out … I'm trying to sleep …'

He opened his eyes. Moonlight was shining through the bars on the window. And someone *was* goggling through the bars at him: a freckle-faced, red-haired, long-nosed someone.

Ron Weasley was outside Harry's window.

CHAPTER THREE

The Burrow

'Ron!' breathed Harry, creeping to the window and pushing it up so they could talk through the bars. 'Ron, how did you – what the –?'

Harry's mouth fell open as the full impact of what he was seeing hit him. Ron was leaning out of the back window of an old turquoise car, which was parked *in mid-air.* Grinning at Harry from the front seats were Fred and George, Ron's elder twin brothers.

'All right, Harry?'

'What's been going on?' said Ron. 'Why haven't you been answering my letters? I've asked you to stay about twelve times, and then Dad came home and said you'd got an official warning for using magic in front of Muggles ...'

'It wasn't me – and how did he know?'

'He works for the Ministry,' said Ron. 'You *know* we're not supposed to do spells outside school –'

'Bit rich coming from you,' said Harry, staring at the floating car.

'Oh, this doesn't count,' said Ron. 'We're only borrowing this, it's Dad's, *we* didn't enchant it. But doing magic in front of those Muggles you live with ...'

'I told you, I didn't – but it'll take too long to explain now. Look, can you explain to them at Hogwarts that the Dursleys have locked me up and won't let me come back, and obviously I can't magic myself out, because the Ministry'll think that's the second spell I've done in three days, so –'

'Stop gibbering,' said Ron, 'we've come to take you home with us.'

'But you can't magic me out either –'

'We don't need to,' said Ron, jerking his head towards the front seats and grinning. 'You forget who I've got with me.'

'Tie that round the bars,' said Fred, throwing the end of a rope to Harry.

'If the Dursleys wake up, I'm dead,' said Harry, as he tied the rope tightly around a bar and Fred revved up the car.

'Don't worry,' said Fred, 'and stand back.'

Harry moved back into the shadows next to Hedwig, who seemed to have realised how important this was and kept still and silent. The car revved louder and louder and suddenly, with a crunching noise, the bars were pulled clean out of the window as Fred drove straight up in the air – Harry ran back to the window to see the bars dangling a few feet above the ground. Panting, Ron hoisted them up into the car. Harry listened anxiously, but there was no sound from the Dursleys' bedroom.

When the bars were safely in the back seat with Ron, Fred reversed as close as possible to Harry's window.

'Get in,' Ron said.

'But all my Hogwarts stuff … my wand … my broomstick …'

'Where is it?'

'Locked in the cupboard under the stairs, and I can't get out of this room –'

'No problem,' said George from the front passenger seat. 'Out of the way, Harry.'

Fred and George climbed carefully through the window into Harry's room. You had to hand it to them, thought Harry, as George took an ordinary hairpin from his pocket and started to pick the lock.

'A lot of wizards think it's a waste of time, knowing this sort of Muggle trick,' said Fred, 'but we feel they're skills worth learning, even if they are a bit slow.'

There was a small click and the door swung open.

'So – we'll get your trunk – you grab anything you need from your room and hand it out to Ron,' whispered George.

'Watch out for the bottom stair, it creaks,' Harry whispered back, as the twins disappeared onto the dark landing.

Harry dashed around his room, collecting his things together and passing them out of the window to Ron. Then he went to help Fred and George heave his trunk up the stairs. Harry heard Uncle Vernon cough.

At last, panting, they reached the landing, then carried the trunk through Harry's room to the open window. Fred climbed back into the car to pull with Ron, and Harry and George pushed from the bedroom side. Inch by inch, the trunk slid through the window.

Uncle Vernon coughed again.

'A bit more,' panted Fred, who was pulling from inside the car, 'one good push ...'

Harry and George threw their shoulders against the trunk and it slid out of the window into the back seat of the car.

'OK, let's go,' George whispered.

But as Harry climbed onto the window-sill there came a sudden loud screech from behind him, followed immediately by the thunder of Uncle Vernon's voice.

'THAT RUDDY OWL!'

'I've forgotten Hedwig!'

Harry tore back across the room as the landing light clicked on. He snatched up Hedwig's cage, dashed to the window and passed it out to Ron. He was scrambling back onto the chest of drawers when Uncle Vernon hammered on the unlocked door – and it crashed open.

For a split second, Uncle Vernon stood framed in the doorway; then he let out a bellow like an angry bull and dived at Harry, grabbing him by the ankle.

Ron, Fred and George seized Harry's arms and pulled as hard as they could.

'Petunia!' roared Uncle Vernon. 'He's getting away! HE'S GETTING AWAY!'

The Weasleys gave a gigantic tug and Harry's leg slid out of Uncle Vernon's grasp. As soon as Harry was in the car and had slammed the door shut, Ron yelled, 'Put your foot down, Fred!' and the car shot suddenly towards the moon.

Harry couldn't believe it – he was free. He wound down the window, the night air whipping his hair, and looked back at the shrinking rooftops of Privet Drive. Uncle Vernon, Aunt Petunia and Dudley were all hanging, dumbstruck, out of Harry's window.

'See you next summer!' Harry yelled.

The Weasleys roared with laughter and Harry settled back in his seat, grinning from ear to ear.

'Let Hedwig out,' he told Ron, 'she can fly behind us. She hasn't had a chance to stretch her wings for ages.'

George handed the hairpin to Ron and a moment later, Hedwig had soared joyfully out of the window to glide alongside them like a ghost.

'So – what's the story, Harry?' said Ron impatiently. 'What's been happening?'

Harry told them all about Dobby, the warning he'd given Harry and the fiasco of the violet pudding. There was a long shocked silence when he had finished.

'Very fishy,' said Fred finally.

'Definitely dodgy,' agreed George. 'So he wouldn't even tell you who's supposed to be plotting all this stuff?'

'I don't think he could,' said Harry. 'I told you, every time he got close to letting something slip, he started banging his head against the wall.'

He saw Fred and George look at each other.

'What, you think he was lying to me?' said Harry.

'Well,' said Fred, 'put it this way – house-elves have got powerful magic of their own, but they can't usually use it without their masters' permission. I reckon old Dobby was sent to stop you coming back to Hogwarts. Someone's idea of a joke. Can you think of anyone at school with a grudge against you?'

'Yes,' said Harry and Ron together, instantly.

'Draco Malfoy,' Harry explained. 'He hates me.'

'Draco Malfoy?' said George, turning round. 'Not Lucius Malfoy's son?'

'Must be, it's not a very common name, is it?' said Harry. 'Why?'

'I've heard Dad talking about him,' said George. 'He was a big supporter of You-Know-Who.'

'And when You-Know-Who disappeared,' said Fred, craning around to look at Harry, 'Lucius Malfoy came back saying he'd never meant any of it. Load of dung – Dad reckons he was right in You-Know-Who's inner circle.'

Harry had heard these rumours about Malfoy's family before, and they didn't surprise him at all. Draco Malfoy made Dudley Dursley look like a kind, thoughtful and sensitive boy.

'I don't know whether the Malfoys own a house-elf ...' said Harry.

'Well, whoever owns him will be an old wizarding family, and they'll be rich,' said Fred.

'Yeah, Mum's always wishing we had a house-elf to do the ironing,' said George. 'But all we've got is a lousy old ghoul in the attic and gnomes all over the garden. House-elves come with big old manors and castles and places like that, you wouldn't catch one in our house ...'

Harry was silent. Judging by the fact that Draco Malfoy usually had the best of everything, his family was rolling in wizard gold; he could just see Malfoy strutting around a large manor house. Sending the family servant to stop Harry going back to Hogwarts also sounded exactly like the sort of thing Malfoy would do. Had Harry been stupid to take Dobby seriously?

'I'm glad we came to get you, anyway,' said Ron. 'I was getting really worried when you didn't answer any of my letters. I thought it was Errol's fault at first –'

'Who's Errol?'

'Our owl. He's ancient. It wouldn't be the first time he'd collapsed on a delivery. So then I tried to borrow Hermes –'

'*Who?*'

'The owl Mum and Dad bought Percy when he was made a prefect,' said Fred from the front.

'But Percy wouldn't lend him to me,' said Ron. 'Said he needed him.'

'Percy's been acting very oddly this summer,' said George, frowning. 'And he *has* been sending a lot of letters and spending a load of time shut up in his room ... I mean, there's only so many times you can polish a prefect badge ... You're driving too far west, Fred,' he added, pointing at a compass on the dashboard. Fred twiddled the steering wheel.

'So, does your dad know you've got the car?' said Harry, guessing the answer.

'Er, no,' said Ron, 'he had to work tonight. Hopefully we'll be able to get it back in the garage without Mum noticing we flew it.'

'What does your dad do at the Ministry of Magic, anyway?'

'He works in the most boring department,' said Ron. 'The Misuse of Muggle Artefacts Office.'

'The *what?*'

'It's all to do with bewitching things that are Muggle-made, you know, in case they end up back in a Muggle shop or house. Like, last year, some old witch died and her tea set was sold to an antiques shop. This Muggle woman bought it, took it home and tried to serve her friends tea in it. It was a nightmare – Dad was working overtime for weeks.'

'What happened?'

'The teapot went berserk and squirted boiling tea all over the place and one man ended up in hospital with the sugar tongs clamped to his nose. Dad was going frantic, it's only him and an old warlock called Perkins in the office, and they had to do Memory Charms and all sorts to cover it up ...'

'But your dad ... this car ...'

Fred laughed. 'Yeah, Dad's mad about everything to do with Muggles, our shed's full of Muggle stuff. He takes it apart, puts spells on it and puts it back together again. If he raided our house he'd have to put himself straight under arrest. It drives Mum mad.'

'That's the main road,' said George, peering down through the windscreen. 'We'll be there in ten minutes ... just as well, it's getting light ...'

A faint pinkish glow was visible along the horizon to the east.

Fred brought the car lower and Harry saw a dark patchwork of fields and clumps of trees.

'We're a little way outside the village,' said George. 'Ottery St Catchpole ...'

Lower and lower went the flying car. The edge of a brilliant red sun was now gleaming through the trees.

'Touchdown!' said Fred as, with a slight bump, they hit the ground. They had landed next to a tumbledown garage in a small yard and Harry looked out for the first time at Ron's house.

It looked as though it had once been a large stone pigsty, but extra rooms had been added here and there until it was several storeys high and so crooked it looked as though it was held up by magic (which, Harry reminded himself, it probably was). Four or five chimneys were perched on top of the red roof. A lop-sided sign stuck in the ground near the entrance read *The Burrow*. Round the front door lay a jumble of wellington boots and a very rusty cauldron. Several fat brown chickens were pecking their way around the yard.

'It's not much,' said Ron.

'It's *brilliant*,' said Harry happily, thinking of Privet Drive.

They got out of the car.

'Now, we'll go upstairs really quietly,' said Fred, 'and wait for Mum to call us for breakfast. Then Ron, you come bounding downstairs going, "Mum, look who turned up in the night!" and she'll be all pleased to see Harry and no one need ever know we flew the car.'

'Right,' said Ron. 'Come on, Harry, I sleep at the –'

Ron had gone a nasty greenish colour, his eyes fixed on the house. The other three wheeled around.

Mrs Weasley was marching across the yard, scattering chickens, and for a short, plump, kind-faced woman, it was remarkable how much she looked like a sabre-toothed tiger.

'*Ah,*' said Fred.

'Oh dear,' said George.

Mrs Weasley came to a halt in front of them, her hands on her hips, staring from one guilty face to the next. She was wearing a flowered apron with a wand sticking out of the pocket.

'*So,*' she said.

'Morning, Mum,' said George, in what he clearly thought was a jaunty, winning voice.

'Have you any idea how worried I've been?' said Mrs Weasley in a deadly whisper.

'Sorry, Mum, but see, we had to –'

All three of Mrs Weasley's sons were taller than she was, but they cowered as her rage broke over them.

'*Beds empty! No note! Car gone … could have crashed … out of my mind with worry … did you care? … never, as long as I've lived … you wait until your father gets home, we never had trouble like this from Bill or Charlie or Percy …*'

'Perfect Percy,' muttered Fred.

'YOU COULD DO WITH TAKING A LEAF OUT OF PERCY'S BOOK!' yelled Mrs Weasley, prodding a finger in

Fred's chest. 'You could have *died*, you could have been *seen*, you could have lost your father his *job* –'

It seemed to go on for hours. Mrs Weasley had shouted herself hoarse before she turned on Harry, who backed away.

'I'm very pleased to see you, Harry, dear,' she said. 'Come in and have some breakfast.'

She turned and walked back into the house and Harry, after a nervous glance at Ron, who nodded encouragingly, followed her.

The kitchen was small and rather cramped. There was a scrubbed wooden table and chairs in the middle and Harry sat down on the edge of his seat, looking around. He had never been in a wizard house before.

The clock on the wall opposite him had only one hand and no numbers at all. Written around the edge were things like 'Time to make tea', 'Time to feed the chickens' and 'You're late'. Books were stacked three deep on the mantelpiece, books with titles like *Charm Your Own Cheese, Enchantment in Baking* and *One Minute Feasts – It's Magic!* And unless Harry's ears were deceiving him, the old radio next to the sink had just announced that coming up was 'Witching Hour, with the popular singing sorceress, Celestina Warbeck'.

Mrs Weasley was clattering around, cooking breakfast a little haphazardly, throwing dirty looks at her sons as she threw sausages into the frying pan. Every now and then she muttered things like 'don't know *what* you were thinking of' and '*never* would have believed it'.

'I don't blame *you*, dear,' she assured Harry, tipping eight or nine sausages onto his plate. 'Arthur and I have been worried about you, too. Just last night we were saying we'd come and get you ourselves if you hadn't written back to Ron by Friday. But really,' (she was now adding three fried eggs to his plate) 'flying an illegal car halfway across the country – anyone could have seen you –'

She flicked her wand casually at the washing-up in the sink, which began to clean itself, clinking gently in the background.

'It was *cloudy*, Mum!' said Fred.

'You keep your mouth closed while you're eating!' Mrs Weasley snapped.

'They were starving him, Mum!' said George.

'And you!' said Mrs Weasley, but it was with a slightly softened expression that she started cutting Harry bread and buttering it for him.

At that moment, there was a diversion in the form of a small, red-headed figure in a long nightdress, who appeared in the kitchen, gave a small squeal, and ran out again.

'Ginny,' said Ron in an undertone to Harry. 'My sister. She's been talking about you all summer.'

'Yeah, she'll be wanting your autograph, Harry,' grinned Fred, but he caught his mother's eye and bent his face over his plate without another word. Nothing more was said until all four plates were clean, which took a surprisingly short time.

'Blimey, I'm tired,' yawned Fred, setting down his knife and fork at last. 'I think I'll go to bed and –'

'You will not,' snapped Mrs Weasley. 'It's your own fault you've been up all night. You're going to de-gnome the garden for me, they're getting completely out of hand again.'

'Oh, Mum –'

'And you two,' she said, glaring at Ron and George. 'You can go up to bed, dear,' she added to Harry. 'You didn't ask them to fly that wretched car.'

But Harry, who felt wide awake, said quickly, 'I'll help Ron, I've never seen a de-gnoming –'

'That's very sweet of you, dear, but it's dull work,' said Mrs Weasley. 'Now, let's see what Lockhart's got to say on the subject.'

And she pulled a heavy book from the stack on the mantelpiece. George groaned.

'Mum, we know how to de-gnome a garden.'

Harry looked at the cover of Mrs Weasley's book. Written across it in fancy gold letters were the words: *Gilderoy Lockhart's Guide to Household Pests.* There was a big photograph on the front of a very good-looking wizard with wavy blond hair and bright blue eyes. As always in the wizarding world, the photograph was moving; the wizard, who Harry supposed was Gilderoy Lockhart, kept winking cheekily up at them all. Mrs Weasley beamed down at him.

'Oh, he is marvellous,' she said, 'he knows his household pests, all right, it's a wonderful book …'

'Mum fancies him,' said Fred, in a very audible whisper.

'Don't be so ridiculous, Fred,' said Mrs Weasley, her cheeks rather pink. 'All right, if you think you know better than

Lockhart, you can go and get on with it, and woe betide you if there's a single gnome in that garden when I come out to inspect it.'

Yawning and grumbling, the Weasleys slouched outside with Harry behind them. The garden was large and, in Harry's eyes, exactly what a garden should be. The Dursleys wouldn't have liked it – there were plenty of weeds, and the grass needed cutting – but there were gnarled trees all around the walls, plants Harry had never seen spilling from every flowerbed and a big green pond full of frogs.

'Muggles have garden gnomes, too, you know,' Harry told Ron as they crossed the lawn.

'Yeah, I've seen those things they think are gnomes,' said Ron, bent double with his head in a peony bush. 'Like fat little Father Christmases with fishing rods ...'

There was a violent scuffling noise, the peony bush shuddered and Ron straightened up. '*This* is a gnome,' he said grimly.

'Gerroff me! Gerroff me!' squealed the gnome.

It was certainly nothing like Father Christmas. It was small and leathery-looking, with a large, knobbly, bald head exactly like a potato. Ron held it at arm's length as it kicked out at him with its horny little feet; he grasped it around the ankles and turned it upside-down.

'This is what you have to do,' he said. He raised the gnome above his head ('Gerroff me!') and started to swing it in great circles like a lasso. Seeing the shocked look on Harry's face, Ron added, 'It doesn't *hurt* them – you've just got to make them really dizzy so they can't find their way back to the gnomeholes.'

He let go of the gnome's ankles: it flew twenty feet into the air and landed with a thud in the field over the hedge.

'Pitiful,' said Fred. 'I bet I can get mine beyond that stump.'

Harry learned quickly not to feel too sorry for the gnomes. He decided just to drop the first one he caught over the hedge, but the gnome, sensing weakness, sank its razor-sharp teeth into Harry's finger and he had a hard job shaking it off until –

'Wow, Harry – that must've been fifty feet …'

The air was soon thick with flying gnomes.

'See, they're not too bright,' said George, seizing five or six gnomes at once. 'The moment they know the de-gnoming's going on they storm up to have a look. You'd think they'd have learned by now just to stay put.'

Soon, the crowd of gnomes in the field started walking away in a straggling line, their little shoulders hunched.

'They'll be back,' said Ron, as they watched the gnomes disappear into the hedge on the other side of the field. 'They love it here … Dad's too soft with them, he thinks they're funny …'

Just then, the front door slammed.

'He's back!' said George. 'Dad's home!'

They hurried through the garden and back into the house.

Mr Weasley was slumped in a kitchen chair with his glasses off and his eyes closed. He was a thin man, going bald, but the little hair he had was as red as any of his children's. He was wearing long green robes which were dusty and travel-worn.

'What a night,' he mumbled, groping for the teapot as they all sat down around him. 'Nine raids. Nine! And old Mundungus Fletcher tried to put a hex on me when I had my back turned ...'

Mr Weasley took a long gulp of tea and sighed.

'Find anything, Dad?' said Fred eagerly.

'All I got were a few shrinking door-keys and a biting kettle,' yawned Mr Weasley. 'There was some pretty nasty stuff that wasn't my department, though. Mortlake was taken away for questioning about some extremely odd ferrets, but that's the Committee on Experimental Charms, thank goodness ...'

'Why would anyone bother making door-keys shrink?' said George.

'Just Muggle-baiting,' sighed Mr Weasley. 'Sell them a key that keeps shrinking to nothing so they can never find it when they need it ... Of course, it's very hard to convict anyone because no Muggle would admit their key keeps shrinking – they'll insist they just keep losing it. Bless them, they'll go to any lengths to ignore magic, even if it's staring them in the face ... but the things our lot have taken to enchanting, you wouldn't believe –'

'LIKE CARS, FOR INSTANCE?'

Mrs Weasley had appeared, holding a long poker like a sword. Mr Weasley's eyes jerked open. He stared guiltily at his wife.

'C-cars, Molly, dear?'

'Yes, Arthur, cars,' said Mrs Weasley, her eyes flashing. 'Imagine a wizard buying a rusty old car and telling his wife all he wanted to do with it was take it apart to see how it worked, while *really* he was enchanting it to make it *fly*.'

Mr Weasley blinked.

'Well, dear, I think you'll find that he would be quite within the law to do that, even if, er, he maybe would have done better to, um, tell his wife the truth … There's a loophole in the law, you'll find … as long as he wasn't *intending* to fly the car, the fact that the car *could* fly wouldn't –'

'Arthur Weasley, you made sure there was a loophole when you wrote that law!' shouted Mrs Weasley. 'Just so you could carry on tinkering with all that Muggle rubbish in your shed! And for your information, Harry arrived this morning in the car you weren't intending to fly!'

'Harry?' said Mr Weasley blankly. 'Harry who?'

He looked around, saw Harry and jumped.

'Good Lord, is it Harry Potter? Very pleased to meet you, Ron's told us so much about –'

'Your sons flew that car to Harry's house and back last night!' shouted Mrs Weasley. 'What have you got to say about that, eh?'

'Did you really?' said Mr Weasley eagerly. 'Did it go all right? I-I mean,' he faltered, as sparks flew from Mrs Weasley's eyes, 'that-that was very wrong, boys – very wrong indeed …'

'Let's leave them to it,' Ron muttered to Harry, as Mrs Weasley swelled like a bullfrog. 'Come on, I'll show you my bedroom.'

They slipped out of the kitchen and down a narrow passageway to an uneven staircase, which zigzagged its way up through the house. On the third landing, a door stood ajar. Harry just caught sight of a pair of bright brown eyes staring at him before it closed with a snap.

'Ginny,' said Ron. 'You don't know how weird it is for her to be this shy, she never shuts up normally –'

They climbed two more flights until they reached a door with peeling paint and a small plaque on it, saying 'Ronald's Room'.

Harry stepped in, his head almost touching the sloping ceiling, and blinked. It was like walking into a furnace: nearly everything in Ron's room seemed to be a violent shade of orange: the bedspread, the walls, even the ceiling. Then Harry realised that Ron had covered nearly every inch of the shabby wallpaper with posters of the same seven witches and wizards, all wearing bright orange robes, carrying broomsticks and waving energetically.

'Your Quidditch team?' said Harry.

'The Chudley Cannons,' said Ron, pointing at the orange bedspread, which was emblazoned with two giant black Cs and a speeding cannonball. 'Ninth in the league.'

Ron's school spellbooks were stacked untidily in a corner, next to a pile of comics which all seemed to feature *The Adventures of Martin Miggs, the Mad Muggle.* Ron's magic wand was lying on top of a fish tank full of frogspawn on the window-sill, next to his fat grey rat, Scabbers, who was snoozing in a patch of sun.

Harry stepped over a pack of Self-Shuffling playing cards on the floor and looked out of the tiny window. In the field far below he could see a gang of gnomes sneaking, one by one, back through the Weasleys' hedge. Then he turned to look at Ron, who was watching him almost nervously, as though waiting for his opinion.

'It's a bit small,' said Ron quickly. 'Not like that room you had with the Muggles. And I'm right underneath the ghoul in the attic, he's always banging on the pipes and groaning …'

But Harry, grinning widely, said, 'This is the best house I've ever been in.'

Ron's ears went pink.

CHAPTER FOUR

At Flourish and Blotts

Life at The Burrow was as different as possible from life in Privet Drive. The Dursleys liked everything neat and ordered; the Weasleys' house burst with the strange and unexpected. Harry got a shock the first time he looked in the mirror over the kitchen mantelpiece and it shouted, *'Tuck your shirt in, scruffy!'* The ghoul in the attic howled and dropped pipes whenever he felt things were getting too quiet, and small explosions from Fred and George's bedroom were considered perfectly normal. What Harry found most unusual about life at Ron's, however, wasn't the talking mirror or the clanking ghoul: it was the fact that everybody there seemed to like him.

Mrs Weasley fussed over the state of his socks and tried to force him to eat fourth helpings at every meal. Mr Weasley liked Harry to sit next to him at the dinner table so that he could bombard him with questions about life with Muggles, asking him to explain how things like plugs and the postal service worked.

'*Fascinating!*' he would say, as Harry talked him through using a telephone. '*Ingenious*, really, how many ways Muggles have found of getting along without magic.'

Harry heard from Hogwarts one sunny morning about a week after he had arrived at The Burrow. He and Ron went down to breakfast to find Mr and Mrs Weasley and Ginny already sitting at the kitchen table. The moment she saw Harry, Ginny accidentally knocked her porridge bowl to the floor with a loud clatter. Ginny seemed very prone to knocking things over whenever Harry entered a room. She dived under the table to retrieve the bowl and emerged with her face glowing like the setting sun. Pretending he hadn't noticed this, Harry sat down and took the toast Mrs Weasley offered him.

'Letters from school,' said Mr Weasley, passing Harry and Ron identical envelopes of yellowish parchment, addressed in green ink. 'Dumbledore already knows you're here, Harry – doesn't miss a trick, that man. You two've got them, too,' he added, as Fred and George ambled in, still in their pyjamas.

For a few minutes there was silence as they all read their letters. Harry's told him to catch the Hogwarts Express as usual from King's Cross station on September the first. There was also a list of the new books he'd need for the coming year.

Second-year students will require:
The Standard Book of Spells, Grade 2 by Miranda Goshawk
Break with a Banshee by Gilderoy Lockhart
Gadding with Ghouls by Gilderoy Lockhart
Holidays with Hags by Gilderoy Lockhart

Travels with Trolls by Gilderoy Lockhart
Voyages with Vampires by Gilderoy Lockhart
Wanderings with Werewolves by Gilderoy Lockhart
Year with the Yeti by Gilderoy Lockhart

Fred, who had finished his own list, peered over at Harry's.

'You've been told to get all Lockhart's books, too!' he said. 'The new Defence Against the Dark Arts teacher must be a fan – bet it's a witch.'

At this point, Fred caught his mother's eye and quickly busied himself with the marmalade.

'That lot won't come cheap,' said George, with a quick look at his parents. 'Lockhart's books are really expensive …'

'Well, we'll manage,' said Mrs Weasley, but she looked worried. 'I expect we'll be able to pick up a lot of Ginny's things second-hand.'

'Oh, are you starting at Hogwarts this year?' Harry asked Ginny.

She nodded, blushing to the roots of her flaming hair, and put her elbow in the butter dish. Fortunately no one saw this except Harry, because just then Ron's elder brother Percy walked in. He was already dressed, his Hogwarts prefect badge pinned to his knitted tank top.

'Morning, all,' said Percy briskly. 'Lovely day.'

He sat down in the only remaining chair but leapt up again almost immediately, pulling from underneath him a moulting, grey feather duster – at least, that was what Harry thought it was, until he saw that it was breathing.

'Errol!' said Ron, taking the limp owl from Percy and extracting a letter from under its wing. '*Finally* – he's got Hermione's answer. I wrote to her saying we were going to try and rescue you from the Dursleys.'

He carried Errol to a perch just inside the back door and tried to stand him on it, but Errol flopped straight off again so Ron laid him on the draining board instead, muttering, 'Pathetic.' Then he ripped open Hermione's letter and read it out loud:

Dear Ron, and Harry if you're there,

I hope everything went all right and that Harry is OK and that you didn't do anything illegal to get him out, Ron, because that would get Harry into trouble, too. I've been really worried and if Harry is all right, will you please let me know at once, but perhaps it would be better if you used a different owl, because I think another delivery might finish your one off.

I'm very busy with school work, of course – 'How *can* she be?' said Ron in horror. 'We're on holiday!' – *and we're going to London next Wednesday to buy my new books. Why don't we meet in Diagon Alley?*

Let me know what's happening as soon as you can, love from Hermione.

'Well, that fits in nicely, we can go and get all your things then, too,' said Mrs Weasley, starting to clear the table. 'What're you all up to today?'

Harry, Ron, Fred and George were planning to go up the hill to a small paddock the Weasleys owned. It was surrounded by trees that blocked it from view of the village below, meaning that they could practise Quidditch there, as long as they didn't fly too high. They couldn't use real Quidditch balls, which would have been hard to explain if they had escaped and flown away over the village; instead they threw apples for each other to catch. They took it in turns to ride Harry's Nimbus Two Thousand, which was easily the best broom; Ron's old Shooting Star was often outstripped by passing butterflies.

Five minutes later they were marching up the hill, broomsticks over their shoulders. They had asked Percy if he wanted to join them, but he had said he was busy. Harry had only seen Percy at meal-times so far; he stayed shut in his room the rest of the time.

'Wish I knew what he was up to,' said Fred, frowning. 'He's not himself. His exam results came the day before you did; twelve O.W.L.s and he hardly gloated at all.'

'Ordinary Wizarding Levels,' George explained, seeing Harry's puzzled look. 'Bill got twelve, too. If we're not careful, we'll have another Head Boy in the family. I don't think I could stand the shame.'

Bill was the oldest Weasley brother. He and the next brother, Charlie, had already left Hogwarts. Harry had never met either of them, but knew that Charlie was in Romania, studying dragons, and Bill in Egypt, working for the wizards' bank, Gringotts.

'Dunno how Mum and Dad are going to afford all our school stuff this year,' said George after a while. 'Five sets of Lockhart books! And Ginny needs robes and a wand and everything ...'

Harry said nothing. He felt a bit awkward. Stored in an underground vault at Gringotts in London was a small fortune that his parents had left him. Of course, it was only in the wizarding world that he had money; you couldn't use Galleons, Sickles and Knuts in Muggle shops. He had never mentioned his Gringotts bank account to the Dursleys; he didn't think their horror of anything connected with magic would stretch to a large pile of gold.

Mrs Weasley woke them all early the following Wednesday. After a quick half a dozen bacon sandwiches each, they pulled on their coats and Mrs Weasley took a flowerpot off the kitchen mantelpiece and peered inside.

'We're running low, Arthur,' she sighed. 'We'll have to buy some more today ... ah well, guests first! After you, Harry dear!'

And she offered him the flowerpot.

Harry stared at them all watching him.

'W-what am I supposed to do?' he stammered.

'He's never travelled by Floo powder,' said Ron suddenly. 'Sorry, Harry, I forgot.'

'Never?' said Mr Weasley. 'But how did you get to Diagon Alley to buy your school things last year?'

'I went on the Underground –'

'Really?' said Mr Weasley eagerly. 'Were there *escapators*? How exactly –'

'Not *now*, Arthur,' said Mrs Weasley. 'Floo powder's a lot quicker, dear, but goodness me, if you've never used it before –'

'He'll be all right, Mum,' said Fred. 'Harry, watch us first.'

He took a pinch of glittering powder out of the flowerpot, stepped up to the fire and threw the powder into the flames.

With a roar, the fire turned emerald green and rose higher than Fred, who stepped right into it, shouted, 'Diagon Alley!' and vanished.

'You must speak clearly, dear,' Mrs Weasley told Harry, as George dipped his hand into the flowerpot. 'And mind you get out at the right grate …'

'The right what?' said Harry nervously, as the fire roared and whipped George out of sight too.

'Well, there are an awful lot of wizard fires to choose from, you know, but as long as you've spoken clearly –'

'He'll be fine, Molly, don't fuss,' said Mr Weasley, helping himself to Floo powder too.

'But dear, if he got lost, how would we ever explain to his aunt and uncle?'

'They wouldn't mind,' Harry reassured her. 'Dudley would think it was a brilliant joke if I got lost up a chimney, don't worry about that.'

'Well … all right … you go after Arthur,' said Mrs Weasley. 'Now, when you get into the fire, say where you're going –'

'And keep your elbows tucked in,' Ron advised.

'And your eyes shut,' said Mrs Weasley. 'The soot –'

'Don't fidget,' said Ron. 'Or you might well fall out of the wrong fireplace –'

'But don't panic and get out too early, wait until you see Fred and George.'

Trying hard to bear all this in mind, Harry took a pinch of Floo powder and walked to the edge of the fire. He took a deep breath, scattered the powder into the flames and stepped forward; the fire felt like a warm breeze; he opened his mouth and immediately swallowed a lot of hot ash.

'D-Dia-gon Alley,' he coughed.

It felt as though he was being sucked down a giant plug hole. He seemed to be spinning very fast … the roaring in his ears was deafening … he tried to keep his eyes open but the whirl of green flames made him feel sick … something hard knocked his elbow and he tucked it in tightly, still spinning and spinning … now it felt as though cold hands were slapping his face … squinting through his glasses he saw a blurred stream of fireplaces and snatched glimpses of the rooms beyond … his bacon sandwiches were churning inside him … He closed his eyes again wishing it would stop, and then – he fell, face forward, onto cold stone and felt his glasses shatter.

Dizzy and bruised, covered in soot, he got gingerly to his feet, holding his broken glasses up to his eyes. He was quite alone, but *where* he was, he had no idea. All he could tell was that he was standing in the stone fireplace of what looked like a large, dimly lit wizard's shop – but nothing in here was ever likely to be on a Hogwarts school list.

A glass case nearby held a withered hand on a cushion,

a blood-stained pack of cards and a staring glass eye. Evil-looking masks leered down from the walls, an assortment of human bones lay upon the counter and rusty, spiked instruments hung from the ceiling. Even worse, the dark, narrow street Harry could see through the dusty shop window was definitely not Diagon Alley.

The sooner he got out of here, the better. Nose still stinging where it had hit the hearth, Harry made his way swiftly and silently towards the door, but before he'd got halfway towards it, two people appeared on the other side of the glass – and one of them was the very last person Harry wanted to meet when he was lost, covered in soot and wearing broken glasses: Draco Malfoy.

Harry looked quickly around and spotted a large black cabinet to his left; he shot inside it and pulled the doors to, leaving a small crack to peer through. Seconds later, a bell clanged, and Malfoy stepped into the shop.

The man who followed could only be his father. He had the same pale, pointed face and identical cold grey eyes. Mr Malfoy crossed the shop, looking lazily at the items on display, and rang a bell on the counter before turning to his son and saying, 'Touch nothing, Draco.'

Malfoy, who had reached for the glass eye, said, 'I thought you were going to buy me a present.'

'I said I would buy you a racing broom,' said his father, drumming his fingers on the counter.

'What's the good of that if I'm not in the house team?' said Malfoy, looking sulky and bad-tempered. 'Harry Potter got a

Nimbus Two Thousand last year. Special permission from Dumbledore so he could play for Gryffindor. He's not even that good, it's just because he's *famous* … famous for having a stupid *scar* on his forehead …'

Malfoy bent down to examine a shelf full of skulls.

'… everyone thinks he's so *smart*, wonderful *Potter* with his *scar* and his *broomstick* –'

'You have told me this at least a dozen times already,' said Mr Malfoy, with a quelling look at his son, 'and I would remind you that it is not – prudent – to appear less than fond of Harry Potter, not when most of our kind regard him as the hero who made the Dark Lord disappear – ah, Mr Borgin.'

A stooping man had appeared behind the counter, smoothing his greasy hair back from his face.

'Mr Malfoy, what a pleasure to see you again,' said Mr Borgin in a voice as oily as his hair. 'Delighted – and young Master Malfoy, too – charmed. How may I be of assistance? I must show you, just in today, and very reasonably priced –'

'I'm not buying today, Mr Borgin, but selling,' said Mr Malfoy.

'Selling?' The smile faded slightly from Mr Borgin's face.

'You have heard, of course, that the Ministry is conducting more raids,' said Mr Malfoy, taking a roll of parchment from his inside pocket and unravelling it for Mr Borgin to read. 'I have a few – ah – items at home that might embarrass me, if the Ministry were to call …'

Mr Borgin fixed a pince-nez to his nose and looked down the list.

'The Ministry wouldn't presume to trouble you, sir, surely?'

Mr Malfoy's lip curled.

'I have not been visited yet. The name Malfoy still commands a certain respect, yet the Ministry grows ever more meddlesome. There are rumours about a new Muggle Protection Act – no doubt that flea-bitten, Muggle-loving fool Arthur Weasley is behind it –'

Harry felt a hot surge of anger.

'– and as you see, certain of these poisons might make it *appear* –'

'I understand, sir, of course,' said Mr Borgin. 'Let me see ...'

'Can I have *that*?' interrupted Draco, pointing at the withered hand on its cushion.

'Ah, the Hand of Glory!' said Mr Borgin, abandoning Mr Malfoy's list and scurrying over to Draco. 'Insert a candle and it gives light only to the holder! Best friend of thieves and plunderers! Your son has fine taste, sir.'

'I hope my son will amount to more than a thief or a plunderer, Borgin,' said Mr Malfoy coldly and Mr Borgin said quickly, 'No offence, sir, no offence meant –'

'Though if his school marks don't pick up,' said Mr Malfoy, more coldly still, 'that may indeed be all he is fit for.'

'It's not my fault,' retorted Draco. 'The teachers all have favourites, that Hermione Granger –'

'I would have thought you'd be ashamed that a girl of no wizard family beat you in every exam,' snapped Mr Malfoy.

'Ha!' said Harry under his breath, pleased to see Draco looking both abashed and angry.

'It's the same all over,' said Mr Borgin, in his oily voice. 'Wizard blood is counting for less everywhere –'

'Not with me,' said Mr Malfoy, his long nostrils flaring.

'No, sir, nor with me, sir,' said Mr Borgin, with a deep bow.

'In that case, perhaps we can return to my list,' said Mr Malfoy shortly. 'I am in something of a hurry, Borgin, I have important business elsewhere today.'

They started to haggle. Harry watched nervously as Draco drew nearer and nearer to his hiding place, examining the objects for sale. He paused to examine a long coil of hangman's rope and to read, smirking, the card propped on a magnificent necklace of opals:

Caution : Do Not Touch.
Cursed – Has Claimed the Lives of
Nineteen Muggle Owners to Date.

Draco turned away and saw the cabinet right in front of him. He walked forward … he stretched out his hand for the handle …

'Done,' said Mr Malfoy at the counter. 'Come, Draco!'

Harry wiped his forehead on his sleeve as Draco turned away.

'Good day to you, Mr Borgin, I'll expect you at the manor tomorrow to pick up the goods.'

The moment the door had closed, Mr Borgin dropped his oily manner.

'Good day yourself, *Mister* Malfoy, and if the stories are true, you haven't sold me half of what's hidden in your *manor* ...'

Muttering darkly, Mr Borgin disappeared into a back room. Harry waited for a minute in case he came back, then, quietly as he could, slipped out of the cabinet, past the glass cases and out of the shop door.

Clutching his broken glasses to his face he stared around. He had emerged into a dingy alleyway that seemed to be made up entirely of shops devoted to the Dark Arts. The one he'd just left, Borgin and Burkes, looked like the largest, but opposite was a nasty window display of shrunken heads, and two doors down, a large cage was alive with gigantic black spiders. Two shabby-looking wizards were watching him from the shadow of a doorway, muttering to each other. Feeling jumpy, Harry set off, trying to hold his glasses on straight and hoping against hope he'd be able to find a way out of there.

An old wooden street sign hanging over a shop selling poisonous candles told him he was in Knockturn Alley. This didn't help, as Harry had never heard of such a place. He supposed he hadn't spoken clearly enough through his mouthful of ashes back in the Weasleys' fire. Trying to stay calm, he wondered what to do.

'Not lost are you, my dear?' said a voice in his ear, making him jump.

An aged witch stood in front of him, holding a tray of what looked horribly like whole human fingernails. She leered at him, showing mossy teeth. Harry backed away.

'I'm fine, thanks,' he said. 'I'm just –'

'HARRY! What d'yeh think yer doin' down there?'

Harry's heart leapt. So did the witch; a load of fingernails cascaded down over her feet and she cursed as the massive form of Hagrid, the Hogwarts gamekeeper, came striding towards them, beetle-black eyes flashing over his great bristling beard.

'Hagrid!' Harry croaked in relief. 'I was lost … Floo powder …'

Hagrid seized Harry by the scruff of the neck and pulled him away from the witch, knocking the tray right out of her hands. Her shrieks followed them all the way along the twisting alleyway out into bright sunlight. Harry saw a familiar, snow-white marble building in the distance: Gringotts bank. Hagrid had steered him right into Diagon Alley.

'Yer a mess!' said Hagrid gruffly, brushing soot off Harry so forcefully he nearly knocked him into a barrel of dragon dung outside an apothecary's. 'Skulkin' around Knockturn Alley, I dunno – dodgy place, Harry – don' want no one ter see yeh down there –'

'I realised *that*,' said Harry, ducking as Hagrid made to brush him off again. 'I told you, I was lost – what were you doing down there, anyway?'

'*I* was lookin' fer a Flesh-Eatin' Slug Repellent,' growled Hagrid. 'They're ruinin' the school cabbages. Yer not on yer own?'

'I'm staying with the Weasleys but we got separated,' Harry explained. 'I've got to go and find them ...'

They set off together down the street.

'How come yeh never wrote back ter me?' said Hagrid, as Harry jogged alongside him (he had to take three steps to every stride of Hagrid's enormous boots). Harry explained all about Dobby and the Dursleys.

'Ruddy Muggles,' growled Hagrid. 'If I'd've known –'

'Harry! Harry! Over here!'

Harry looked up and saw Hermione Granger standing at the top of the white flight of steps to Gringotts. She ran down to meet them, her bushy brown hair flying behind her.

'What happened to your glasses? Hello, Hagrid ... Oh, it's *wonderful* to see you two again ... Are you coming into Gringotts, Harry?'

'As soon as I've found the Weasleys,' said Harry.

'Yeh won't have long ter wait,' grinned Hagrid.

Harry and Hermione looked around; sprinting up the crowded street were Ron, Fred, George, Percy and Mr Weasley.

'Harry,' Mr Weasley panted. 'We *hoped* you'd only gone one grate too far ...' He mopped his glistening bald patch. 'Molly's frantic – she's coming now.'

'Where did you come out?' Ron asked.

'Knockturn Alley,' said Hagrid grimly.

'Brilliant!' said Fred and George together.

'We've never been allowed in,' said Ron enviously.

'I should ruddy well think not,' growled Hagrid.

Mrs Weasley now came galloping into view, her handbag swinging wildly in one hand, Ginny just clinging onto the other.

'Oh, Harry – oh, my dear – you could have been anywhere –'

Gasping for breath she pulled a large clothes brush out of her bag and began sweeping off the soot Hagrid hadn't managed to beat away. Mr Weasley took Harry's glasses, gave them a tap of his wand and returned them, good as new.

'Well, gotta be off,' said Hagrid, who was having his hand wrung by Mrs Weasley ('Knockturn Alley! If you hadn't found him, Hagrid!'). 'See yer at Hogwarts!' And he strode away, head and shoulders taller than anyone else in the packed street.

'Guess who I saw in Borgin and Burkes?' Harry asked Ron and Hermione as they climbed the Gringotts steps. 'Malfoy and his father.'

'Did Lucius Malfoy buy anything?' said Mr Weasley sharply behind them.

'No, he was selling.'

'So he's worried,' said Mr Weasley with grim satisfaction. 'Oh, I'd love to get Lucius Malfoy for something …'

'You be careful, Arthur,' said Mrs Weasley sharply, as they were ushered into the bank by a bowing goblin at the door. 'That family's trouble, don't go biting off more than you can chew.'

'So you don't think I'm a match for Lucius Malfoy?' said Mr Weasley indignantly, but he was distracted almost at once by the sight of Hermione's parents, who were standing nervously at the counter that ran all along the great marble hall, waiting for Hermione to introduce them.

'But you're *Muggles*!' said Mr Weasley delightedly. 'We must have a drink! What's that you've got there? Oh, you're changing Muggle money. Molly, look!' He pointed excitedly at the ten-pound notes in Mr Granger's hand.

'Meet you back here,' Ron said to Hermione, as the Weasleys and Harry were led off to their underground vaults by another Gringotts goblin.

The vaults were reached by means of small, goblin-driven carts that sped along miniature train-tracks through the bank's underground tunnels. Harry enjoyed the breakneck journey down to the Weasleys' vault, but felt dreadful, far worse than he had in Knockturn Alley, when it was opened. There was a very small pile of silver Sickles inside, and just one gold Galleon. Mrs Weasley felt right into the corners before sweeping the whole lot into her bag. Harry felt even worse when they reached his vault. He tried to block the contents from view as he hastily shoved handfuls of coins into a leather bag.

Back outside on the marble steps, they all separated. Percy muttered vaguely about needing a new quill. Fred and George had spotted their friend from Hogwarts, Lee Jordan. Mrs Weasley and Ginny were going to a second-hand robe shop. Mr Weasley was insisting on taking the Grangers off to the Leaky Cauldron for a drink.

'We'll all meet at Flourish and Blotts in an hour to buy your school books,' said Mrs Weasley, setting off with Ginny. 'And not one step down Knockturn Alley!' she shouted at the twins' retreating backs.

Harry, Ron and Hermione strolled off along the winding, cobbled street. The bag of gold, silver and bronze jangling cheerfully in Harry's pocket was clamouring to be spent, so he bought three large strawberry and peanut-butter ice-creams which they slurped happily as they wandered up the alley, examining the fascinating shop windows. Ron gazed longingly at a full set of Chudley Cannon robes in the windows of 'Quality Quidditch Supplies' until Hermione dragged them off to buy ink and parchment next door. In Gambol and Japes Wizarding Joke Shop, they met Fred, George and Lee Jordan, who were stocking up on 'Dr Filibuster's Fabulous Wet-Start, No-Heat Fireworks', and in a tiny junk shop full of broken wands, wonky brass scales and old cloaks covered in potion stains they found Percy, deeply immersed in a small and deeply boring book called *Prefects Who Gained Power*.

'A study of Hogwarts Prefects and their later careers,' Ron read aloud off the back cover. 'That sounds *fascinating* ...'

'Go away,' Percy snapped.

'Course, he's very ambitious, Percy, he's got it all planned out ... he wants to be Minister of Magic ...' Ron told Harry and Hermione in an undertone, as they left Percy to it.

An hour later, they headed for Flourish and Blotts. They were by no means the only ones making their way to the bookshop. As they approached it, they saw to their surprise a large crowd jostling outside the doors, trying to get in. The reason for this was proclaimed by a large banner stretched across the upper windows:

Gilderoy Lockhart

will be signing copies of his autobiography

☆ MAGICAL ME ☆

today 12.30 – 4.30 pm

'We can actually meet him!' Hermione squealed. 'I mean, he's written almost the whole booklist!'

The crowd seemed to be made up mostly of witches around Mrs Weasley's age. A harassed-looking wizard stood at the door, saying, 'Calmly, please, ladies ... don't push, there ... mind the books, now ...'

Harry, Ron and Hermione squeezed inside. A long queue wound right to the back of the shop, where Gilderoy Lockhart was signing his books. They each grabbed a copy of *Break with a Banshee*, and sneaked up the line to where the rest of the Weasleys were standing with Mr and Mrs Granger.

'Oh, there you are, good,' said Mrs Weasley. She sounded breathless and kept patting her hair. 'We'll be able to see him in a minute ...'

Gilderoy Lockhart came slowly into view, seated at a table surrounded by large pictures of his own face, all winking and flashing dazzlingly white teeth at the crowd. The real Lockhart was wearing robes of forget-me-not blue which exactly matched his eyes; his pointed wizard's hat was set at a jaunty angle on his wavy hair.

A short, irritable-looking man was dancing around taking photographs with a large black camera that emitted puffs of purple smoke with every blinding flash.

'Out of the way, there,' he snarled at Ron, moving back to get a better shot. 'This is for the *Daily Prophet*.'

'Big deal,' said Ron, rubbing his foot where the photographer had stepped on it.

Gilderoy Lockhart heard him. He looked up. He saw Ron – and then he saw Harry. He stared. Then he leapt to his feet and positively shouted, 'It *can't* be Harry Potter?'

The crowd parted, whispering excitedly. Lockhart dived forward, seized Harry's arm and pulled him to the front. The crowd burst into applause. Harry's face burned as Lockhart shook his hand for the photographer, who was clicking away madly, wafting thick smoke over the Weasleys.

'Nice big smile, Harry,' said Lockhart, through his own gleaming teeth. 'Together, you and I are worth the front page.'

When he finally let go of Harry's hand, Harry could hardly feel his fingers. He tried to sidle back over to the Weasleys, but Lockhart threw an arm around his shoulders and clamped him tightly to his side.

'Ladies and gentlemen,' he said loudly, waving for quiet. 'What an extraordinary moment this is! The perfect moment for me to make a little announcement I've been sitting on for some time!

'When young Harry here stepped into Flourish and Blotts today, he only wanted to buy my autobiography – which I shall be happy to present him now, free of charge –' the crowd applauded again, '– he had *no idea,*' Lockhart continued, giving Harry a little shake that made his glasses slip to the end of his nose, 'that he would shortly be getting much, much more than my book, *Magical Me*. He and his school fellows will, in fact, be getting the real, magical me. Yes, ladies and gentlemen, I have great pleasure and pride in announcing that, this September, I will be taking up the post of Defence Against the Dark Arts teacher at Hogwarts School of Witchcraft and Wizardry!'

The crowd cheered and clapped and Harry found himself being presented with the entire works of Gilderoy Lockhart. Staggering slightly under their weight, he managed to make his way out of the limelight to the edge of the room, where Ginny was standing next to her new cauldron.

'You have these,' Harry mumbled to her, tipping the books into the cauldron. 'I'll buy my own –'

'Bet you loved that, didn't you, Potter?' said a voice Harry had no trouble recognising. He straightened up and found himself face to face with Draco Malfoy, who was wearing his usual sneer.

'*Famous* Harry Potter,' said Malfoy. 'Can't even go into a *bookshop* without making the front page.'

'Leave him alone, he didn't want all that!' said Ginny. It was the first time she had spoken in front of Harry. She was glaring at Malfoy.

'Potter, you've got yourself a *girlfriend*!' drawled Malfoy. Ginny went scarlet as Ron and Hermione fought their way over, both clutching stacks of Lockhart's books.

'Oh, it's you,' said Ron, looking at Malfoy as if he were something unpleasant on the sole of his shoe. 'Bet you're surprised to see Harry here, eh?'

'Not as surprised as I am to see you in a shop, Weasley,' retorted Malfoy. 'I suppose your parents will go hungry for a month to pay for that lot.'

Ron went as red as Ginny. He dropped his books into the cauldron, too, and started towards Malfoy, but Harry and Hermione grabbed the back of his jacket.

'Ron!' said Mr Weasley, struggling over with Fred and George. 'What are you doing? It's mad in here, let's go outside.'

'Well, well, well – Arthur Weasley.'

It was Mr Malfoy. He stood with his hand on Draco's shoulder, sneering in just the same way.

'Lucius,' said Mr Weasley, nodding coldly.

'Busy time at the Ministry, I hear,' said Mr Malfoy. 'All those raids … I hope they're paying you overtime?'

He reached into Ginny's cauldron and extracted, from amidst the glossy Lockhart books, a very old, very battered copy of *A Beginner's Guide to Transfiguration*.

'Obviously not,' he said. 'Dear me, what's the use of being a disgrace to the name of wizard if they don't even pay you well for it?'

Mr Weasley flushed darker than either Ron or Ginny.

'We have a very different idea of what disgraces the name of wizard, Malfoy,' he said.

'Clearly,' said Mr Malfoy, his pale eyes straying to Mr and Mrs Granger, who were watching apprehensively. 'The company you keep, Weasley ... and I thought your family could sink no lower –'

There was a thud of metal as Ginny's cauldron went flying; Mr Weasley had thrown himself at Mr Malfoy, knocking him backwards into a bookshelf. Dozens of heavy spellbooks came thundering down on all their heads; there was a yell of 'Get him, Dad!' from Fred or George; Mrs Weasley was shrieking, 'No, Arthur, no!'; the crowd stampeded backwards, knocking more shelves over; 'Gentlemen, please – please!' cried the assistant and then, louder than all, 'Break it up, there, gents, break it up –'

Hagrid was wading towards them through the sea of books. In an instant he had pulled Mr Weasley and Mr Malfoy apart. Mr Weasley had a cut lip and Mr Malfoy had been hit in the eye by an *Encyclopedia of Toadstools*. He was still holding Ginny's old transfiguration book. He thrust it at her, his eyes glittering with malice.

'Here, girl – take your book – it's the best your father can give you –'

Pulling himself out of Hagrid's grip he beckoned to Draco and swept from the shop.

'Yeh should've ignored him, Arthur,' said Hagrid, almost lifting Mr Weasley off his feet as he straightened his robes. 'Rotten ter the core, the whole family, everyone knows that.

No Malfoy's worth listenin' ter. Bad blood, that's what it is. Come on now – let's get outta here.'

The assistant looked as though he wanted to stop them leaving, but he barely came up to Hagrid's waist and seemed to think better of it. They hurried up the street, the Grangers shaking with fright and Mrs Weasley beside herself with fury.

'A *fine* example to set to your children … *brawling* in public … *what* Gilderoy Lockhart must've thought …'

'He was pleased,' said Fred. 'Didn't you hear him as we were leaving? He was asking that bloke from the *Daily Prophet* if he'd be able to work the fight into his report – said it was all publicity.'

But it was a subdued group who headed back to the fireside in the Leaky Cauldron, where Harry, the Weasleys and all their shopping would be travelling back to The Burrow using Floo powder. They said goodbye to the Grangers, who were leaving the pub for the Muggle street on the other side. Mr Weasley started to ask them how bus stops worked, but stopped quickly at the look on Mrs Weasley's face.

Harry took off his glasses and put them safely in his pocket before helping himself to Floo powder. It definitely wasn't his favourite way to travel.

CHAPTER FIVE

The Whomping Willow

The end of the summer holidays came too quickly for Harry's liking. He was looking forward to getting back to Hogwarts, but his month at The Burrow had been the happiest of his life. It was difficult not to feel jealous of Ron when he thought of the Dursleys and the sort of welcome he could expect next time he turned up in Privet Drive.

On their last evening, Mrs Weasley conjured up a sumptuous dinner which included all of Harry's favourite things, ending with a mouthwatering treacle pudding. Fred and George rounded off the evening with a display of Filibuster fireworks; they filled the kitchen with red and blue stars that bounced from ceiling to wall for at least half an hour. Then it was time for a last mug of hot chocolate and bed.

It took a long while to get started next morning. They were up at cock-crow, but somehow they still seemed to have a great deal to do. Mrs Weasley dashed about in a bad mood looking for spare socks and quills, people kept colliding on the stairs, half-dressed with bits of toast in their hands, and Mr Weasley nearly broke his neck, tripping over a stray chicken as he crossed the yard carrying Ginny's trunk to the car.

Harry couldn't see how eight people, six large trunks, two owls and a rat were going to fit into one small Ford Anglia. He had reckoned, of course, without the special features which Mr Weasley had added.

'Not a word to Molly,' he whispered to Harry as he opened the boot and showed him how it had been magically expanded so that the trunks fitted easily.

When at last they were all in the car, Mrs Weasley glanced into the back seat, where Harry, Ron, Fred, George and Percy were all sitting comfortably side by side, and said, 'Muggles *do* know more than we give them credit for, don't they?' She and Ginny got into the front seat, which had been stretched so that it resembled a park bench. 'I mean, you'd never know it was this roomy from the outside, would you?'

Mr Weasley started up the engine and they trundled out of the yard, Harry turning back for a last look at the house. He barely had time to wonder when he'd see it again when they were back: George had forgotten his box of Filibuster fireworks. Five minutes after that, they skidded to a halt in the yard so that Fred could run in for his broomstick. They had almost reached the motorway when Ginny shrieked that she'd left her diary. By the time she had clambered back into the car, they were running very late, and tempers were running high.

Mr Weasley glanced at his watch and then at his wife.

'Molly, dear –'

'*No*, Arthur.'

'No one would see. This little button here is an Invisibility Booster I installed – that'd get us up in the air – then we fly above the clouds. We'd be there in ten minutes and no one would be any the wiser …'

'I said *no*, Arthur, not in broad daylight.'

They reached King's Cross at a quarter to eleven. Mr Weasley dashed across the road to get trolleys for their trunks and they all hurried into the station.

Harry had caught the Hogwarts Express the previous year. The tricky bit was getting onto platform nine and three-quarters, which wasn't visible to the Muggle eye. What you had to do was walk through the solid barrier dividing platforms nine and ten. It didn't hurt, but it had to be done carefully so that none of the Muggles noticed you vanishing.

'Percy first,' said Mrs Weasley, looking nervously at the clock overhead, which showed they had only five minutes to disappear casually through the barrier.

Percy strode briskly forward and vanished. Mr Weasley went next, Fred and George followed.

'I'll take Ginny and you two come right after us,' Mrs Weasley told Harry and Ron, grabbing Ginny's hand and setting off. In the blink of an eye they were gone.

'Let's go together, we've only got a minute,' Ron said to Harry.

Harry made sure that Hedwig's cage was safely wedged on top of his trunk and wheeled his trolley about to face the barrier. He felt perfectly confident; this wasn't nearly as uncomfortable as using Floo powder. Both of them bent low over the handles of their trolleys and walked purposefully towards the barrier, gathering speed. A few feet away from it, they broke into a run and –

CRASH.

Both trolleys hit the barrier and bounced backwards. Ron's trunk fell off with a loud thump, Harry was knocked off his feet, and Hedwig's cage bounced onto the shiny floor and she rolled away, shrieking indignantly. People all around them stared and a guard nearby yelled, 'What in blazes d'you think you're doing?'

'Lost control of the trolley,' Harry gasped, clutching his ribs as he got up. Ron ran to pick up Hedwig, who was causing such a scene that there was a lot of muttering about cruelty to animals from the surrounding crowd.

'Why can't we get through?' Harry hissed to Ron.

'I dunno –'

Ron looked wildly around. A dozen curious people were still watching them.

'We're going to miss the train,' Ron whispered. 'I don't understand why the gateway's sealed itself …'

Harry looked up at the giant clock with a sickening feeling in the pit of his stomach. Ten seconds … nine seconds …

He wheeled his trolley forward cautiously until it was right against the barrier, and pushed with all his might. The metal remained solid.

Three seconds … two seconds … one second …

'It's gone,' said Ron, sounding stunned. 'The train's left. What if Mum and Dad can't get back through to us? Have you got any Muggle money?'

Harry gave a hollow laugh. 'The Dursleys haven't given me pocket money for about six years.'

Ron pressed his ear to the cold barrier.

'Can't hear a thing,' he said tensely. 'What're we going to do? I don't know how long it'll take Mum and Dad to get back to us.'

They looked around. People were still watching them, mainly because of Hedwig's continuing screeches.

'I think we'd better go and wait by the car,' said Harry. 'We're attracting too much atten–'

'Harry!' said Ron, his eyes gleaming. 'The car!'

'What about it?'

'We can fly the car to Hogwarts!'

'But I thought –'

'We're stuck, right? And we've got to get to school, haven't we? And even underage wizards are allowed to use magic if it's a real emergency, section nineteen or something of the Restriction of Thingy …'

Harry's feeling of panic turned suddenly to excitement.

'Can you fly it?'

'No problem,' said Ron, wheeling his trolley around to face the exit. 'C'mon, let's go, if we hurry we'll be able to follow the Hogwarts Express.'

And they marched off through the crowd of curious Muggles, out of the station and back into the side road where the old Ford Anglia was parked.

Ron unlocked the cavernous boot with a series of taps from his wand. They heaved their trunks back in, put Hedwig on the back seat and got into the front.

'Check no one's watching,' said Ron, starting the ignition with another tap of his wand. Harry stuck his head out of the window: traffic was rumbling along the main road ahead, but their street was empty.

'OK,' he said.

Ron pressed a tiny silver button on the dashboard. The car around them vanished – and so did they. Harry could feel the seat vibrating beneath him, hear the engine, feel his hands on his knees and his glasses on his nose, but for all he could see, he had become a pair of eyeballs, floating a few feet above the ground in a dingy street full of parked cars.

'Let's go,' said Ron's voice from his right.

The ground and the dirty buildings on either side fell away, dropping out of sight as the car rose; in seconds, the whole of London lay, smoky and glittering, below them.

Then there was a popping noise and the car, Harry and Ron reappeared.

'Uh oh,' said Ron, jabbing at the Invisibility Booster. 'It's faulty –'

Both of them pummelled it. The car vanished. Then it flickered back again.

'Hold on!' Ron yelled, and he slammed his foot on the accelerator; they shot straight into the low woolly clouds and everything turned dull and foggy.

'Now what?' said Harry, blinking at the solid mass of cloud pressing in on them from all sides.

'We need to see the train to know what direction to go in,' said Ron.

'Dip back down again – quickly –'

They dropped back beneath the clouds and twisted around in their seats, squinting at the ground –

'I can see it!' Harry yelled. 'Right ahead – there!'

The Hogwarts Express was streaking along below them like a scarlet snake.

'Due north,' said Ron, checking the compass on the dashboard. 'OK, we'll just have to check on it every half an hour or so. Hold on ...' And they shot up through the clouds. A minute later, they burst out into a blaze of sunlight.

It was a different world. The wheels of the car skimmed the sea of fluffy cloud, the sky a bright, endless blue under the blinding white sun.

'All we've got to worry about now are aeroplanes,' said Ron.

They looked at each other and started to laugh; for a long time, they couldn't stop.

It was as though they had been plunged into a fabulous dream. This, thought Harry, was surely the only way to travel: past swirls and turrets of snowy cloud, in a car full of hot, bright sunlight, with a fat pack of toffees in the glove compartment, and the prospect of seeing Fred and George's jealous faces when they landed smoothly and spectacularly on the sweeping lawn in front of Hogwarts castle.

They made regular checks on the train as they flew further and further north, each dip beneath the clouds showing them a different view. London was soon far behind them, replaced by neat green fields which gave way in turn to wide, purplish moors, villages with tiny toy churches and a great city alive with cars like multi-coloured ants.

Several uneventful hours later, however, Harry had to admit that some of the fun was wearing off. The toffees had made them extremely thirsty and they had nothing to drink. He and Ron had pulled off their jumpers, but Harry's T-shirt was sticking to the back of his seat and his glasses kept sliding down to the end of his sweaty nose. He had stopped noticing the fantastic cloud shapes now, and was thinking longingly of the train miles below, where you could buy ice-cold pumpkin juice from a trolley pushed by a plump witch. *Why* hadn't they been able to get onto platform nine and three-quarters?

'Can't be much further, can it?' croaked Ron, hours later still, as the sun started to sink into their floor of cloud, staining it a deep pink. 'Ready for another check on the train?'

It was still right below them, winding its way past a snow-capped mountain. It was much darker beneath the canopy of clouds.

Ron put his foot on the accelerator and drove them upwards again, but as he did so, the engine began to whine.

Harry and Ron exchanged nervous glances.

'It's probably just tired,' said Ron. 'It's never been this far before ...'

And they both pretended not to notice the whining growing louder and louder as the sky became steadily darker. Stars were blossoming in the blackness. Harry pulled his jumper back on, trying to ignore the way the windscreen wipers were now waving feebly, as though in protest.

'Not far,' said Ron, more to the car than to Harry, 'not far now,' and he patted the dashboard nervously.

When they flew back beneath the clouds a little while later, they had to squint through the darkness for a landmark they knew.

'*There!*' Harry shouted, making Ron and Hedwig jump. 'Straight ahead!'

Silhouetted on the dark horizon, high on the cliff over the lake, stood the many turrets and towers of Hogwarts castle.

But the car had begun to shudder and was losing speed.

'Come on,' Ron said cajolingly, giving the steering wheel a little shake, 'nearly there, come on –'

The engine groaned. Narrow jets of steam were issuing from under the bonnet. Harry found himself gripping the edges of his seat very hard as they flew towards the lake.

The car gave a nasty wobble. Glancing out of his window, Harry saw the smooth, black, glassy surface of the water, a mile below. Ron's knuckles were white on the steering wheel. The car wobbled again.

'Come *on*,' Ron muttered.

They were over the lake … the castle was right ahead … Ron put his foot down.

There was a loud clunk, a splutter, and the engine died completely.

'Uh oh,' said Ron, into the silence.

The nose of the car dropped. They were falling, gathering speed, heading straight for the solid castle wall.

'Noooooo!' Ron yelled, swinging the steering wheel around; they missed the dark stone wall by inches as the car turned in a great arc, soaring over the dark greenhouses, then the vegetable patch and then out over the black lawns, losing height all the time.

Ron let go of the steering wheel completely and pulled his wand out of his back pocket.

'STOP! STOP!' he yelled, whacking the dashboard and the windscreen, but they were still plummeting, the ground flying up towards them ...

'MIND THAT TREE!' Harry bellowed, lunging for the steering wheel, but too late –

CRUNCH.

With an ear-splitting bang of metal on wood, they hit the thick tree trunk and dropped to the ground with a heavy jolt. Steam was billowing from under the crumpled bonnet; Hedwig was shrieking in terror, a golf-ball-sized lump was throbbing on Harry's head where he had hit the windscreen, and to his right, Ron let out a low, despairing groan.

'Are you OK?' Harry said urgently.

'My wand,' said Ron, in a shaky voice. 'Look at my wand.'

It had snapped, almost in two; the tip was dangling limply, held on by a few splinters.

Harry opened his mouth to say he was sure they'd be able to mend it up at the school, but he never even got started. At that very moment, something hit his side of the car with the force of a charging bull, sending him lurching sideways into Ron, just as an equally heavy blow hit the roof.

'What's happen–?'

Ron gasped, staring through the windscreen, and Harry looked around just in time to see a branch as thick as a python smash into it. The tree they had hit was attacking them. Its trunk was bent almost double, and its gnarled boughs were pummelling every inch of the car it could reach.

'Aaargh!' said Ron, as another twisted limb punched a large dent into his door; the windscreen was now trembling under a hail of blows from knuckle-like twigs and a branch as thick as a battering ram was pounding furiously on the roof, which seemed to be caving in –

'Run for it!' Ron shouted, throwing his full weight against his door, but next second he had been knocked backwards into Harry's lap by a vicious upper cut from another branch.

'We're done for!' he moaned, as the ceiling sagged, but suddenly the floor of the car was vibrating – the engine had restarted.

'Reverse!' Harry yelled, and the car shot backwards. The tree was still trying to hit them; they could hear its roots creaking as it almost ripped itself up, lashing out at them as they sped out of reach.

'That,' panted Ron, 'was close. Well done, car.'

The car, however, had reached the end of its tether. With two smart clunks, the doors flew open and Harry felt his seat tip sideways: next thing he knew he was sprawled on the damp ground. Loud thuds told him that the car was ejecting their luggage from the boot. Hedwig's cage flew through the air and burst open; she rose out of it with a loud, angry screech and sped off towards the castle without a backwards look. Then, dented, scratched and steaming, the car rumbled off into the darkness, its rear lights blazing angrily.

'Come back!' Ron yelled after it, brandishing his broken wand. 'Dad'll kill me!'

But the car disappeared from view with one last snort from its exhaust.

'Can you *believe* our luck?' said Ron miserably, bending down to pick up Scabbers the rat. 'Of all the trees we could've hit, we had to get one that hits back.'

He glanced over his shoulder at the ancient tree, which was still flailing its branches threateningly.

'Come on,' said Harry wearily, 'we'd better get up to the school ...'

It wasn't at all the triumphant arrival they had pictured. Stiff, cold and bruised, they seized the ends of their trunks and began dragging them up the grassy slope, towards the great oak front doors.

'I think the feast's already started,' said Ron, dropping his trunk at the foot of the front steps and crossing quietly to look through a brightly lit window. 'Hey, Harry, come and look – it's the Sorting!'

Harry hurried over and, together, he and Ron peered in at the Great Hall.

Innumerable candles were hovering in mid-air over four long, crowded tables, making the golden plates and goblets sparkle. Overhead, the bewitched ceiling which always mirrored the sky outside, sparkled with stars.

Through the forest of pointed black Hogwarts hats, Harry saw a long line of scared-looking first-years filing into the Hall. Ginny was amongst them, easily visible because of her vivid Weasley hair. Meanwhile, Professor McGonagall, a bespectacled witch with her hair in a tight bun, was placing the famous Hogwarts Sorting Hat on a stool before the newcomers.

Every year, this aged old hat, patched, frayed and dirty, sorted new students into the four Hogwarts houses (Gryffindor, Hufflepuff, Ravenclaw and Slytherin). Harry well remembered putting it on, exactly one year ago, and waiting, petrified, for its decision as it muttered aloud in his ear. For a few horrible seconds he had feared that the hat was going to put him in Slytherin, the house which had turned out more dark witches and wizards than any other – but he had ended up in Gryffindor, along with Ron, Hermione and the rest of the Weasleys. Last term, Harry and Ron had helped Gryffindor win the House Championship, beating Slytherin for the first time in seven years.

A very small, mousey-haired boy had been called forward to place the hat on his head. Harry's eyes wandered past him to where Professor Dumbledore, the Headmaster, sat watching the Sorting from the staff table, his long silver beard and half-moon glasses shining brightly in the candlelight. Several seats along, Harry saw Gilderoy Lockhart, dressed in robes of aquamarine. And there at the end was Hagrid, huge and hairy, drinking deeply from his goblet.

'Hang on …' Harry muttered to Ron. 'There's an empty chair at the staff table … Where's Snape?'

Professor Severus Snape was Harry's least favourite teacher. Harry also happened to be Snape's least favourite student. Cruel, sarcastic and disliked by everybody except the students from his own house (Slytherin), Snape taught Potions.

'Maybe he's ill!' said Ron hopefully.

'Maybe he's *left*,' said Harry, 'because he missed out on the Defence Against the Dark Arts job *again*!'

'Or he might have been *sacked*!' said Ron enthusiastically. 'I mean, everyone hates him –'

'Or maybe,' said a very cold voice right behind them, 'he's waiting to hear why you two didn't arrive on the school train.'

Harry spun around. There, his black robes rippling in a cold breeze, stood Severus Snape. He was a thin man with sallow skin, a hooked nose and greasy, shoulder-length black hair, and at this moment, he was smiling in a way that told Harry he and Ron were in very deep trouble.

'Follow me,' said Snape.

Not daring even to look at each other, Harry and Ron followed Snape up the steps into the vast, echoing Entrance Hall, which was lit with flaming torches. A delicious smell of food was wafting from the Great Hall, but Snape led them away from the warmth and light, down a narrow stone staircase that led into the dungeons.

'In!' he said, opening a door halfway down the cold passageway and pointing.

They entered Snape's office, shivering. The shadowy walls were lined with shelves of large glass jars, in which floated all manner of revolting things Harry didn't really want to know the name of at the moment. The fireplace was dark and empty. Snape closed the door and turned to look at them.

'So,' he said softly, 'the train isn't good enough for the famous Harry Potter and his faithful sidekick Weasley. Wanted to arrive with a *bang*, did we, boys?'

'No, sir, it was the barrier at King's Cross, it –'

'Silence!' said Snape coldly. 'What have you done with the car?'

Ron gulped. This wasn't the first time Snape had given Harry the impression of being able to read minds. But a moment later, he understood, as Snape unrolled today's issue of the *Evening Prophet*.

'You were seen,' he hissed, showing them the headline: FLYING FORD ANGLIA MYSTIFIES MUGGLES. He began to read aloud. ' "Two Muggles in London, convinced they saw an old car flying over the Post Office tower … at noon in Norfolk, Mrs Hetty Bayliss, while hanging out her washing … Mr Angus Fleet, of Peebles, reported to police" … six or seven Muggles in all. I believe *your* father works in the Misuse of Muggle Artefacts Office?' he said, looking up at Ron and smiling still more nastily. 'Dear, dear … his own son …'

Harry felt as though he'd just been walloped in the stomach by one of the mad tree's larger branches. If anyone found out Mr Weasley had bewitched the car ... he hadn't thought of that ...

'I noticed, in my search of the park, that considerable damage seems to have been done to a very valuable Whomping Willow,' Snape went on.

'That tree did more damage to *us* than we –' Ron blurted out.

'Silence!' snapped Snape again. 'Most unfortunately, you are not in my house and the decision to expel you does not rest with me. I shall go and fetch the people who *do* have that happy power. You will wait here.'

Harry and Ron stared at each other, white-faced. Harry didn't feel hungry any more. He now felt extremely sick. He tried not to look at a large, slimy something suspended in green liquid on a shelf behind Snape's desk. If Snape had gone to fetch Professor McGonagall, Head of Gryffindor house, they were hardly any better off. She might be fairer than Snape, but she was still extremely strict.

Ten minutes later, Snape returned, and sure enough it was Professor McGonagall who accompanied him. Harry had seen Professor McGonagall angry on several occasions, but either he had forgotten just how thin her mouth could go, or he had never seen her this angry before. She raised her wand the moment she entered. Harry and Ron both flinched, but she merely pointed it at the empty fireplace, where flames suddenly erupted.

'Sit,' she said, and they both backed into chairs by the fire.

'Explain,' she said, her glasses glinting ominously.

Ron launched into the story, starting with the barrier at the station refusing to let them through.

'... so we had no choice, Professor, we couldn't get on the train.'

'Why didn't you send us a letter by owl? I believe *you* have an owl?' Professor McGonagall said coldly to Harry.

Harry gaped at her. Now she said it, that seemed the obvious thing to have done.

'I – I didn't think –'

'That,' said Professor McGonagall, 'is obvious.'

There was a knock on the office door and Snape, now looking happier than ever, opened it. There stood the Headmaster, Professor Dumbledore.

Harry's whole body went numb. Dumbledore was looking unusually grave. He stared down his very crooked nose at them and Harry suddenly found himself wishing he and Ron were still being beaten up by the Whomping Willow.

There was a long silence. Then Dumbledore said, 'Please explain why you did this.'

It would have been better if he had shouted. Harry hated the disappointment in his voice. For some reason, he was unable to look Dumbledore in the eyes, and spoke instead to his knees. He told Dumbledore everything except that Mr Weasley owned the bewitched car, making it sound as though he and Ron had happened to find a flying car parked outside the station. He knew Dumbledore would see through this at once, but Dumbledore asked no questions about the car. When Harry had finished, he merely continued to peer at them through his spectacles.

'We'll go and get our stuff,' said Ron in a hopeless sort of voice.

'What are you talking about, Weasley?' barked Professor McGonagall.

'Well, you're expelling us, aren't you?' said Ron.

Harry looked quickly at Dumbledore.

'Not today, Mr Weasley,' said Dumbledore. 'But I must impress upon both of you the seriousness of what you have done. I will be writing to both your families tonight. I must also warn you that if you do anything like this again, I will have no choice but to expel you.'

Snape looked as though Christmas had been cancelled. He cleared his throat and said, 'Professor Dumbledore, these boys have flouted the Decree for the Restriction of Underage Wizardry, caused serious damage to an old and valuable tree ... surely acts of this nature ...'

'It will be for Professor McGonagall to decide on these boys' punishments, Severus,' said Dumbledore calmly. 'They are in her house and are therefore her responsibility.' He turned to Professor McGonagall. 'I must go back to the feast, Minerva, I've got to give out a few notices. Come, Severus, there's a delicious-looking custard tart I want to sample.'

Snape shot a look of pure venom at Harry and Ron as he allowed himself to be swept out of his office, leaving them alone with Professor McGonagall, who was still eyeing them like a wrathful eagle.

'You'd better get along to the hospital wing, Weasley, you're bleeding.'

'Not much,' said Ron, hastily wiping the cut over his eye with his sleeve. 'Professor, I wanted to watch my sister being Sorted –'

'The Sorting Ceremony is over,' said Professor McGonagall. 'Your sister is also in Gryffindor.'

'Oh, good,' said Ron.

'And speaking of Gryffindor –' Professor McGonagall said sharply, but Harry cut in: 'Professor, when we took the car, term hadn't started, so – so Gryffindor shouldn't really have points taken from it, should it?' he finished, watching her anxiously.

Professor McGonagall gave him a piercing look, but he was sure she had almost smiled. Her mouth looked less thin, anyway.

'I will not take any points from Gryffindor,' she said, and Harry's heart lightened considerably. 'But you will both get a detention.'

It was better than Harry had expected. As for Dumbledore's writing to the Dursleys, that was nothing. Harry knew perfectly well they'd just be disappointed that the Whomping Willow hadn't squashed him flat.

Professor McGonagall raised her wand again and pointed it at Snape's desk. A large plate of sandwiches, two silver goblets and a jug of iced pumpkin juice appeared with a *pop*.

'You will eat in here and then go straight up to your dormitory,' she said. 'I must also return to the feast.'

When the door had closed behind her, Ron let out a long, low whistle.

'I thought we'd had it,' he said, grabbing a sandwich.

'So did I,' said Harry, taking one too.

'Can you believe our luck, though?' said Ron thickly through a mouthful of chicken and ham. 'Fred and George must've flown that car five or six times and no Muggle ever saw *them*.' He swallowed and took another huge bite. '*Why* couldn't we get through the barrier?'

Harry shrugged. 'We'll have to watch our step from now on, though,' he said, taking a grateful swig of pumpkin juice. 'Wish we could've gone up to the feast ...'

'She didn't want us showing off,' said Ron sagely. 'Doesn't want people to think it's clever, arriving by flying car.'

When they had eaten as many sandwiches as they could (the plate kept refilling itself) they rose and left the office, treading the familiar path to Gryffindor Tower. The castle was quiet; it seemed that the feast was over. They walked past muttering portraits and creaking suits of armour, and climbed narrow flights of stone stairs, until at last they reached the passage where the secret entrance to Gryffindor Tower was hidden, behind an oil painting of a very fat woman in a pink silk dress.

'Password?' she said, as they approached.

'Er –' said Harry.

They didn't know the new year's password, not having met a Gryffindor Prefect yet, but help came almost immediately;

they heard hurrying feet behind them and turned to see Hermione dashing towards them.

'*There* you are! Where have you *been*? The most *ridiculous* rumours – someone said you'd been expelled for crashing a flying *car*.'

'Well, we haven't been expelled,' Harry assured her.

'You're not telling me you *did* fly here?' said Hermione, sounding almost as severe as Professor McGonagall.

'Skip the lecture,' said Ron impatiently, 'and tell us the new password.'

'It's "wattlebird",' said Hermione impatiently, 'but that's not the point –'

Her words were cut short, however, as the portrait of the fat lady swung open and there was a sudden storm of clapping. It looked as though the whole of Gryffindor house was still awake, packed into the circular common room, standing on the lop-sided tables and squashy armchairs, waiting for them to arrive. Arms reached through the portrait hole to pull Harry and Ron inside, leaving Hermione to scramble in after them.

'Brilliant!' yelled Lee Jordan. 'Inspired! What an entrance! Flying a car right into the Whomping Willow, people'll be talking about that one for years!'

'Good on you,' said a fifth-year Harry had never spoken to; someone was patting him on the back as though he'd just won a marathon. Fred and George pushed their way to the front of the crowd and said together, 'Why couldn't you've called us back, eh?' Ron was scarlet in the face, grinning embarrassedly, but Harry could see one person who didn't look happy at all. Percy was visible over the heads of some excited first-years, and he seemed to be trying to get near enough to start telling them off. Harry nudged Ron in the ribs and nodded in Percy's direction. Ron got the point at once.

'Got to get upstairs – bit tired,' he said, and the two of them started pushing their way towards the door on the other side of the room, which led to a spiral staircase and the dormitories.

'Night,' Harry called back to Hermione, who was wearing a scowl just like Percy's.

They managed to get to the other side of the common room, still having their backs slapped, and gained the peace of the staircase. They hurried up it, right to the top, and at last reached the door of their old dormitory, which now had a sign on it saying 'second-years'. They entered the familiar, circular room, with its five four-posters hung with red velvet and its high, narrow windows. Their trunks had been brought up for them and placed at the ends of their beds.

Ron grinned guiltily at Harry.

'I know I shouldn't've enjoyed that or anything, but –'

The dormitory door flew open and in came the other second-year Gryffindor boys, Seamus Finnigan, Dean Thomas and Neville Longbottom.

'*Unbelievable!*' beamed Seamus.

'Cool,' said Dean.

'Amazing,' said Neville, awestruck.

Harry couldn't help it. He grinned, too.

CHAPTER SIX

Gilderoy Lockhart

The next day, however, Harry barely grinned once. Things started to go downhill from breakfast in the Great Hall. The four long house tables were laden with tureens of porridge, plates of kippers, mountains of toast and dishes of eggs and bacon, beneath the enchanted ceiling (today, a dull, cloudy grey). Harry and Ron sat down at the Gryffindor table next to Hermione, who had her copy of *Voyages with Vampires* propped open against a milk jug. There was a slight stiffness in the way she said 'Morning' which told Harry that she was still disapproving of the way they had arrived. Neville Longbottom, on the other hand, greeted them cheerfully. Neville was a round-faced and accident-prone boy with the worst memory of anyone Harry had ever met.

'Post's due any minute – I think Gran's sending on a few things I forgot.'

Harry had only just started his porridge when, sure enough, there was a rushing sound overhead and a hundred or so owls streamed in, circling the Hall and dropping letters and packages into the chattering crowd. A big, lumpy parcel bounced off Neville's head, and a second later, something large and grey fell into Hermione's jug, spraying them all with milk and feathers.

'Errol!' said Ron, pulling the bedraggled owl out by the feet. Errol slumped, unconscious, onto the table, his legs in the air and a damp red envelope in his beak.

'Oh no –' Ron gasped.

'It's all right, he's still alive,' said Hermione, prodding Errol gently with the tip of her finger.

'It's not that – it's *that.*'

Ron was pointing at the red envelope. It looked quite ordinary to Harry, but Ron and Neville were both looking at it as though they expected it to explode.

'What's the matter?' said Harry.

'She's – she's sent me a Howler,' said Ron faintly.

'You'd better open it, Ron,' said Neville, in a timid whisper. 'It'll be worse if you don't. My Gran sent me one once, and I ignored it and –' he gulped, 'it was horrible.'

Harry looked from their petrified faces to the red envelope.

'What's a Howler?' he said.

But Ron's whole attention was fixed on the letter, which had begun to smoke at the corners.

'Open it,' Neville urged. 'It'll all be over in a few minutes …'

Ron stretched out a shaking hand, eased the envelope from Errol's beak and slit it open. Neville stuffed his fingers in his ears. A split second later, Harry knew why. He thought for a moment it *had* exploded; a roar of sound filled the huge Hall, shaking dust from the ceiling.

'... *STEALING THE CAR, I WOULDN'T HAVE BEEN SURPRISED IF THEY'D EXPELLED YOU, YOU WAIT TILL I GET HOLD OF YOU, I DON'T SUPPOSE YOU STOPPED TO THINK WHAT YOUR FATHER AND I WENT THROUGH WHEN WE SAW IT HAD GONE* ...'

Mrs Weasley's yells, a hundred times louder than usual, made the plates and spoons rattle on the table, and echoed deafeningly off the stone walls. People throughout the Hall were swivelling around to see who had received the Howler and Ron sank so low in his chair that only his crimson forehead could be seen.

'... *LETTER FROM DUMBLEDORE LAST NIGHT, I THOUGHT YOUR FATHER WOULD DIE OF SHAME, WE DIDN'T BRING YOU UP TO BEHAVE LIKE THIS, YOU AND HARRY COULD BOTH HAVE DIED* ...'

Harry had been wondering when his name was going to crop up. He tried very hard to look as though he couldn't hear the voice that was making his eardrums throb.

'... *ABSOLUTELY DISGUSTED, YOUR FATHER'S FACING AN INQUIRY AT WORK, IT'S ENTIRELY YOUR FAULT AND IF YOU PUT ANOTHER TOE OUT OF LINE WE'LL BRING YOU STRAIGHT BACK HOME.*'

A ringing silence fell. The red envelope, which had dropped from Ron's hand, burst into flames and curled into ashes. Harry and Ron sat stunned, as though a tidal wave had just passed over them. A few people laughed and, gradually, a babble of talk broke out again.

Hermione closed *Voyages with Vampires* and looked down at the top of Ron's head.

'Well, I don't know what you expected, Ron, but you –'

'Don't tell me I deserved it,' snapped Ron.

Harry pushed his porridge away. His insides were burning with guilt. Mr Weasley was facing an inquiry at work. After all Mr and Mrs Weasley had done for him over the summer …

But he had no time to dwell on this; Professor McGonagall was moving along the Gryffindor table, handing out timetables. Harry took his, and saw that they had double Herbology with the Hufflepuffs first.

Harry, Ron and Hermione left the castle together, crossed the vegetable patch and made for the greenhouses, where the magical plants were kept. At least the Howler had done one good thing: Hermione seemed to think they had now been punished enough and was being perfectly friendly again.

As they neared the greenhouses they saw the rest of the class standing outside, waiting for Professor Sprout. Harry, Ron and Hermione had only just joined them when she came striding into view across the lawn, accompanied by Gilderoy Lockhart. Professor Sprout's arms were full of bandages, and with another twinge of guilt, Harry spotted the Whomping Willow in the distance, several of its branches now in slings.

Professor Sprout was a squat little witch who wore a patched hat over her flyaway hair; there was usually a large amount of earth on her clothes, and her fingernails would have made Aunt Petunia faint. Gilderoy Lockhart, however, was immaculate in sweeping robes of turquoise, his golden hair shining under a perfectly positioned turquoise hat with gold trimming.

'Oh, hello there!' Lockhart called, beaming around at the assembled students. 'Just been showing Professor Sprout the right way to doctor a Whomping Willow! But I don't want you running away with the idea that I'm better at Herbology than she is! I just happen to have met several of these exotic plants on my travels ...'

'Greenhouse Three today, chaps!' said Professor Sprout, who was looking distinctly disgruntled, not at all her usual cheerful self.

There was a murmur of interest. They had only ever worked in Greenhouse One before – Greenhouse Three housed far more interesting and dangerous plants. Professor Sprout took a large key from her belt and unlocked the door. Harry caught a whiff of damp earth and fertiliser, mingling with the heavy perfume of some giant, umbrella-sized flowers dangling from the ceiling. He was about to follow Ron and Hermione inside when Lockhart's hand shot out.

'Harry! I've been wanting a word – you don't mind if he's a couple of minutes late, do you, Professor Sprout?'

Judging by Professor Sprout's scowl, she did mind, but Lockhart said, 'That's the ticket,' and closed the greenhouse door in her face.

'Harry,' said Lockhart, his large white teeth gleaming in the sunlight as he shook his head. 'Harry, Harry, Harry.'

Completely nonplussed, Harry said nothing.

'When I heard – well, of course, it was all my fault. Could have kicked myself.'

Harry had no idea what he was talking about. He was about to say so when Lockhart went on, 'Don't know when I've been more shocked. Flying a car to Hogwarts! Well, of course, I knew at once why you'd done it. Stood out a mile. Harry, Harry, *Harry*.'

It was remarkable how he could show every one of those brilliant teeth even when he wasn't talking.

'Gave you a taste for publicity, didn't I?' said Lockhart. 'Gave you the *bug*. You got onto the front page of the paper with me and you couldn't wait to do it again.'

'Oh – no, Professor, see –'

'Harry, Harry, Harry,' said Lockhart, reaching out and grasping his shoulder. '*I understand*. Natural to want a bit more once you've had that first taste – and I blame myself for giving you that, because it was bound to go to your head – but see here, young man, you can't start *flying cars* to try and get yourself noticed. Just calm down, all right? Plenty of time for all that when you're older. Yes, yes, I know what you're thinking! "It's all right for him, he's an internationally famous wizard already!" But when I was twelve, I was just as much of a nobody as you are now. In fact, I'd say I was even more of a nobody! I mean, a few people have heard of you, haven't they? All that business with He Who Must Not Be Named!' He glanced at the lightning scar on Harry's forehead. 'I know, I know, it's not quite as good as winning *Witch Weekly*'s Most-Charming-Smile

Award five times in a row, as I have – but it's a *start*, Harry, it's a *start*.'

He gave Harry a hearty wink and strode off. Harry stood stunned for a few seconds, then, remembering he was supposed to be in the greenhouse, he opened the door and slid inside.

Professor Sprout was standing behind a trestle bench in the centre of the greenhouse. About twenty pairs of different-coloured earmuffs were lying on the bench. When Harry had taken his place between Ron and Hermione, she said, 'We'll be repotting Mandrakes today. Now, who can tell me the properties of the Mandrake?'

To nobody's surprise, Hermione's hand was first into the air.

'Mandrake, or Mandragora, is a powerful restorative,' said Hermione, sounding as usual as though she had swallowed the textbook. 'It is used to return people who have been transfigured or cursed, to their original state.'

'Excellent. Ten points to Gryffindor,' said Professor Sprout. 'The Mandrake forms an essential part of most antidotes. It is also, however, dangerous. Who can tell me why?'

Hermione's hand narrowly missed Harry's glasses as it shot up again.

'The cry of the Mandrake is fatal to anyone who hears it,' she said promptly.

'Precisely. Take another ten points,' said Professor Sprout. 'Now, the Mandrakes we have here are still very young.'

She pointed to a row of deep trays as she spoke and everyone shuffled forward for a better look. A hundred or so tufty little plants, purplish green in colour, were growing there in rows. They looked quite unremarkable to Harry, who didn't have the slightest idea what Hermione meant by the 'cry' of the Mandrake.

'Everyone take a pair of earmuffs,' said Professor Sprout.

There was a scramble as everyone tried to seize a pair that wasn't pink and fluffy.

'When I tell you to put them on, make sure your ears are *completely* covered,' said Professor Sprout. 'When it is safe to remove them, I will give you the thumbs-up. Right – earmuffs *on*.'

Harry snapped the earmuffs over his ears. They shut out sound completely. Professor Sprout put a pink fluffy pair over her own ears, rolled up the sleeves of her robes, grasped one of the tufty plants firmly, and pulled hard.

Harry let out a gasp of surprise that no one could hear.

Instead of roots, a small, muddy and extremely ugly baby popped out of the earth. The leaves were growing right out of his head. He had pale green, mottled skin, and was clearly bawling at the top of his lungs.

Professor Sprout took a large plant pot from under the table and plunged the Mandrake into it, burying him in dark, damp compost until only the tufted leaves were visible. Professor Sprout dusted off her hands, gave them all the thumbs-up and removed her own earmuffs.

'As our Mandrakes are only seedlings, their cries won't kill yet,' she said calmly, as though she'd just done nothing more exciting than water a begonia. 'However, they *will* knock you out for several hours, and as I'm sure none of you want to miss your first day back, make sure your earmuffs are securely in place while you work. I will attract your attention when it is time to pack up.

'Four to a tray – there is a large supply of pots here – compost in the sacks over there – and be careful of the Venomous Tentacula, it's teething.'

She gave a sharp slap to a spiky, dark red plant as she spoke, making it draw in the long feelers that had been inching sneakily over her shoulder.

Harry, Ron and Hermione were joined at their tray by a curly-haired Hufflepuff boy Harry knew by sight, but had never spoken to.

'Justin Finch-Fletchley,' he said brightly, shaking Harry by the hand. 'Know who you are, of course, the famous Harry Potter … and you're Hermione Granger – always top in everything …' (Hermione beamed as she had her hand shaken, too) 'and Ron Weasley. Wasn't that your flying car?'

Ron didn't smile. The Howler was obviously still on his mind.

'That Lockhart's something, isn't he?' said Justin happily, as they began filling their plant pots with dragon-dung compost. 'Awfully brave chap. Have you read his books? I'd have died of fear if I'd been cornered in a telephone box by a werewolf, but he stayed cool and – zap – just *fantastic*.

'My name was down for Eton, you know, I can't tell you how glad I am I came here instead. Of course, mother was slightly disappointed, but since I made her read Lockhart's books I think she's begun to see how useful it'll be to have a fully trained wizard in the family …'

After that they didn't have much chance to talk. Their earmuffs were back on and they needed to concentrate on the Mandrakes. Professor Sprout had made it look extremely easy, but it wasn't. The Mandrakes didn't like coming out of the earth, but didn't seem to want to go back into it either. They squirmed, kicked, flailed their sharp little fists and gnashed their teeth; Harry spent ten whole minutes trying to squash a particularly fat one into a pot.

By the end of the class, Harry, like everyone else, was sweaty, aching and covered in earth. They traipsed back to the castle for a quick wash and then the Gryffindors hurried off to Transfiguration.

Professor McGonagall's classes were always hard work, but today was especially difficult. Everything Harry had learned last year seemed to have leaked out of his head during the summer. He was supposed to be turning a beetle into a button, but all he managed to do was give his beetle a lot of exercise as it scuttled over the desk top avoiding his wand.

Ron was having far worse problems. He had patched up his wand with some borrowed Spellotape, but it seemed to be damaged beyond repair. It kept crackling and sparking at odd moments, and every time Ron tried to transfigure his beetle it engulfed him in thick grey smoke which smelled of rotten eggs. Unable to see what he was doing, Ron accidentally squashed his beetle with his elbow and had to ask for a new one. Professor McGonagall wasn't pleased.

Harry was relieved to hear the lunch bell. His brain felt like a wrung sponge. Everyone filed out of the classroom except him and Ron, who was whacking his wand furiously on the desk.

'Stupid ... useless ... thing ...'

'Write home for another one,' Harry suggested, as the wand let off a volley of bangs like a firecracker.

'Oh yeah, and get another Howler back,' said Ron, stuffing the now hissing wand into his bag. *'It's your own fault your wand got snapped –'*

They went down to lunch, where Ron's mood was not improved by Hermione showing them the handful of perfect coat buttons she had produced in Transfiguration.

'What've we got this afternoon?' said Harry, hastily changing the subject.

'Defence Against the Dark Arts,' said Hermione at once.

'*Why,*' demanded Ron, seizing her timetable, 'have you outlined all Lockhart's lessons in little hearts?'

Hermione snatched the timetable back, flushing furiously.

They finished lunch and went outside into the overcast courtyard. Hermione sat down on a stone step and buried her nose in *Voyages with Vampires* again. Harry and Ron stood talking about Quidditch for several minutes before Harry became aware that he was being closely watched. Looking up, he saw the very small, mousey-haired boy he'd seen trying on the Sorting Hat last night, staring at Harry as though transfixed. He was clutching what looked like an ordinary Muggle camera, and the moment Harry looked at him, he went bright red.

'All right, Harry? I'm – I'm Colin Creevey,' he said breathlessly, taking a tentative step forward. 'I'm in Gryffindor, too. D'you think – would it be all right if – can I have a picture?' he said, raising the camera hopefully.

'A picture?' Harry repeated blankly.

'So I can prove I've met you,' said Colin Creevey eagerly, edging further forwards. 'I know all about you. Everyone's told me. About how you survived when You-Know-Who tried to kill you and how he disappeared and everything and how you've still got a lightning scar on your forehead,' (his eyes raked Harry's hairline) 'and a boy in my dormitory said if I develop the film in the right potion, the pictures'll *move*.' Colin drew a great shuddering breath of excitement and said, 'It's *brilliant* here, isn't it? I never knew all the odd stuff I could do was magic till I got the letter from Hogwarts. My dad's a milkman, he couldn't believe it either. So I'm taking loads of pictures to send home to him. And it'd be really good if I had one of you –' he looked imploringly at Harry, '– maybe your friend could take it and I could stand next to you? And then, could you sign it?'

'*Signed photos*? You're giving out *signed photos*, Potter?'

Loud and scathing, Draco Malfoy's voice echoed around the courtyard. He had stopped right behind Colin, flanked, as he always was at Hogwarts, by his large and thuggish cronies, Crabbe and Goyle.

'Everyone queue up!' Malfoy roared to the crowd. 'Harry Potter's giving out signed photos!'

'No, I'm not,' said Harry angrily, his fists clenching. 'Shut up, Malfoy.'

'You're just jealous,' piped up Colin, whose entire body was about as thick as Crabbe's neck.

'*Jealous?*' said Malfoy, who didn't need to shout any more; half the courtyard was listening in. 'Of what? I don't want a foul scar right across my head, thanks. I don't think getting your head cut open makes you that special, myself.'

Crabbe and Goyle were sniggering stupidly.

'Eat slugs, Malfoy,' said Ron angrily. Crabbe stopped laughing and started rubbing his conker-like knuckles in a menacing way.

'Be careful, Weasley,' sneered Malfoy. 'You don't want to start any trouble or your mummy'll have to come and take you away from school.' He put on a shrill, piercing voice. '*If you put another toe out of line –*'

A knot of Slytherin fifth-years nearby laughed loudly at this.

'Weasley would like a signed photo, Potter,' smirked Malfoy. 'It'd be worth more than his family's whole house.'

Ron whipped out his Spellotaped wand, but Hermione shut *Voyages with Vampires* with a snap and whispered, 'Look out!'

'What's all this, what's all this?' Gilderoy Lockhart was striding towards them, his turquoise robes swirling behind him. 'Who's giving out signed photos?'

Harry started to speak but he was cut short as Lockhart flung an arm around his shoulders and thundered jovially, 'Shouldn't have asked! We meet again, Harry!'

Pinned to Lockhart's side and burning with humiliation, Harry saw Malfoy slide smirking back into the crowd.

'Come on then, Mr Creevey,' said Lockhart, beaming at Colin. 'A double portrait, can't say fairer than that, and we'll *both* sign it for you.'

Colin fumbled for his camera and took the picture as the bell rang behind them, signalling the start of afternoon classes.

'Off you go, move along there,' Lockhart called to the crowd, and he set off back to the castle with Harry, who was wishing he knew a good vanishing spell, still clasped to his side.

'A word to the wise, Harry,' said Lockhart paternally as they entered the building through a side door. 'I covered up for you back there with young Creevey – if he was photographing me, too, your schoolfellows won't think you're setting yourself up so much …'

Deaf to Harry's stammers, Lockhart swept him down a corridor lined with staring students and up a staircase.

'Let me just say that handing out signed pictures at this stage of your career isn't sensible – looks a tad bigheaded, Harry, to be frank. There may well come a time when, like me, you'll need to keep a stack handy wherever you go, but –' he gave a little chortle, 'I don't think you're quite there yet.'

They had reached Lockhart's classroom and he let Harry go at last. Harry yanked his robes straight and headed for a seat at the very back of the class, where he busied himself with piling all seven of Lockhart's books in front of him, so that he could avoid looking at the real thing.

The rest of the class came clattering in and Ron and Hermione sat down on either side of Harry.

'You could've fried an egg on your face' said Ron. 'You'd better hope Creevey doesn't meet Ginny, they'll be starting a Harry Potter fan club.'

'Shut up,' snapped Harry. The last thing he needed was for Lockhart to hear the phrase 'Harry Potter fan club'.

When the whole class was seated, Lockhart cleared his throat loudly and silence fell. He reached forward, picked up Neville Longbottom's copy of *Travels with Trolls* and held it up to show his own, winking portrait on the front.

'Me,' he said, pointing at it and winking as well, 'Gilderoy Lockhart, Order of Merlin, Third Class, Honorary Member of the Dark Force Defence League and five times winner of *Witch Weekly*'s Most-Charming-Smile Award – but I don't talk about that. I didn't get rid of the Bandon Banshee by *smiling* at her!'

He waited for them to laugh; a few people smiled weakly.

'I see you've all bought a complete set of my books – well done. I thought we'd start today with a little quiz. Nothing to worry about – just to check how well you've read them, how much you've taken in ...'

When he had handed out the test papers he returned to the front of the class and said, 'You have thirty minutes. Start – *now*!'

Harry looked down at his paper and read:

1. **What is Gilderoy Lockhart's favourite colour?**
2. **What is Gilderoy Lockhart's secret ambition?**
3. **What, in your opinion, is Gilderoy Lockhart's greatest achievement to date?**

On and on it went, over three sides of paper, right down to:

> **54. When is Gilderoy Lockhart's birthday, and what would his ideal gift be?**

Half an hour later, Lockhart collected in the papers and rifled through them in front of the class.

'Tut, tut – hardly any of you remembered that my favourite colour is lilac. I say so in *Year with a Yeti*. And a few of you need to read *Wanderings with Werewolves* more carefully – I clearly state in chapter twelve that my ideal birthday gift would be harmony between all magic and non-magic peoples – though I wouldn't say no to a large bottle of Ogden's Old Firewhisky!'

He gave them another roguish wink. Ron was now staring at Lockhart with an expression of disbelief on his face; Seamus Finnigan and Dean Thomas, who were sitting in front, were shaking with silent laughter. Hermione, on the other hand, was listening to Lockhart with rapt attention, and gave a start when he mentioned her name.

'... but Miss Hermione Granger knew my secret ambition is to rid the world of evil and market my own range of hair-care potions – good girl! In fact –' he flipped her paper over, 'full marks! Where is Miss Hermione Granger?'

Hermione raised a trembling hand.

'Excellent!' beamed Lockhart. 'Quite excellent! Take ten points for Gryffindor! And so, to business ...'

He bent down behind his desk and lifted a large, covered cage onto it.

'Now – be warned! It is my job to arm you against the foulest creatures known to wizardkind! You may find yourselves facing your worst fears in this room. Know only that no harm can befall you whilst I am here. All I ask is that you remain calm.'

In spite of himself, Harry leaned around his pile of books for a better look at the cage. Lockhart placed a hand on the cover. Dean and Seamus had stopped laughing now. Neville was cowering in his front-row seat.

'I must ask you not to scream,' said Lockhart in a low voice. 'It might provoke them.'

As the whole class held its breath, Lockhart whipped off the cover.

'Yes,' he said dramatically. *'Freshly caught Cornish pixies.'*

Seamus Finnigan couldn't control himself. He let out a snort of laughter which even Lockhart couldn't mistake for a scream of terror.

'Yes?' he smiled at Seamus.

'Well, they're not – they're not very – *dangerous*, are they?' Seamus choked.

'Don't be so sure!' said Lockhart, waggling a finger annoyingly at Seamus. 'Devilish tricky little blighters they can be!'

The pixies were electric blue and about eight inches high, with pointed faces and voices so shrill it was like listening to a lot of budgies arguing. The moment the cover had been removed, they had started jabbering and rocketing around, rattling the bars and pulling bizarre faces at the people nearest them.

'Right then,' Lockhart said loudly. 'Let's see what you make of them!' And he opened the cage.

It was pandemonium. The pixies shot in every direction like rockets. Two of them seized Neville by the ears and lifted him into the air. Several shot straight through the window, showering the back row with broken glass. The rest proceeded to wreck the classroom more effectively than a rampaging rhino. They grabbed ink bottles and sprayed the class with them, shredded books and papers, tore pictures from the walls, upended the waste bin, grabbed bags and books and threw them out of the smashed window; within minutes, half the class was sheltering under desks and Neville was swinging from the candelabra in the ceiling.

'Come on now, round them up, round them up, they're only pixies ...' Lockhart shouted.

He rolled up his sleeves, brandished his wand and bellowed, *'Peskipiksi Pesternomi!'*

It had absolutely no effect; one of the pixies seized Lockhart's wand and threw it out of the window, too. Lockhart gulped and dived under his own desk, narrowly avoiding being squashed by Neville, who fell a second later as the candelabra gave way.

The bell rang and there was a mad rush towards the exit. In the relative calm that followed, Lockhart straightened up, caught sight of Harry, Ron and Hermione, who were almost at the door, and said, 'Well, I'll ask you three to just nip the rest of them back into their cage.' He swept past them and shut the door quickly behind him.

'Can you *believe* him?' roared Ron, as one of the remaining pixies bit him painfully on the ear.

'He just wants to give us some hands-on experience,' said Hermione, immobilising two pixies at once with a clever Freezing Charm and stuffing them back into their cage.

'Hands on?' said Harry, who was trying to grab a pixie dancing out of reach with its tongue out. 'Hermione, he didn't have a clue what he was doing.'

'Rubbish,' said Hermione. 'You've read his books – look at all those amazing things he's done ...'

'He *says* he's done,' Ron muttered.

CHAPTER SEVEN

Mudbloods and Murmurs

Harry spent a lot of time over the next few days dodging out of sight whenever he saw Gilderoy Lockhart coming down a corridor. Harder to avoid was Colin Creevey, who seemed to have memorised Harry's timetable. Nothing seemed to give Colin a bigger thrill than to say, 'All right, Harry?' six or seven times a day and hear, 'Hullo, Colin,' back, however exasperated Harry sounded when he said it.

Hedwig was still angry with Harry about the disastrous car journey and Ron's wand was still malfunctioning, surpassing itself on Friday morning by shooting out of Ron's hand in Charms and hitting tiny old Professor Flitwick squarely between the eyes, creating a large, throbbing green boil where it had struck. So, with one thing and another, Harry was quite glad to reach the weekend. He, Ron and Hermione were planning to visit Hagrid on Saturday morning. Harry, however, was shaken awake several hours earlier than he would have liked by Oliver Wood, captain of the Gryffindor Quidditch team.

'Whassamatter?' said Harry groggily.

'Quidditch practice!' said Wood. 'Come on!'

Harry squinted at the window. There was a thin mist hanging across the pink and gold sky. Now he was awake, he couldn't understand how he could have slept through the racket the birds were making.

'Oliver,' Harry croaked, 'it's the crack of dawn.'

'Exactly,' said Wood. He was a tall and burly sixth-year and, at the moment, his eyes were gleaming with a mad enthusiasm. 'It's part of our new training programme. Come on, grab your broom and let's go,' said Wood heartily. 'None of the other teams have started training yet, we're going to be first off the mark this year ...'

Yawning and shivering slightly, Harry climbed out of bed and tried to find his Quidditch robes.

'Good man,' said Wood. 'Meet you on the pitch in fifteen minutes.'

When he'd found his scarlet team robes and pulled on his cloak for warmth, Harry scribbled a note to Ron explaining where he'd gone and went down the spiral staircase to the common room, his Nimbus Two Thousand on his shoulder. He had just reached the portrait hole when there was a clatter behind him and Colin Creevey came dashing down the spiral staircase, his camera swinging madly around his neck and something clutched in his hand.

'I heard someone saying your name on the stairs, Harry! Look what I've got here! I've had it developed, I wanted to show you –'

Harry looked bemusedly at the photograph Colin was brandishing under his nose.

A moving, black and white Lockhart was tugging hard on an arm Harry recognised as his own. He was pleased to see that his photographic self was putting up a good fight and refusing to be dragged into view. As Harry watched, Lockhart gave up and slumped, panting, against the white edge of the picture.

'Will you sign it?' said Colin eagerly.

'No,' said Harry flatly, glancing around to check that the room was really deserted. 'Sorry, Colin, I'm in a hurry – Quidditch practice.'

He climbed through the portrait hole.

'Oh wow! Wait for me! I've never watched a Quidditch game before!'

Colin scrambled through the hole after him.

'It'll be really boring,' Harry said quickly, but Colin ignored him, his face shining with excitement.

'You were the youngest house player in a hundred years, weren't you, Harry? Weren't you?' said Colin, trotting alongside him. 'You must be brilliant. I've never flown. Is it easy? Is that your own broom? Is that the best one there is?'

Harry didn't know how to get rid of him. It was like having an extremely talkative shadow.

'I don't really understand Quidditch,' said Colin breathlessly. 'Is it true there are four balls? And two of them fly round trying to knock people off their brooms?'

'Yes,' said Harry heavily, resigned to explaining the complicated rules of Quidditch. 'They're called Bludgers.

There are two Beaters on each team, who carry clubs to beat the Bludgers away from their side. Fred and George Weasley are the Gryffindor Beaters.'

'And what are the other balls for?' Colin asked, tripping down a couple of steps because he was gazing open-mouthed at Harry.

'Well, the Quaffle – that's the biggish red one – is the one that scores goals. Three Chasers on each team throw the Quaffle to each other and try and get it through the goalposts at the end of the pitch – they're three long poles with hoops on the end.'

'And the fourth ball –'

'– is the Golden Snitch,' said Harry, 'and it's very small, very fast and difficult to catch. But that's what the Seeker's got to do, because a game of Quidditch doesn't end until the Snitch has been caught. And whichever team's Seeker gets the Snitch earns his team an extra hundred and fifty points.'

'And you're Gryffindor Seeker, aren't you?' said Colin in awe.

'Yes,' said Harry, as they left the castle and started across the dew-drenched grass. 'And there's the Keeper, too. He guards the goalposts. That's it, really.'

But Colin didn't stop questioning Harry all the way down the sloping lawns to the Quidditch pitch, and Harry only shook him off when he reached the changing rooms. Colin called after him in a piping voice, 'I'll go and get a good seat, Harry!' and hurried off to the stands.

The rest of the Gryffindor team were already in the changing room. Wood was the only person who looked truly awake. Fred and George Weasley were sitting, puffy-eyed and tousle-haired, next to fourth-year Alicia Spinnet, who seemed to be nodding off against the wall behind her. Her fellow Chasers, Katie Bell and Angelina Johnson, were yawning, side by side, opposite them.

'There you are, Harry, what kept you?' said Wood briskly. 'Now, I wanted a quick talk with you all before we actually get onto the pitch, because I spent the summer devising a whole new training programme, which I really think will make all the difference …'

Wood was holding up a large diagram of a Quidditch pitch, on which were drawn many lines, arrows and crosses in different-coloured inks. He took out his wand, tapped the board and the arrows began to wiggle over the diagram like caterpillars. As Wood launched into a speech about his new tactics, Fred Weasley's head drooped right onto Alicia Spinnet's shoulder and he began to snore.

The first board took nearly twenty minutes to explain, but there was another board under that, and a third under that one. Harry sank into a stupor as Wood droned on and on.

'So,' said Wood, at long last, jerking Harry from a wistful fantasy about what he could be eating for breakfast at this very moment up at the castle, 'is that clear? Any questions?'

'I've got a question, Oliver,' said George, who had woken with a start. 'Why couldn't you have told us all this yesterday when we were awake?'

Wood wasn't pleased.

'Now, listen here, you lot,' he said, glowering at them all, 'we should have won the Quidditch Cup last year. We're easily the best team. But unfortunately, owing to circumstances beyond our control ...'

Harry shifted guiltily in his seat. He had been unconscious in the hospital wing for the final match of the previous year, meaning that Gryffindor had been a player short and had suffered their worst defeat in three hundred years.

Wood took a moment to regain control of himself. Their last defeat was clearly still torturing him.

'So, this year, we train harder than ever before ... OK, let's go and put our new theories into practice!' Wood shouted, seizing his broomstick and leading the way out of the changing rooms. Stiff-legged and still yawning, his team followed.

They had been in the changing room so long that the sun was up properly now, although remnants of mist hung over the grass in the stadium. As Harry walked onto the pitch, he saw Ron and Hermione sitting in the stands.

'Aren't you finished yet?' called Ron incredulously.

'Haven't even started,' said Harry, looking jealously at the toast and marmalade Ron and Hermione had brought out of the Great Hall. 'Wood's been teaching us new moves.'

He mounted his broomstick and kicked at the ground, soaring up into the air. The cool morning air whipped his face, waking him far more effectively than Wood's long talk. It felt wonderful to be back on the Quidditch pitch. He soared right around the stadium at full speed, racing Fred and George.

'What's that funny clicking noise?' called Fred, as they hurtled around the corner.

Harry looked into the stands. Colin was sitting in one of the highest seats, his camera raised, taking picture after picture, the sound strangely magnified in the deserted stadium.

'Look this way, Harry! This way!' he cried shrilly.

'Who's that?' said Fred.

'No idea,' Harry lied, putting on a spurt of speed that took him as far away as possible from Colin.

'What's going on?' said Wood, frowning, as he skimmed through the air towards them. 'Why's that first-year taking pictures? I don't like it. He could be a Slytherin spy, trying to find out about our new training programme.'

'He's in Gryffindor,' said Harry quickly.

'And the Slytherins don't need a spy, Oliver,' said George.

'What makes you say that?' said Wood testily.

'Because they're here in person,' said George, pointing.

Several people in green robes were walking onto the pitch, broomsticks in their hands.

'I don't believe it!' Wood hissed in outrage. 'I booked the pitch for today! We'll see about this!'

Wood shot towards the ground, landing rather harder than he meant to in his anger, staggering slightly as he dismounted. Harry, Fred and George followed.

'Flint!' Wood bellowed at the Slytherin captain. 'This is our practice time! We got up specially! You can clear off now!'

Marcus Flint was even larger than Wood. He had a look of trollish cunning on his face as he replied, 'Plenty of room for all of us, Wood.'

Angelina, Alicia and Katie had come over, too. There were no girls on the Slytherin team – who stood, shoulder to shoulder, facing the Gryffindors, leering to a man.

'But I booked the pitch!' said Wood, positively spitting with rage. 'I booked it!'

'Ah,' said Flint, 'but I've got a specially signed note here from Professor Snape. *I, Professor S. Snape, give the Slytherin team permission to practise today on the Quidditch pitch, owing to the need to train their new Seeker.*'

'You've got a new Seeker?' said Wood, distracted. 'Where?'

And from behind the six large figures before them came a seventh, smaller boy, smirking all over his pale, pointed face. It was Draco Malfoy.

'Aren't you Lucius Malfoy's son?' said Fred, looking at Malfoy with dislike.

'Funny you should mention Draco's father,' said Flint, as the whole Slytherin team smiled still more broadly. 'Let me show you the generous gift he's made to the Slytherin team.'

All seven of them held out their broomsticks. Seven highly polished, brand-new handles and seven sets of fine gold lettering spelling the words 'Nimbus Two Thousand and One' gleamed under the Gryffindors' noses in the early-morning sun.

'Very latest model. Only came out last month,' said Flint carelessly, flicking a speck of dust from the end of his own. 'I believe it outstrips the old Two Thousand series by a considerable amount. As for the old Cleansweeps,' he smiled nastily at Fred and George, who were both clutching Cleansweep Fives, 'sweeps the board with them.'

None of the Gryffindor team could think of anything to say for a moment. Malfoy was smirking so broadly his cold eyes were reduced to slits.

'Oh look,' said Flint. 'A pitch invasion.'

Ron and Hermione were crossing the grass to see what was going on.

'What's happening?' Ron asked Harry. 'Why aren't you playing? And what's *he* doing here?'

He was looking at Malfoy, taking in his Slytherin Quidditch robes.

'I'm the new Slytherin Seeker, Weasley,' said Malfoy, smugly. 'Everyone's just been admiring the brooms my father's bought our team.'

Ron gaped, open-mouthed, at the seven superb broomsticks in front of him.

'Good, aren't they?' said Malfoy smoothly. 'But perhaps the Gryffindor team will be able to raise some gold and get new brooms, too. You could raffle off those Cleansweep Fives, I expect a museum would bid for them.'

The Slytherin team howled with laughter.

'At least no one on the Gryffindor team had to *buy* their way in,' said Hermione sharply. '*They* got in on pure talent.'

The smug look on Malfoy's face flickered.

'No one asked your opinion, you filthy little Mudblood,' he spat.

Harry knew at once that Malfoy had said something really bad because there was an instant uproar at his words. Flint had to dive in front of Malfoy to stop Fred and George jumping on him, Alicia shrieked, *'How dare you!'* and Ron plunged his hand into his robes, pulled out his wand, yelling, 'You'll pay for that one, Malfoy!' and pointed it furiously under Flint's arm at Malfoy's face.

A loud bang echoed around the stadium and a jet of green light shot out of the wrong end of Ron's wand, hitting him in the stomach and sending him reeling backwards onto the grass.

'Ron! Ron! Are you all right?' squealed Hermione.

Ron opened his mouth to speak, but no words came out. Instead he gave an almighty belch and several slugs dribbled out of his mouth onto his lap.

The Slytherin team were paralysed with laughter. Flint was doubled up, hanging on to his new broomstick for support. Malfoy was on all fours, banging the ground with his fist. The Gryffindors were gathered around Ron, who kept belching large, glistening slugs. Nobody seemed to want to touch him.

'We'd better get him to Hagrid's, it's nearest,' said Harry to Hermione, who nodded bravely, and the pair of them pulled Ron up by the arms.

'What happened, Harry? What happened? Is he ill? But you can cure him, can't you?' Colin had run down from his seat and was now dancing alongside them as they left the pitch. Ron gave a huge heave and more slugs dribbled down his front.

'Oooh,' said Colin, fascinated and raising his camera. 'Can you hold him still, Harry?'

'Get out of the way, Colin!' said Harry angrily. He and Hermione supported Ron out of the stadium and across the grounds towards the edge of the Forest.

'Nearly there, Ron,' said Hermione, as the gamekeeper's cabin came into view. 'You'll be all right in a minute … almost there …'

They were within twenty feet of Hagrid's house when the front door opened, but it wasn't Hagrid who emerged. Gilderoy Lockhart, wearing robes of palest mauve today, came striding out.

'Quick, behind here,' Harry hissed, dragging Ron behind a nearby bush. Hermione followed, somewhat reluctantly.

'It's a simple matter if you know what you're doing!' Lockhart was saying loudly to Hagrid. 'If you need help, you know where I am! I'll let you have a copy of my book – I'm surprised you haven't already got one. I'll sign one tonight and send it over. Well, goodbye!' And he strode away towards the castle.

Harry waited until Lockhart was out of sight, then pulled Ron out of the bush and up to Hagrid's front door. They knocked urgently.

Hagrid appeared at once, looking very grumpy, but his expression brightened when he saw who it was.

'Bin wonderin' when you'd come ter see me – come in, come in – thought you mighta bin Professor Lockhart back again.'

Harry and Hermione supported Ron over the threshold, into the one-roomed cabin, which had an enormous bed in one corner, a fire crackling merrily in another. Hagrid didn't seem perturbed by Ron's slug problem, which Harry hastily explained as he lowered Ron into a chair.

'Better out than in,' he said cheerfully, plonking a large copper basin in front of him. 'Get 'em all up, Ron.'

'I don't think there's anything to do except wait for it to stop,' said Hermione anxiously, watching Ron bend over the basin. 'That's a difficult curse to work at the best of times, but with a broken wand ...'

Hagrid was bustling around, making them tea. His boarhound, Fang, was slobbering over Harry.

'What did Lockhart want with you, Hagrid?' Harry asked, scratching Fang's ears.

'Givin' me advice on gettin' kelpies out of a well,' growled Hagrid, moving a half-plucked rooster off his scrubbed table and setting down the teapot. 'Like I don' know. An' bangin' on about some Banshee he banished. If one word of it was true, I'll eat my kettle.'

It was most unlike Hagrid to criticise a Hogwarts teacher and Harry looked at him in surprise. Hermione, however, said in a voice somewhat higher than usual, 'I think you're being a bit unfair. Professor Dumbledore obviously thought he was the best man for the job –'

'He was the *on'y* man for the job,' said Hagrid, offering them a plate of treacle toffee, while Ron coughed squelchily into his basin. 'An' I mean the *on'y* one. Gettin' very difficult ter find anyone fer the Dark Arts job. People aren't too keen ter take it on, see. They're startin' ter think it's jinxed. No one's lasted long fer a while now. So tell me,' said Hagrid, jerking his head at Ron, 'who was he tryin' ter curse?'

'Malfoy called Hermione something. It must've been really bad, because everyone went mad.'

'It *was* bad,' said Ron hoarsely, emerging over the table top, looking pale and sweaty. 'Malfoy called her "Mudblood", Hagrid –'

Ron dived out of sight again as a fresh wave of slugs made their appearance. Hagrid looked outraged.

'He didn't!' he growled at Hermione.

'He did,' she said. 'But I don't know what it means. I could tell it was really rude, of course ...'

'It's about the most insulting thing he could think of,' gasped Ron, coming back up. 'Mudblood's a really foul name for someone who was Muggle-born – you know, non-magic parents. There are some wizards – like Malfoy's family – who think they're better than everyone else because they're what people call pure-blood.' He gave a small burp, and a single slug fell into his outstretched hand. He threw it into the basin and continued, 'I mean, the rest of us know it doesn't make any difference at all. Look at Neville Longbottom – he's pure-blood and he can hardly stand a cauldron the right way up.'

'An' they haven't invented a spell our Hermione can't do,' said Hagrid proudly, making Hermione go a brilliant shade of magenta.

'It's a disgusting thing to call someone,' said Ron, wiping his sweaty brow with a shaking hand. 'Dirty blood, see. Common blood. It's mad. Most wizards these days are half-blood anyway. If we hadn't married Muggles we'd've died out.'

He retched and ducked out of sight again.

'Well, I don' blame yeh fer tryin' ter curse him, Ron,' said Hagrid loudly over the thuds of more slugs hitting the basin. 'Bu' maybe it was a good thing yer wand backfired. 'Spect Lucius Malfoy would've come marchin' up ter school if yeh'd cursed his son. Least yer not in trouble.'

Harry would have pointed out that trouble didn't come much worse than having slugs pouring out of your mouth, but he couldn't; Hagrid's treacle toffee had cemented his jaws together.

'Harry,' said Hagrid suddenly, as though struck by a sudden thought, 'gotta bone ter pick with yeh. I've heard you've bin givin' out signed photos. How come I haven't got one?'

Furious, Harry wrenched his teeth apart.

'I have *not* been giving out signed photos,' he said hotly. 'If Lockhart's still putting that about –'

But then he saw that Hagrid was laughing.

'I'm on'y jokin',' he said, patting Harry genially on the back and sending him, face first, into the table. 'I knew yeh hadn't really. I told Lockhart yeh didn' need teh. Yer more famous than him without tryin'.'

'Bet he didn't like that,' said Harry, sitting up and rubbing his chin.

'Don' think he did,' said Hagrid, his eyes twinkling. 'An' then I told him I'd never read one o' his books an' he decided ter go. Treacle toffee, Ron?' he added, as Ron reappeared.

'No thanks,' said Ron weakly. 'Better not risk it.'

'Come an' see what I've bin growin',' said Hagrid, as Harry and Hermione finished the last of their tea.

In the small vegetable patch behind Hagrid's house were a dozen of the largest pumpkins Harry had ever seen. Each was the size of a large boulder.

'Gettin' on well, aren't they?' said Hagrid happily. 'Fer the Hallowe'en feast ... should be big enough by then.'

'What've you been feeding them?' said Harry.

Hagrid looked over his shoulder to check that they were alone.

'Well, I've bin givin' them – you know – a bit o' help.'

Harry noticed Hagrid's flowery pink umbrella leaning against the back wall of the cabin. Harry had had reason to believe before now that this umbrella was not all it looked; in fact, he had the strong impression that Hagrid's old school wand was concealed inside it. Hagrid wasn't supposed to use magic. He had been expelled from Hogwarts in his third year, but Harry had never found out why – any mention of the matter and Hagrid would clear his throat loudly and become mysteriously deaf until the subject was changed.

'An Engorgement Charm, I suppose?' said Hermione, halfway between disapproval and amusement. 'Well, you've done a good job on them.'

'That's what yer little sister said,' said Hagrid, nodding at Ron. 'Met her jus' yesterday.' Hagrid looked sideways at Harry, his beard twitching. 'Said she was jus' lookin' round the grounds, but I reckon she was hopin' she might run inter someone else at my house.' He winked at Harry. 'If yeh ask me, *she* wouldn' say no ter a signed –'

'Oh, shut up,' said Harry. Ron snorted with laughter and the ground was sprayed with slugs.

'Watch it!' Hagrid roared, pulling Ron away from his precious pumpkins.

It was nearly lunchtime and as Harry had only had one bit of treacle toffee since dawn, he was keen to go back to school to eat. They said goodbye to Hagrid and walked back up to the castle, Ron hiccoughing occasionally, but only bringing up two, very small slugs.

They had barely set foot in the cool Entrance Hall when a voice rang out. 'There you are, Potter, Weasley.' Professor McGonagall was walking towards them, looking stern. 'You will both do your detentions this evening.'

'What are we doing, Professor?' said Ron, nervously suppressing a burp.

'*You* will be polishing the silver in the trophy room with Mr Filch,' said Professor McGonagall. 'And no magic, Weasley – elbow grease.'

Ron gulped. Argus Filch, the caretaker, was loathed by every student in the school.

'And you, Potter, will be helping Professor Lockhart answer his fan mail,' said Professor McGonagall.

'Oh no – can't I go and do the trophy room, too?' said Harry desperately.

'Certainly not,' said Professor McGonagall, raising her eyebrows. 'Professor Lockhart requested you particularly. Eight o'clock sharp, both of you.'

Harry and Ron slouched into the Great Hall in states of deepest gloom, Hermione behind them, wearing a *well-you-did-break-school-rules* sort of expression. Harry didn't fancy his shepherd's pie as much as he'd thought. Both he and Ron felt they'd got the worse deal.

'Filch'll have me there all night,' said Ron heavily. 'No magic! There must be about a hundred cups in that room. I'm no good at Muggle cleaning.'

'I'd swap any time,' said Harry hollowly. 'I've had loads of practice with the Dursleys. Answering Lockhart's fan mail … he'll be a nightmare …'

Saturday afternoon seemed to melt away, and in what seemed like no time, it was five minutes to eight, and Harry was dragging his feet along the second-floor corridor to Lockhart's office. He gritted his teeth and knocked.

The door flew open at once. Lockhart beamed down at him.

'Ah, here's the scallywag!' he said. 'Come in, Harry, come in.'

Shining brightly on the walls by the light of many candles were countless framed photographs of Lockhart. He had even signed a few of them. Another large pile lay on his desk.

'You can address the envelopes!' Lockhart told Harry, as though this was a huge treat. 'This first one's to Gladys Gudgeon, bless her – huge fan of mine.'

The minutes snailed by. Harry let Lockhart's voice wash over him, occasionally saying, 'Mmm' and 'Right' and 'Yeah'. Now and then he caught a phrase like 'Fame's a fickle friend, Harry' or 'Celebrity is as celebrity does, remember that'.

The candles burned lower and lower, making the light dance over the many moving faces of Lockhart watching him. Harry moved his aching hand over what felt like the thousandth envelope, writing out Veronica Smethley's address. 'It must be nearly time to leave,' Harry thought miserably. 'Please let it be nearly time … '

And then he heard something – something quite apart from the spitting of the dying candles and Lockhart's prattle about his fans.

It was a voice, a voice to chill the bone-marrow, a voice of breath-taking, ice-cold venom.

'Come … come to me … let me rip you … let me tear you … let me kill you …'

Harry gave a huge jump and a large lilac blot appeared on Veronica Smethley's street.

'*What?*' he said loudly.

'I know!' said Lockhart. 'Six solid months at the top of the bestseller list! Broke all records!'

'No,' said Harry frantically. 'That voice!'

'Sorry?' said Lockhart, looking puzzled. 'What voice?'

'That – that voice that said – didn't you hear it?'

Lockhart was looking at Harry in high astonishment.

'What *are* you talking about, Harry? Perhaps you're getting a little drowsy? Great Scott – look at the time! We've been here nearly four hours! I'd never have believed it – the time's flown, hasn't it?'

Harry didn't answer. He was straining his ears to hear the voice again, but there was no sound now except for Lockhart telling him he mustn't expect a treat like this every time he got detention. Feeling dazed, Harry left.

It was so late that the Gryffindor common room was almost empty. Harry went straight up to the dormitory. Ron wasn't back yet. Harry pulled on his pyjamas, got into bed and waited. Half an hour later, Ron arrived, nursing his right arm and bringing a strong smell of polish into the darkened room.

'My muscles have all seized up,' he groaned, sinking on his bed. 'Fourteen times he made me buff up that Quidditch Cup before he was satisfied. And then I had another slug attack all over a Special Award for Services to the School. Took ages to shift the slime … How was it with Lockhart?'

Keeping his voice low so as not to wake Neville, Dean and Seamus, Harry told Ron exactly what he had heard.

'And Lockhart said he couldn't hear it?' said Ron. Harry could see him frowning in the moonlight. 'D'you think he was lying? But I don't get it – even someone invisible would've had to open the door.'

'I know,' said Harry, lying back in his four-poster and staring at the canopy above him. 'I don't get it, either.'

CHAPTER EIGHT

The Deathday Party

October arrived, spreading a damp chill over the grounds and into the castle. Madam Pomfrey, the matron, was kept busy by a sudden spate of colds among the staff and students. Her Pepperup Potion worked instantly, though it left the drinker smoking at the ears for several hours afterwards. Ginny Weasley, who had been looking peaky, was bullied into taking some by Percy. The steam pouring from under her vivid hair gave the impression that her whole head was on fire.

Raindrops the size of bullets thundered on the castle windows for days on end; the lake rose, the flowerbeds turned into muddy streams and Hagrid's pumpkins swelled to the size of garden sheds. Oliver Wood's enthusiasm for regular training sessions, however, was not dampened, which was why Harry was to be found, late one stormy Saturday afternoon a few days before Hallowe'en, returning to Gryffindor Tower, drenched to the skin and splattered with mud.

Even aside from the rain and wind it hadn't been a happy practice session. Fred and George, who had been spying on the Slytherin team, had seen for themselves the speed of those new Nimbus Two Thousand and Ones. They reported that the Slytherin team were no more than seven greenish blurs, shooting through the air like jump-jets.

As Harry squelched along the deserted corridor he came across somebody who looked just as preoccupied as he was. Nearly Headless Nick, the ghost of Gryffindor Tower, was staring morosely out of a window, muttering under his breath, '… don't fulfil their requirements … half an inch, if that …'

'Hello, Nick,' said Harry.

'Hello, hello,' said Nearly Headless Nick, starting and looking round. He wore a dashing, plumed hat on his long curly hair, and a tunic with a ruff, which concealed the fact that his neck was almost completely severed. He was pale as smoke, and Harry could see right through him to the dark sky and torrential rain outside.

'You look troubled, young Potter,' said Nick, folding a transparent letter as he spoke and tucking it inside his doublet.

'So do you,' said Harry.

'Ah,' Nearly Headless Nick waved an elegant hand, 'a matter of no importance … it's not as though I really wanted to join … thought I'd apply, but apparently I "don't fulfil requirements".'

In spite of his airy tone, there was a look of great bitterness on his face.

'But you would think, wouldn't you,' he erupted suddenly, pulling the letter back out of his pocket, 'that getting hit forty-five times in the neck with a blunt axe would qualify you to join the Headless Hunt?'

'Oh – yes,' said Harry, who was obviously supposed to agree.

'I mean, nobody wishes more than I do that it had all been quick and clean, and my head had come off properly, I mean, it would have saved me a great deal of pain and ridicule. However ...' Nearly Headless Nick shook his letter open and read furiously.

'We can only accept huntsmen whose heads have parted company with their bodies. You will appreciate that it would be impossible otherwise for members to participate in hunt activities such as Horseback Head-Juggling and Head Polo. It is with the greatest regret, therefore, that I must inform you that you do not fulfil our requirements. With very best wishes, Sir Patrick Delaney-Podmore.'

Fuming, Nearly Headless Nick stuffed the letter away.

'Half an inch of skin and sinew holding my neck on, Harry! Most people would think that's good and beheaded, but oh no, it's not enough for Sir Properly Decapitated-Podmore.'

Nearly Headless Nick took several deep breaths and then said, in a far calmer tone, 'So – what's bothering you? Anything I can do?'

'No,' said Harry. 'Not unless you know where we can get seven free Nimbus Two Thousand and Ones for our match against Sly–'

The rest of Harry's sentence was drowned by a high-pitched mewing from somewhere near his ankles. He looked down and found himself gazing into a pair of lamp-like yellow eyes. It was Mrs Norris, the skeletal grey cat who was used by the caretaker, Argus Filch, as a sort of deputy in his endless battle against students.

'You'd better get out of here, Harry,' said Nick quickly. 'Filch isn't in a good mood. He's got flu and some third-years accidentally plastered frog brains all over the ceiling in dungeon five; he's been cleaning all morning, and if he sees you dripping mud all over the place ...'

'Right,' said Harry, backing away from the accusing stare of Mrs Norris, but not quickly enough. Drawn to the spot by the mysterious power that seemed to connect him with his foul cat, Argus Filch burst suddenly through a tapestry to Harry's right, wheezing and looking wildly about for the rule-breaker. There was a thick tartan scarf bound around his head, and his nose was unusually purple.

'Filth!' he shouted, his jowls aquiver, his eyes popping alarmingly as he pointed at the muddy puddle that had dripped from Harry's Quidditch robes. 'Mess and muck everywhere! I've had enough of it, I tell you! Follow me, Potter!'

So Harry waved a gloomy goodbye to Nearly Headless Nick, and followed Filch back downstairs, doubling the number of muddy footprints on the floor.

Harry had never been inside Filch's office before; it was a place most students avoided. The room was dingy and windowless, lit by a single oil lamp dangling from the low ceiling. A faint smell of fried fish lingered about the place. Wooden filing cabinets stood around the walls; from their labels, Harry could see that they contained details of every pupil Filch had ever punished. Fred and George Weasley had an entire drawer to themselves. A highly polished collection of chains and manacles hung on the wall behind Filch's desk. It was common knowledge that he was always begging Dumbledore to let him suspend students by their ankles from the ceiling.

Filch grabbed a quill from a pot on his desk and began shuffling around looking for parchment.

'Dung,' he muttered furiously, 'great sizzling dragon bogies … frog brains … rat intestines … I've had enough of it … make an *example* … where's the form … yes …'

He retrieved a large roll of parchment from his desk drawer and stretched it out in front of him, dipping his long black quill into the ink pot.

'*Name* … Harry Potter. *Crime* …'

'It was only a bit of mud!' said Harry.

'It's only a bit of mud to you, boy, but to me it's an extra hour scrubbing!' shouted Filch, a drip shivering unpleasantly at the end of his bulbous nose. '*Crime* … befouling the castle … *suggested sentence* …'

Dabbing at his streaming nose, Filch squinted unpleasantly at Harry, who waited with bated breath for his sentence to fall.

But as Filch lowered his quill, there was a great BANG! on the ceiling of the office, which made the oil lamp rattle.

'PEEVES!' Filch roared, flinging down his quill in a transport of rage. 'I'll have you this time, I'll have you!'

And without a backwards glance at Harry, Filch ran flat-footed from the office, Mrs Norris streaking alongside him.

Peeves was the school poltergeist, a grinning, airborne menace who lived to cause havoc and distress. Harry didn't much like Peeves, but couldn't help feeling grateful for his timing. Hopefully, whatever Peeves had done (and it sounded as though he'd wrecked something very big this time) would distract Filch from Harry.

Thinking that he should probably wait for Filch to come back, Harry sank into a moth-eaten chair next to the desk. There was only one thing on it apart from his half-completed form: a large, glossy, purple envelope with silver lettering on the front. With a quick glance at the door to check that Filch wasn't on his way back, Harry picked up the envelope and read:

*** *Kwikspell* ***

A Correspondence Course in
Beginners' Magic

Intrigued, Harry flicked the envelope open and pulled out the sheaf of parchment inside. More curly silver writing on the front page said:

Feel out of step in the world of modern magic?
Find yourself making excuses not to perform simple spells?
Ever been taunted for your woeful wandwork?
There is an answer!

Kwikspell is an all-new, fail-safe, quick-result, easy-learn course. Hundreds of witches and wizards have benefited from the Kwikspell method!

Madam Z. Nettles of Topsham writes:

'I had no memory for incantations and my potions were a family joke! Now, after a Kwikspell course, I am the centre of attention at parties and friends beg for the recipe of my Scintillation Solution!'

Warlock D. J. Prod of Didsbury says:

'My wife used to sneer at my feeble charms but one month into your fabulous Kwikspell course I succeeded in turning her into a yak! Thank you, Kwikspell!'

Fascinated, Harry thumbed through the rest of the envelope's contents. Why on earth did Filch want a Kwikspell course? Did this mean he wasn't a proper wizard? Harry was just reading 'Lesson One: Holding Your Wand (Some Useful Tips)' when shuffling footsteps outside told him Filch was coming back. Stuffing the parchment back into the envelope, Harry threw it back onto the desk just as the door opened.

Filch was looking triumphant.

'That vanishing cabinet was extremely valuable!' he was saying gleefully to Mrs Norris. 'We'll have Peeves out this time, my sweet.'

His eyes fell on Harry and then darted to the Kwikspell

envelope which, Harry realised too late, was lying two feet away from where it had started.

Filch's pasty face went brick red. Harry braced himself for a tidal wave of fury. Filch hobbled across to his desk, snatched up the envelope and threw it into a drawer.

'Have you – did you read –?' he spluttered.

'No,' Harry lied quickly.

Filch's knobbly hands were twisting together.

'If I thought you'd read my private … not that it's mine … for a friend … be that as it may … however …'

Harry was staring at him, alarmed; Filch had never looked madder. His eyes were popping, a tic was going in one of his pouchy cheeks and the tartan scarf didn't help.

'Very well … go … and don't breathe a word … not that … however, if you didn't read … go now, I have to write up Peeves' report … go …'

Amazed at his luck, Harry sped out of the office, up the corridor and back upstairs. To escape from Filch's office without punishment was probably some kind of school record.

'Harry! Harry! Did it work?'

Nearly Headless Nick came gliding out of a classroom. Behind him, Harry could see the wreckage of a large black and gold cabinet which appeared to have been dropped from a great height.

'I persuaded Peeves to crash it right over Filch's office,' said Nick eagerly. 'Thought it might distract him –'

'Was that you?' said Harry gratefully. 'Yeah, it worked, I didn't even get detention. Thanks, Nick!'

They set off up the corridor together. Nearly Headless Nick, Harry noticed, was still holding Sir Patrick's rejection letter.

'I wish there was something I could do for you about the Headless Hunt,' Harry said.

Nearly Headless Nick stopped in his tracks and Harry walked right through him. He wished he hadn't; it was like stepping through an icy shower.

'But there *is* something you could do for me,' said Nick excitedly. 'Harry – would I be asking too much – but no, you wouldn't want –'

'What is it?' said Harry.

'Well, this Hallowe'en will be my five hundredth deathday,' said Nearly Headless Nick, drawing himself up and looking dignified.

'Oh,' said Harry, not sure whether he should look sorry or happy about this. 'Right.'

'I'm holding a party down in one of the roomier dungeons. Friends will be coming from all over the country. It would be such an *honour* if you would attend. Mr Weasley and Miss Granger would be most welcome too, of course – but I dare say you'd rather go to the school feast?' He watched Harry on tenterhooks.

'No,' said Harry quickly, 'I'll come –'

'My dear boy! Harry Potter, at my Deathday Party! And,' he hesitated, looking excited, 'do you think you could *possibly* mention to Sir Patrick how *very* frightening and impressive you find me?'

'Of – of course,' said Harry.

Nearly Headless Nick beamed at him.

'A Deathday Party?' said Hermione keenly, when Harry had changed at last and joined her and Ron in the common room. 'I bet there aren't many living people who can say they've been to one of those – it'll be fascinating!'

'Why would anyone want to celebrate the day they died?' said Ron, who was halfway through his Potions homework and grumpy. 'Sounds dead depressing to me ...'

Rain was still lashing the windows, which were now inky black, but inside, all looked bright and cheerful. The firelight glowed over the countless squashy armchairs where people sat reading, talking, doing homework or, in the case of Fred and George Weasley, trying to find out what would happen if you fed a Filibuster Firework to a Salamander. Fred had 'rescued' the brilliant orange, fire-dwelling lizard from a Care of Magical Creatures class and it was now smouldering gently on a table surrounded by a knot of curious people.

Harry was on the point of telling Ron and Hermione about Filch and the Kwikspell course when the Salamander suddenly whizzed into the air, emitting loud sparks and bangs as it whirled wildly round the room. The sight of Percy bellowing himself hoarse at Fred and George, the spectacular display of tangerine stars showering from the Salamander's mouth, and its escape into the fire, with accompanying explosions, drove both Filch and the Kwikspell envelope from Harry's mind.

* * *

By the time Hallowe'en arrived, Harry was regretting his rash promise to go to the Deathday Party. The rest of the school were happily anticipating their Hallowe'en feast; the Great Hall had been decorated with the usual live bats, Hagrid's vast pumpkins had been carved into lanterns large enough for three men to sit in and there were rumours that Dumbledore had booked a troupe of dancing skeletons for the entertainment.

'A promise is a promise,' Hermione reminded Harry bossily. 'You *said* you'd go to the Deathday Party.'

So, at seven o'clock, Harry, Ron and Hermione walked straight past the doorway to the packed Great Hall, which was glittering invitingly with gold plates and candles, and directed their steps instead towards the dungeons.

The passageway leading to Nearly Headless Nick's party had been lined with candles too, though the effect was far from cheerful: these were long, thin, jet-black tapers, all burning bright blue, casting a dim, ghostly light even over their own living faces. The temperature dropped with every step they took. As Harry shivered and drew his robes tightly around him, he heard what sounded like a thousand fingernails scraping an enormous blackboard.

'Is that supposed to be *music?*' Ron whispered. They turned a corner and saw Nearly Headless Nick standing at a doorway hung with black velvet drapes.

'My dear friends,' he said mournfully, 'welcome, welcome … so pleased you could come …'

He swept off his plumed hat and bowed them inside.

It was an incredible sight. The dungeon was full of hundreds of pearly-white, translucent people, mostly drifting around a crowded dance floor, waltzing to the dreadful, quavering sound of thirty musical saws, played by an orchestra on a black-draped platform. A chandelier overhead blazed midnight blue with a thousand more black candles. Their breath rose in a mist before them; it was like stepping into a freezer.

'Shall we have a look around?' Harry suggested, wanting to warm up his feet.

'Careful not to walk through anyone,' said Ron nervously, and they set off around the edge of the dance floor. They passed a group of gloomy nuns, a ragged man wearing chains, and the Fat Friar, a cheerful Hufflepuff ghost, who was talking to a knight with an arrow sticking out of his forehead. Harry wasn't surprised to see that the Bloody Baron, a gaunt, staring Slytherin ghost covered in silver bloodstains, was being given a wide berth by the other ghosts.

'Oh no,' said Hermione, stopping abruptly. 'Turn back, turn back, I don't want to talk to Moaning Myrtle –'

'Who?' said Harry, as they backtracked quickly.

'She haunts the girls' toilet on the first floor,' said Hermione.

'She haunts a *toilet*?'

'Yes. It's been out of order all year because she keeps having tantrums and flooding the place. I never went in there anyway if I could avoid it, it's awful trying to go to the loo with her wailing at you –'

'Look, food!' said Ron.

On the other side of the dungeon was a long table, also covered in black velvet. They approached it eagerly, but next moment had stopped in their tracks, horrified. The smell was quite disgusting. Large, rotten fish were laid on handsome silver platters; cakes, burned charcoal black, were heaped on salvers; there was a great maggoty haggis, a slab of cheese covered in furry green mould and, in pride of place, an enormous grey cake in the shape of a tombstone, with tar-like icing forming the words,

Sir Nicholas de Mimsy-Porpington
died 31st October, 1492

Harry watched, amazed, as a portly ghost approached the table, crouched low and walked through it, his mouth held wide so that it passed through one of the stinking salmon.

'Can you taste it if you walk through it?' Harry asked him.

'Almost,' said the ghost sadly, and he drifted away.

'I expect they've let it rot to give it a stronger flavour,' said Hermione knowledgeably, pinching her nose and leaning closer to look at the putrid haggis.

'Can we move? I feel sick,' said Ron.

They had barely turned around, however, when a little man swooped suddenly from under the table and came to a halt in mid-air before them.

'Hello, Peeves,' said Harry cautiously.

Unlike the ghosts around them, Peeves the poltergeist was

the very reverse of pale and transparent. He was wearing a bright orange party hat, a revolving bow-tie and a broad grin on his wide, wicked face.

'Nibbles?' he said sweetly, offering them a bowl of peanuts covered in fungus.

'No thanks,' said Hermione.

'Heard you talking about poor Myrtle,' said Peeves, his eyes dancing. '*Rude* you was about poor Myrtle.' He took a deep breath and bellowed, 'OY! MYRTLE!'

'Oh, no, Peeves, don't tell her what I said, she'll be really upset,' Hermione whispered frantically. 'I didn't mean it, I don't mind her – er, hello, Myrtle.'

The squat ghost of a girl had glided over. She had the glummest face Harry had ever seen, half-hidden behind lank hair and thick, pearly spectacles.

'What?' she said sulkily.

'How are you, Myrtle?' said Hermione, in a falsely bright voice. 'It's nice to see you out of the toilet.'

Myrtle sniffed.

'Miss Granger was just talking about you –' said Peeves slyly in Myrtle's ear.

'Just saying – saying – how nice you look tonight,' said Hermione, glaring at Peeves.

Myrtle eyed Hermione suspiciously.

'You're making fun of me,' she said, silver tears welling rapidly in her small, see-through eyes.

'No – honestly – didn't I just say how nice Myrtle's looking?' said Hermione, nudging Harry and Ron painfully in the ribs.

'Oh, yeah ...'

'She did ...'

'Don't lie to me,' Myrtle gasped, tears now flooding down her face, while Peeves chuckled happily over her shoulder. 'D'you think I don't know what people call me behind my back? Fat Myrtle! Ugly Myrtle! Miserable, moaning, moping Myrtle!'

'You've missed out "spotty",' Peeves hissed in her ear.

Moaning Myrtle burst into anguished sobs and fled from the dungeon. Peeves shot after her, pelting her with mouldy peanuts, yelling, *'Spotty! Spotty!'*

'Oh, dear,' said Hermione sadly.

Nearly Headless Nick now drifted towards them through the crowd.

'Enjoying yourselves?'

'Oh, yes,' they lied.

'Not a bad turnout,' said Nearly Headless Nick proudly. 'The Wailing Widow came all the way up from Kent ... It's nearly time for my speech, I'd better go and warn the orchestra ...'

The orchestra, however, stopped playing at that very moment. They, and everyone else in the dungeon, fell silent, looking around in excitement, as a hunting horn sounded.

'Oh, here we go,' said Nearly Headless Nick bitterly.

Through the dungeon wall burst a dozen ghost horses, each ridden by a headless horseman. The assembly clapped wildly; Harry started to clap too, but stopped quickly at the sight of Nick's face.

The horses galloped into the middle of the dance floor and halted, rearing and plunging; a large ghost at the front, whose bearded head was under his arm, blowing the horn, leapt down, lifted his head high in the air so he could see over the crowd (everyone laughed) and strode over to Nearly Headless Nick, squashing his head back onto his neck.

'Nick!' he roared. 'How are you? Head still hanging in there?'

He gave a hearty guffaw and clapped Nearly Headless Nick on the shoulder.

'Welcome, Patrick,' said Nick stiffly.

'Live 'uns!' said Sir Patrick, spotting Harry, Ron and Hermione and giving a huge, fake jump of astonishment, so that his head fell off again (the crowd howled with laughter).

'Very amusing,' said Nearly Headless Nick darkly.

'Don't mind Nick!' shouted Sir Patrick's head from the floor. 'Still upset we won't let him join the Hunt! But I mean to say – look at the fellow –'

'I think,' said Harry hurriedly, at a meaningful look from Nick, 'Nick's very – frightening and – er –'

'Ha!' yelled Sir Patrick's head. 'Bet he asked you to say that!'

'If I could have everyone's attention, it's time for my speech!' said Nearly Headless Nick loudly, striding towards the podium and climbing into an icy-blue spotlight.

'My late lamented lords, ladies and gentlemen, it is my great sorrow …'

But nobody heard much more. Sir Patrick and the rest of the Headless Hunt had just started a game of Head Hockey and the crowd were turning to watch. Nearly Headless Nick tried vainly to recapture his audience, but gave up as Sir Patrick's head went sailing past him to loud cheers.

Harry was very cold by now, not to mention hungry.

'I can't stand much more of this,' Ron muttered, his teeth chattering, as the orchestra ground back into action and the ghosts swept back onto the dance floor.

'Let's go,' Harry agreed.

They backed towards the door, nodding and beaming at anyone who looked at them, and a minute later were hurrying back up the passageway full of black candles.

'Pudding might not be finished yet,' said Ron hopefully, leading the way towards the steps to the Entrance Hall.

And then Harry heard it.

'... rip ... tear ... kill ...'

It was the same voice, the same cold, murderous voice he had heard in Lockhart's office.

He stumbled to a halt, clutching at the stone wall, listening with all his might, looking around, squinting up and down the dimly lit passageway.

'Harry, what're you –?'

'It's that voice again – shut up a minute –'

'... soo hungry ... for so long ...'

'Listen!' said Harry urgently, and Ron and Hermione froze, watching him.

'... kill ... time to kill ...'

The voice was growing fainter. Harry was sure it was moving away – moving upwards. A mixture of fear and excitement gripped him as he stared at the dark ceiling; how could it be moving upwards? Was it a phantom, to whom stone ceilings didn't matter?

'This way,' he shouted, and he began to run, up the stairs, into the Entrance Hall. It was no good hoping to hear anything here, the babble of talk from the Hallowe'en feast was echoing out of the Great Hall. Harry sprinted up the marble staircase to the first floor, Ron and Hermione clattering behind him.

'Harry, what are we –'

'SHH!'

Harry strained his ears. Distantly, from the floor above, and growing fainter still, he heard the voice: '*… I smell blood … I SMELL BLOOD!*'

His stomach lurched. 'It's going to kill someone!' he shouted, and ignoring Ron and Hermione's bewildered faces, he ran up the next flight of steps three at a time, trying to listen over his own pounding footsteps.

Harry hurtled around the whole of the second floor, Ron and Hermione panting behind him, not stopping until they turned a corner into the last, deserted passage.

'Harry, *what* was that all about?' said Ron, wiping sweat off his face. 'I couldn't hear anything …'

But Hermione gave a sudden gasp, pointing down the corridor.

'Look!'

Something was shining on the wall ahead. They approached, slowly, squinting through the darkness. Foot-high words had been daubed on the wall between two windows, shimmering in the light cast by the flaming torches.

THE CHAMBER OF SECRETS
HAS BEEN OPENED.
ENEMIES OF THE HEIR,
BEWARE.

'What's that thing – hanging underneath?' said Ron, a slight quiver in his voice.

As they edged nearer, Harry almost slipped over: there was a large puddle of water on the floor. Ron and Hermione grabbed him, and they inched towards the message, eyes fixed on a dark shadow beneath it. All three of them realised what it was at once, and leapt backwards with a splash.

Mrs Norris, the caretaker's cat, was hanging by her tail from the torch bracket. She was stiff as a board, her eyes wide and staring.

For a few seconds, they didn't move. Then Ron said, 'Let's get out of here.'

'Shouldn't we try and help –' Harry began awkwardly.

'Trust me,' said Ron. 'We don't want to be found here.'

But it was too late. A rumble, as though of distant thunder, told them that the feast had just ended. From either end of the corridor where they stood came the sound of hundreds of feet climbing the stairs, and the loud, happy talk of well-fed people; next moment, students were crashing into the passage from both ends.

The chatter, the bustle, the noise died suddenly as the people in front spotted the hanging cat. Harry, Ron and Hermione stood alone, in the middle of the corridor, as silence fell among the mass of students, pressing forward to see the grisly sight.

Then someone shouted through the quiet.

'Enemies of the heir, beware! You'll be next, Mudbloods!'

It was Draco Malfoy. He had pushed to the front of the crowd, his cold eyes alive, his usually bloodless face flushed, as he grinned at the sight of the hanging, immobile cat.

CHAPTER NINE

The Writing on the Wall

'What's going on here? What's going on?'

Attracted no doubt by Malfoy's shout, Argus Filch came shouldering his way through the crowd. Then he saw Mrs Norris and fell back, clutching his face in horror.

'My cat! My cat! What's happened to Mrs Norris?' he shrieked.

And his popping eyes fell on Harry.

'You!' he screeched, *'You!* You've murdered my cat! You've killed her! I'll kill you! I'll –'

'Argus!'

Dumbledore had arrived on the scene, followed by a number of other teachers. In seconds, he had swept past Harry, Ron and Hermione and detached Mrs Norris from the torch bracket.

'Come with me, Argus,' he said to Filch. 'You too, Mr Potter, Mr Weasley, Miss Granger.'

Lockhart stepped forward eagerly.

'My office is nearest, Headmaster – just upstairs – please feel free –'

'Thank you, Gilderoy,' said Dumbledore.

The silent crowd parted to let them pass. Lockhart, looking excited and important, hurried after Dumbledore; so did Professors McGonagall and Snape.

As they entered Lockhart's darkened office there was a flurry of movement across the walls; Harry saw several of the Lockharts in the pictures dodging out of sight, their hair in rollers. The real Lockhart lit the candles on his desk and stood back. Dumbledore laid Mrs Norris on the polished surface and began to examine her. Harry, Ron and Hermione exchanged tense looks and sank into chairs outside the pool of candlelight, watching.

The tip of Dumbledore's long, crooked nose was barely an inch from Mrs Norris's fur. He was looking at her closely through his half-moon spectacles, his long fingers gently prodding and poking. Professor McGonagall was bent almost as close, her eyes narrowed. Snape loomed behind them, half in shadow, wearing a most peculiar expression: it was as though he was trying hard not to smile. And Lockhart was hovering around all of them, making suggestions.

'It was definitely a curse that killed her – probably the Transmogrifian Torture. I've seen it used many times, so unlucky I wasn't there, I know the very counter-curse that would have saved her …'

Lockhart's comments were punctuated by Filch's dry, racking sobs. He was slumped in a chair by the desk, unable to look at Mrs Norris, his face in his hands. Much as he detested Filch, Harry couldn't help feeling a bit sorry for him, though not nearly as sorry as he felt for himself. If Dumbledore believed Filch, he would be expelled for sure.

Dumbledore was now muttering strange words under his breath and tapping Mrs Norris with his wand, but nothing happened: she continued to look as though she had been recently stuffed.

'... I remember something very similar happening in Ouagadougou,' said Lockhart, 'a series of attacks, the full story's in my autobiography. I was able to provide the townsfolk with various amulets which cleared the matter up at once ...'

The photographs of Lockhart on the walls were all nodding in agreement as he talked. One of them had forgotten to remove his hairnet.

At last Dumbledore straightened up.

'She's not dead, Argus,' he said softly.

Lockhart stopped abruptly in the middle of counting the number of murders he had prevented.

'Not dead?' choked Filch, looking through his fingers at Mrs Norris. 'But why's she all – all stiff and frozen?'

'She has been Petrified,' said Dumbledore ('Ah! I thought so!' said Lockhart). 'But how, I cannot say ...'

'Ask *him*!' shrieked Filch, turning his blotched and tear-stained face to Harry.

'No second-year could have done this,' said Dumbledore firmly. 'It would take Dark Magic of the most advanced –'

'He did it, he did it!' Filch spat, his pouchy face purpling. 'You saw what he wrote on the wall! He found – in my office – he knows I'm a – I'm a –' Filch's face worked horribly. 'He knows I'm a Squib!' he finished.

'I never *touched* Mrs Norris!' Harry said loudly, uncomfortably aware of everyone looking at him, including all the Lockharts on the walls. 'And I don't even know what a Squib *is*.'

'Rubbish!' snarled Filch. 'He saw my Kwikspell letter!'

'If I might speak, Headmaster,' said Snape from the shadows, and Harry's sense of foreboding increased; he was sure nothing Snape had to say was going to do him any good.

'Potter and his friends may have simply been in the wrong place at the wrong time,' he said, a slight sneer curling his mouth as though he doubted it, 'but we do have a set of suspicious circumstances here. Why were they in the upstairs corridor at all? Why weren't they at the Hallowe'en feast?'

Harry, Ron and Hermione all launched into an explanation about the Deathday Party, '... there were hundreds of ghosts, they'll tell you we were there –'

'But why not join the feast afterwards?' said Snape, his black eyes glittering in the candlelight. 'Why go up to that corridor?'

Ron and Hermione looked at Harry.

'Because – because –' Harry said, his heart thumping very fast; something told him it would sound very far-fetched if he told them he had been led there by a bodiless voice no one but he could hear, 'because we were tired and wanted to go to bed,' he said.

'Without any supper?' said Snape, a triumphant smile flickering across his gaunt face. 'I didn't think ghosts provided food fit for living people at their parties.'

'We weren't hungry,' said Ron loudly, as his stomach gave a huge rumble.

Snape's nasty smile widened.

'I suggest, Headmaster, that Potter is not being entirely truthful,' he said. 'It might be a good idea if he were deprived of certain privileges until he is ready to tell us the whole story. I personally feel he should be taken off the Gryffindor Quidditch team until he is ready to be honest.'

'Really, Severus,' said Professor McGonagall sharply, 'I see no reason to stop the boy playing Quidditch. This cat wasn't hit over the head with a broomstick. There is no evidence at all that Potter has done anything wrong.'

Dumbledore was giving Harry a searching look. His twinkling light-blue gaze made Harry feel as though he was being X-rayed.

'Innocent until proven guilty, Severus,' he said firmly.

Snape looked furious. So did Filch.

'My cat has been Petrified!' he shrieked, his eyes popping. 'I want to see some *punishment*!'

'We will be able to cure her, Argus,' said Dumbledore patiently. 'Professor Sprout recently managed to procure some Mandrakes. As soon as they have reached their full size, I will have a potion made which will revive Mrs Norris.'

'I'll make it,' Lockhart butted in. 'I must have done it a hundred times, I could whip up a Mandrake Restorative Draught in my sleep –'

'Excuse me,' said Snape icily, 'but I believe I am the Potions master at this school.'

There was a very awkward pause.

'You may go,' Dumbledore said to Harry, Ron and Hermione.

They went, as quickly as they could without actually running. When they were a floor up from Lockhart's office, they turned into an empty classroom and closed the door quietly behind them. Harry squinted at his friends' darkened faces.

'D'you think I should have told them about that voice I heard?'

'No,' said Ron, without hesitation. 'Hearing voices no one else can hear isn't a good sign, even in the wizarding world.'

Something in Ron's voice made Harry ask, 'You do believe me, don't you?'

'Course I do,' said Ron quickly. 'But – you must admit it's weird ...'

'I know it's weird,' said Harry. 'The whole thing's weird. What was that writing on the wall about? *The Chamber has been opened* ... what's that supposed to mean?'

'You know, it rings a sort of bell,' said Ron slowly. 'I think someone told me a story about a secret chamber at Hogwarts once ... might've been Bill ...'

'And what on earth's a Squib?' said Harry.

To his surprise, Ron stifled a snigger.

'Well – it's not funny really – but as it's Filch …' he said. 'A Squib is someone who was born into a wizarding family but hasn't got any magic powers. Kind of the opposite of Muggle-born wizards, but Squibs are quite unusual. If Filch's trying to learn magic from a Kwikspell course, I reckon he must be a Squib. It would explain a lot. Like why he hates students so much.' Ron gave a satisfied smile. 'He's bitter.'

A clock chimed somewhere.

'Midnight,' said Harry. 'We'd better get to bed before Snape comes along and tries to frame us for something else.'

For a few days, the school could talk of little but the attack on Mrs Norris. Filch kept it fresh in everyone's minds by pacing the spot where she had been attacked, as though he thought the attacker might come back. Harry had seen him scrubbing the message on the wall with 'Mrs Skower's All-Purpose Magical Mess Remover', but to no effect; the words still gleamed as brightly as ever on the stone. When Filch wasn't guarding the scene of the crime, he was skulking red-eyed through the corridors, lunging out at unsuspecting students and trying to put them in detention for things like 'breathing loudly' and 'looking happy'.

Ginny Weasley seemed very disturbed by Mrs Norris's fate. According to Ron, she was a great cat-lover.

'But you hadn't really got to know Mrs Norris,' Ron told her bracingly. 'Honestly, we're much better off without her.'

Ginny's lip trembled. 'Stuff like this doesn't often happen at Hogwarts,' Ron assured her. 'They'll catch the nutter who did it and have him out of here in no time. I just hope he's got time to Petrify Filch before he's expelled. I'm only joking –' Ron added hastily, as Ginny blanched.

The attack had also had an effect on Hermione. It was quite usual for Hermione to spend a lot of time reading, but she was now doing almost nothing else. Nor could Harry and Ron get much response from her when they asked what she was up to, and not until the following Wednesday did they find out.

Harry had been held back in Potions, where Snape had made him stay behind to scrape tubeworms off the desks. After a hurried lunch, he went upstairs to meet Ron in the library, and saw Justin Finch-Fletchley, the Hufflepuff boy from Herbology, coming towards him. Harry had just opened his mouth to say hello when Justin caught sight of him, turned abruptly and sped off in the opposite direction.

Harry found Ron at the back of the library, measuring his History of Magic homework. Professor Binns had asked for a three-foot long composition on 'The Medieval Assembly of European Wizards'.

'I don't believe it, I'm still eight inches short …' said Ron furiously, letting go of his parchment, which sprang back into a roll, 'and Hermione's done four feet seven inches and her writing's *tiny*.'

'Where is she?' asked Harry, grabbing the tape measure and unrolling his own homework.

'Somewhere over there,' said Ron, pointing along the shelves, 'looking for another book. I think she's trying to read the whole library before Christmas.'

Harry told Ron about Justin Finch-Fletchley running away from him.

'Dunno why you care, I thought he was a bit of an idiot,' said Ron, scribbling away, making his writing as large as possible. 'All that rubbish about Lockhart being so great –'

Hermione emerged from between the bookshelves. She looked irritable and at last seemed ready to talk to them.

'*All* the copies of *Hogwarts: A History* have been taken out,' she said, sitting down next to Harry and Ron. 'And there's a two-week waiting list. I *wish* I hadn't left my copy at home, but I couldn't fit it in my trunk with all the Lockhart books.'

'Why do you want it?' said Harry.

'The same reason everyone else wants it,' said Hermione, 'to read up on the legend of the Chamber of Secrets.'

'What's that?' said Harry quickly.

'That's just it. I can't remember,' said Hermione, biting her lip. 'And I can't find the story anywhere else –'

'Hermione, let me read your composition,' said Ron desperately, checking his watch.

'No, I won't,' said Hermione, suddenly severe. 'You've had ten days to finish it.'

'I only need another two inches, go on …'

The bell rang. Ron and Hermione led the way to History of Magic, bickering.

History of Magic was the dullest subject on their timetable. Professor Binns, who taught it, was their only ghost teacher, and the most exciting thing that ever happened in his classes was his entering the room through the blackboard. Ancient and shrivelled, many people said he hadn't noticed he was dead. He had simply got up to teach one day and left his body behind him in an armchair in front of the staff-room fire; his routine had not varied in the slightest since.

Today was as boring as ever. Professor Binns opened his notes and began to read in a flat drone like an old vacuum cleaner until nearly everyone in the class was in a deep stupor, occasionally coming round long enough to copy down a name or date, then falling asleep again. He had been speaking for half an hour when something happened that had never happened before. Hermione put up her hand.

Professor Binns, glancing up in the middle of a deadly dull lecture on the International Warlock Convention of 1289, looked amazed.

'Miss – er –?'

'Granger, Professor. I was wondering if you could tell us anything about the Chamber of Secrets,' said Hermione in a clear voice.

Dean Thomas, who had been sitting with his mouth hanging open, gazing out of the window, jerked out of his trance; Lavender Brown's head came up off her arms and Neville's elbow slipped off his desk.

Professor Binns blinked.

'My subject is History of Magic,' he said in his dry, wheezy voice. 'I deal with *facts*, Miss Granger, not myths and legends.' He cleared his throat with a small noise like chalk snapping and continued, 'In September of that year, a sub-committee of Sardinian sorcerers –'

He stuttered to a halt. Hermione's hand was waving in the air again.

'Miss Grant?'

'Please, sir, don't legends always have a basis in fact?'

Professor Binns was looking at her in such amazement, Harry was sure no student had ever interrupted him before, alive or dead.

'Well,' said Professor Binns slowly, 'yes, one could argue that, I suppose.' He peered at Hermione as though he had never seen a student properly before. 'However, the legend of which you speak is such a very *sensational*, even *ludicrous* tale ...'

But the whole class was now hanging on Professor Binns's every word. He looked dimly at them all, every face turned to his. Harry could tell he was completely thrown by such an unusual show of interest.

'Oh, very well,' he said slowly. 'Let me see ... the Chamber of Secrets ...

'You all know, of course, that Hogwarts was founded over a thousand years ago – the precise date is uncertain – by the four greatest witches and wizards of the age. The four school houses are named after them: Godric Gryffindor, Helga Hufflepuff, Rowena Ravenclaw and Salazar Slytherin. They built this castle together, far from prying Muggle eyes, for it was an age when magic was feared by common people, and witches and wizards suffered much persecution.'

He paused, gazed blearily around the room, and continued, 'For a few years, the founders worked in harmony together, seeking out youngsters who showed signs of magic and bringing them to the castle to be educated. But then disagreements sprang up between them. A rift began to grow between Slytherin and the others. Slytherin wished to be more *selective* about the students admitted to Hogwarts. He believed that magical learning should be kept within all-magic families. He disliked taking students of Muggle parentage, believing them to be untrustworthy. After a while, there was a serious argument on the subject between Slytherin and Gryffindor, and Slytherin left the school.'

Professor Binns paused again, pursing his lips, looking like a wrinkled old tortoise.

'Reliable historical sources tell us this much,' he said, 'but these honest facts have been obscured by the fanciful legend of the Chamber of Secrets. The story goes that Slytherin had built a hidden chamber in the castle, of which the other founders knew nothing.

'Slytherin, according to the legend, sealed the Chamber of Secrets so that none would be able to open it until his own true heir arrived at the school. The heir alone would be able to unseal the Chamber of Secrets, unleash the horror within, and use it to purge the school of all who were unworthy to study magic.'

There was silence as he finished telling the story, but it wasn't the usual, sleepy silence that filled Professor Binns's classes. There was unease in the air as everyone continued to watch him, hoping for more. Professor Binns looked faintly annoyed.

'The whole thing is arrant nonsense, of course,' he said. 'Naturally, the school has been searched for evidence of such a chamber, many times, by the most learned witches and wizards. It does not exist. A tale told to frighten the gullible.'

Hermione's hand was back in the air.

'Sir – what exactly do you mean by the "horror within" the Chamber?'

'That is believed to be some sort of monster, which the heir of Slytherin alone can control,' said Professor Binns in his dry, reedy voice.

The class exchanged nervous looks.

'I tell you, the thing does not exist,' said Professor Binns, shuffling his notes. 'There is no Chamber and no monster.'

'But, sir,' said Seamus Finnigan, 'if the Chamber can only be opened by Slytherin's true heir, no one else *would* be able to find it, would they?'

'Nonsense, O'Flaherty,' said Professor Binns in an aggravated tone. 'If a long succession of Hogwarts headmasters and headmistresses haven't found the thing –'

'But, Professor,' piped up Parvati Patil, 'you'd probably have to use Dark Magic to open it –'

'Just because a wizard *doesn't* use Dark Magic, doesn't mean he *can't*, Miss Pennyfeather,' snapped Professor Binns. 'I repeat, if the likes of Dumbledore –'

'But maybe you've got to be related to Slytherin, so Dumbledore couldn't –' began Dean Thomas, but Professor Binns had had enough.

'That will do,' he said sharply. 'It is a myth! It does not exist! There is not a shred of evidence that Slytherin ever built so much as a secret broom cupboard! I regret telling you such a foolish story! We will return, if you please, to *history*, to solid, believable, verifiable *fact*!'

And within five minutes, the class had sunk back into its usual torpor.

'I always knew Salazar Slytherin was a twisted old loony,' Ron told Harry and Hermione, as they fought their way through the teeming corridors at the end of the lesson to drop off their bags before dinner. 'But I never knew he started all this pure-blood stuff. I wouldn't be in his house if you paid me. Honestly, if the Sorting Hat had tried to put me in Slytherin, I'd've got the train straight back home ...'

Hermione nodded fervently, but Harry didn't say anything. His stomach had just dropped unpleasantly.

Harry had never told Ron and Hermione that the Sorting Hat had seriously considered putting *him* in Slytherin. He could remember, as though it was yesterday, the small voice that had spoken in his ear when he'd placed the Hat on his head a year before.

'You could be great, you know, it's all here in your head, and Slytherin would help you on the way to greatness, no doubt about that ...'

But Harry, who had already heard of Slytherin house's reputation for turning out Dark wizards, had thought desperately, 'Not Slytherin!' and the Hat had said, '*Oh, well, if you're sure … better be Gryffindor …*'

As they were shunted along in the throng, Colin Creevey went past.

'Hiya, Harry!'

'Hullo, Colin,' said Harry automatically.

'Harry – Harry – a boy in my class has been saying you're –'

But Colin was so small he couldn't fight against the tide of people bearing him towards the Great Hall; they heard him squeak, 'See you, Harry!' and he was gone.

'What's a boy in his class saying about you?' Hermione wondered.

'That I'm Slytherin's heir, I expect,' said Harry, his stomach dropping another inch or so, as he suddenly remembered the way Justin Finch-Fletchley had run away from him at lunchtime.

'People here'll believe anything,' said Ron in disgust.

The crowd thinned and they were able to climb the next staircase without difficulty.

'D'you *really* think there's a Chamber of Secrets?' Ron asked Hermione.

'I don't know,' she said, frowning. 'Dumbledore couldn't cure Mrs Norris, and that makes me think that whatever attacked her might not be – well – human.'

As she spoke, they turned a corner and found themselves at the end of the very corridor where the attack had happened.

They stopped and looked. The scene was just as it had been that night, except that there was no stiff cat hanging from the torch bracket, and an empty chair stood against the wall bearing the message 'The Chamber has been opened.'

'That's where Filch has been keeping guard,' Ron muttered.

They looked at each other. The corridor was deserted.

'Can't hurt to have a poke around,' said Harry, dropping his bag and getting to his hands and knees so that he could crawl along, searching for clues.

'Scorch marks!' he said. 'Here – and here –'

'Come and look at this!' said Hermione. 'This is funny …'

Harry got up and crossed to the window next to the message on the wall. Hermione was pointing at the topmost pane, where around twenty spiders were scuttling, apparently fighting to get through a small crack in the glass. A long, silvery thread was dangling like a rope, as though they had all climbed it in their hurry to get outside.

'Have you ever seen spiders act like that?' said Hermione wonderingly.

'No,' said Harry, 'have you, Ron? Ron?'

He looked over his shoulder. Ron was standing well back, and seemed to be fighting the impulse to run.

'What's up?' said Harry.

'I – don't – like – spiders,' said Ron tensely.

'I never knew that,' said Hermione, looking at Ron in surprise. 'You've used spiders in potions loads of times …'

'I don't mind them dead,' said Ron, who was carefully

looking anywhere but at the window, 'I just don't like the way they move …'

Hermione giggled.

'It's not funny,' said Ron, fiercely. 'If you must know, when I was three, Fred turned my – my teddy bear into a dirty great spider because I broke his toy broomstick. You wouldn't like them either if you'd been holding your bear and suddenly it had too many legs and …'

He broke off, shuddering. Hermione was obviously still trying not to laugh. Feeling they had better get off the subject, Harry said, 'Remember all that water on the floor? Where did that come from? Someone's mopped it up.'

'It was about here,' said Ron, recovering himself to walk a few paces past Filch's chair and pointing. 'Level with this door.'

He reached for the brass doorknob but suddenly withdrew his hand as though he'd been burned.

'What's the matter?' said Harry.

'Can't go in there,' said Ron gruffly, 'that's a girls' toilet.'

'Oh, Ron, there won't be anyone in there,' said Hermione, standing up and coming over. 'That's Moaning Myrtle's place. Come on, let's have a look.'

And ignoring the large 'Out of Order' sign, she opened the door.

It was the gloomiest, most depressing bathroom Harry had ever set foot in. Under a large, cracked and spotted mirror was a row of chipped, stone sinks. The floor was damp and reflected the dull light given off by the stubs of a few candles, burning low in their holders; the wooden doors to the cubicles were flaking and scratched and one of them was dangling off its hinges.

Hermione put her fingers to her lips and set off towards the end cubicle. When she reached it she said, 'Hello, Myrtle, how are you?'

Harry and Ron went to look. Moaning Myrtle was floating on the cistern of the toilet, picking a spot on her chin.

'This is a *girls'* bathroom,' she said, eyeing Ron and Harry suspiciously. '*They're* not girls.'

'No,' Hermione agreed. 'I just wanted to show them how – er – nice it is in here.'

She waved vaguely at the dirty old mirror and the damp floor.

'Ask her if she saw anything,' Harry mouthed at Hermione.

'What are you whispering?' said Myrtle, staring at him.

'Nothing,' said Harry quickly. 'We wanted to ask –'

'I wish people would stop talking behind my back!' said Myrtle, in a voice choked with tears. 'I *do* have feelings, you know, even if I *am* dead.'

'Myrtle, no one wants to upset you,' said Hermione. 'Harry only –'

'No one wants to upset me! That's a good one!' howled Myrtle. 'My life was nothing but misery at this place and now people come along ruining my death!'

'We wanted to ask you if you'd seen anything funny lately,' said Hermione quickly, 'because a cat was attacked right outside your front door on Hallowe'en.'

'Did you see anyone near here that night?' said Harry.

'I wasn't paying attention,' said Myrtle dramatically. 'Peeves upset me so much I came in here and tried to *kill* myself. Then, of course, I remembered that I'm – that I'm –'

'Already dead,' said Ron helpfully.

Myrtle gave a tragic sob, rose up in the air, turned over and dived head first into the toilet, splashing water all over them and vanishing from sight; from the direction of her muffled sobs, she had come to rest somewhere in the U-bend.

Harry and Ron stood with their mouths open, but Hermione shrugged wearily and said, 'Honestly, that was almost cheerful for Myrtle ... come on, let's go.'

Harry had barely closed the door on Myrtle's gurgling sobs when a loud voice made all three of them jump.

'RON!'

Percy Weasley had stopped dead at the head of the stairs, prefect badge agleam, an expression of complete shock on his face.

'That's a *girls'* bathroom!' he gasped. 'What were *you* –?'

'Just having a look around,' Ron shrugged. 'Clues, you know ...'

Percy swelled in a manner that reminded Harry forcefully of Mrs Weasley.

'Get – away – from – there –' he said, striding towards them and starting to chivvy them along, flapping his arms. 'Don't you *care* what this looks like? Coming back here while everyone's at dinner ...'

'Why shouldn't we be here?' said Ron hotly, stopping short and glaring at Percy. 'Listen, we never laid a finger on that cat!'

'That's what I told Ginny,' said Percy fiercely, 'but she still seems to think you're going to be expelled; I've never seen her so upset, crying her eyes out. You might think of *her*, all the first-years are thoroughly over-excited by this business –'

'*You* don't care about Ginny,' said Ron, whose ears were reddening now. '*You're* just worried I'm going to mess up your chances of being Head Boy.'

'Five points from Gryffindor!' Percy said tersely, fingering his prefect badge. 'And I hope it teaches you a lesson! No more *detective work*, or I'll write to Mum!'

And he strode off, the back of his neck as red as Ron's ears.

Harry, Ron and Hermione chose seats as far as possible from Percy in the common room that night. Ron was still in a very bad temper and kept blotting his Charms homework. When he reached absently for his wand to remove the smudges, it ignited the parchment. Fuming almost as much as his homework, Ron slammed *The Standard Book of Spells, Grade 2* shut. To Harry's surprise, Hermione followed suit.

'Who can it be, though?' she said in a quiet voice, as though continuing a conversation they had just been having. 'Who'd *want* all the Squibs and Muggle-borns out of Hogwarts?'

'Let's think,' said Ron in mock puzzlement. 'Who do we know who thinks Muggle-borns are scum?'

He looked at Hermione. Hermione looked back, unconvinced.

'If you're talking about Malfoy –'

'Of course I am!' said Ron. 'You heard him: *"You'll be next, Mudbloods!"* Come on, you've only got to look at his foul rat face to know it's him –'

'Malfoy, the heir of Slytherin?' said Hermione sceptically.

'Look at his family,' said Harry, closing his books, too. 'The whole lot of them have been in Slytherin, he's always boasting about it. They could easily be Slytherin's descendants. His father's definitely evil enough.'

'They could've had the key to the Chamber of Secrets for centuries!' said Ron. 'Handing it down, father to son …'

'Well,' said Hermione cautiously, 'I suppose it's possible …'

'But how do we prove it?' said Harry darkly.

'There might be a way,' said Hermione slowly, dropping her voice still further with a quick glance across the room at Percy. 'Of course, it would be difficult. And dangerous, very dangerous. We'd be breaking about fifty school rules, I expect.'

'If, in a month or so, you feel like explaining, you will let us know, won't you?' said Ron irritably.

'All right,' said Hermione coldly. 'What we'd need to do is to get inside the Slytherin common room and ask Malfoy a few questions without him realising it's us.'

'But that's impossible,' Harry said, as Ron laughed.

'No, it's not,' said Hermione. 'All we'd need would be some Polyjuice Potion.'

'What's that?' said Ron and Harry together.

'Snape mentioned it in class a few weeks ago –'

'D'you think we've got nothing better to do in Potions than listen to Snape?' muttered Ron.

'It transforms you into somebody else. Think about it! We could change into three of the Slytherins. No one would know it was us. Malfoy would probably tell us anything. He's probably boasting about it in the Slytherin common room right now, if only we could hear him.'

'This Polyjuice stuff sounds a bit dodgy to me,' said Ron, frowning. 'What if we were stuck looking like three of the Slytherins for ever?'

'It wears off after a while,' said Hermione, waving her hand impatiently, 'but getting hold of the recipe will be very difficult. Snape said it was in a book called *Moste Potente Potions* and it's bound to be in the Restricted Section of the library.'

There was only one way to get out a book from the Restricted Section: you needed a signed note of permission from a teacher.

'Hard to see why we'd want the book, really,' said Ron, 'if we weren't going to try and make one of the potions.'

'I think,' said Hermione, 'that if we made it sound as though we were just interested in the theory, we might stand a chance …'

'Oh, come on, no teacher's going to fall for that,' said Ron. 'They'd have to be really thick …'

CHAPTER TEN

The Rogue Bludger

Since the disastrous episode of the pixies, Professor Lockhart had not brought live creatures to class. Instead, he read passages from his books to them, and sometimes re-enacted some of the more dramatic bits. He usually picked Harry to help him with these reconstructions; so far, Harry had been forced to play a simple Transylvanian villager whom Lockhart had cured of a Babbling Curse, a yeti with a head-cold, and a vampire who had been unable to eat anything except lettuce since Lockhart had dealt with him.

Harry was hauled to the front of the class during their very next Defence Against the Dark Arts lesson, this time acting a werewolf. If he hadn't had a very good reason for keeping Lockhart in a good mood, he would have refused to do it.

'Nice loud howl, Harry – exactly – and then, if you'll believe it, I pounced – like this – *slammed* him to the floor – thus – with one hand, I managed to hold him down – with my other, I put my wand to his throat – I then screwed up my remaining strength and performed the immensely complex Homorphus Charm – he let out a piteous moan – go on, Harry – higher than that – good – the fur vanished – the fangs shrank – and he turned back into a man. Simple, yet effective – and another village will remember me forever as the hero who delivered them from the monthly terror of werewolf attacks.'

The bell rang and Lockhart got to his feet.

'Homework: compose a poem about my defeat of the Wagga Wagga werewolf! Signed copies of *Magical Me* to the author of the best one!'

The class began to leave. Harry returned to the back of the room, where Ron and Hermione were waiting.

'Ready?' Harry muttered.

'Wait till everyone's gone,' said Hermione nervously. 'All right …'

She approached Lockhart's desk, a piece of paper clutched tightly in her hand, Harry and Ron right behind her.

'Er – Professor Lockhart?' Hermione stammered. 'I wanted to – to get this book out of the library. Just for background reading.' She held out the piece of paper, her hand shaking slightly. 'But the thing is, it's in the Restricted Section of the library, so I need a teacher to sign for it – I'm sure it would help me understand what you say in *Gadding with Ghouls* about slow-acting venoms …'

'Ah, *Gadding with Ghouls*!' said Lockhart, taking the note from Hermione and smiling widely at her. 'Possibly my very favourite book. You enjoyed it?'

'Oh, yes,' said Hermione eagerly. 'So clever, the way you trapped that last one with the tea-strainer …'

'Well, I'm sure no one will mind me giving the best student in the year a little extra help,' said Lockhart warmly, and he pulled out an enormous peacock quill. 'Yes, nice, isn't it?' he said, misreading the revolted look on Ron's face. 'I usually save it for book-signings.'

He scrawled an enormous loopy signature on the note and handed it back to Hermione.

'So, Harry,' said Lockhart, while Hermione folded the note with fumbling fingers and slipped it into her bag, 'tomorrow's the first Quidditch match of the season, I believe? Gryffindor against Slytherin, is it not? I hear you're a useful player. I was a Seeker, too. I was asked to try for the National Squad, but preferred to dedicate my life to the eradication of the Dark Forces. Still, if ever you feel the need for a little private training, don't hesitate to ask. Always happy to pass on my expertise to less able players …'

Harry made an indistinct noise in his throat and then hurried off after Ron and Hermione.

'I don't believe it,' he said, as the three of them examined the signature on the note. 'He didn't even *look* at the book we wanted.'

'That's because he's a brainless git,' said Ron. 'But who cares, we've got what we needed.'

'He is *not* a brainless git,' said Hermione shrilly, as they half ran towards the library.

'Just because he said you were the best student in the year …'

They dropped their voices as they entered the muffled stillness of the library. Madam Pince, the librarian, was a thin, irritable woman who looked like an underfed vulture.

'*Moste Potente Potions?*' she repeated suspiciously, trying to take the note from Hermione; but Hermione wouldn't let go.

'I was wondering if I could keep it,' she said breathlessly.

'Oh, come on,' said Ron, wrenching it from her grasp and thrusting it at Madam Pince. 'We'll get you another autograph. Lockhart'll sign anything if it stands still long enough.'

Madam Pince held the note up to the light, as though determined to detect a forgery, but it passed the test. She stalked away between the lofty shelves and returned several minutes later carrying a large and mouldy-looking book. Hermione put it carefully into her bag and they left, trying not to walk too quickly or look too guilty.

Five minutes later, they were barricaded in Moaning Myrtle's out-of-order bathroom once again. Hermione had overridden Ron's objections by pointing out that it was the last place anyone in their right minds would go, so they were guaranteed some privacy. Moaning Myrtle was crying noisily in her cubicle, but they were ignoring her, and she them.

Hermione opened *Moste Potente Potions* carefully, and the three of them bent over the damp-spotted pages. It was clear from a glance why it belonged in the Restricted Section. Some of the potions had effects almost too gruesome to think about, and there were some very unpleasant illustrations, which included a man who seemed to have been turned inside out and a witch sprouting several extra pairs of arms out of her head.

'Here it is,' said Hermione excitedly, as she found the page headed *The Polyjuice Potion*. It was decorated with drawings of people halfway through transforming into other people. Harry sincerely hoped the artist had imagined the looks of intense pain on their faces.

'This is the most complicated potion I've ever seen,' said Hermione, as they scanned the recipe. 'Lacewing flies, leeches, fluxweed and knotgrass,' she murmured, running her finger down the list of ingredients. 'Well, they're easy enough, they're in the student store-cupboard, we can help ourselves. Oooh, look, powdered horn of a Bicorn – don't know where we're going to get that … Shredded skin of a Boomslang – that'll be tricky, too – and of course a bit of whoever we want to change into.'

'Excuse me?' said Ron sharply. 'What d'you mean, a bit of whoever we're changing into? I'm drinking *nothing* with Crabbe's toenails in it …'

Hermione continued as though she hadn't heard him.

'We don't have to worry about that yet, though, because we add those bits last …'

Ron turned, speechless, to Harry, who had another worry.

'D'you realise how much we're going to have to steal, Hermione? Shredded skin of Boomslang, that's definitely not in the students' cupboard. What're we going to do, break into Snape's private stores? I don't know if this is a good idea …'

Hermione shut the book with a snap.

'Well, if you two are going to chicken out, fine,' she said. There were bright pink patches on her cheeks and her eyes were brighter than usual. '*I* don't want to break rules, you know. *I* think threatening Muggle-borns is far worse than brewing up a difficult potion. But if you don't want to find out if it's Malfoy, I'll go straight to Madam Pince now and hand the book back in ...'

'I never thought I'd see the day when you'd be persuading us to break rules,' said Ron. 'All right, we'll do it. But not toenails, OK?'

'How long will it take to make, anyway?' said Harry, as Hermione, looking happier, opened the book again.

'Well, as the fluxweed has got to be picked at the full moon and the lacewings have got to be stewed for twenty-one days ... I'd say it'd be ready in about a month, if we can get all the ingredients.'

'A month?' said Ron. 'Malfoy could have attacked half the Muggle-borns in the school by then!' But Hermione's eyes narrowed dangerously again, and he added swiftly, 'But it's the best plan we've got, so full steam ahead, I say.'

However, while Hermione was checking that the coast was clear for them to leave the bathroom, Ron muttered to Harry, 'It'll be a lot less hassle if you can just knock Malfoy off his broom tomorrow.'

Harry woke early on Saturday morning and lay for a while thinking about the coming Quidditch match. He was nervous, mainly at the thought of what Wood would say if Gryffindor lost, but also at the idea of facing a team mounted on the fastest racing brooms gold could buy. He had never wanted to beat Slytherin so badly. After half an hour of lying there with his insides churning, he got up, dressed, and went down to breakfast early, where he found the rest of the Gryffindor team huddled at the long, empty table, all looking uptight and not speaking much.

As eleven o'clock approached, the whole school started to make its way down to the Quidditch stadium. It was a muggy sort of day with a hint of thunder in the air. Ron and Hermione came hurrying over to wish Harry good luck as he entered the changing rooms. The team pulled on their scarlet Gryffindor robes, then sat down to listen to Wood's usual pre-match pep talk.

'Slytherin have better brooms than us,' he began, 'no point denying it. But we've got better *people* on our brooms. We've trained harder than they have, we've been flying in all weathers –' ('Too true,' muttered George Weasley. 'I haven't been properly dry since August') '– and we're going to make them rue the day they let that little bit of slime, Malfoy, buy his way onto their team.'

Chest heaving with emotion, Wood turned to Harry.

'It'll be down to you, Harry, to show them that a Seeker has to have something more than a rich father. Get to that Snitch before Malfoy or die trying, Harry, because we've got to win today, we've got to.'

'So no pressure, Harry,' said Fred, winking at him.

As they walked out onto the pitch, a roar of noise greeted them; mainly cheers, because Ravenclaw and Hufflepuff were anxious to see Slytherin beaten, but the Slytherins in the crowd made their boos and hisses heard too. Madam Hooch, the Quidditch teacher, asked Flint and Wood to shake hands, which they did, giving each other threatening stares and gripping rather harder than was necessary.

'On my whistle,' said Madam Hooch, 'three … two … one …'

With a roar from the crowd to speed them upwards, the fourteen players rose towards the leaden sky. Harry flew higher than any of them, squinting around for the Snitch.

'All right there, Scarhead?' yelled Malfoy, shooting underneath him as though to show off the speed of his broom.

Harry had no time to reply. At that very moment, a heavy black Bludger came pelting towards him; he avoided it so narrowly that he felt it ruffle his hair as it passed.

'Close one, Harry!' said George, streaking past him with his club in his hand, ready to knock the Bludger back towards a Slytherin. Harry saw George give the Bludger a powerful whack in the direction of Adrian Pucey, but the Bludger changed direction in mid-air and shot straight for Harry again.

Harry dropped quickly to avoid it, and George managed to hit it hard towards Malfoy. Once again, the Bludger swerved like a boomerang and shot at Harry's head.

Harry put on a burst of speed and zoomed towards the other end of the pitch. He could hear the Bludger whistling along behind him. What was going on? Bludgers never concentrated on one player like this, it was their job to try and unseat as many people as possible …

Fred Weasley was waiting for the Bludger at the other end. Harry ducked as Fred swung at the Bludger with all his might; the Bludger was knocked off course.

'That's done it!' Fred yelled happily, but he was wrong; as though it was magnetically attracted towards Harry, the Bludger pelted after him once more and Harry was forced to fly off at full speed.

It had started to rain; Harry felt heavy drops fall onto his face, splattering onto his glasses. He didn't have a clue what was going on in the rest of the game until he heard Lee Jordan, who was commentating, say, 'Slytherin lead, sixty points to zero.'

The Slytherins' superior brooms were clearly doing their jobs, and meanwhile the mad Bludger was doing all it could to knock Harry out of the air. Fred and George were now flying so close to him on either side that Harry could see nothing at all except their flailing arms and had no chance to look for the Snitch, let alone catch it.

'Someone's – tampered – with – this – Bludger –' Fred grunted, swinging his bat with all his might at it as it launched a new attack on Harry.

'We need time out,' said George, trying to signal to Wood and stop the Bludger breaking Harry's nose at the same time.

Wood had obviously got the message. Madam Hooch's whistle rang out and Harry, Fred and George dived for the ground, still trying to avoid the mad Bludger.

'What's going on?' said Wood, as the Gryffindor team

huddled together, while Slytherins in the crowd jeered. 'We're being flattened. Fred, George, where were you when that Bludger stopped Angelina scoring?'

'We were twenty feet above her, stopping the other Bludger murdering Harry, Oliver,' said George angrily. 'Someone's fixed it – it won't leave Harry alone, it hasn't gone for anyone else all game. The Slytherins must have done something to it.'

'But the Bludgers have been locked in Madam Hooch's office since our last practice, and there was nothing wrong with them then ...' said Wood, anxiously.

Madam Hooch was walking towards them. Over her shoulder, Harry could see the Slytherin team jeering and pointing in his direction.

'Listen,' said Harry, as she came nearer and nearer, 'with you two flying round me all the time the only way I'm going to catch the Snitch is if it flies up my sleeve. Go back to the rest of the team and let me deal with the rogue one.'

'Don't be thick,' said Fred. 'It'll take your head off.'

Wood was looking from Harry to the Weasleys.

'Oliver, this is mad,' said Alicia Spinnet angrily. 'You can't let Harry deal with that thing on his own. Let's ask for an inquiry –'

'If we stop now, we'll have to forfeit the match!' said Harry. 'And we're not losing to Slytherin just because of a mad Bludger! Come on, Oliver, tell them to leave me alone!'

'This is all your fault,' George said angrily to Wood. '"Get the Snitch or die trying" – what a stupid thing to tell him!'

Madam Hooch had joined them.

'Ready to resume play?' she asked Wood.

Wood looked at the determined look on Harry's face.

'All right,' he said. 'Fred, George, you heard Harry – leave him alone and let him deal with the Bludger on his own.'

The rain was falling more heavily now. On Madam Hooch's whistle, Harry kicked hard into the air and heard the tell-tale whoosh of the Bludger behind him. Higher and higher Harry climbed. He looped and swooped, spiralled, zigzagged and rolled. Slightly dizzy, he nevertheless kept his eyes wide open. Rain was speckling his glasses and ran up his nostrils as he hung upside down, avoiding another fierce dive from the Bludger. He could hear laughter from the crowd; he knew he must look very stupid, but the rogue Bludger was heavy and couldn't change direction as quickly as he could. He began a kind of roller-coaster ride around the edges of the stadium, squinting through the silver sheets of rain to the Gryffindor goalposts, where Adrian Pucey was trying to get past Wood …

A whistling in Harry's ear told him the Bludger had just missed him again; he turned right over and sped in the opposite direction.

'Training for the ballet, Potter?' yelled Malfoy, as Harry was forced to do a stupid kind of twirl in mid-air to dodge the Bludger. Off Harry fled, the Bludger trailing a few feet behind him: and then, glaring back at Malfoy in hatred, he saw it, *the Golden Snitch*. It was hovering inches above Malfoy's left ear – and Malfoy, busy laughing at Harry, hadn't seen it.

For an agonising moment, Harry hung in mid-air, not daring to speed towards Malfoy in case he looked up and saw the Snitch.

WHAM!

He had stayed still a second too long. The Bludger had hit him at last, smashed into his elbow, and Harry felt his arm break. Dimly, dazed by the searing pain in his arm, he slid sideways on his rain-drenched broom, one knee still crooked over it, his right arm dangling useless at his side. The Bludger came pelting back for a second attack, this time aiming at his face. Harry swerved out of the way, one idea firmly lodged in his numb brain: *get to Malfoy*.

Through a haze of rain and pain he dived for the shimmering, sneering face below him and saw its eyes widen with fear: Malfoy thought Harry was attacking him.

'What the –' he gasped, careering out of Harry's way.

Harry took his remaining hand off his broom and made a wild snatch; he felt his fingers close on the cold Snitch but was now only gripping the broom with his legs and there was a yell from the crowd below as he headed straight for the ground, trying hard not to pass out.

With a splattering thud he hit the mud and rolled off his broom. His arm was hanging at a very strange angle. Riddled with pain, he heard, as though from a distance, a good deal of whistling and shouting. He focused on the Snitch clutched in his good hand.

'Aha,' he said vaguely, 'we've won.'

And he fainted.

He came round, rain falling on his face, still lying on the pitch, with someone leaning over him. He saw a glitter of teeth.

'Oh no, not you,' he moaned.

'Doesn't know what he's saying,' said Lockhart loudly, to the anxious crowd of Gryffindors pressing around them. 'Not to worry, Harry. I'm about to fix your arm.'

'No!' said Harry. 'I'll keep it like this, thanks ...'

He tried to sit up, but the pain was terrible. He heard a familiar clicking noise nearby.

'I don't want a photo of this, Colin,' he said loudly.

'Lie back, Harry,' said Lockhart soothingly. 'It's a simple charm I've used countless times.'

'Why can't I just go to the hospital wing?' said Harry through clenched teeth.

'He should really, Professor,' said a muddy Wood, who couldn't help grinning even though his Seeker was injured. 'Great capture, Harry, really spectacular, your best yet, I'd say.'

Through the thicket of legs around him, Harry spotted Fred and George Weasley wrestling the rogue Bludger into a box. It was still putting up a terrific fight.

'Stand back,' said Lockhart, who was rolling up his jade-green sleeves.

'No – don't –' said Harry weakly, but Lockhart was twirling his wand and a second later had directed it straight at Harry's arm.

A strange and unpleasant sensation started at Harry's shoulder and spread all the way down to his fingertips. It felt as though his arm was being deflated. He didn't dare look at what was happening. He had shut his eyes, his face turned away from his arm, but his worst fears were realised as the people above him gasped and Colin Creevey began clicking away madly. His arm didn't hurt any more – but nor did it feel remotely like an arm.

'Ah,' said Lockhart. 'Yes. Well, that can sometimes happen. But the point is, the bones are no longer broken. That's the thing to bear in mind. So, Harry, just toddle up to the Hospital Wing – ah, Mr Weasley, Miss Granger, would you escort him? – and Madam Pomfrey will be able to – er – tidy you up a bit.'

As Harry got to his feet, he felt strangely lopsided. Taking a deep breath he looked down at his right side. What he saw nearly made him pass out again.

Poking out of the end of his robes was what looked like a thick, flesh-coloured rubber glove. He tried to move his fingers. Nothing happened.

Lockhart hadn't mended Harry's bones. He had removed them.

Madam Pomfrey wasn't at all pleased.

'You should have come straight to me!' she raged, holding up the sad, limp remainder of what, half an hour before, had been a working arm. 'I can mend bones in a second – but growing them back –'

'You will be able to, won't you?' said Harry desperately.

'I'll be able to, certainly, but it will be painful,' said Madam Pomfrey grimly, throwing Harry a pair of pyjamas. 'You'll have to stay the night ...'

Hermione waited outside the curtain drawn around Harry's bed while Ron helped him into his pyjamas. It took a while to stuff the rubbery, boneless arm into a sleeve.

'How can you stick up for Lockhart now, Hermione, eh?' Ron called through the curtain as he pulled Harry's limp fingers through the cuff. 'If Harry had wanted de-boning he would have asked.'

'Anyone can make a mistake,' said Hermione. 'And it doesn't hurt any more, does it, Harry?'

'No,' said Harry, 'but it doesn't do anything else, either.'

As he swung himself onto the bed, his arm flapped pointlessly.

Hermione and Madam Pomfrey came around the curtain. Madam Pomfrey was holding a large bottle of something labelled 'Skele-Gro'.

'You're in for a rough night,' she said, pouring out a steaming beakerful and handing it to him. 'Regrowing bones is a nasty business.'

So was taking the Skele-Gro. It burned Harry's mouth and throat as it went down, making him cough and splutter. Still tut-tutting about dangerous sports and inept teachers, Madam Pomfrey retreated, leaving Ron and Hermione to help Harry gulp down some water.

'We won, though,' said Ron, a grin breaking across his face. 'That was some catch you made. Malfoy's face … he looked ready to kill!'

'I want to know how he fixed that Bludger,' said Hermione darkly.

'We can add that to the list of questions we'll ask him when we've taken the Polyjuice Potion,' said Harry, sinking back onto his pillows. 'I hope it tastes better than this stuff …'

'If it's got bits of Slytherins in it? You've got to be joking,' said Ron.

The door of the hospital wing burst open at that moment. Filthy and soaking wet, the rest of the Gryffindor team had arrived to see Harry.

'Unbelievable flying, Harry,' said George. 'I've just seen Marcus Flint yelling at Malfoy. Something about having the Snitch on top of his head and not noticing. Malfoy didn't seem too happy.'

They had brought cakes, sweets and bottles of pumpkin juice; they gathered around Harry's bed and were just getting started on what promised to be a good party when Madam Pomfrey came storming over, shouting, 'This boy needs rest, he's got thirty-three bones to regrow! Out! OUT!'

And Harry was left alone, with nothing to distract him from the stabbing pains in his limp arm.

Hours and hours later, Harry woke quite suddenly in the pitch blackness and gave a small yelp of pain: his arm now felt full of large splinters. For a second, he thought it was that which had woken him. Then, with a thrill of horror, he realised that someone was sponging his forehead in the dark.

'Get off!' he said loudly, and then, *'Dobby!'*

The house-elf's goggling tennis-ball eyes were peering at Harry through the darkness. A single tear was running down his long, pointed nose.

'Harry Potter came back to school,' he whispered miserably. 'Dobby warned and warned Harry Potter. Ah, sir, why didn't you heed Dobby? Why didn't Harry Potter go back home when he missed the train?'

Harry heaved himself up on his pillows and pushed Dobby's sponge away.

'What're you doing here?' he said. 'And how did you know I missed the train?'

Dobby's lip trembled and Harry was seized by a sudden suspicion.

'It was *you*!' he said slowly. '*You* stopped the barrier letting us through!'

'Indeed yes, sir,' said Dobby, nodding his head vigorously, ears flapping. 'Dobby hid and watched for Harry Potter and sealed the gateway and Dobby had to iron his hands afterwards –' he showed Harry ten, long, bandaged fingers, '– but Dobby didn't care, sir, for he thought Harry Potter was safe, and *never* did Dobby dream that Harry Potter would get to school another way!'

He was rocking backwards and forwards, shaking his ugly head.

'Dobby was so shocked when he heard Harry Potter was back at Hogwarts, he let his master's dinner burn! Such a flogging Dobby never had, sir ...'

Harry slumped back onto his pillows.

'You nearly got Ron and me expelled,' he said fiercely. 'You'd better clear off before my bones come back, Dobby, or I might strangle you.'

Dobby smiled weakly.

'Dobby is used to death threats, sir. Dobby gets them five times a day at home.'

He blew his nose on a corner of the filthy pillowcase he wore, looking so pathetic that Harry felt his anger ebb away in spite of himself.

'Why d'you wear that thing, Dobby?' he asked curiously.

'This, sir?' said Dobby, plucking at the pillowcase. ''Tis a mark of the house-elf's enslavement, sir. Dobby can only be freed if his masters present him with clothes, sir. The family is careful not to pass Dobby even a sock, sir, for then he would be free to leave their house for ever.'

Dobby mopped his bulging eyes and said suddenly, 'Harry Potter *must* go home! Dobby thought his Bludger would be enough to make –'

'*Your* Bludger?' said Harry, anger rising once more. 'What d'you mean, *your* Bludger? *You* made that Bludger try and kill me?'

'Not kill you, sir, never kill you!' said Dobby, shocked. 'Dobby wants to save Harry Potter's life! Better sent home, grievously injured, than remain here, sir! Dobby only wanted Harry Potter hurt enough to be sent home!'

'Oh, is that all?' said Harry angrily. 'I don't suppose you're going to tell me *why* you wanted me sent home in pieces?'

'Ah, if Harry Potter only knew!' Dobby groaned, more tears dripping onto his ragged pillowcase. 'If he knew what he means to us, to the lowly, the enslaved, us dregs of the magical world! Dobby remembers how it was when He Who Must Not Be Named was at the height of his powers, sir! We house-elves were treated like vermin, sir! Of course, Dobby is still treated like that, sir,' he admitted, drying his face on the pillowcase. 'But mostly, sir, life has improved for my kind since you triumphed over He Who Must Not Be Named. Harry Potter survived, and the Dark Lord's power was broken, and it was a new dawn, sir, and Harry Potter shone like a beacon of hope for those of us who thought the dark days would never end, sir ... And now, at Hogwarts, terrible things are to happen, are perhaps happening already, and Dobby cannot let Harry Potter stay here now that history is to repeat itself, now that the Chamber of Secrets is open once more –'

Dobby froze, horror-struck, then grabbed Harry's water jug from his bedside table and cracked it over his own head, toppling out of sight. A second later, he crawled back onto the bed, cross-eyed, muttering, 'Bad Dobby, very bad Dobby ...'

'So there *is* a Chamber of Secrets?' Harry whispered. 'And – did you say it's been opened *before? Tell* me, Dobby!'

He seized the elf's bony wrist as Dobby's hand inched towards the water jug. 'But I'm not Muggle-born – how can I be in danger from the Chamber?'

'Ah, sir, ask no more, ask no more of poor Dobby,' stammered the elf, his eyes huge in the dark. 'Dark deeds are planned in this place, but Harry Potter must not be here when they happen. Go home, Harry Potter. Go home. Harry Potter must not meddle in this, sir, 'tis too dangerous –'

'Who is it, Dobby?' Harry said, keeping a firm hold on Dobby's wrist to stop him hitting himself with the water jug again. 'Who's opened it? Who opened it last time?'

'Dobby can't, sir, Dobby can't, Dobby mustn't tell!' squealed the elf. 'Go home, Harry Potter, go home!'

'I'm not going anywhere!' said Harry fiercely. 'One of my best friends is Muggle-born, she'll be first in line if the Chamber really has been opened –'

'Harry Potter risks his own life for his friends!' moaned Dobby, in a kind of miserable ecstasy. 'So noble! So valiant! But he must save himself, he must, Harry Potter must not –'

Dobby suddenly froze, his bat ears quivering. Harry heard it, too. There were footsteps coming down the passageway outside.

'Dobby must go!' breathed the elf, terrified; there was a loud crack, and Harry's fist was suddenly clenched on thin air. He slumped back into bed, his eyes on the dark doorway to the hospital wing as the footsteps drew nearer.

Next moment, Dumbledore was backing into the dormitory, wearing a long woolly dressing gown and a nightcap. He was carrying one end of what looked like a statue. Professor McGonagall appeared a second later, carrying its feet. Together, they heaved it onto a bed.

'Get Madam Pomfrey,' whispered Dumbledore, and Professor McGonagall hurried past the end of Harry's bed out of sight. Harry lay quite still, pretending to be asleep. He heard urgent voices, and then Professor McGonagall swept back into view, closely followed by Madam Pomfrey, who was pulling a cardigan on over her nightdress. He heard a sharp intake of breath.

'What happened?' Madam Pomfrey whispered to Dumbledore, bending over the statue on the bed.

'Another attack,' said Dumbledore. 'Minerva found him on the stairs.'

'There was a bunch of grapes next to him,' said Professor McGonagall. 'We think he was trying to sneak up here to visit Potter.'

Harry's stomach gave a horrible lurch. Slowly and carefully, he raised himself a few inches so he could look at the statue on the bed. A ray of moonlight lay across its staring face.

It was Colin Creevey. His eyes were wide and his hands were stuck up in front of him, holding his camera.

'Petrified?' whispered Madam Pomfrey.

'Yes,' said Professor McGonagall. 'But I shudder to think … If Albus hadn't been on the way downstairs for hot chocolate, who knows what might have …'

The three of them stared down at Colin. Then Dumbledore leaned forward and prised the camera out of Colin's rigid grip.

'You don't think he managed to get a picture of his attacker?' said Professor McGonagall eagerly.

Dumbledore didn't answer. He prised open the back of the camera.

'Good gracious!' said Madam Pomfrey.

A jet of steam had hissed out of the camera. Harry, three beds away, caught the acrid smell of burnt plastic.

'Melted,' said Madam Pomfrey wonderingly, 'all melted …'

'What does this *mean*, Albus?' Professor McGonagall asked urgently.

'It means,' said Dumbledore, 'that the Chamber of Secrets is indeed open again.'

Madam Pomfrey clapped a hand to her mouth. Professor McGonagall stared at Dumbledore.

'But Albus … surely … *who?*'

'The question is not *who*,' said Dumbledore, his eyes on Colin. 'The question is, *how* …'

And from what Harry could see of Professor McGonagall's shadowy face, she didn't understand this any better than he did.

CHAPTER ELEVEN

The Duelling Club

Harry woke up on Sunday morning to find the dormitory blazing with winter sunlight and his arm reboned but very stiff. He sat up quickly and looked over at Colin's bed, but it had been blocked from view by the high curtains Harry had changed behind yesterday. Seeing that he was awake, Madam Pomfrey came bustling over with a breakfast tray and then began bending and stretching his arm and fingers.

'All in order,' she said, as he clumsily fed himself porridge left-handed. 'When you've finished eating, you may leave.'

Harry dressed as quickly as he could and hurried off to Gryffindor Tower, desperate to tell Ron and Hermione about Colin and Dobby, but they weren't there. Harry left to look for them, wondering where they could have got to and feeling slightly hurt that they weren't interested in whether he had his bones back or not.

As Harry passed the library, Percy Weasley strolled out of it, looking in far better spirits than last time they'd met.

'Oh, hello, Harry,' he said. 'Excellent flying yesterday, really excellent. Gryffindor have just taken the lead for the House Cup – you earned fifty points!'

'You haven't seen Ron or Hermione, have you?' said Harry.

'No, I haven't,' said Percy, his smile fading. 'I hope Ron's not in another *girls' toilet ...*'

Harry forced a laugh, watched Percy out of sight and then headed straight for Moaning Myrtle's bathroom. He couldn't see why Ron and Hermione would be in there again, but after making sure that neither Filch nor any Prefects were around, he opened the door and heard their voices coming from a locked cubicle.

'It's me,' he said, closing the door behind him. There was a clunk, a splash and a gasp from within the cubicle and he saw Hermione's eye peering through the keyhole.

'Harry!' she said. 'You gave us such a fright. Come in – how's your arm?'

'Fine,' said Harry, squeezing into the cubicle. An old cauldron was perched on the toilet, and a crackling from under the rim told Harry they had lit a fire beneath it. Conjuring up portable, waterproof fires was a speciality of Hermione's.

'We'd've come to meet you, but we decided to get started on the Polyjuice Potion,' Ron explained, as Harry, with difficulty, locked the cubicle again. 'We've decided this is the safest place to hide it.'

Harry started to tell them about Colin, but Hermione interrupted. 'We already know, we heard Professor McGonagall telling Professor Flitwick this morning. That's why we decided we'd better get going –'

'The sooner we get a confession out of Malfoy, the better,' snarled Ron. 'D'you know what I think? He was in such a foul temper after the Quidditch match, he took it out on Colin.'

'There's something else,' said Harry, watching Hermione tearing bundles of knotgrass and throwing them into the potion. 'Dobby came to visit me in the middle of the night.'

Ron and Hermione looked up, amazed. Harry told them everything Dobby had told him – or hadn't told him. Ron and Hermione listened with their mouths open.

'The Chamber of Secrets has been opened *before?*' said Hermione.

'This settles it,' said Ron in a triumphant voice. 'Lucius Malfoy must've opened the Chamber when he was at school here and now he's told dear old Draco how to do it. It's obvious. Wish Dobby'd told you what kind of monster's in there, though. I want to know how come nobody's noticed it sneaking round the school.'

'Maybe it can make itself invisible,' said Hermione, prodding leeches to the bottom of the cauldron. 'Or maybe it can disguise itself – pretend to be a suit of armour or something. I've read about Chameleon Ghouls …'

'You read too much, Hermione,' said Ron, pouring dead lacewings on top of the leeches. He crumpled up the empty lacewing bag and looked round at Harry.

'So Dobby stopped us getting on the train and broke your arm …' He shook his head. 'You know what, Harry? If he doesn't stop trying to save your life he's going to kill you.'

The news that Colin Creevey had been attacked and was now lying as though dead in the hospital wing had spread through the entire school by Monday morning. The air was suddenly thick with rumour and suspicion. The first-years were now moving around the castle in tight-knit groups, as though scared they would be attacked if they ventured forth alone.

Ginny Weasley, who sat next to Colin Creevey in Charms, was distraught, but Harry felt that Fred and George were going the wrong way about cheering her up. They were taking it in turns to cover themselves with fur or boils and jump out at her from behind statues. They only stopped when Percy, apoplectic with rage, told them he was going to write to Mrs Weasley and tell her Ginny was having nightmares.

Meanwhile, hidden from the teachers, a roaring trade in talismans, amulets and other protective devices was sweeping the school. Neville Longbottom bought a large, evil-smelling green onion, a pointed purple crystal and a rotting newt-tail before the other Gryffindor boys pointed out that he was in no danger: he was a pure-blood, and therefore unlikely to be attacked.

'They went for Filch first,' Neville said, his round face fearful, 'and everyone knows I'm almost a Squib.'

* * *

In the second week of December Professor McGonagall came around as usual, collecting names of those who would be staying at school for Christmas. Harry, Ron and Hermione signed her list; they had heard that Malfoy was staying, which struck them as very suspicious. The holidays would be the perfect time to use the Polyjuice Potion and try to worm a confession out of him.

Unfortunately, the potion was only half-finished. They still needed the Bicorn horn and the Boomslang skin, and the only place they were going to get them was from Snape's private stores. Harry privately felt he'd rather face Slytherin's legendary monster than have Snape catch him robbing his office.

'What we need,' said Hermione briskly, as Thursday afternoon's double Potions lesson loomed nearer, 'is a diversion. Then one of us can sneak into Snape's office and take what we need.'

Harry and Ron looked at her nervously.

'I think I'd better do the actual stealing,' Hermione continued, in a matter-of-fact tone. 'You two will be expelled if you get in any more trouble, and I've got a clean record. So all you need to do is cause enough mayhem to keep Snape busy for five minutes or so.'

Harry smiled feebly. Deliberately causing mayhem in Snape's Potions class was about as safe as poking a sleeping dragon in the eye.

Potions lessons took place in one of the large dungeons. Thursday afternoon's lesson proceeded in the usual way. Twenty cauldrons stood steaming between the wooden desks, on which stood brass scales and jars of ingredients. Snape prowled through the fumes, making waspish remarks about the Gryffindors' work while the Slytherins sniggered appreciatively. Draco Malfoy, who was Snape's favourite student, kept flicking puffer-fish eyes at Ron and Harry, who knew that if they retaliated they would get detention faster than you could say 'unfair'.

Harry's Swelling Solution was far too runny, but he had his mind on more important things. He was waiting for Hermione's signal, and he hardly listened as Snape paused to sneer at his watery potion. When Snape turned and walked off to bully Neville, Hermione caught Harry's eye and nodded.

Harry ducked swiftly down behind his cauldron, pulled one of Fred's Filibuster fireworks out of his pocket and gave it a quick prod with his wand. The firework began to fizz and sputter. Knowing he had only seconds, Harry straightened up, took aim, and lobbed it into the air; it landed right on target in Goyle's cauldron.

Goyle's potion exploded, showering the whole class. People shrieked as splashes of the Swelling Solution hit them. Malfoy got a faceful and his nose began to swell like a balloon; Goyle blundered around, his hands over his eyes, which had expanded to the size of dinner plates, while Snape was trying to restore calm and find out what had happened. Through the confusion, Harry saw Hermione slip quietly out of the door.

'Silence! SILENCE!' Snape roared. 'Anyone who has been splashed, come here for a Deflating Draught. When I find out who did this …'

Harry tried not to laugh as he watched Malfoy hurry forward, his head drooping with the weight of a nose like a small melon. As half the class lumbered up to Snape's desk, some weighed down with arms like clubs, others unable to talk through gigantic puffed-up lips, Harry saw Hermione slide back into the dungeon, the front of her robes bulging.

When everyone had taken a swig of antidote and the various swellings had subsided, Snape swept over to Goyle's cauldron and scooped out the twisted black remains of the firework. There was a sudden hush.

'If I ever find out who threw this,' Snape whispered, 'I shall *make sure* that person is expelled.'

Harry arranged his face into what he hoped was a puzzled expression. Snape was looking right at him, and the bell which rang ten minutes later could not have been more welcome.

'He knew it was me,' Harry told Ron and Hermione, as they hurried back to Moaning Myrtle's bathroom. 'I could tell.'

Hermione threw the new ingredients into the cauldron and began to stir feverishly.

'It'll be ready in a fortnight,' she said happily.

'Snape can't prove it was you,' said Ron reassuringly to Harry. 'What can he do?'

'Knowing Snape, something foul,' said Harry, as the potion frothed and bubbled.

A week later, Harry, Ron and Hermione were walking across the Entrance Hall when they saw a small knot of people gathered around the noticeboard, reading a piece of parchment that had just been pinned up. Seamus Finnigan and Dean Thomas beckoned them over, looking excited.

'They're starting a Duelling Club!' said Seamus. 'First meeting tonight! I wouldn't mind duelling lessons, they might come in handy one of these days …'

'What, you reckon Slytherin's monster can duel?' said Ron, but he too read the sign with interest.

'Could be useful,' he said to Harry and Hermione as they went into dinner. 'Shall we go?'

Harry and Hermione were all for it, so at eight o'clock that evening they hurried back to the Great Hall. The long dining tables had vanished and a golden stage had appeared along one wall, lit by thousands of candles floating overhead. The ceiling was velvety black once more and most of the school seemed to be packed beneath it, all carrying their wands and looking excited.

'I wonder who'll be teaching us?' said Hermione, as they edged into the chattering crowd. 'Someone told me Flitwick was a duelling champion when he was young, maybe it'll be him.'

'As long as it's not –' Harry began, but he ended on a groan: Gilderoy Lockhart was walking onto the stage, resplendent in robes of deep plum and accompanied by none other than Snape, wearing his usual black.

Lockhart waved an arm for silence and called, 'Gather round, gather round! Can everyone see me? Can you all hear me? Excellent!

'Now, Professor Dumbledore has granted me permission to start this little Duelling Club, to train you all up in case you ever need to defend yourselves as I myself have done on countless occasions – for full details, see my published works.

'Let me introduce my assistant Professor Snape,' said Lockhart, flashing a wide smile. 'He tells me he knows a tiny little bit about duelling himself and has sportingly agreed to help me with a short demonstration before we begin. Now, I don't want any of you youngsters to worry – you'll still have your Potions master when I'm through with him, never fear!'

'Wouldn't it be good if they finished each other off?' Ron muttered in Harry's ear.

Snape's upper lip was curling. Harry wondered why Lockhart was still smiling; if Snape had been looking at *him* like that he'd have been running as fast as he could in the opposite direction.

Lockhart and Snape turned to face each other and bowed; at least, Lockhart did, with much twirling of his hands, whereas Snape jerked his head irritably. Then they raised their wands like swords in front of them.

'As you see, we are holding our wands in the accepted combative position,' Lockhart told the silent crowd. 'On the count of three, we will cast our first spells. Neither of us will be aiming to kill, of course.'

'I wouldn't bet on that,' Harry murmured, watching Snape baring his teeth.

'One – two – three –'

Both of them swung their wands up and over their shoulders. Snape cried: *'Expelliarmus!'* There was a dazzling flash of scarlet light and Lockhart was blasted off his feet: he flew backwards off the stage, smashed into the wall and slid down it to sprawl on the floor.

Malfoy and some of the other Slytherins cheered. Hermione was dancing on tiptoes. 'Do you think he's all right?' she squealed through her fingers.

'Who cares?' said Harry and Ron together.

Lockhart was getting unsteadily to his feet. His hat had fallen off and his wavy hair was standing on end.

'Well, there you have it!' he said, tottering back onto the platform. 'That was a Disarming Charm – as you see, I've lost my wand – ah, thank you, Miss Brown. Yes, an excellent idea to show them that, Professor Snape, but if you don't mind my saying so, it was very obvious what you were about to do. If I had wanted to stop you it would have been only too easy. However, I felt it would be instructive to let them see …'

Snape was looking murderous. Possibly Lockhart had noticed, because he said, 'Enough demonstrating! I'm going to come amongst you now and put you all into pairs. Professor Snape, if you'd like to help me …'

They moved through the crowd, matching up partners. Lockhart teamed Neville with Justin Finch-Fletchley, but Snape reached Harry and Ron first.

'Time to split up the dream team, I think,' he sneered. 'Weasley, you can partner Finnigan. Potter –'

Harry moved automatically towards Hermione.

'I don't think so,' said Snape, smiling coldly. 'Mr Malfoy, come over here. Let's see what you make of the famous Potter. And you, Miss Granger – you can partner Miss Bulstrode.'

Malfoy strutted over, smirking. Behind him walked a Slytherin girl who reminded Harry of a picture he'd seen in *Holidays with Hags*. She was large and square and her heavy jaw jutted aggressively. Hermione gave her a weak smile which she did not return.

'Face your partners!' called Lockhart, back on the platform, 'and bow!'

Harry and Malfoy barely inclined their heads, not taking their eyes off each other.

'Wands at the ready!' shouted Lockhart. 'When I count to three, cast your charms to disarm your opponent – *only* to disarm them – we don't want any accidents. One … two … three …'

Harry swung his wand over his shoulder, but Malfoy had already started on 'two': his spell hit Harry so hard he felt as though he'd been hit over the head with a saucepan. He stumbled, but everything still seemed to be working, and wasting no more time, Harry pointed his wand straight at Malfoy and shouted, *'Rictusempra!'*

A jet of silver light hit Malfoy in the stomach and he doubled up, wheezing.

'I said disarm only!' Lockhart shouted in alarm over the heads of the battling crowd, as Malfoy sank to his knees; Harry had hit him with a Tickling Charm, and he could barely move for

laughing. Harry hung back, with a vague feeling it would be unsporting to bewitch Malfoy while he was on the floor, but this was a mistake. Gasping for breath, Malfoy pointed his wand at Harry's knees, choked, *'Tarantallegra!'* and next second Harry's legs had begun to jerk around out of his control in a kind of quickstep.

'Stop! Stop!' screamed Lockhart, but Snape took charge.

'Finite Incantatem!' he shouted; Harry's feet stopped dancing, Malfoy stopped laughing and they were able to look up.

A haze of greenish smoke was hovering over the scene. Both Neville and Justin were lying on the floor, panting; Ron was holding up an ashen-faced Seamus, apologising for whatever his broken wand had done; but Hermione and Millicent Bulstrode were still moving; Millicent had Hermione in a headlock and Hermione was whimpering in pain. Both their wands lay forgotten on the floor. Harry leapt forward and pulled Millicent off. It was difficult; she was a lot bigger than he was.

'Dear, dear,' said Lockhart, skittering through the crowd, looking at the aftermath of the duels. 'Up you get, Macmillan ... careful there, Miss Fawcett ... pinch it hard, it'll stop bleeding in a second, Boot ...

'I think I'd better teach you how to *block* unfriendly spells,' said Lockhart, standing flustered in the midst of the hall. He glanced at Snape, whose black eyes glinted, and looked quickly away. 'Let's have a volunteer pair – Longbottom and Finch-Fletchley, how about you?'

'A bad idea, Professor Lockhart,' said Snape, gliding over like a large and malevolent bat. 'Longbottom causes devastation with the simplest spells. We'll be sending what's left of Finch-Fletchley up to the hospital wing in a matchbox.' Neville's round pink face went pinker. 'How about Malfoy and Potter?' said Snape with a twisted smile.

'Excellent idea!' said Lockhart, gesturing Harry and Malfoy into the middle of the Hall as the crowd backed away to give them room.

'Now, Harry,' said Lockhart, 'when Draco points his wand at you, you do *this*.'

He raised his own wand, attempted a complicated sort of wiggling action and dropped it. Snape smirked as Lockhart quickly picked it up, saying, 'Whoops – my wand is a little over-excited.'

Snape moved closer to Malfoy, bent down and whispered something in his ear. Malfoy smirked, too. Harry looked nervously up at Lockhart and said, 'Professor, could you show me that blocking thing again?'

'Scared?' muttered Malfoy, so that Lockhart couldn't hear him.

'You wish,' said Harry out of the corner of his mouth.

Lockhart cuffed Harry merrily on the shoulder. 'Just do what I did, Harry!'

'What, drop my wand?'

But Lockhart wasn't listening.

'Three – two – one – go!' he shouted.

Malfoy raised his wand quickly and bellowed, *'Serpensortia!'*

The end of his wand exploded. Harry watched, aghast, as a long black snake shot out of it, fell heavily onto the floor between them and raised itself, ready to strike. There were screams as the crowd backed swiftly away, clearing the floor.

'Don't move, Potter,' said Snape lazily, clearly enjoying the sight of Harry standing motionless, eye to eye with the angry snake. 'I'll get rid of it ...'

'Allow me!' shouted Lockhart. He brandished his wand at the snake and there was a loud bang; the snake, instead of vanishing, flew ten feet into the air and fell back to the floor with a loud smack. Enraged, hissing furiously, it slithered straight towards Justin Finch-Fletchley and raised itself again, fangs exposed, poised to strike.

Harry wasn't sure what made him do it. He wasn't even aware of deciding to do it. All he knew was that his legs were carrying him forward as though he was on castors and that he had shouted stupidly at the snake, 'Leave him!' And miraculously – inexplicably – the snake slumped to the floor, docile as a thick black garden hose, its eyes now on Harry. Harry felt the fear drain out of him. He knew the snake wouldn't attack anyone now, though how he knew it, he couldn't have explained.

He looked up at Justin, grinning, expecting to see Justin looking relieved, or puzzled, or even grateful – but certainly not angry and scared.

'What do you think you're playing at?' he shouted, and before Harry could say anything, Justin had turned and stormed out of the Hall.

Snape stepped forward, waved his wand and the snake vanished in a small puff of black smoke. Snape, too, was looking at Harry in an unexpected way: it was a shrewd and calculating look, and Harry didn't like it. He was also dimly aware of an ominous muttering all around the walls. Then he felt a tugging on the back of his robes.

'Come on,' said Ron's voice in his ear. 'Move – come *on* …'

Ron steered him out of the Hall, Hermione hurrying alongside them. As they went through the doors, the people on either side drew away as though they were frightened of catching something. Harry didn't have a clue what was going on, and neither Ron nor Hermione explained anything until they had dragged him all the way up to the empty Gryffindor common room. Then Ron pushed Harry into an armchair and said, 'You're a Parselmouth. Why didn't you tell us?'

'I'm a what?' said Harry.

'*A Parselmouth!*' said Ron. 'You can talk to snakes!'

'I know,' said Harry. 'I mean, that's only the second time I've ever done it. I accidentally set a boa constrictor on my cousin Dudley at the zoo once – long story – but it was telling me it had never seen Brazil and I sort of set it free without meaning to. That was before I knew I was a wizard …'

'A boa constrictor told you it had never seen Brazil?' Ron repeated faintly.

'So?' said Harry. 'I bet loads of people here can do it.'

'Oh no they can't,' said Ron. 'It's not a very common gift. Harry, this is bad.'

'What's bad?' said Harry, starting to feel quite angry. 'What's wrong with everyone? Listen, if I hadn't told that snake not to attack Justin –'

'Oh, that's what you said to it?'

'What d'you mean? You were there … you heard me.'

'I heard you speaking Parseltongue,' said Ron, 'snake language. You could have been saying anything. No wonder Justin panicked, you sounded like you were egging the snake on or something. It was creepy, you know.'

Harry gaped at him.

'I spoke a different language? But – I didn't realise – how can I speak a language without knowing I can speak it?'

Ron shook his head. Both he and Hermione were looking as though someone had died. Harry couldn't see what was so terrible.

'D'you want to tell me what's wrong with stopping a dirty great snake biting Justin's head off?' he said. 'What does it matter *how* I did it as long as Justin doesn't have to join the Headless Hunt?'

'It matters,' said Hermione, speaking at last in a hushed voice, 'because being able to talk to snakes was what Salazar Slytherin was famous for. That's why the symbol of Slytherin house is a serpent.'

Harry's mouth fell open.

'Exactly,' said Ron. 'And now the whole school's going to think you're his great-great-great-great-grandson or something …'

'But I'm not,' said Harry, with a panic he couldn't quite explain.

'You'll find that hard to prove,' said Hermione. 'He lived about a thousand years ago; for all we know, you could be.'

* * *

Harry lay awake for hours that night. Through a gap in the hangings round his four-poster he watched snow starting to drift past the tower window, and wondered.

Could he be a descendant of Salazar Slytherin? He didn't know anything about his father's family, after all. The Dursleys had always forbidden questions about his wizarding relatives.

Quietly, Harry tried to say something in Parseltongue. The words wouldn't come. It seemed he had to be face to face with a snake to do it.

'But I'm in *Gryffindor*,' Harry thought. 'The Sorting Hat wouldn't have put me in here if I had Slytherin blood …'

'*Ah*,' said a nasty little voice in his brain, 'But the Sorting Hat *wanted* to put you in Slytherin, don't you remember?'

Harry turned over. He'd see Justin next day in Herbology and he'd explain that he'd been calling the snake off, not egging it on, which (he thought angrily, pummelling his pillow) any fool should have realised.

By next morning, however, the snow that had begun in the night had turned into a blizzard so thick that the last Herbology lesson of term was cancelled: Professor Sprout wanted to fit socks and scarves on the Mandrakes, a tricky operation she would entrust to no one else, now that it was so important for the Mandrakes to grow quickly and revive Mrs Norris and Colin Creevey.

Harry fretted about this next to the fire in the Gryffindor common room, while Ron and Hermione used their lesson off to play a game of wizard chess.

'For heaven's sake, Harry,' said Hermione, exasperated, as one of Ron's bishops wrestled her knight off his horse and dragged him off the board. 'Go and *find* Justin if it's so important to you.'

So Harry got up and left through the portrait hole, wondering where Justin might be.

The castle was darker than it usually was in daytime, because of the thick, swirling grey snow at every window. Shivering, Harry walked past classrooms where lessons were taking place, catching snatches of what was happening within. Professor McGonagall was shouting at someone who, by the sound of it, had turned his friend into a badger. Resisting the urge to take a look, Harry walked on by, thinking that Justin might be using his free lesson to catch up on some work, and deciding to check the library first.

A group of the Hufflepuffs who should have been in Herbology were indeed sitting at the back of the library, but they didn't seem to be working. Between the long lines of high bookshelves, Harry could see that their heads were close together and they were having what looked like an absorbing conversation. He couldn't see whether Justin was among them. He was walking towards them when something of what they were saying met his ears, and he paused to listen, hidden in the Invisibility section.

'So anyway,' a stout boy was saying, 'I told Justin to hide up in our dormitory. I mean to say, if Potter's marked him down as his next victim, it's best if he keeps a low profile for a while. Of course, Justin's been waiting for something like this to happen ever since he let slip to Potter he was Muggle-born. Justin actually *told* him he'd been down for Eton. That's not the kind of thing you bandy about with Slytherin's heir on the loose, is it?'

'You definitely think it *is* Potter, then, Ernie?' said a girl with blonde pigtails anxiously.

'Hannah,' said the stout boy solemnly, 'he's a Parselmouth. Everyone knows that's the mark of a Dark wizard. Have you ever heard of a decent one who could talk to snakes? They called Slytherin himself Serpent-tongue.'

There was some heavy murmuring at this, and Ernie went on, 'Remember what was written on the wall? *Enemies of the Heir Beware*. Potter had some sort of run-in with Filch. Next thing we know, Filch's cat's attacked. That first-year, Creevey, was annoying Potter at the Quidditch match, taking pictures of him while he was lying in the mud. Next thing we know, Creevey's been attacked.'

'He always seems so nice, though,' said Hannah uncertainly, 'and, well, he's the one who made You-Know-Who disappear. He can't be all bad, can he?'

Ernie lowered his voice mysteriously, the Hufflepuffs bent closer, and Harry edged nearer so that he could catch Ernie's words.

'No one knows how he survived that attack by You-Know-Who. I mean to say, he was only a baby when it happened. He should have been blasted into smithereens. Only a really powerful Dark wizard could have survived a curse like that.' He dropped his voice until it was barely more than a whisper, and said, '*That's* probably why You-Know-Who wanted to kill him in the first place. Didn't want another Dark Lord *competing* with him. I wonder what other powers Potter's been hiding?'

Harry couldn't take any more. Clearing his throat loudly, he stepped out from behind the bookshelves. If he hadn't been feeling so angry, he would have found the sight that greeted him funny: every one of the Hufflepuffs looked as though they had been Petrified by the sight of him, and the colour was draining out of Ernie's face.

'Hello,' said Harry. 'I'm looking for Justin Finch-Fletchley.'

The Hufflepuffs' worst fears had clearly been confirmed. They all looked fearfully at Ernie.

'What do you want with him?' said Ernie, in a quavering voice.

'I wanted to tell him what really happened with that snake at the Duelling Club,' said Harry.

Ernie bit his white lips and then, taking a deep breath, said, 'We were all there. We saw what happened.'

'Then you noticed that, after I spoke to it, the snake backed off?' said Harry.

'All I saw,' said Ernie stubbornly, though he was trembling as he spoke, 'was you speaking Parseltongue and chasing the snake towards Justin.'

'I didn't chase it at him!' Harry said, his voice shaking with anger. 'It didn't even *touch* him!'

'It was a very near miss,' said Ernie. 'And in case you're getting ideas,' he added hastily, 'I might tell you that you can trace my family back through nine generations of witches and warlocks and my blood's as pure as anyone's, so –'

'I don't care what sort of blood you've got!' said Harry fiercely. 'Why would I want to attack Muggle-borns?'

'I've heard you hate those Muggles you live with,' said Ernie swiftly.

'It's not possible to live with the Dursleys and not hate them,' said Harry. 'I'd like to see you try it.'

He turned on his heel and stormed out of the library, earning himself a reproving glare from Madam Pince, who was polishing the gilded cover of a large spellbook.

Harry blundered up the corridor, barely noticing where he was going, he was in such a fury. The result was that he walked into something very large and solid, which knocked him backwards onto the floor.

'Oh, hullo, Hagrid,' Harry said, looking up.

Hagrid's face was entirely hidden by a woolly, snow-covered balaclava, but it couldn't possibly be anyone else, as he filled most of the corridor in his moleskin overcoat. A dead rooster was hanging from one of his massive, gloved hands.

'All righ', Harry?' he said, pulling up the balaclava so he could speak. 'Why aren't yeh in class?'

'Cancelled,' said Harry, getting up. 'What're you doing in here?'

Hagrid held up the limp rooster.

'Second one killed this term,' he explained. 'It's either foxes or a Blood-Suckin' Bugbear, an' I need the Headmaster's permission ter put a charm round the hen-coop.'

He peered more closely at Harry from under his thick, snow-flecked eyebrows.

'Yeh sure yeh're all righ'? Yeh look all hot an' bothered.'

Harry couldn't bring himself to repeat what Ernie and the rest of the Hufflepuffs had been saying about him.

'It's nothing,' he said. 'I'd better get going, Hagrid, it's Transfiguration next and I've got to pick up my books.'

He walked off, his mind still full of what Ernie had said about him.

'Justin's been waiting for something like this to happen ever since he let slip to Potter he was Muggle-born ...'

Harry stamped up the stairs and turned along another corridor, which was particularly dark; the torches had been extinguished by a strong, icy draught which was blowing through a loose window pane. He was halfway down the passage when he tripped headlong over something lying on the floor.

He turned to squint at what he'd fallen over, and felt as though his stomach had dissolved.

Justin Finch-Fletchley was lying on the floor, rigid and cold, a look of shock frozen on his face, his eyes staring blankly at the ceiling. And that wasn't all. Next to him was another figure, the strangest sight Harry had ever seen.

It was Nearly Headless Nick, no longer pearly-white and transparent, but black and smoky, floating immobile and horizontal, six inches off the floor. His head was half off and his face wore an expression of shock identical to Justin's.

Harry got to his feet, his breathing fast and shallow, his heart doing a kind of drum-roll against his ribs. He looked wildly up and down the deserted corridor and saw a line of spiders scuttling as fast as they could away from the bodies. The only sounds were the muffled voices of teachers from the classes on either side.

He could run, and no one would ever know he had been there. But he couldn't just leave them lying here … he had to get help. Would anyone believe he hadn't had anything to do with this?

As he stood there, panicking, a door right next to him opened with a bang. Peeves the poltergeist came shooting out.

'Why, it's potty wee Potter!' cackled Peeves, knocking Harry's glasses askew as he bounced past him. 'What's Potter up to? Why's Potter lurking –'

Peeves stopped, halfway through a mid-air somersault. Upside-down, he spotted Justin and Nearly Headless Nick. He flipped the right way up, filled his lungs and, before Harry could stop him, screamed, 'ATTACK! ATTACK! ANOTHER ATTACK! NO MORTAL OR GHOST IS SAFE! RUN FOR YOUR LIVES! ATTAAAACK!'

Crash – crash – crash: door after door flew open along the corridor and people flooded out. For several long minutes, there was a scene of such confusion that Justin was in danger of being squashed and people kept standing in Nearly Headless Nick. Harry found himself pinned against the wall as the teachers shouted for quiet. Professor McGonagall came running, followed by her own class, one of whom still had black and white striped hair. She used her wand to set off a loud bang, which restored silence, and ordered everyone back into their classes. No sooner had the scene cleared somewhat than Ernie the Hufflepuff arrived, panting, on the scene.

'*Caught in the act!*' Ernie yelled, his face stark white, pointing his finger dramatically at Harry.

'That will do, Macmillan!' said Professor McGonagall sharply.

Peeves was bobbing overhead, now grinning wickedly, surveying the scene; Peeves always loved chaos. As the teachers bent over Justin and Nearly Headless Nick, examining them, Peeves broke into song:

'*Oh Potter, you rotter, oh what have you done?*

You're killing off students, you think it's good fun –'

'That's enough Peeves!' barked Professor McGonagall, and Peeves zoomed away backwards, with his tongue out at Harry.

Justin was carried up to the hospital wing by Professor Flitwick and Professor Sinistra of the Astronomy department, but nobody seemed to know what to do for Nearly Headless Nick. In the end, Professor McGonagall conjured a large fan out of thin air, which she gave to Ernie with instructions to waft Nearly Headless Nick up the stairs. This Ernie did, fanning Nick along like a silent black hovercraft. This left Harry and Professor McGonagall alone together.

'This way, Potter,' she said.

'Professor,' said Harry at once, 'I swear I didn't –'

'This is out of my hands, Potter,' said Professor McGonagall curtly.

They marched in silence around a corner and she stopped before a large and extremely ugly stone gargoyle.

'Sherbet lemon!' she said. This was evidently a password, because the gargoyle sprang suddenly to life, and hopped aside as the wall behind him split in two. Even full of dread for what was coming, Harry couldn't fail to be amazed. Behind the wall was a spiral staircase which was moving smoothly upwards, like an escalator. As he and Professor McGonagall stepped onto it, Harry heard the wall thud closed behind them. They rose upwards in circles, higher and higher, until at last, slightly dizzy, Harry could see a gleaming oak door ahead, with a brass knocker in the shape of a griffon.

He knew where he was being taken. This must be where Dumbledore lived.

CHAPTER TWELVE

The Polyjuice Potion

They stepped off the stone staircase at the top and Professor McGonagall rapped on the door. It opened silently and they entered. Professor McGonagall told Harry to wait, and left him there, alone.

Harry looked around. One thing was certain: of all the teachers' offices Harry had visited so far this year, Dumbledore's was by far the most interesting. If he hadn't been scared out of his wits that he was about to be thrown out of school, he would have been very pleased to have a chance to look around it.

It was a large and beautiful circular room, full of funny little noises. A number of curious silver instruments stood on spindle-legged tables, whirring and emitting little puffs of smoke. The walls were covered with portraits of old headmasters and headmistresses, all of whom were snoozing gently in their frames. There was also an enormous, claw-footed desk, and, sitting on a shelf behind it, a shabby, tattered wizard's hat – the *Sorting Hat*.

Harry hesitated. He cast a wary eye around the sleeping witches and wizards on the walls. Surely it couldn't hurt if he took the Hat down and tried it on again? Just to see ... just to make sure it *had* put him in the right house.

He walked quietly around the desk, lifted the Hat from its shelf, and lowered it slowly onto his head. It was much too large and slipped down over his eyes, just as it had done the last time he'd put it on. Harry stared at the black inside of the Hat, waiting. Then a small voice said in his ear, 'Bee in your bonnet, Harry Potter?'

'Er, yes,' Harry muttered. 'Er – sorry to bother you – I wanted to ask –'

'You've been wondering whether I put you in the right house,' said the Hat smartly. 'Yes ... you were particularly difficult to place. But I stand by what I said before –' Harry's heart leapt '– you *would* have done well in Slytherin.'

Harry's stomach plummeted. He grabbed the point of the Hat and pulled it off. It hung limply in his hand, grubby and faded. Harry pushed it back onto its shelf, feeling sick.

'You're wrong,' he said aloud to the still and silent Hat. It didn't move. Harry backed away, watching it. Then a strange, gagging noise behind him made him wheel around.

He wasn't alone after all. Standing on a golden perch behind the door was a decrepit-looking bird which resembled a half-plucked turkey. Harry stared at it and the bird looked balefully back, making its gagging noise again. Harry thought it looked very ill. Its eyes were dull and, even as Harry watched, a couple more feathers fell out of its tail.

Harry was just thinking that all he needed was for Dumbledore's pet bird to die while he was alone in the office with it, when the bird burst into flames.

Harry yelled in shock and backed away into the desk. He looked feverishly around in case there was a glass of water somewhere, but couldn't see one. The bird, meanwhile, had become a fireball; it gave one loud shriek and next second there was nothing but a smouldering pile of ash on the floor.

The office door opened. Dumbledore came in, looking very sombre.

'Professor,' Harry gasped, 'your bird – I couldn't do anything – he just caught fire –'

To Harry's astonishment, Dumbledore smiled.

'About time, too,' he said. 'He's been looking dreadful for days, I've been telling him to get a move on.'

He chuckled at the stunned look on Harry's face.

'Fawkes is a phoenix, Harry. Phoenixes burst into flame when it is time for them to die and are reborn from the ashes. Watch him …'

Harry looked down in time to see a tiny, wrinkled, newborn bird poke its head out of the ashes. It was quite as ugly as the old one.

'It's a shame you had to see him on a Burning Day,' said Dumbledore, seating himself behind his desk. 'He's really very handsome most of the time: wonderful red and gold plumage. Fascinating creatures, phoenixes. They can carry immensely heavy loads, their tears have healing powers and they make highly *faithful* pets.'

In the shock of Fawkes catching fire, Harry had forgotten what he was there for, but it all came back to him as Dumbledore settled himself in the high-backed chair behind the desk and fixed Harry with his penetrating, light-blue stare.

Before Dumbledore could speak another word, however, the door of the office flew open with an almighty bang and Hagrid burst in, a wild look in his eyes, his balaclava perched on top of his shaggy black head and the dead rooster still swinging from his hand.

'It wasn' Harry, Professor Dumbledore!' said Hagrid urgently. 'I was talkin' ter him *seconds* before that kid was found, he never had time, sir ...'

Dumbledore tried to say something, but Hagrid went ranting on, waving the rooster around in his agitation, sending feathers everywhere.

'... It can't've bin him, I'll swear it in front o' the Ministry o' Magic if I have to ...'

'Hagrid, I –'

'... Yeh've got the wrong boy, sir, I *know* Harry never –'

'Hagrid!' said Dumbledore loudly. 'I do *not* think that Harry attacked those people.'

'Oh,' said Hagrid, the rooster falling limply at his side. 'Right. I'll wait outside then, Headmaster.'

And he stomped out looking embarrassed.

'You don't think it was me, Professor?' Harry repeated hopefully, as Dumbledore brushed rooster feathers off his desk.

'No, Harry, I don't,' said Dumbledore, though his face was sombre again. 'But I still want to talk to you.'

Harry waited nervously while Dumbledore considered him, the tips of his long fingers together.

'I must ask you, Harry, whether there is anything you'd like to tell me,' he said gently. 'Anything at all.'

Harry didn't know what to say. He thought of Malfoy shouting, 'You'll be next, Mudbloods!' and of the Polyjuice Potion, simmering away in Moaning Myrtle's bathroom. Then he thought of the disembodied voice he had heard twice and remembered what Ron had said: *'Hearing voices no one else can hear isn't a good sign, even in the wizarding world.'* He thought, too, about what everyone was saying about him, and his growing dread that he was somehow connected with Salazar Slytherin …

'No,' said Harry, 'there isn't anything, Professor.'

The double attack on Justin and Nearly Headless Nick turned what had hitherto been nervousness into real panic. Curiously, it was Nearly Headless Nick's fate that seemed to worry people most. What could possibly do that to a ghost, people asked each other; what terrible power could harm someone who was already dead? There was almost a stampede to book seats on the Hogwarts Express so that students could go home for Christmas.

'At this rate, we'll be the only ones left,' Ron told Harry and Hermione. 'Us, Malfoy, Crabbe and Goyle. What a jolly holiday it's going to be.'

Crabbe and Goyle, who always did whatever Malfoy did, had signed up to stay over the holidays too. But Harry was glad that most people were leaving. He was tired of people skirting around him in the corridors, as though he was about to sprout fangs or spit poison; tired of all the muttering, pointing and hissing as he passed.

Fred and George, however, found all this very funny. They went out of their way to march ahead of Harry down the corridors, shouting, 'Make way for the heir of Slytherin, seriously evil wizard coming through …'

Percy was deeply disapproving of this behaviour.

'It is *not* a laughing matter,' he said coldly.

'Oh, get out of the way, Percy,' said Fred. 'Harry's in a hurry.'

'Yeah, he's nipping off to the Chamber of Secrets for a cup of tea with his fanged servant,' said George, chortling.

Ginny didn't find it amusing either.

'Oh, *don't*,' she wailed every time Fred asked Harry loudly who he was planning to attack next, or George pretended to ward Harry off with a large clove of garlic when they met.

Harry didn't mind; it made him feel better that Fred and George, at least, thought the idea of his being Slytherin's heir was quite ludicrous. But their antics seemed to be aggravating Draco Malfoy, who looked increasingly sour each time he saw them at it.

'It's because he's *bursting* to say it's really him,' said Ron knowingly. 'You know how he hates anyone beating him at anything, and you're getting all the credit for his dirty work.'

'Not for long,' said Hermione in a satisfied tone. 'The Polyjuice Potion's nearly ready. We'll be getting the truth out of him any day now.'

* * *

At last the term ended, and a silence deep as the snow on the grounds descended on the castle. Harry found it peaceful, rather than gloomy, and enjoyed the fact that he, Hermione and the Weasleys had the run of Gryffindor Tower, which meant they could play Exploding Snap loudly without bothering anyone, and practise duelling in private. Fred, George and Ginny had chosen to stay at school rather than visit Bill in Egypt with Mr and Mrs Weasley. Percy, who disapproved of what he termed their childish behaviour, didn't spend much time in the Gryffindor common room. He had already told them pompously that *he* was only staying over Christmas because it was his duty as a Prefect to support the teachers during this troubled time.

Christmas morning dawned, cold and white. Harry and Ron, the only ones left in their dormitory, were woken very early by Hermione, who burst in, fully dressed and carrying presents for them both.

'Wake up,' she said loudly, pulling back the curtains at the window.

'Hermione – you're not supposed to be in here,' said Ron, shielding his eyes against the light.

'Merry Christmas to you, too,' said Hermione, throwing him his present. 'I've been up for nearly an hour, adding more lacewings to the Potion. It's ready.'

Harry sat up, suddenly wide awake.

'Are you sure?'

'Positive,' said Hermione, shifting Scabbers the rat so that she could sit down on the end of his four-poster. 'If we're going to do it, I say it should be tonight.'

At that moment, Hedwig swooped into the room, carrying a very small package in her beak.

'Hello,' said Harry happily, as she landed on his bed, 'are you speaking to me again?'

She nibbled his ear in an affectionate sort of way, which was a far better present than the one which she had brought him, which turned out to be from the Dursleys. They had sent Harry a toothpick and a note telling him to find out whether he'd be able to stay at Hogwarts for the summer holidays, too.

The rest of Harry's Christmas presents were far more satisfactory. Hagrid had sent him a large tin of treacle fudge, which Harry decided to soften by the fire before eating; Ron had given him a book called *Flying with the Cannons*, a book of interesting facts about his favourite Quidditch team; and Hermione had bought him a luxury eagle-feather quill. Harry opened the last present to find a new, hand-knitted jumper from Mrs Weasley, and a large plum cake. He put up her card with a fresh surge of guilt, thinking about Mr Weasley's car, which hadn't been seen since its crash with the Whomping Willow, and the bout of rule-breaking he and Ron were planning next.

No one, not even someone dreading taking Polyjuice Potion later, could fail to enjoy Christmas dinner at Hogwarts.

The Great Hall looked magnificent. Not only were there a dozen frost-covered Christmas trees and thick streamers of holly and mistletoe criss-crossing the ceiling, but enchanted snow was falling, warm and dry, from the ceiling. Dumbledore led them in a few of his favourite carols, Hagrid booming more and more loudly with every goblet of eggnog he consumed. Percy, who hadn't noticed that Fred had bewitched his prefect badge so that it now read 'Pinhead', kept asking them all what they were sniggering at. Harry didn't even care that Draco Malfoy was making loud, snide remarks about his new jumper from the Slytherin table. With a bit of luck, Malfoy would be getting his come-uppance in a few hours' time.

Harry and Ron had barely finished their third helpings of Christmas pudding when Hermione ushered them out of the Hall to finalise their plans for the evening.

'We still need a bit of the people you're changing into,' said Hermione matter-of-factly, as though she was sending them to the supermarket for washing-powder. 'And obviously, it'll be best if you can get something of Crabbe and Goyle's; they're Malfoy's best friends, he'll tell them anything. And we also need to make sure the real Crabbe and Goyle can't burst in on us while we're interrogating him.

'I've got it all worked out,' she went on smoothly, ignoring Harry and Ron's stupefied faces. She held up two plump chocolate cakes. 'I've filled these with a simple Sleeping Draught. All you have to do is make sure Crabbe and Goyle find them. You know how greedy they are, they're bound to eat them. Once they're asleep, pull out a few of their hairs and hide them in a broom cupboard.'

Harry and Ron looked incredulously at each other.

'Hermione, I don't think –'

'That could go seriously wrong –'

But Hermione had a steely glint in her eye not unlike the one Professor McGonagall sometimes had.

'The Potion will be useless without Crabbe and Goyle's hair,' she said sternly. 'You do *want* to investigate Malfoy, don't you?'

'Oh, all right, all right,' said Harry. 'But what about you? Whose hair are you ripping out?'

'I've already got mine!' said Hermione brightly, pulling a tiny bottle out of her pocket and showing them the single hair inside it. 'Remember Millicent Bulstrode wrestling with me at the Duelling Club? She left this on my robes when she was trying to strangle me! And she's gone home for Christmas – so I'll just have to tell the Slytherins I've decided to come back.'

When Hermione had bustled off to check on the Polyjuice Potion again, Ron turned to Harry with a doom-laden expression.

'Have you ever heard of a plan where so many things could go wrong?'

But to Harry and Ron's utter amazement, stage one of the operation went just as smoothly as Hermione had said. They lurked in the deserted Entrance Hall after Christmas tea, waiting for Crabbe and Goyle, who had remained alone at the Slytherin table, shovelling down fourth helpings of trifle. Harry had perched the chocolate cakes on the end of the banisters. When they spotted Crabbe and Goyle coming out of the Great Hall, Harry and Ron hid quickly behind a suit of armour next to the front door.

'How thick can you get?' Ron whispered ecstatically, as Crabbe gleefully pointed out the cakes to Goyle and grabbed them. Grinning stupidly, they stuffed the cakes whole into their large mouths. For a moment, both of them chewed greedily, looks of triumph on their faces. Then, without the smallest change of expression, they both keeled over backwards onto the floor.

Much the most difficult bit was hiding them in the cupboard across the hall. Once they were safely stowed amongst the buckets and mops, Harry yanked out a couple of the bristles that covered Goyle's forehead and Ron pulled out several of Crabbe's hairs. They also stole their shoes, because their own were far too small for Crabbe- and Goyle-sized feet. Then, still stunned at what they had just done, they sprinted up to Moaning Myrtle's bathroom.

They could hardly see for the thick black smoke issuing from the cubicle in which Hermione was stirring the cauldron. Pulling their robes up over their faces, Harry and Ron knocked softly on the door.

'Hermione?'

They heard the scrape of the lock and Hermione emerged, shiny-faced and looking anxious. Behind her they heard the *gloop gloop* of the bubbling, treacle-thick Potion. Three glass tumblers stood ready on the toilet seat.

'Did you get them?' Hermione asked breathlessly.

Harry showed her Goyle's hair.

'Good. And I sneaked these spare robes out of the laundry,' Hermione said, holding up a small sack. 'You'll need bigger sizes once you're Crabbe and Goyle.'

The three of them stared into the cauldron. Close up, the Potion looked like thick, dark mud, bubbling sluggishly.

'I'm sure I've done everything right,' said Hermione, nervously rereading the splotched page of *Moste Potente Potions*. 'It looks like the book says it should … Once we've drunk it, we'll have exactly an hour before we change back into ourselves.'

'Now what?' Ron whispered.

'We separate it into three glasses and add the hairs.'

Hermione ladled large dollops of the Potion into each of the glasses. Then, her hand trembling, she shook Millicent Bulstrode's hair out of its bottle into the first glass.

The Potion hissed loudly like a boiling kettle and frothed madly. A second later, it had turned a sick sort of yellow.

'Urgh – essence of Millicent Bulstrode,' said Ron, eyeing it with loathing. 'Bet it tastes disgusting.'

'Add yours, then,' said Hermione.

Harry dropped Goyle's hair into the middle glass and Ron put Crabbe's into the last one. Both glasses hissed and frothed: Goyle's turned the khaki colour of a bogey, Crabbe's a dark, murky brown.

'Hang on,' said Harry, as Ron and Hermione reached for their glasses. 'We'd better not all drink them in here: once we turn into Crabbe and Goyle we won't fit. And Millicent Bulstrode's no pixie.'

'Good thinking,' said Ron, unlocking the door. 'We'll take separate cubicles.'

Careful not to spill a drop of his Polyjuice Potion, Harry slipped into the middle cubicle.

'Ready?' he called.

'Ready,' came Ron and Hermione's voices.

'One … two … three …'

Pinching his nose, Harry drank the Potion down in two large gulps. It tasted like overcooked cabbage.

Immediately, his insides started writhing as though he'd just swallowed live snakes – doubled up, he wondered whether he was going to be sick – then a burning sensation spread rapidly from his stomach to the very ends of his fingers and toes. Next, bringing him gasping to all fours, came a horrible melting feeling, as the skin all over his body bubbled like hot wax, and before his eyes, his hands began to grow, the fingers thickened, the nails broadened and the knuckles were bulging like bolts. His shoulders stretched painfully and a prickling on his forehead told him that hair was creeping down towards his eyebrows; his robes ripped as his chest expanded like a barrel bursting its hoops; his feet were agony in shoes four sizes too small …

As suddenly as it had started, everything stopped. Harry lay face down on the cold stone floor, listening to Myrtle gurgling morosely in the end toilet. With difficulty, he kicked off his shoes and stood up. So this was what it felt like, being Goyle. His large hands trembling, he pulled off his old robes, which were hanging a foot above his ankles, pulled on the spare ones and laced up Goyle's boat-like shoes. He reached up to brush his hair out of his eyes and met only the short growth of wiry bristles, low on his forehead. Then he realised that his glasses were clouding his eyes, because Goyle obviously didn't need them. He took them off and called, 'Are you two OK?' Goyle's low rasp of a voice issued from his mouth.

'Yeah,' came the deep grunt of Crabbe from his right.

Harry unlocked his door and stepped in front of the cracked mirror. Goyle stared back at him out of dull, deep-set eyes. Harry scratched his ear. So did Goyle.

Ron's door opened. They stared at each other. Except that he looked pale and shocked, Ron was indistinguishable from Crabbe, from the pudding-basin haircut to the long, gorilla arms.

'This is unbelievable,' said Ron, approaching the mirror and prodding Crabbe's flat nose. *'Unbelievable.'*

'We'd better get going,' said Harry, loosening the watch that was cutting into Goyle's thick wrist. 'We've still got to find out where the Slytherin common room is, I only hope we can find someone to follow ...'

Ron, who had been gazing at Harry, said, 'You don't know how bizarre it is to see Goyle *thinking*.' He banged on Hermione's door. 'C'mon, we need to go ...'

A high-pitched voice answered him. 'I – I don't think I'm going to come after all. You go on without me.'

'Hermione, we know Millicent Bulstrode's ugly, no one's going to know it's you.'

'No – really – I don't think I'll come. You two hurry up, you're wasting time.'

Harry looked at Ron, bewildered.

'*That* looks more like Goyle,' said Ron. 'That's how he looks every time a teacher asks him a question.'

'Hermione, are you OK?' said Harry through the door.

'Fine – I'm fine … Go on –'

Harry looked at his watch. Five of their precious sixty minutes had already passed.

'We'll meet you back here, all right?' he said.

Harry and Ron opened the door of the bathroom carefully, checked that the coast was clear and set off.

'Don't swing your arms like that,' Harry muttered to Ron.

'Eh?'

'Crabbe holds them sort of stiff …'

'How's this?'

'Yeah, that's better.'

They went down the marble staircase. All they needed now was a Slytherin whom they could follow to the Slytherin common room, but there was nobody around.

'Any ideas?' muttered Harry.

'The Slytherins always come up to breakfast from over there,' said Ron, nodding at the entrance to the dungeons. The words had barely left his mouth when a girl with long curly hair emerged from the entrance.

'Excuse me,' said Ron, hurrying up to her, 'we've forgotten the way to our common room.'

'I beg your pardon?' said the girl stiffly. '*Our* common room? *I'm* a Ravenclaw.'

She walked away, looking suspiciously back at them.

Harry and Ron hurried down the stone steps into the darkness, their footsteps echoing particularly loudly as Crabbe and Goyle's huge feet hit the floor, feeling that this wasn't going to be as easy as they had hoped.

The labyrinthine passages were deserted. They walked deeper and deeper under the school, constantly checking their watches to see how much time they had left. After a quarter of an hour, just when they were getting desperate, they heard a sudden movement ahead.

'Ha!' said Ron excitedly. 'There's one of them now!'

The figure was emerging from a side room. As they hurried nearer, however, their hearts sank. It wasn't a Slytherin, it was Percy.

'What're you doing down here?' said Ron in surprise.

Percy looked affronted.

'That,' he said stiffly, 'is none of your business. It's Crabbe, isn't it?'

'Wh– oh, yeah,' said Ron.

'Well, get off to your dormitories,' said Percy sternly. 'It's not safe to go wandering around dark corridors these days.'

'*You* are,' Ron pointed out.

'I,' said Percy, drawing himself up, 'am a Prefect. Nothing's about to attack *me*.'

A voice suddenly echoed behind Harry and Ron. Draco

Malfoy was strolling towards them, and for the first time in his life, Harry was pleased to see him.

'There you are,' he drawled, looking at them. 'Have you two been pigging out in the Great Hall all this time? I've been looking for you, I want to show you something really funny.'

Malfoy glanced witheringly at Percy.

'And what're you doing down here, Weasley?' he sneered.

Percy looked outraged.

'You want to show a bit more respect to a school Prefect!' he said. 'I don't like your attitude!'

Malfoy sneered and motioned Harry and Ron to follow him. Harry almost said something apologetic to Percy but caught himself just in time. He and Ron hurried after Malfoy, who said as they turned into the next passage, 'That Peter Weasley –'

'Percy,' Ron corrected him automatically.

'Whatever,' said Malfoy. 'I've noticed him sneaking around a lot lately. And I bet I know what he's up to. He thinks he's going to catch Slytherin's heir single-handed.'

He gave a short, derisive laugh. Harry and Ron exchanged excited looks.

Malfoy paused by a stretch of bare, damp stone wall.

'What's the new password again?' he said to Harry.

'Er –' said Harry.

'Oh yeah – *pure-blood*!' said Malfoy, not listening, and a stone door concealed in the wall slid open. Malfoy marched through it and Harry and Ron followed him.

The Slytherin common room was a long, low underground room with rough stone walls and ceiling, from which round, greenish lamps were hanging on chains. A fire was crackling under an elaborately carved mantelpiece ahead of them, and several Slytherins were silhouetted around it in carved chairs.

'Wait here,' said Malfoy to Harry and Ron, motioning them to a pair of empty chairs set back from the fire. 'I'll go and get it – my father's just sent it to me –'

Wondering what Malfoy was going to show them, Harry and Ron sat down, doing their best to look at home.

Malfoy came back a minute later, holding what looked like a newspaper cutting. He thrust it under Ron's nose.

'That'll give you a laugh,' he said.

Harry saw Ron's eyes widen in shock. He read the cutting quickly, gave a very forced laugh and handed it to Harry.

It had been clipped out of the *Daily Prophet*, and it said:

ENQUIRY AT THE MINISTRY OF MAGIC

Arthur Weasley, Head of the Misuse of Muggle Artefacts Office, was today fined fifty Galleons for bewitching a Muggle car.

Mr Lucius Malfoy, a governor of Hogwarts School of Witchcraft and Wizardry, where the enchanted car crashed earlier this year, called today for Mr Weasley's resignation.

'Weasley has brought the Ministry into disrepute,' Mr Malfoy told our reporter. 'He is clearly unfit to draw up our laws and his ridiculous Muggle Protection Act should be scrapped immediately.'

Mr Weasley was unavailable for comment, although his wife told reporters to clear off or she'd set the family ghoul on them.

'Well?' said Malfoy impatiently, as Harry handed the cutting back to him. 'Don't you think it's funny?'

'Ha, ha,' said Harry bleakly.

'Arthur Weasley loves Muggles so much he should snap his wand in half and go and join them,' said Malfoy scornfully. 'You'd never know the Weasleys were pure-bloods, the way they behave.'

Ron's – or rather, Crabbe's – face was contorted with fury.

'What's up with you, Crabbe?' snapped Malfoy.

'Stomach ache,' Ron grunted.

'Well, go up to the hospital wing and give all those Mud-bloods a kick from me,' said Malfoy, snickering. 'You know, I'm surprised the *Daily Prophet* hasn't reported all these attacks yet,' he went on thoughtfully. 'I suppose Dumbledore's trying to hush it all up. He'll be sacked if it doesn't stop soon. Father's always said Dumbledore's the worst thing that's ever happened to this place. He loves Muggle-borns. A decent Headmaster would never've let slime like that Creevey in.'

Malfoy started taking pictures with an imaginary camera and did a cruel but accurate impression of Colin: 'Potter, can I have your picture, Potter? Can I have your autograph? Can I lick your shoes, please, Potter?'

He dropped his hands and looked at Harry and Ron.

'What's the *matter* with you two?'

Far too late, Harry and Ron forced themselves to laugh, but Malfoy seemed satisfied; perhaps Crabbe and Goyle were always slow on the uptake.

'Saint Potter, the Mudbloods' friend,' said Malfoy slowly. 'He's another one with no proper wizard feeling, or he wouldn't go around with that jumped-up Granger Mudblood. And people think *he*'s Slytherin's heir!'

Harry and Ron waited with bated breath: Malfoy was surely seconds away from telling them it was him. But then –

'I *wish* I knew who it *is*,' said Malfoy petulantly. 'I could help them.'

Ron's jaw dropped so that Crabbe's face looked even more gormless than usual. Fortunately, Malfoy didn't notice, and Harry, thinking fast, said, 'You must have some idea who's behind it all ...'

'You know I haven't, Goyle, how many times do I have to tell you?' snapped Malfoy. 'And father won't tell me *anything* about the last time the Chamber was opened, either. Of course, it was fifty years ago, so it was before his time, but he knows all about it, and he says that it was all kept quiet and it'll look suspicious if I know too much about it. But I know one thing: last time the Chamber of Secrets was opened, a Mudblood *died*. So I bet it's only a matter of time before one of them's killed this time … I hope it's Granger,' he said with relish.

Ron was clenching Crabbe's gigantic fists. Feeling that it would be a bit of a give-away if Ron punched Malfoy, Harry shot him a warning look and said, 'D'you know if the person who opened the Chamber last time was caught?'

'Oh, yeah … whoever it was was expelled,' said Malfoy. 'They're probably still in Azkaban.'

'Azkaban?' said Harry, puzzled.

'Azkaban – *the wizard prison,* Goyle,' said Malfoy, looking at him in disbelief. 'Honestly, if you were any slower, you'd be going backwards.'

He shifted restlessly in his chair and said, 'Father says to keep my head down and let the heir of Slytherin get on with it. He says the school needs ridding of all the Mudblood filth, but not to get mixed up in it. Of course, he's got a lot on his plate at the moment. You know the Ministry of Magic raided our Manor last week?'

Harry tried to force Goyle's dull face into a look of concern.

'Yeah …' said Malfoy. 'Luckily, they didn't find much. Father's got some *very* valuable Dark Arts stuff. But luckily, we've got our own secret chamber under the drawing-room floor –'

'Ho!' said Ron.

Malfoy looked at him. So did Harry. Ron blushed. Even his hair was turning red. His nose was also slowly lengthening –

their hour was up. Ron was turning back into himself, and from the look of horror he was suddenly giving Harry, he must be, too.

They both jumped to their feet.

'Medicine for my stomach,' Ron grunted, and without further ado they sprinted the length of the Slytherin common room, hurled themselves at the stone wall and dashed up the passage, hoping against hope that Malfoy hadn't noticed anything. Harry could feel his feet slipping around in Goyle's huge shoes and had to hoist up his robes as he shrank; they crashed up the steps into the dark Entrance Hall, which was full of a muffled pounding coming from the cupboard where they'd locked Crabbe and Goyle. Leaving their shoes outside the cupboard door, they sprinted in their socks up the marble staircase towards Moaning Myrtle's bathroom.

'Well, it wasn't a complete waste of time,' Ron panted, closing the bathroom door behind them. 'I know we still haven't found out who's doing the attacks, but I'm going to write to Dad tomorrow and tell him to check under the Malfoys' drawing room.'

Harry checked his face in the cracked mirror. He was back to normal. He put his glasses on as Ron hammered on the door of Hermione's cubicle.

'Hermione, come out, we've got loads to tell you –'

'Go away!' Hermione squeaked.

Harry and Ron looked at each other.

'What's the matter?' said Ron. 'You must be back to normal by now, we are …'

But Moaning Myrtle glided suddenly through the cubicle door. Harry had never seen her looking so happy.

'Ooooooh, wait till you see,' she said. 'It's *awful*!'

They heard the lock slide back and Hermione emerged, sobbing, her robes pulled up over her head.

'What's up?' said Ron uncertainly. 'Have you still got Millicent's nose or something?'

Hermione let her robes fall and Ron backed into the sink.

Her face was covered in black fur. Her eyes had gone yellow and there were long pointed ears poking through her hair.

'It was a c-cat hair!' she howled. 'M-Millicent Bulstrode m-must have a cat! And the P-Potion isn't supposed to be used for animal transformations!'

'Uh oh,' said Ron.

'You'll be teased something *dreadful*,' said Myrtle happily.

'It's OK, Hermione,' said Harry quickly. 'We'll take you up to the hospital wing. Madam Pomfrey never asks too many questions …'

It took a long time to persuade Hermione to leave the bathroom. Moaning Myrtle sped them on their way with a hearty guffaw.

'Wait till everyone finds out you've got a *tail*!'

CHAPTER THIRTEEN

The Very Secret Diary

Hermione remained in the hospital wing for several weeks. There was a flurry of rumour about her disappearance when the rest of the school arrived back from their Christmas holidays, because of course everyone thought that she had been attacked. So many students filed past the hospital wing trying to catch a glimpse of her that Madam Pomfrey took out her curtains again and placed them around Hermione's bed, to spare her the shame of being seen with a furry face.

Harry and Ron went to visit her every evening. When the new term started, they brought her each day's homework.

'If I'd sprouted whiskers, I'd take a break from work,' said Ron, tipping a stack of books onto Hermione's bedside table one evening.

'Don't be silly, Ron, I've got to keep up,' said Hermione briskly. Her spirits were greatly improved by the fact that all the hair had gone from her face and her eyes were turning slowly back to brown. 'I don't suppose you've got any new leads?' she added in a whisper, so that Madam Pomfrey couldn't hear her.

'Nothing,' said Harry gloomily.

'I was so *sure* it was Malfoy,' said Ron, for about the hundredth time.

'What's that?' asked Harry, pointing to something gold sticking out from under Hermione's pillow.

'Just a Get Well card,' said Hermione hastily, trying to poke it out of sight, but Ron was too quick for her. He pulled it out, flicked it open and read aloud:

'To Miss Granger, wishing you a speedy recovery, from your concerned teacher, Professor Gilderoy Lockhart, Order of Merlin, Third Class, Honorary Member of the Dark Force Defence League and five times winner of Witch Weekly*'s Most-Charming-Smile Award.'*

Ron looked up at Hermione, disgusted.

'You sleep with this under your *pillow*?'

But Hermione was spared answering by Madam Pomfrey sweeping over with her evening dose of medicine.

'Is Lockhart the smarmiest bloke you've ever met, or what?' Ron said to Harry as they left the dormitory and started up the stairs towards Gryffindor Tower. Snape had given them so much homework, Harry thought he was likely to be in the sixth year before he finished it. Ron was just saying he wished he had asked Hermione how many rat tails you were supposed to add to a Hair-Raising Potion, when an angry outburst from the floor above reached their ears.

'That's Filch,' Harry muttered, as they hurried up the stairs and paused, out of sight, listening hard.

'You don't think someone else's been attacked?' said Ron tensely.

They stood still, their heads inclined towards Filch's voice, which sounded quite hysterical.

'*... even more work for me! Mopping all night, like I haven't got enough to do! No, this is the final straw, I'm going to Dumbledore ...*'

His footsteps receded and they heard a distant door slam.

They poked their heads around the corner. Filch had clearly been manning his usual lookout post: they were once again on the spot where Mrs Norris had been attacked. They saw at a glance what Filch had been shouting about. A great flood of water stretched over half the corridor, and it looked as though it was still seeping from under the door of Moaning Myrtle's bathroom. Now Filch had stopped shouting, they could hear Myrtle's wails echoing off the bathroom walls.

'*Now* what's up with her?' said Ron.

'Let's go and see,' said Harry, and holding their robes over their ankles they stepped through the great wash of water to the door bearing its 'Out of Order' sign, ignored it as always, and entered.

Moaning Myrtle was crying, if possible, louder and harder than ever before. She seemed to be hiding down her usual toilet. It was dark in the bathroom, because the candles had been extinguished in the great rush of water that had left both walls and floor soaking wet.

'What's up, Myrtle?' said Harry.

'Who's that?' glugged Myrtle miserably. 'Come to throw something else at me?'

Harry waded across to her cubicle and said, 'Why would I throw something at you?'

'Don't ask me,' Myrtle shouted, emerging with a wave of yet more water, which splashed onto the already sopping floor. 'Here I am, minding my own business, and someone thinks it's funny to throw a book at me ...'

'But it can't hurt you if someone throws something at you,' said Harry, reasonably. 'I mean, it'd just go right through you, wouldn't it?'

He had said the wrong thing. Myrtle puffed herself up and shrieked, 'Let's all throw books at Myrtle, because *she* can't feel it! Ten points if you can get it through her stomach! Fifty points if it goes through her head! Well, ha ha ha! What a lovely game, I *don't* think!'

'Who threw it at you, anyway?' asked Harry.

'*I* don't know ... I was just sitting in the U-bend, thinking about death, and it fell right through the top of my head,' said Myrtle, glaring at them. 'It's over there, it got washed out.'

Harry and Ron looked under the sink, where Myrtle was pointing. A small, thin book lay there. It had a shabby black cover and was as wet as everything else in the bathroom. Harry stepped forward to pick it up, but Ron suddenly flung out an arm to hold him back.

'What?' said Harry.

'Are you mad?' said Ron. 'It could be dangerous.'

'*Dangerous?*' said Harry, laughing. 'Come off it, how could it be dangerous?'

'You'd be surprised,' said Ron, who was looking apprehensively at the book. 'Some of the books the Ministry's confiscated – Dad's told me – there was one that burned your eyes out. And everyone who read *Sonnets of a Sorcerer* spoke in limericks for the rest of their lives. And some old witch in Bath had a book that you could *never stop reading*! You just had to wander around with your nose in it, trying to do everything one-handed. And –'

'All right, I've got the point,' said Harry.

The little book lay on the floor, nondescript and soggy.

'Well, we won't find out unless we look at it,' he said, and he ducked round Ron and picked it off the floor.

Harry saw at once that it was a diary, and the faded year on the cover told him it was fifty years old. He opened it eagerly. On the first page he could just make out the name 'T. M. Riddle' in smudged ink.

'Hang on,' said Ron, who had approached cautiously and was looking over Harry's shoulder. 'I know that name … T. M. Riddle got an award for special services to the school fifty years ago.'

'How on earth d'you know that?' said Harry in amazement.

'Because Filch made me polish his shield about fifty times in detention,' said Ron resentfully. 'That was the one I burped slugs all over. If you'd wiped slime off a name for an hour, you'd remember it, too.'

Harry peeled the wet pages apart. They were completely blank. There wasn't the faintest trace of writing on any of them, not even 'Auntie Mabel's birthday', or 'dentist, half past three'.

'He never wrote in it,' said Harry, disappointed.

'I wonder why someone wanted to flush it away?' said Ron curiously.

Harry turned to the back cover of the book and saw the printed name of a newsagent's in Vauxhall Road, London.

'He must've been Muggle-born,' said Harry thoughtfully, 'to have bought a diary from Vauxhall Road …'

'Well, it's not much use to you,' said Ron. He dropped his voice. 'Fifty points if you can get it through Myrtle's nose.'

Harry, however, pocketed it.

Hermione left the hospital wing, de-whiskered, tail-less and fur-free, at the beginning of February. On her first evening back in Gryffindor Tower, Harry showed her T. M. Riddle's diary and told her the story of how they had found it.

'Oooh, it might have hidden powers,' said Hermione enthusiastically, taking the diary and looking at it closely.

'If it has, it's hiding them very well,' said Ron. 'Maybe it's shy. I don't know why you don't chuck it, Harry.'

'I wish I knew why someone *did* try to chuck it,' said Harry. 'I wouldn't mind knowing how Riddle got an award for special services to Hogwarts, either.'

'Could've been anything,' said Ron. 'Maybe he got thirty O.W.L.s or saved a teacher from the giant squid. Maybe he murdered Myrtle, that would've done everyone a favour …'

But Harry could tell from the arrested look on Hermione's face that she was thinking what he was thinking.

'What?' said Ron, looking from one to the other.

'Well, the Chamber of Secrets was opened fifty years ago, wasn't it?' he said. 'That's what Malfoy said.'

'Yeah …' said Ron slowly.

'And *this diary* is fifty years old,' said Hermione, tapping it excitedly.

'So?'

'Oh, Ron, wake up,' snapped Hermione. 'We know the person who opened the Chamber last time was expelled *fifty years ago*. We know T. M. Riddle got an award for special services to the school *fifty years ago*. Well, what if Riddle got his special award for *catching the heir of Slytherin*? His diary would probably tell us everything: where the Chamber is, and how to open it, and what sort of creature lives in it. The person who's behind the attacks this time wouldn't want that lying around, would they?'

'That's a *brilliant* theory, Hermione,' said Ron, 'with just one tiny little flaw. *There's nothing written in his diary*.'

But Hermione was pulling her wand out of her bag.

'It might be invisible ink!' she whispered.

She tapped the diary three times and said, '*Aparecium!*'

Nothing happened. Undaunted, Hermione shoved her hand back into her bag and pulled out what appeared to be a bright red eraser.

'It's a Revealer, I got it in Diagon Alley,' she said.

She rubbed hard on 'January the first'. Nothing happened.

'I'm telling you, there's nothing to find in there,' said Ron. 'Riddle just got a diary for Christmas and couldn't be bothered filling it in.'

* * *

Harry couldn't explain, even to himself, why he didn't just throw Riddle's diary away. The fact was that even though he *knew* the diary was blank, he kept absent-mindedly picking it up and turning the pages, as though it was a story he wanted to finish. And while Harry was sure he had never heard the name T. M. Riddle before, it still seemed to mean something to him, almost as though Riddle was a friend he'd had when he was very small, and half-forgotten. But this was absurd. He'd never had friends before Hogwarts, Dudley had made sure of that.

Nevertheless, Harry was determined to find out more about Riddle, so, next day at break, he headed for the trophy room to examine Riddle's special award, accompanied by an interested Hermione and a thoroughly unconvinced Ron, who told them he'd seen enough of the trophy room to last him a lifetime.

Riddle's burnished gold shield was tucked away in a corner cabinet. It didn't carry details of why it had been given to him ('Good thing, too, or it'd be even bigger and I'd still be polishing it,' said Ron). However, they did find Riddle's name on an old Medal for Magical Merit, and on a list of old Head Boys.

'He sounds like Percy,' said Ron, wrinkling his nose in disgust. 'Prefect, Head Boy – probably top of every class.'

'You say that like it's a bad thing,' said Hermione, in a slightly hurt voice.

The sun had now begun to shine weakly on Hogwarts again. Inside the castle, the mood had grown more hopeful.

There had been no more attacks since those on Justin and Nearly Headless Nick, and Madam Pomfrey was pleased to report that the Mandrakes were becoming moody and secretive, meaning that they were fast leaving childhood.

'The moment their acne clears up, they'll be ready for repotting again,' Harry heard her telling Filch kindly one afternoon. 'And after that, it won't be long until we're cutting them up and stewing them. You'll have Mrs Norris back in no time.'

Perhaps the heir of Slytherin had lost his or her nerve, thought Harry. It must be getting riskier and riskier to open the Chamber of Secrets, with the school so alert and suspicious. Perhaps the monster, whatever it was, was even now settling itself down to hibernate for another fifty years …

Ernie Macmillan of Hufflepuff didn't take this cheerful view. He was still convinced that Harry was the guilty one, that he had 'given himself away' at the Duelling Club. Peeves wasn't helping matters: he kept popping up in the crowded corridors singing 'Oh Potter, you rotter …', now with a dance-routine to match.

Gilderoy Lockhart seemed to think he himself had made the attacks stop. Harry overheard him telling Professor McGonagall so while the Gryffindors were lining up for Transfiguration.

'I don't think there'll be any more trouble, Minerva,' he said, tapping his nose knowingly and winking. 'I think the

Chamber has been locked for good this time. The culprit must have known it was only a matter of time before I caught them. Rather sensible to stop now, before I came down hard on them.

'You know, what the school needs now is a morale-booster. Wash away the memories of last term! I won't say any more just now, but I think I know just the thing ...'

He tapped his nose again and strode off.

Lockhart's idea of a morale-booster became clear at breakfast time on February the fourteenth. Harry hadn't had much sleep because of a late-running Quidditch practice the night before, and he hurried down to the Great Hall slightly late. He thought, for a moment, that he'd walked through the wrong doors.

The walls were all covered with large, lurid pink flowers. Worse still, heart-shaped confetti was falling from the pale blue ceiling. Harry went over to the Gryffindor table, where Ron was sitting looking sickened, and Hermione seemed to have come over rather giggly.

'What's going on?' Harry asked them, sitting down, and wiping confetti off his bacon.

Ron pointed to the teachers' table, apparently too disgusted to speak. Lockhart, wearing lurid pink robes to match the decorations, was waving for silence. The teachers on either side of him were looking stony-faced. From where he sat, Harry could see a muscle going in Professor McGonagall's cheek. Snape looked as though someone had just fed him a large beaker of Skele-Gro.

'Happy Valentine's Day!' Lockhart shouted. 'And may I thank the forty-six people who have so far sent me cards! Yes, I have taken the liberty of arranging this little surprise for you all – and it doesn't end here!'

Lockhart clapped his hands and through the doors to the Entrance Hall marched a dozen surly-looking dwarfs. Not just any dwarfs, however. Lockhart had them all wearing golden wings and carrying harps.

'My friendly, card-carrying cupids!' beamed Lockhart. 'They will be roving around the school today delivering your Valentines! And the fun doesn't stop here! I'm sure my colleagues will want to enter into the spirit of the occasion! Why not ask Professor Snape to show you how to whip up a Love Potion! And while you're at it, Professor Flitwick knows more about Entrancing Enchantments than any wizard I've ever met, the sly old dog!'

Professor Flitwick buried his face in his hands. Snape was looking as though the first person to ask him for a Love Potion would be force-fed poison.

'Please, Hermione, tell me you weren't one of the forty-six,' said Ron, as they left the Great Hall for their first lesson. Hermione suddenly became very interested in searching her bag for her timetable and didn't answer.

All day long, the dwarfs kept barging into their classes to deliver Valentines, to the annoyance of the teachers, and late that afternoon, as the Gryffindors were walking upstairs for Charms, one of them caught up with Harry.

'Oy, you! 'Arry Potter!' shouted a particularly grim-looking dwarf, elbowing people out of the way to get to Harry.

Hot all over at the thought of being given a Valentine in front of a queue of first-years, which happened to include Ginny Weasley, Harry tried to escape. The dwarf, however, cut his way through the crowd by kicking people's shins, and reached him before he'd gone two paces.

'I've got a musical message to deliver to 'Arry Potter in person,' he said, twanging his harp in a threatening sort of way.

'Not here,' Harry hissed, trying to escape.

'Stay *still*!' grunted the dwarf, grabbing hold of Harry's bag and pulling him back.

'Let me go!' Harry snarled, tugging.

With a loud ripping noise, his bag split in two. His books, wand, parchment and quill spilled onto the floor and his ink bottle smashed over the lot.

Harry scrambled around, trying to pick it all up before the dwarf started singing, causing something of a hold-up in the corridor.

'What's going on here?' came the cold, drawling voice of Draco Malfoy. Harry started stuffing everything feverishly into his ripped bag, desperate to get away before Malfoy could hear his musical Valentine.

'What's all this commotion?' said another familiar voice, as Percy Weasley arrived.

Losing his head, Harry tried to make a run for it, but the dwarf seized him around the knees and brought him crashing to the floor.

'Right,' he said, sitting on Harry's ankles, 'here is your singing Valentine:

'His eyes are as green as a fresh pickled toad,
His hair is as dark as a blackboard.
I wish he was mine, he's really divine,
The hero who conquered the Dark Lord.'

Harry would have given all the gold in Gringotts to evaporate on the spot. Trying valiantly to laugh along with everyone else, he got up, his feet numb from the weight of the dwarf, as Percy Weasley did his best to disperse the crowd, some of whom were crying with mirth.

'Off you go, off you go, the bell rang five minutes ago, off to class, now,' he said, shooing some of the younger students away. '*And* you, Malfoy.'

Harry, glancing over, saw Malfoy stoop and snatch up something. Leering, he showed it to Crabbe and Goyle, and Harry realised that he'd got Riddle's diary.

'Give that back,' said Harry quietly.

'Wonder what Potter's written in this?' said Malfoy, who obviously hadn't noticed the year on the cover, and thought he had Harry's own diary. A hush fell over the onlookers. Ginny was staring from the diary to Harry, looking terrified.

'Hand it over, Malfoy,' said Percy sternly.

'When I've had a look,' said Malfoy, waving the diary tauntingly at Harry.

Percy said, 'As a school Prefect –', but Harry had lost his temper. He pulled out his wand and shouted, *'Expelliarmus!'* and just as Snape had disarmed Lockhart, so Malfoy found the diary shooting out of his hand into the air. Ron, grinning broadly, caught it.

'Harry!' said Percy loudly. 'No magic in the corridors. I'll have to report this, you know!'

But Harry didn't care, he'd got one over on Malfoy, and that was worth five points from Gryffindor any day. Malfoy was looking furious, and as Ginny passed him to enter her classroom, he yelled spitefully after her, 'I don't think Potter liked your Valentine much!'

Ginny covered her face with her hands and ran into class. Snarling, Ron pulled out his wand, too, but Harry pulled him away. Ron didn't need to spend the whole of Charms belching slugs.

It wasn't until they had reached Professor Flitwick's class that Harry noticed something rather odd about Riddle's diary. All his other books were drenched in scarlet ink. The diary, however, was as clean as it had been before the ink bottle had smashed all over it. He tried to point this out to Ron, but Ron was having trouble with his wand again; large purple bubbles were blossoming out of the end, and he wasn't much interested in anything else.

Harry went to bed before anyone else in his dormitory that night. This was partly because he didn't think he could stand Fred and George singing, *'His eyes are as green as a fresh pickled toad'*, one more time, and partly because he wanted to examine Riddle's diary again, and knew that Ron thought he was wasting his time.

Harry sat on his four-poster and flicked through the blank pages, not one of which had a trace of scarlet ink on it. Then he pulled a new bottle out of his bedside cabinet, dipped his quill into it, and dropped a blot onto the first page of the diary.

The ink shone brightly on the paper for a second and then, as though it was being sucked into the page, vanished. Excited, Harry loaded up his quill a second time and wrote, 'My name is Harry Potter.'

The words shone momentarily on the page and they too sank without trace. Then, at last, something happened.

Oozing back out of the page, in his very own ink, came words Harry had never written.

'Hello, Harry Potter. My name is Tom Riddle. How did you come by my diary?'

These words, too, faded away, but not before Harry had started to scribble back.

'Someone tried to flush it down a toilet.'

He waited eagerly for Riddle's reply.

'Lucky that I recorded my memories in some more lasting way than ink. But I always knew that there would be those who would not want this diary read.'

'What do you mean?' Harry scrawled, blotting the page in his excitement.

'I mean that this diary holds memories of terrible things. Things which

were covered up. Things which happened at Hogwarts School of Witchcraft and Wizardry.'

'That's where I am now,' Harry wrote quickly. 'I'm at Hogwarts, and horrible stuff's been happening. Do you know anything about the Chamber of Secrets?'

His heart was hammering. Riddle's reply came quickly, his writing becoming untidier, as though he was hurrying to tell all he knew.

'Of course I know about the Chamber of Secrets. In my day, they told us it was a legend, that it did not exist. But this was a lie. In my fifth year, the Chamber was opened and the monster attacked several students, finally killing one. I caught the person who'd opened the Chamber and he was expelled. But the Headmaster, Professor Dippet, ashamed that such a thing had happened at Hogwarts, forbade me to tell the truth. A story was given out that the girl had died in a freak accident. They gave me a nice, shiny, engraved trophy for my trouble and warned me to keep my mouth shut. But I knew it could happen again. The monster lived on, and the one who had the power to release it was not imprisoned.'

Harry nearly upset his ink bottle in his hurry to write back.

'It's happening again now. There have been three attacks and no one seems to know who's behind them. Who was it last time?'

'I can show you, if you like,' came Riddle's reply. *'You don't have to take my word for it. I can take you inside my memory of the night when I caught him.'*

Harry hesitated, his quill suspended over the diary. What did Riddle mean? How could he be taken inside somebody else's memory? He glanced nervously at the door to the dormitory, which was growing dark. When he looked back at the diary, he saw fresh words forming.

'Let me show you.'

Harry paused for a fraction of a second and then wrote two letters.

'OK.'

The pages of the diary began to blow as though caught in a high wind, stopping halfway through the month of June. Mouth hanging open, Harry saw that the little square for June the thirteenth seemed to have turned into a minuscule television screen. His hands trembling slightly, he raised the book to press his eye against the little window, and before he knew what was happening, he was tilting forwards; the window was widening, he felt his body leave his bed and he was pitched headfirst through the opening in the page, into a whirl of colour and shadow.

He felt his feet hit solid ground, and stood, shaking, as the blurred shapes around him came suddenly into focus.

He knew immediately where he was. This circular room with the sleeping portraits was Dumbledore's office – but it wasn't Dumbledore who was sitting behind the desk. A wizened, frail-looking wizard, bald except for a few wisps of white hair, was reading a letter by candlelight. Harry had never seen this man before.

'I'm sorry,' he said shakily, 'I didn't mean to butt in ...'

But the wizard didn't look up. He continued to read,

frowning slightly. Harry drew nearer to his desk and stammered, 'Er – I'll just go, shall I?'

Still the wizard ignored him. He didn't seem even to have heard him. Thinking that the wizard might be deaf, Harry raised his voice.

'Sorry I disturbed you, I'll go now,' he half shouted.

The wizard folded up the letter with a sigh, stood up, walked past Harry without glancing at him and went to draw the curtains at his window.

The sky outside the window was ruby red; it seemed to be sunset. The wizard went back to the desk, sat down and twiddled his thumbs, watching the door.

Harry looked around the office. No Fawkes the phoenix; no whirring silver contraptions. This was Hogwarts as Riddle had known it, meaning that this unknown wizard was Headmaster, not Dumbledore, and he, Harry, was little more than a phantom, completely invisible to the people of fifty years ago.

There was a knock on the office door.

'Enter,' said the old wizard in a feeble voice.

A boy of about sixteen entered, taking off his pointed hat. A silver Prefect's badge was glinting on his chest. He was much taller than Harry, but he, too, had jet-black hair.

'Ah, Riddle,' said the Headmaster.

'You wanted to see me, Professor Dippet?' said Riddle. He looked nervous.

'Sit down,' said Dippet. 'I've just been reading the letter you sent me.'

'Oh,' said Riddle. He sat down, gripping his hands together very tightly.

'My dear boy,' said Dippet kindly, 'I cannot possibly let you stay at school over the summer. Surely you want to go home for the holidays?'

'No,' said Riddle at once, 'I'd much rather stay at Hogwarts than go back to that – to that –'

'You live in a Muggle orphanage during the holidays, I believe?' said Dippet curiously.

'Yes, sir,' said Riddle, reddening slightly.

'You are Muggle-born?'

'Half-blood, sir,' said Riddle. 'Muggle father, witch mother.'

'And are both your parents –?'

'My mother died just after I was born, sir. They told me at the orphanage she lived just long enough to name me: Tom after my father, Marvolo after my grandfather.'

Dippet clucked his tongue sympathetically.

'The thing is, Tom,' he sighed, 'special arrangements might have been made for you, but in the current circumstances …'

'You mean all these attacks, sir?' said Riddle, and Harry's heart leapt, and he moved closer, scared of missing anything.

'Precisely,' said the Headmaster. 'My dear boy, you must see how foolish it would be of me to allow you to remain at the castle when term ends. Particularly in the light of the recent tragedy … the death of that poor little girl … You will be safer by far at your orphanage. As a matter of fact, the Ministry of

Magic is even now talking about closing the school. We are no nearer locating the – er – source of all this unpleasantness …'

Riddle's eyes had widened.

'Sir – if the person was caught … If it all stopped …'

'What do you mean?' said Dippet, with a squeak in his voice, sitting up in his chair. 'Riddle do you mean you know something about these attacks?'

'No, sir,' said Riddle quickly.

But Harry was sure it was the same sort of 'no' that he himself had given Dumbledore.

Dippet sank back, looking faintly disappointed.

'You may go, Tom …'

Riddle slid off his chair and stumped out of the room. Harry followed him.

Down the moving spiral staircase they went, emerging next to the gargoyle in the darkening corridor. Riddle stopped, and so did Harry, watching him. Harry could tell that Riddle was doing some serious thinking. He was biting his lip, his forehead furrowed.

Then, as though he had suddenly reached a decision, he hurried off, Harry gliding noiselessly behind him. They didn't see another person until they reached the Entrance Hall, when a tall wizard with long, sweeping auburn hair and beard called to Riddle from the marble staircase.

'What are you doing, wandering around this late, Tom?'

Harry gaped at the wizard. He was none other than a fifty-year-younger Dumbledore.

'I had to see the Headmaster, sir,' said Riddle.

'Well, hurry off to bed,' said Dumbledore, giving Riddle exactly the kind of penetrating stare Harry knew so well. 'Best not to roam the corridors these days. Not since ...'

He sighed heavily, bade Riddle goodnight and strode off. Riddle watched him out of sight and then, moving quickly, headed straight down the stone steps to the dungeons, with Harry in hot pursuit.

But to Harry's disappointment, Riddle led him not into a hidden passageway or a secret tunnel but the very dungeon in which Harry had Potions with Snape. The torches hadn't been lit, and when Riddle pushed the door almost closed, Harry could only just see Riddle, standing stock-still by the door, watching the passage outside.

It felt to Harry that they were there for at least an hour. All he could see was the figure of Riddle at the door, staring through the crack, waiting like a statue. And just when Harry had stopped feeling expectant and tense, and started wishing he could return to the present, he heard something move beyond the door.

Someone was creeping along the passage. He heard whoever it was pass the dungeon where he and Riddle were hidden. Riddle, quiet as a shadow, edged through the door and followed, Harry tiptoeing behind him, forgetting that he couldn't be heard.

For perhaps five minutes they followed the footsteps, until Riddle stopped suddenly, his head inclined in the direction of new noises. Harry heard a door creak open, and then someone speaking in a hoarse whisper.

'C'mon … gotta get yeh outta here … c'mon now … in the box …'

There was something familiar about that voice.

Riddle suddenly jumped around the corner. Harry stepped out behind him. He could see the dark outline of a huge boy who was crouching in front of an open door, a very large box next to it.

'Evening, Rubeus,' said Riddle sharply.

The boy slammed the door shut and stood up.

'What yer doin' down here, Tom?'

Riddle stepped closer.

'It's all over,' he said. 'I'm going to have to turn you in, Rubeus. They're talking about closing Hogwarts if the attacks don't stop.'

'What d'yeh –'

'I don't think you meant to kill anyone. But monsters don't make good pets. I suppose you just let it out for exercise and –'

'It never killed no one!' said the large boy, backing against the closed door. From behind him, Harry could hear a funny rustling and clicking.

'Come on, Rubeus,' said Riddle, moving yet closer. 'The dead girl's parents will be here tomorrow. The least Hogwarts can do is make sure that the thing that killed their daughter is slaughtered …'

'It wasn' him!' roared the boy, his voice echoing in the dark passage. 'He wouldn'! He never!'

'Stand aside,' said Riddle, drawing out his wand.

His spell lit the corridor with a sudden flaming light. The door behind the large boy flew open with such force it knocked him into the wall opposite. And out of it came something that made Harry let out a long, piercing scream no one but he seemed to hear.

A vast, low-slung, hairy body and a tangle of black legs; a gleam of many eyes and a pair of razor-sharp pincers – Riddle raised his wand again, but he was too late. The thing bowled him over as it scuttled away, tearing up the corridor and out of sight. Riddle scrambled to his feet, looking after it; he raised his wand, but the huge boy leapt on him, seized his wand and threw him back down, yelling, 'NOOOOOOO!'

The scene whirled, the darkness became complete, Harry felt himself falling and, with a crash, he landed spread-eagled on his four-poster in the Gryffindor dormitory, Riddle's diary lying open on his stomach.

Before he had had time to regain his breath, the dormitory door opened and Ron came in.

'There you are,' he said.

Harry sat up. He was sweating and shaking.

'What's up?' said Ron, looking at him with concern.

'It was Hagrid, Ron. Hagrid opened the Chamber of Secrets fifty years ago.'

CHAPTER FOURTEEN

Cornelius Fudge

Harry, Ron and Hermione had always known that Hagrid had an unfortunate liking for large and monstrous creatures. During their first year at Hogwarts he had tried to raise a dragon in his little wooden house, and it would be a long time before they forgot the giant, three-headed dog he'd christened 'Fluffy'. And if, as a boy, Hagrid had heard that a monster was hidden somewhere in the castle, Harry was sure he'd have gone to any lengths for a glimpse of it. He'd probably thought it was a shame that the monster had been cooped up so long, and thought it deserved the chance to stretch its many legs; Harry could just imagine the thirteen-year-old Hagrid trying to fit a lead and collar on it. But he was equally certain that Hagrid would never have meant to kill anybody.

Harry half wished he hadn't found out how to work Riddle's diary. Again and again Ron and Hermione made him recount what he'd seen, until he was heartily sick of telling them and sick of the long, circular conversations that followed.

'Riddle *might* have got the wrong person,' said Hermione. 'Maybe it was some other monster that was attacking people ...'

'How many monsters d'you think this place can hold?' Ron asked dully.

'We always knew Hagrid had been expelled,' said Harry miserably. 'And the attacks must've stopped after Hagrid was kicked out. Otherwise, Riddle wouldn't have got his award.'

Ron tried a different tack.

'Riddle *does* sound like Percy – who asked him to grass on Hagrid, anyway?'

'But the monster had *killed* someone, Ron,' said Hermione.

'And Riddle was going to go back to some Muggle orphanage if they closed Hogwarts,' said Harry. 'I don't blame him for wanting to stay here ...'

Ron bit his lip, then said tentatively, 'You met Hagrid down Knockturn Alley, didn't you, Harry?'

'He was buying a Flesh-Eating Slug Repellent,' said Harry quickly.

The three of them fell silent. After a long pause, Hermione voiced the knottiest question of all in a hesitant voice: 'Do you think we should go and *ask* Hagrid about it all?'

'That'd be a cheerful visit,' said Ron. 'Hello, Hagrid, tell us, have you been setting anything mad and hairy loose in the castle lately?'

In the end, they decided that they wouldn't say anything to Hagrid unless there was another attack, and as more and more days went by with no whisper from the disembodied voice, they became hopeful that they would never need to talk to him about why he had been expelled. It was now nearly four months since Justin and Nearly Headless Nick had been Petrified, and nearly everybody seemed to think that the attacker, whoever it was, had retired for good. Peeves had finally got bored of his 'Oh Potter you rotter' song, Ernie Macmillan asked Harry quite politely to pass a bucket of leaping toadstools in Herbology one day, and in March several of the Mandrakes threw a loud and raucous party in Greenhouse Three. This made Professor Sprout very happy.

'The moment they start trying to move into each other's pots, we'll know they're fully mature,' she told Harry. 'Then we'll be able to revive those poor people in the hospital wing.'

The second-years were given something new to think about during their Easter holidays. The time had come to choose their subjects for the third year, a matter that Hermione, at least, took very seriously.

'It could affect our whole future,' she told Harry and Ron, as they pored over lists of new subjects, marking them with ticks.

'I just want to give up Potions,' said Harry.

'We can't,' said Ron gloomily. 'We keep all our old subjects, or I'd've ditched Defence Against the Dark Arts.'

'But that's very important!' said Hermione, shocked.

'Not the way Lockhart teaches it,' said Ron. 'I haven't learned anything from him except not to set pixies loose.'

Neville Longbottom had been sent letters from all the witches and wizards in his family, all giving him different advice on what to choose. Confused and worried, he sat reading the subject lists with his tongue poking out, asking people whether they thought Arithmancy sounded more difficult than Study of Ancient Runes. Dean Thomas, who, like Harry, had grown up with Muggles, ended up closing his eyes and jabbing his wand at the list, then picking the subjects it landed on. Hermione took nobody's advice but signed up for everything.

Harry smiled grimly to himself at the thought of what Uncle Vernon and Aunt Petunia would say if he tried to discuss his career in wizardry with them. Not that he didn't get any guidance: Percy Weasley was eager to share his experience.

'Depends where you want to *go*, Harry,' he said. 'It's never too early to think about the future, so I'd recommend Divination. People say Muggle Studies is a soft option, but I personally think wizards should have a thorough understanding of the non-magical community, particularly if they're thinking of working in close contact with them – look at my father, he has to deal with Muggle business all the time. My brother Charlie was always more of an outdoor type, so he went for Care of Magical Creatures. Play to your strengths, Harry.'

But the only thing Harry felt he was really good at was Quidditch. In the end, he chose the same new subjects as

Ron, feeling that if he was rubbish at them, at least he'd have someone friendly to help him.

Gryffindor's next Quidditch match would be against Hufflepuff. Wood was insisting on team practices every night after dinner, so that Harry barely had time for anything but Quidditch and homework. However, the training sessions were getting better, or at least drier, and the evening before Saturday's match, he went up to his dormitory to drop off his broomstick, feeling Gryffindor's chances for the Quidditch Cup had never been better.

But his cheerful mood didn't last long. At the top of the stairs to the dormitory, he met Neville Longbottom, who was looking frantic.

'Harry – I don't know who did it. I just found –'

Watching Harry fearfully, Neville pushed open the door.

The contents of Harry's trunk had been thrown everywhere. His cloak lay ripped on the floor. The bedclothes had been pulled off his four-poster and the drawer had been pulled out of his bedside cabinet, the contents strewn over the mattress.

Harry walked over to the bed, open-mouthed, treading on a few loose pages of *Travels with Trolls*.

As he and Neville pulled the blankets back onto his bed, Ron, Dean and Seamus came in. Dean swore loudly.

'What happened, Harry?'

'No idea,' said Harry. But Ron was examining Harry's robes. All the pockets were hanging out.

'Someone's been looking for something,' said Ron. 'Is there anything missing?'

Harry started to pick up all his things and throw them into his trunk. It was only as he threw the last of the Lockhart books back into it that he realised what wasn't there.

'Riddle's diary's gone,' he said in an undertone to Ron.

'*What?*'

Harry jerked his head towards the dormitory door and Ron followed him out. They hurried back down to the Gryffindor common room, which was half-empty, and joined Hermione, who was sitting alone, reading a book called *Ancient Runes Made Easy*.

Hermione looked aghast at the news.

'But – only a Gryffindor could have stolen – nobody else knows our password ...'

'Exactly,' said Harry.

They woke next day to brilliant sunshine and a light, refreshing breeze.

'Perfect Quidditch conditions!' said Wood enthusiastically at the Gryffindor table, loading the team's plates with scrambled eggs. 'Harry, buck up there, you need a decent breakfast.'

Harry had been staring down the packed Gryffindor table, wondering if the new owner of Riddle's diary was right in front of his eyes. Hermione had been urging him to report the robbery, but Harry didn't like the idea. He'd have to tell a teacher all about the diary and how many people knew why

Hagrid had been expelled fifty years ago? He didn't want to be the one who brought it all up again.

As he left the Great Hall with Ron and Hermione to go and collect his Quidditch things, another, very serious worry was added to Harry's growing list. He had just set foot on the marble staircase when he heard it yet again: *'Kill this time … let me rip … tear …'*

He shouted aloud and Ron and Hermione both jumped away from him in alarm.

'The voice!' said Harry, looking over his shoulder. 'I just heard it again – didn't you?'

Ron shook his head, wide-eyed. Hermione, however, clapped a hand to her forehead.

'Harry – I think I've just understood something! I've got to go to the library!'

And she sprinted away, up the stairs.

'*What* does she understand?' said Harry distractedly, still looking around, trying to tell where the voice had come from.

'Loads more than I do,' said Ron, shaking his head.

'But why's she got to go to the library?'

'Because that's what Hermione does,' said Ron, shrugging. 'When in doubt, go to the library.'

Harry stood, irresolute, trying to catch the voice again but people were now emerging from the Great Hall behind him, talking loudly, exiting through the front doors on their way to the Quidditch pitch.

'You'd better get moving,' said Ron. 'It's nearly eleven – the match.'

Harry raced up to Gryffindor Tower, collected his Nimbus Two Thousand and joined the large crowd swarming across the grounds, but his mind was still in the castle, along with the bodiless voice, and as he pulled on his scarlet robes in the changing room, his only comfort was that everyone was now outside to watch the game.

The teams walked onto the pitch to tumultuous applause. Oliver Wood took off for a warm-up flight around the goalposts, Madam Hooch released the balls. The Hufflepuffs, who played in canary yellow, were standing in a huddle, having a last-minute discussion of tactics.

Harry was just mounting his broom when Professor McGonagall came half marching, half running across the pitch, carrying an enormous purple megaphone.

Harry's heart dropped like a stone.

'This match has been cancelled,' Professor McGonagall called through the megaphone, addressing the packed stadium. There were boos and shouts. Oliver Wood, looking devastated, landed and ran towards Professor McGonagall without getting off his broomstick.

'But Professor!' he shouted. 'We've got to play … the Cup … *Gryffindor* …'

Professor McGonagall ignored him and continued to shout through her megaphone: 'All students are to make their way back to the house common rooms, where their Heads of Houses will give them further information. As quickly as you can, please!'

Then she lowered the megaphone and beckoned Harry over to her.

'Potter, I think you'd better come with me …'

Wondering how she could possibly suspect him this time, Harry saw Ron detach himself from the complaining crowd; he came running up to them as they set off towards the castle. To Harry's surprise, Professor McGonagall didn't object.

'Yes, perhaps you'd better come too, Weasley.'

Some of the students swarming around them were grumbling about the match being cancelled, others looked worried. Harry and Ron followed Professor McGonagall back into the school and up the marble staircase. But they weren't taken to anybody's office this time.

'This will be a bit of a shock,' said Professor McGonagall in a surprisingly gentle voice as they approached the hospital wing. 'There has been another attack … another *double* attack.'

Harry's insides did a horrible somersault. Professor McGonagall pushed the door open and he and Ron entered.

Madam Pomfrey was bending over a sixth-year girl with long curly hair. Harry recognised her as the Ravenclaw they'd accidentally asked for directions to the Slytherin common room. And on the bed next to her was –

'Hermione!' Ron groaned.

Hermione lay utterly still, her eyes open and glassy.

'They were found near the library,' said Professor McGonagall. 'I don't suppose either of you can explain this? It was on the floor next to them …'

She was holding up a small, circular mirror.

Harry and Ron shook their heads, both staring at Hermione.

'I will escort you back to Gryffindor Tower,' said Professor McGonagall heavily. 'I need to address the students in any case.'

'All students will return to their house common rooms by six o'clock in the evening. No student is to leave the dormitories after that time. You will be escorted to each lesson by a teacher. No student is to use the bathroom unaccompanied by a teacher. All further Quidditch training and matches are to be postponed. There will be no more evening activities.'

The Gryffindors packed inside the common room listened to Professor McGonagall in silence. She rolled up the parchment from which she had been reading and said in a somewhat choked voice, 'I need hardly add that I have rarely been so distressed. It is likely that the school will be closed unless the culprit behind these attacks is caught. I would urge anyone who thinks they might know anything about them to come forward.'

She climbed somewhat awkwardly out of the portrait hole, and the Gryffindors began talking immediately.

'That's two Gryffindors down, not counting a Gryffindor ghost, one Ravenclaw and one Hufflepuff,' said the Weasley twins' friend Lee Jordan, counting on his fingers. 'Haven't *any* of the teachers noticed that the Slytherins are all safe? Isn't it *obvious* all this stuff's coming from Slytherin? The *heir* of Slytherin, the *monster* of Slytherin – why don't they just chuck all the Slytherins out?' he roared, to nods and scattered applause.

Percy Weasley was sitting in a chair behind Lee, but for once he didn't seem keen to make his views heard. He was looking pale and stunned.

'Percy's in shock,' George told Harry quietly. 'That Ravenclaw girl – Penelope Clearwater – she's a Prefect. I don't think he thought the monster would dare attack a *Prefect*.'

But Harry was only half listening. He didn't seem to be able to get rid of the picture of Hermione, lying on the hospital bed as though carved out of stone. And if the culprit wasn't caught soon, he was looking at a lifetime back with the Dursleys. Tom Riddle had turned Hagrid in because he was faced with the prospect of a Muggle orphanage if the school closed. Harry now knew exactly how he had felt.

'What're we going to do?' said Ron quietly in Harry's ear. 'D'you think they suspect Hagrid?'

'We've got to go and talk to him,' said Harry, making up his mind. 'I can't believe it's him this time, but if he set the monster loose last time he'll know how to get inside the Chamber of Secrets, and that's a start.'

'But McGonagall said we've got to stay in our tower unless we're in class –'

'I think,' said Harry, more quietly still, 'it's time to get my dad's old Cloak out again.'

Harry had inherited just one thing from his father: a long and silvery Invisibility Cloak. It was their only chance of sneaking out of the school to visit Hagrid without anyone knowing about it. They went to bed at the usual time, waited until Neville, Dean and Seamus had stopped discussing the Chamber of Secrets and finally fallen asleep, then got up, dressed again, and threw the Cloak over themselves.

The journey through the dark and deserted castle corridors wasn't enjoyable. Harry, who had wandered the castle at night several times before, had never seen it so crowded after sunset. Teachers, Prefects and ghosts were marching the corridors in pairs, staring around for any unusual activity. Their Invisibility Cloak didn't stop them making any noise, and there was a particularly tense moment when Ron stubbed his toe only yards from the spot where Snape was standing guard. Thankfully, Snape sneezed at almost exactly the moment Ron swore. It was with relief that they reached the oak front doors and eased them open.

It was a clear, starry night. They hurried towards the lighted windows of Hagrid's house, and pulled off the Cloak only when they were right outside his front door.

Seconds after they had knocked, Hagrid flung it open. They found themselves face to face, with him aiming a crossbow at them, Fang the boarhound barking loudly behind him.

'Oh,' he said, lowering the weapon and staring at them. 'What're you two doin' here?'

'What's that for?' said Harry, pointing at the crossbow as they stepped inside.

'Nothin' … nothin',' Hagrid muttered. 'I've bin expectin' … doesn' matter … Sit down … I'll make tea …'

He hardly seemed to know what he was doing. He nearly extinguished the fire, spilling water from the kettle on it, and then smashed the teapot with a nervous jerk of his massive hand.

'Are you OK, Hagrid?' said Harry. 'Did you hear about Hermione?'

'Oh, I heard, all righ',' said Hagrid, a slight break in his voice.

He kept glancing nervously at the windows. He poured them both large mugs of boiling water (he had forgotten to add tea bags) and was just putting a slab of fruitcake on a plate, when there was a loud knock on the door.

Hagrid dropped the fruitcake. Harry and Ron exchanged panic-stricken looks, then threw the Invisibility Cloak back over themselves and retreated into a corner. Hagrid checked that they were hidden, seized his crossbow and flung open his door once more.

'Good evening, Hagrid.'

It was Dumbledore. He entered, looking deadly serious, and was followed by a second, very odd-looking man.

The stranger was a short, portly man with rumpled grey hair and an anxious expression. He was wearing a strange mixture of clothes: a pin-striped suit, a scarlet tie, a long black cloak and pointed purple boots. Under his arm he carried a lime-green bowler.

'That's Dad's boss!' Ron breathed. 'Cornelius Fudge, the Minister of Magic!'

Harry elbowed Ron hard to make him shut up.

Hagrid had gone pale and sweaty. He dropped into one of his chairs and looked from Dumbledore to Cornelius Fudge.

'Bad business, Hagrid,' said Fudge, in rather clipped tones. 'Very bad business. Had to come. Four attacks on Muggle-borns. Things've gone far enough. Ministry's got to act.'

'I never,' said Hagrid, looking imploringly at Dumbledore, 'you know I never, Professor Dumbledore, sir ...'

'I want it understood, Cornelius, that Hagrid has my full confidence,' said Dumbledore, frowning at Fudge.

'Look, Albus,' said Fudge, uncomfortably. 'Hagrid's record's against him. Ministry's got to do something – the school governors have been in touch.'

'Yet again, Cornelius, I tell you that taking Hagrid away will not help in the slightest,' said Dumbledore. His blue eyes were full of a fire Harry had never seen before.

'Look at it from my point of view,' said Fudge, fidgeting with his bowler. 'I'm under a lot of pressure. Got to be seen to be doing something. If it turns out it wasn't Hagrid, he'll be back and no more said. But I've got to take him. Got to. Wouldn't be doing my duty –'

'Take me?' said Hagrid, who was trembling. 'Take me where?'

'For a short stretch only,' said Fudge, not meeting Hagrid's eyes. 'Not a punishment, Hagrid, more a precaution. If someone else is caught, you'll be let out with a full apology ...'

'Not Azkaban?' croaked Hagrid.

Before Fudge could answer, there was another loud rap on the door.

Dumbledore answered it. It was Harry's turn for an elbow in the ribs: he'd let out an audible gasp.

Mr Lucius Malfoy strode into Hagrid's hut, swathed in a long black travelling cloak, smiling a cold and satisfied smile. Fang started to growl.

'Already here, Fudge,' he said approvingly. 'Good, good ...'

'What're you doin' here?' said Hagrid furiously. 'Get outta my house!'

'My dear man, please believe me, I have no pleasure at all in being inside your – er – d'you call this a house?' said Lucius Malfoy, sneering as he looked around the small cabin. 'I simply called at the school and was told that the Headmaster was here.'

'And what exactly did you want with me, Lucius?' said Dumbledore. He spoke politely, but the fire was still blazing in his blue eyes.

'Dreadful thing, Dumbledore,' said Mr Malfoy lazily, taking out a long roll of parchment, 'but the governors feel it's time for you to step aside. This is an Order of Suspension – you'll find all twelve signatures on it. I'm afraid we feel you're losing your touch. How many attacks have there been now? Two more this afternoon, wasn't it? At this rate, there'll be no Muggle-borns left at Hogwarts, and we all know what an *awful* loss that would be to the school.'

'Oh, now, see here, Lucius,' said Fudge, looking alarmed, 'Dumbledore suspended ... no, no ... last thing we want just now ...'

'The appointment – or suspension – of the Headmaster is a matter for the governors, Fudge,' said Mr Malfoy smoothly. 'And as Dumbledore has failed to stop these attacks ...'

'Now look, Lucius, if *Dumbledore* can't stop them –' said Fudge, whose upper lip was sweating now, 'I mean to say, who *can?*'

'That remains to be seen,' said Mr Malfoy, with a nasty smile. 'But as all twelve of us have voted ...'

Hagrid leapt to his feet, his shaggy black head grazing the ceiling.

'An' how many did yeh have ter threaten an' blackmail before they agreed, Malfoy, eh?' he roared.

'Dear, dear, you know, that temper of yours will lead you into trouble one of these days, Hagrid,' said Mr Malfoy. 'I would advise you not to shout at the Azkaban guards like that. They won't like it at all.'

'Yeh can' take Dumbledore!' yelled Hagrid, making Fang the boarhound cower and whimper in his basket. 'Take him away, an' the Muggle-borns won' stand a chance! There'll be killin's next!'

'Calm yourself, Hagrid,' said Dumbledore sharply. He looked at Lucius Malfoy.

'If the governors want my removal, Lucius, I shall of course step aside.'

'But –' stuttered Fudge.

'No!' growled Hagrid.

Dumbledore had not taken his bright blue eyes off Lucius Malfoy's cold grey ones.

'However,' said Dumbledore, speaking very slowly and clearly, so that none of them could miss a word, 'you will find that I will only *truly* have left this school when none here are loyal to me. You will also find that help will always be given at Hogwarts to those who ask for it.'

For a second, Harry was almost sure Dumbledore's eyes flickered towards the corner where he and Ron stood hidden.

'Admirable sentiments,' said Malfoy, bowing. 'We shall all miss your – er – highly individual way of running things, Albus, and only hope that your successor will manage to prevent any – ah – *"killin's"*.'

He strode to the cabin door, opened it and bowed Dumbledore out. Fudge, fiddling with his bowler, waited for Hagrid to go ahead of him, but Hagrid stood his ground, took a deep breath and said carefully, 'If anyone wanted ter find out some *stuff*, all they'd have ter do would be ter follow the *spiders*. That'd lead 'em right! That's all I'm sayin'.'

Fudge stared at him in amazement.

'All right, I'm comin',' said Hagrid, pulling on his moleskin overcoat. But as he was about to follow Fudge through the door, he stopped again and said loudly, 'An' someone'll need ter feed Fang while I'm away.'

The door banged shut and Ron pulled the Invisibility Cloak off.

'We're in trouble now,' he said hoarsely. 'No Dumbledore. They might as well close the school tonight. There'll be an attack a day with him gone.'

Fang started howling, scratching at the closed door.

CHAPTER FIFTEEN

Aragog

Summer was creeping over the grounds around the castle; sky and lake alike turned periwinkle blue and flowers large as cabbages burst into bloom in the greenhouses. But with no Hagrid visible from the castle windows, striding the grounds with Fang at his heels, the scene didn't look right to Harry; no better, in fact, than the inside of the castle, where things were so horribly wrong.

Harry and Ron had tried to visit Hermione, but visitors were now barred from the hospital wing.

'We're taking no more chances,' Madam Pomfrey told them severely through a crack in the hospital door. 'No, I'm sorry, there's every chance the attacker might come back to finish these people off …'

With Dumbledore gone, fear had spread as never before, so that the sun warming the castle walls outside seemed to stop at the mullioned windows. There was barely a face to be seen in the school that didn't look worried and tense, and any laughter that rang through the corridors sounded shrill and unnatural and was quickly stifled.

Harry constantly repeated Dumbledore's final words to himself. *'I will only truly have left this school when none here are loyal to me … Help will always be given at Hogwarts to those who ask for it.'* But what good were these words? Who exactly were they supposed to ask for help, when everyone was just as confused and scared as they were?

Hagrid's hint about the spiders was far easier to understand – the trouble was, there didn't seem to be a single spider left in the castle to follow. Harry looked everywhere he went, helped (rather reluctantly) by Ron. They were hampered, of course, by the fact that they weren't allowed to wander off on their own, but had to move around the castle in a pack with the other Gryffindors. Most of their fellow students seemed glad that they were being shepherded from class to class by teachers, but Harry found it very irksome.

One person, however, seemed to be thoroughly enjoying the atmosphere of terror and suspicion. Draco Malfoy was strutting around the school as though he had just been appointed Head Boy. Harry didn't realise what he was so pleased about until the Potions lesson about a fortnight after Dumbledore and Hagrid had left, when, sitting right behind Malfoy, Harry overheard him gloating to Crabbe and Goyle.

'I always thought Father might be the one who got rid of Dumbledore,' he said, not troubling to keep his voice down. 'I told you he thinks Dumbledore's the worst Headmaster the school's ever had. Maybe we'll get a decent Headmaster now.

Someone who won't *want* the Chamber of Secrets closed. McGonagall won't last long, she's only filling in ...'

Snape swept past Harry, making no comment about Hermione's empty seat and cauldron.

'Sir,' said Malfoy loudly. 'Sir, why don't *you* apply for the Headmaster's job?'

'Now, now, Malfoy,' said Snape, though he couldn't suppress a thin-lipped smile. 'Professor Dumbledore has only been suspended by the governors. I dare say he'll be back with us soon enough.'

'Yeah, right,' said Malfoy, smirking. 'I expect you'd have Father's vote, sir, if you wanted to apply for the job. *I'll* tell Father you're the best teacher here, sir ...'

Snape smirked as he swept off around the dungeon, fortunately not spotting Seamus Finnigan, who was pretending to vomit into his cauldron.

'I'm quite surprised the Mudbloods haven't all packed their bags by now,' Malfoy went on. 'Bet you five Galleons the next one dies. Pity it wasn't Granger ...'

The bell rang at that moment, which was lucky; at Malfoy's last words, Ron had leapt off his stool, and in the scramble to collect bags and books, his attempts to reach Malfoy went unnoticed.

'Let me at him,' Ron growled, as Harry and Dean hung onto his arms. 'I don't care, I don't need my wand, I'm going to kill him with my bare hands –'

'Hurry up, I've got to take you all to Herbology,' barked Snape over the class's heads, and off they went, crocodile fashion, with Harry, Ron and Dean bringing up the rear, Ron still trying to get loose. It was only safe to let go of him when Snape had seen them out of the castle, and they were making their way across the vegetable patch towards the greenhouses.

The Herbology class was very subdued; there were now two missing from their number, Justin and Hermione.

Professor Sprout set them all to work pruning the Abyssinian Shrivelfigs. Harry went to tip an armful of withered stalks onto the compost heap and found himself face to face with Ernie Macmillan. Ernie took a deep breath and said, very formally, 'I just want to say, Harry, that I'm sorry I ever suspected you. I know you'd never attack Hermione Granger, and I apologise for all the stuff I said. We're all in the same boat now, and, well –'

He held out a pudgy hand, and Harry shook it.

Ernie and his friend Hannah came to work at the same Shrivelfig as Harry and Ron.

'That Draco Malfoy character,' said Ernie, breaking off dead twigs, 'he seems very pleased about all this, doesn't he? D'you know, I think *he* might be Slytherin's heir.'

'That's clever of you,' said Ron, who didn't seem to have forgiven Ernie as readily as Harry.

'Do *you* think it's Malfoy, Harry?' Ernie asked.

'No,' said Harry, so firmly that Ernie and Hannah stared.

A second later, Harry spotted something that made him hit Ron over the hand with his pruning shears.

'*Ouch!* What're you –'

Harry was pointing at the ground a few feet away. Several large spiders were scurrying across the earth.

'Oh, yeah,' said Ron, trying, and failing, to look pleased. 'But we can't follow them now …'

Ernie and Hannah were listening curiously.

Harry watched the spiders running away.

'Looks like they're heading for the Forbidden Forest …'

And Ron looked even unhappier about that.

At the end of the lesson Professor Sprout escorted the class to their Defence Against the Dark Arts lesson. Harry and Ron lagged behind the others so they could talk out of earshot.

'We'll have to use the Invisibility Cloak again,' Harry told Ron. 'We can take Fang with us. He's used to going into the Forest with Hagrid, he might be some help.'

'Right,' said Ron, who was twirling his wand nervously in his fingers. 'Er – aren't there – aren't there supposed to be werewolves in the Forest?' he added, as they took their usual places at the back of Lockhart's classroom.

Preferring not to answer that question, Harry said, 'There are good things in there, too. The centaurs are all right, and the unicorns.'

Ron had never been into the Forbidden Forest before. Harry had entered it only once, and had hoped never to do so again.

Lockhart bounded into the room and the class stared at him. Every other teacher in the place was looking grimmer than usual, but Lockhart appeared nothing short of buoyant.

'Come now,' he cried, beaming around him, 'why all these long faces?'

People swapped exasperated looks, but nobody answered.

'Don't you people realise,' said Lockhart, speaking slowly, as though they were all a bit dim, 'the danger has passed! The culprit has been taken away.'

'Says who?' said Dean Thomas loudly.

'My dear young man, the Minister of Magic wouldn't have taken Hagrid if he hadn't been one hundred per cent sure that he was guilty,' said Lockhart, in the tone of someone explaining that one and one made two.

'Oh, yes he would,' said Ron, even more loudly than Dean.

'I flatter myself I know a *touch* more about Hagrid's arrest than you do, Mr Weasley,' said Lockhart in a self-satisfied tone.

Ron started to say that he didn't think so, somehow, but stopped in mid-sentence when Harry kicked him hard under the desk.

'We weren't there, remember?' Harry muttered.

But Lockhart's disgusting cheeriness, his hints that he had always thought Hagrid was no good, his confidence that the whole business was now at an end, irritated Harry so much that he yearned to throw *Gadding with Ghouls* right in Lockhart's stupid face. Instead he contented himself with scrawling a note to Ron: *'Let's do it tonight.'*

Ron read the message, swallowed hard and looked sideways at the empty seat usually filled by Hermione. The sight seemed to stiffen his resolve, and he nodded.

* * *

The Gryffindor common room was always very crowded these days, because from six o'clock onwards, the Gryffindors had nowhere else to go. They also had plenty to talk about, with the result that the common room often didn't empty until past midnight.

Harry went to get the Invisibility Cloak out of his trunk right after dinner, and spent the evening sitting on it, waiting for the room to clear. Fred and George challenged Harry and Ron to a few games of Exploding Snap and Ginny sat watching them, very subdued in Hermione's usual chair. Harry and Ron kept losing on purpose, trying to finish the games quickly, but even so, it was well past midnight when Fred, George and Ginny finally went to bed.

Harry and Ron waited for the distant sounds of two dormitory doors closing before seizing the Cloak, throwing it over themselves, and climbing through the portrait hole.

It was another difficult journey through the castle, dodging all the teachers. At last they reached the Entrance Hall, slid back the lock on the oak front doors, squeezed between them, trying to stop any creaking, and stepped out into the moonlit grounds.

'Course,' said Ron abruptly, as they strode across the black grass, 'we might get to the Forest and find there's nothing to follow. Those spiders might not've been going there at all. I know it looked like they were moving in that sort of general direction, but …'

His voice tailed away hopefully.

They reached Hagrid's house, sad and sorry-looking with its blank windows. When Harry pushed the door open, Fang went mad with joy at the sight of them. Worried he might wake everyone at the castle with his deep, booming barks, they hastily fed him treacle fudge from a tin on the mantelpiece, which glued his teeth together.

Harry left the Invisibility Cloak on Hagrid's table. There would be no need for it in the pitch-dark Forest.

'C'mon, Fang, we're going for a walk,' said Harry, patting his leg, and Fang bounded happily out of the house behind them, dashed to the edge of the Forest and lifted his leg against a large sycamore tree.

Harry took out his wand, murmured, *'Lumos!'* and a tiny light appeared at the end of it, just enough to let them watch the path for signs of spiders.

'Good thinking,' said Ron. 'I'd light mine too, but you know – it'd probably blow up or something …'

Harry tapped Ron on the shoulder, pointing at the grass. Two solitary spiders were hurrying away from the wandlight into the shade of the trees.

'OK,' Ron sighed, as though resigned to the worst, 'I'm ready. Let's go.'

So, with Fang scampering around them, sniffing tree roots and leaves, they entered the Forest. By the glow of Harry's wand, they followed the steady trickle of spiders moving along the path. They walked for about twenty minutes, not speaking, listening hard for noises other than breaking twigs and rustling leaves. Then, when the trees had become thicker than ever, so that the stars overhead were no longer visible, and Harry's wand shone alone in the sea of dark, they saw their spider guides leaving the path.

Harry paused, trying to see where the spiders were going, but everything outside his little sphere of light was pitch black. He had never been this deep into the Forest before. He could vividly remember Hagrid advising him not to leave the Forest path last time he'd been in here. But Hagrid was miles away now, probably sitting in a cell in Azkaban, and he had also said to follow the spiders.

Something wet touched Harry's hand and he jumped backwards, crushing Ron's foot, but it was only Fang's nose.

'What d'you reckon?' Harry said to Ron, whose eyes he could just make out, reflecting the light from his wand.

'We've come this far,' said Ron.

So they followed the darting shadows of the spiders into the trees. They couldn't move very quickly now; there were tree roots and stumps in their way, barely visible in the near blackness. Harry could feel Fang's hot breath on his hand. More than once, they had to stop, so that Harry could crouch down and find the spiders in the wandlight.

They walked for what seemed like at least half an hour, their robes snagging on low-slung branches and brambles. After a while, they noticed that the ground seemed to be sloping downwards, though the trees were as thick as ever.

Then Fang suddenly let loose a great, echoing bark, making both Harry and Ron jump out of their skins.

'What?' said Ron loudly, looking around into the pitch dark, and gripping Harry's elbow very hard.

'There's something moving over there,' Harry breathed. 'Listen … Sounds like something big.'

They listened. Some distance to their right, the something big was snapping branches as it carved a path through the trees.

'Oh no,' said Ron. 'Oh no, oh no, oh –'

'Shut up,' said Harry frantically. 'It'll hear you.'

'Hear *me*?' said Ron in an unnaturally high voice. 'It's already heard Fang!'

The darkness seemed to be pressing on their eyeballs as they stood, terrified, waiting. There was a strange rumbling noise and then silence.

'What d'you think it's doing?' said Harry.

'Probably getting ready to pounce,' said Ron.

They waited, shivering, hardly daring to move.

'D'you think it's gone?' Harry whispered.

'Dunno –'

Then, to their right, came a sudden blaze of light, so bright in the darkness that both of them flung up their hands to shield their eyes. Fang yelped and tried to run, but got lodged in a tangle of thorns and yelped even louder.

'Harry!' Ron shouted, his voice breaking with relief. 'Harry, it's our car!'

'*What?*'

'Come on!'

Harry blundered after Ron towards the light, stumbling and tripping, and a moment later they had emerged into a clearing.

Mr Weasley's car was standing, empty, in the middle of a circle of thick trees under a roof of dense branches, its headlamps ablaze. As Ron walked, open-mouthed, towards it, it moved slowly towards him, exactly like a large, turquoise dog greeting its owner.

'It's been here all the time!' said Ron delightedly, walking around the car. 'Look at it. The Forest's turned it wild …'

The wings of the car were scratched and smeared with mud. Apparently it had taken to trundling around the Forest on its own. Fang didn't seem at all keen on it; he kept close to Harry, who could feel him quivering. His breathing slowing down again, Harry stuffed his wand back into his robes.

'And we thought it was going to attack us!' said Ron, leaning against the car and patting it. 'I wondered where it had gone!'

Harry squinted around on the floodlit ground for signs of more spiders, but they had all scuttled away from the glare of the headlights.

'We've lost the trail,' he said. 'C'mon, let's go and find them.'

Ron didn't speak. He didn't move. His eyes were fixed on a point some ten feet above the Forest floor, right behind Harry. His face was livid with terror.

Harry didn't even have time to turn around. There was a loud clicking noise and suddenly he felt something long and hairy seize him around the middle and lift him off the ground, so that he was hanging, face down. Struggling, terrified, he heard more clicking, and saw Ron's legs leave the ground too, heard Fang whimpering and howling – next moment, he was being swept away into the dark trees.

Head hanging, Harry saw that what had hold of him was marching on six immensely long, hairy legs, the front two clutching him tightly below a pair of shining black pincers. Behind him, he could hear another of the creatures, no doubt carrying Ron. They were moving into the very heart of the Forest. Harry could hear Fang fighting to free himself from a third monster, whining loudly, but Harry couldn't have yelled even if he had wanted to; he seemed to have left his voice back with the car in the clearing.

He never knew how long he was in the creature's clutches; he only knew that the darkness suddenly lifted enough for him to see that the leaf-strewn ground was now swarming with spiders. Craning his neck sideways, he realised that they had reached the rim of a vast hollow, a hollow which had been cleared of trees, so that the stars shone brightly onto the worst scene he had ever clapped eyes upon.

Spiders. Not tiny spiders like those surging over the leaves below. Spiders the size of carthorses, eight-eyed, eight-legged, black, hairy, gigantic. The massive specimen that was carrying Harry made its way down the steep slope, towards a misty domed web in the very centre of the hollow, while its fellows closed in all around it, clicking their pincers excitedly at the sight of its load.

Harry fell to the ground on all fours as the spider released him. Ron and Fang thudded down next to him. Fang wasn't howling any more, but cowering silently on the spot. Ron looked exactly like Harry felt. His mouth was stretched wide in a kind of silent scream and his eyes were popping.

Harry suddenly realised that the spider which had dropped him was saying something. It had been hard to tell, because he clicked his pincers with every word he spoke.

'Aragog!' it called. 'Aragog!'

And from the middle of the misty domed web, a spider the size of a small elephant emerged, very slowly. There was grey in the black of his body and legs, and each of the eyes on his ugly, pincered head was milky white. He was blind.

'What is it?' he said, clicking his pincers rapidly.

'Men,' clicked the spider who had caught Harry.

'Is it Hagrid?' said Aragog, moving closer, his eight milky eyes wandering vaguely.

'Strangers,' clicked the spider who had brought Ron.

'Kill them,' clicked Aragog fretfully. 'I was sleeping …'

'We're friends of Hagrid's,' Harry shouted. His heart seemed to have left his chest to pound in his throat.

Click, click, click went the pincers of the spiders all around the hollow.

Aragog paused.

'Hagrid has never sent men into our hollow before,' he said slowly.

'Hagrid's in trouble,' said Harry, breathing very fast. 'That's why we've come.'

'In trouble?' said the aged spider, and Harry thought he heard concern beneath the clicking pincers. 'But why has he sent you?'

Harry thought of getting to his feet, but decided against it; he didn't think his legs would support him. So he spoke from the ground, as calmly as he could.

'They think, up at the school, that Hagrid's been setting a – a – something on students. They've taken him to Azkaban.'

Aragog clicked his pincers furiously, and all around the hollow the sound was echoed by the crowd of spiders; it was like applause, except applause didn't usually make Harry feel sick with fear.

'But that was years ago,' said Aragog fretfully. 'Years and years ago. I remember it well. That's why they made him leave the school. They believed that *I* was the monster that dwells in what they call the Chamber of Secrets. They thought that Hagrid had opened the Chamber and set me free.'

'And you … you didn't come from the Chamber of Secrets?' said Harry, who could feel cold sweat on his forehead.

'I!' said Aragog, clicking angrily. 'I was not born in the castle. I come from a distant land. A traveller gave me to Hagrid when I was an egg. Hagrid was only a boy, but he cared for me, hidden in a cupboard in the castle, feeding me on scraps from the table. Hagrid is my good friend, and a good man. When I was discovered, and blamed for the death of a girl, he protected me. I have lived here in the Forest ever since, where Hagrid still visits me. He even found me a wife, Mosag, and you see how our family has grown, all through Hagrid's goodness …'

Harry summoned what remained of his courage.

'So you never – never attacked anyone?'

'Never,' croaked the old spider. 'It would have been my instinct, but from respect of Hagrid, I never harmed a human. The body of the girl who was killed was discovered in a bathroom. I never saw any part of the castle but the cupboard in which I grew up. Our kind like the dark and the quiet ...'

'But then ... Do you know what *did* kill that girl?' said Harry. 'Because whatever it is, it's back and attacking people again –'

His words were drowned by a loud outbreak of clicking and the rustling of many long legs shifting angrily; large black shapes shifted all around him.

'The thing that lives in the castle,' said Aragog, 'is an ancient creature we spiders fear above all others. Well do I remember how I pleaded with Hagrid to let me go, when I sensed the beast moving about the school.'

'What is it?' said Harry urgently.

More loud clicking, more rustling; the spiders seemed to be closing in.

'We do not speak of it!' said Aragog fiercely. 'We do not name it! I never even told Hagrid the name of that dread creature, though he asked me, many times.'

Harry didn't want to press the subject, not with the spiders pressing closer on all sides. Aragog seemed to be tired of talking. He was backing slowly into his domed web, but his fellow spiders continued to inch slowly towards Harry and Ron.

'We'll just go, then,' Harry called desperately to Aragog, hearing leaves rustling behind him.

'Go?' said Aragog slowly. 'I think not …'

'But – but –'

'My sons and daughters do not harm Hagrid, on my command. But I cannot deny them fresh meat, when it wanders so willingly into our midst. Goodbye, friend of Hagrid.'

Harry spun around. Feet away, towering above him, was a solid wall of spiders, clicking, their many eyes gleaming in their ugly black heads …

Even as he reached for his wand, Harry knew it was no good, there were too many of them, but as he tried to stand, ready to die fighting, a loud, long note sounded, and a blaze of light flamed through the hollow.

Mr Weasley's car was thundering down the slope, headlamps glaring, its horn screeching, knocking spiders aside; several were thrown onto their backs, their endless legs waving in the air. The car screeched to a halt in front of Harry and Ron and the doors flew open.

'Get Fang!' Harry yelled, diving into the front seat; Ron seized the boarhound round the middle and threw him, yelping, into the back of the car. The doors slammed shut. Ron didn't touch the accelerator but the car didn't need him; the engine roared and they were off, hitting more spiders. They sped up the slope, out of the hollow, and they were soon crashing through the Forest, branches whipping the windows as the car wound its way cleverly through the widest gaps, following a path it obviously knew.

Harry looked sideways at Ron. His mouth was still open in the silent scream, but his eyes weren't popping any more.

'Are you OK?'

Ron stared straight ahead, unable to speak.

They smashed their way through the undergrowth, Fang howling loudly in the back seat, and Harry saw the wing mirror snap off as they squeezed past a large oak. After ten noisy, rocky minutes, the trees thinned, and Harry could again see patches of sky.

The car stopped so suddenly that they were nearly thrown into the windscreen. They had reached the edge of the Forest. Fang flung himself at the window in his anxiety to get out and when Harry opened the door, he shot off through the trees to Hagrid's house, tail between his legs. Harry got out too, and after a minute or so, Ron seemed to regain the feeling in his limbs and followed, still stiff-necked and staring. Harry gave the car a grateful pat as it reversed back into the Forest and disappeared from view.

Harry went back into Hagrid's cabin to get the Invisibility Cloak. Fang was trembling under a blanket in his basket. When Harry got outside again, he found Ron being violently sick in the pumpkin patch.

'Follow the spiders,' said Ron weakly, wiping his mouth on his sleeve. 'I'll never forgive Hagrid. We're lucky to be alive.'

'I bet he thought Aragog wouldn't hurt friends of his,' said Harry.

'That's exactly Hagrid's problem!' said Ron, thumping the wall of the cabin. 'He always thinks monsters aren't as bad as they're made out, and look where it's got him! A cell in Azkaban!' He was shivering uncontrollably now. 'What was the point of sending us in there? What have we found out, I'd like to know?'

'That Hagrid never opened the Chamber of Secrets,' said Harry, throwing the cloak over Ron and prodding him in the arm to make him walk. 'He was innocent.'

Ron gave a loud snort. Evidently, hatching Aragog out in a cupboard wasn't his idea of being innocent.

As the castle loomed nearer Harry twitched the Cloak to make sure their feet were hidden, then pushed the creaking front doors ajar. They walked carefully back across the Entrance Hall and up the marble staircase, holding their breath as they passed corridors where watchful sentries were walking. At last they reached the safety of the Gryffindor common room, where the fire had burned itself into glowing ash. They took off the Cloak and climbed the winding staircase to their dormitory.

Ron fell onto his bed without bothering to get undressed. Harry, however, didn't feel very sleepy. He sat on the edge of his four-poster, thinking hard about everything Aragog had said.

The creature that was lurking somewhere in the castle, he thought, sounded like a sort of monster Voldemort – even other monsters didn't want to name it. But he and Ron were no closer to finding out what it was, or how it Petrified its victims. Even Hagrid had never known what was in the Chamber of Secrets.

Harry swung his legs up onto his bed and leaned back against his pillows, watching the moon glinting at him through the tower window.

He couldn't see what else they could do. They had hit dead ends everywhere. Riddle had caught the wrong person, the heir of Slytherin had got off, and no one could tell whether it was the same person, or a different one, who had opened the Chamber this time. There was nobody else to ask. Harry lay down, still thinking about what Aragog said.

He was becoming drowsy when what seemed like their very last hope occurred to him and he suddenly sat bolt upright.

'Ron,' he hissed through the dark. 'Ron!'

Ron woke with a yelp like Fang's, stared wildly around and saw Harry.

'Ron – that girl who died. Aragog said she was found in a bathroom,' said Harry, ignoring Neville's snuffling snores from the corner. 'What if she never left the bathroom? What if she's still there?'

Ron rubbed his eyes, frowning through the moonlight. And then he understood.

'You *don't* think – not *Moaning Myrtle*?'

CHAPTER SIXTEEN

The Chamber of Secrets

'All those times we were in that bathroom, and she was just three toilets away,' said Ron bitterly at breakfast next day, 'and we could've asked her, and now ...'

It had been hard enough trying to look for spiders. Escaping their teachers long enough to sneak into a girls' bathroom, the girls' bathroom, moreover, right next to the scene of the first attack, was going to be almost impossible.

But something happened in their first lesson, Transfiguration, which drove the Chamber of Secrets out of their minds for the first time in weeks. Ten minutes into the class, Professor McGonagall told them that their exams would start on the first of June, one week from today.

'*Exams?*' howled Seamus Finnigan. 'We're still getting *exams?*'

There was a loud bang behind Harry as Neville Longbottom's wand slipped, vanishing one of the legs on his desk. Professor McGonagall restored it with a wave of her own wand, and turned, frowning, to Seamus.

'The whole point of keeping the school open at this time is for you to receive your education,' she said sternly. 'The exams will therefore take place as usual, and I trust you are all revising hard.'

Revising hard! It had never occurred to Harry that there would be exams with the castle in this state. There was a great deal of mutinous muttering around the room, which made Professor McGonagall scowl even more darkly.

'Professor Dumbledore's instructions were to keep the school running as normally as possible,' she said. 'And that, I need hardly point out, means finding out how much you have learned this year.'

Harry looked down at the pair of white rabbits he was supposed to be turning into slippers. What had he learned so far this year? He couldn't seem to think of anything that would be useful in an exam.

Ron looked as though he'd just been told he had to go and live in the Forbidden Forest.

'Can you imagine me taking exams with this?' he asked Harry, holding up his wand, which had just started whistling loudly.

Three days before their first exam, Professor McGonagall made another announcement at breakfast.

'I have good news,' she said, and the Great Hall, instead of falling silent, erupted.

'Dumbledore's coming back!' several people yelled joyfully.

'You've caught the heir of Slytherin!' squealed a girl on the Ravenclaw table.

'Quidditch matches are back on!' roared Wood excitedly.

When the hubbub had subsided, Professor McGonagall said, 'Professor Sprout has informed me that the Mandrakes are ready for cutting at last. Tonight, we will be able to revive those people who have been Petrified. I need hardly remind you all that one of them may well be able to tell us who, or what, attacked them. I am hopeful that this dreadful year will end with our catching the culprit.'

There was an explosion of cheering. Harry looked over at the Slytherin table and wasn't at all surprised to see that Draco Malfoy hadn't joined in. Ron, however, was looking happier than he'd looked in days.

'It won't matter that we never asked Myrtle, then!' he said to Harry. 'Hermione'll probably have all the answers when they wake her up! Mind you, she'll go mad when she finds out we've got exams in three days' time. She hasn't revised. It might be kinder to leave her where she is till they're over.'

Just then, Ginny Weasley came over and sat down next to Ron. She looked tense and nervous, and Harry noticed that her hands were twisting in her lap.

'What's up?' said Ron, helping himself to more porridge.

Ginny didn't say anything, but glanced up and down the Gryffindor table with a scared look on her face that reminded Harry of someone, though he couldn't think who.

'Spit it out,' said Ron, watching her.

Harry suddenly realised who Ginny looked like. She was rocking backwards and forwards slightly in her chair, exactly like Dobby did when he was teetering on the edge of revealing forbidden information.

'I've got to tell you something,' Ginny mumbled, carefully not looking at Harry.

'What is it?' said Harry.

Ginny looked as though she couldn't find the right words.

'*What?*' said Ron.

Ginny opened her mouth, but no sound came out. Harry leaned forward and spoke quietly, so that only Ginny and Ron could hear him.

'Is it something about the Chamber of Secrets? Have you seen something? Someone acting oddly?'

Ginny drew a deep breath and, at that precise moment, Percy Weasley appeared, looking tired and wan.

'If you've finished eating, I'll take that seat, Ginny. I'm starving, I've only just come off patrol duty.'

Ginny jumped up as though her chair had just been electrified, gave Percy a fleeting, frightened look, and scarpered away. Percy sat down and grabbed a mug from the centre of the table.

'Percy!' said Ron angrily. 'She was just about to tell us something important!'

Halfway through a gulp of tea, Percy choked.

'What sort of thing?' he said, coughing.

'I just asked her if she'd seen anything odd, and she started to say –'

'Oh – that – that's nothing to do with the Chamber of Secrets,' said Percy at once.

'How do you know?' said Ron, his eyebrows raised.

'Well, er, if you must know, Ginny, er, walked in on me the other day when I was – well, never mind – the point is, she spotted me doing something and I, um, I asked her not to mention it to anybody. I must say, I did think she'd keep her word. It's nothing, really, I'd just rather –'

Harry had never seen Percy look so uncomfortable.

'What were you doing, Percy?' said Ron, grinning. 'Go on, tell us, we won't laugh.'

Percy didn't smile back.

'Pass me those rolls, Harry, I'm starving.'

Harry knew the whole mystery might be solved tomorrow without their help, but he wasn't about to pass up a chance to speak to Myrtle if it turned up – and to his delight it did, mid-morning, when they were being led to History of Magic by Gilderoy Lockhart.

Lockhart, who had so often assured them that all danger had passed, only to be proved wrong straight away, was now whole-heartedly convinced that it was hardly worth the trouble to see them safely down the corridors. His hair wasn't as sleek as usual; it seemed he had been up most of the night, patrolling the fourth floor.

'Mark my words,' he said, ushering them around a corner, 'the first words out of those poor Petrified people's mouths will be, "*It was Hagrid.*" Frankly, I'm astounded Professor McGonagall thinks all these security measures are necessary.'

'I agree, sir,' said Harry, making Ron drop his books in surprise.

'Thank you, Harry,' said Lockhart graciously, while they waited for a long line of Hufflepuffs to pass. 'I mean, we teachers have quite enough to be getting on with, without walking students to classes and standing guard all night …'

'That's right,' said Ron, catching on. 'Why don't you leave us here, sir, we've only got one more corridor to go.'

'You know, Weasley, I think I will,' said Lockhart. 'I really should go and prepare my next class.'

And he hurried off.

'Prepare his class,' Ron sneered after him. 'Gone to curl his hair, more like.'

They let the rest of the Gryffindors draw ahead of them, then darted down a side passage and hurried off towards Moaning Myrtle's bathroom. But just as they were congratulating each other on their brilliant scheme …

'Potter! Weasley! What are you doing?'

It was Professor McGonagall, and her mouth was the thinnest of thin lines.

'We were – we were –' Ron stammered, 'we were going to – to go and see –'

'Hermione,' said Harry. Ron and Professor McGonagall both looked at him.

'We haven't seen her for ages, Professor,' Harry went on hurriedly, treading on Ron's foot, 'and we thought we'd sneak into the hospital wing, you know, and tell her the Mandrakes are nearly ready and, er, not to worry.'

Professor McGonagall was still staring at him, and for a moment, Harry thought she was going to explode, but when she spoke, it was in a strangely croaky voice.

'Of course,' she said, and Harry, amazed, saw a tear glistening in her beady eye. 'Of course, I realise this has all been hardest on the friends of those who have been … I quite understand. Yes, Potter, of course you may visit Miss Granger. I will inform Professor Binns where you've gone. Tell Madam Pomfrey I have given my permission.'

Harry and Ron walked away, hardly daring to believe that they'd avoided detention. As they turned the corner, they distinctly heard Professor McGonagall blow her nose.

'That,' said Ron fervently, 'was the best story you've ever come up with.'

They had no choice now but to go to the hospital wing and tell Madam Pomfrey that they had Professor McGonagall's permission to visit Hermione.

Madam Pomfrey let them in, but reluctantly.

'There's just no *point* talking to a Petrified person,' she said, and they had to admit she was right when they'd taken their seats next to Hermione. It was plain that Hermione didn't have the faintest inkling that she had visitors, and that they might just as well tell her bedside cabinet not to worry for all the good it would do.

'Wonder if she did see the attacker, though?' said Ron, looking sadly at Hermione's rigid face. 'Because if he sneaked up on them all, no one'll ever know …'

But Harry wasn't looking at Hermione's face. He was more

interested in her right hand. It lay clenched on top of her blankets, and bending closer, he saw that a piece of paper was scrunched inside her fist.

Making sure that Madam Pomfrey was nowhere near, he pointed this out to Ron.

'Try and get it out,' Ron whispered, shifting his chair so that he blocked Harry from Madam Pomfrey's view.

It was no easy task. Hermione's hand was clamped so tightly around the paper that Harry was sure he was going to tear it. While Ron kept watch he tugged and twisted, and at last, after several tense minutes, the paper came free.

It was a page torn from a very old library book. Harry smoothed it out eagerly and Ron leaned close to read it too.

Of the many fearsome beasts and monsters that roam our land, there is none more curious or more deadly than the Basilisk, known also as the King of Serpents. This snake, which may reach gigantic size, and live many hundreds of years, is born from a chicken's egg, hatched beneath a toad. Its methods of killing are most wondrous, for aside from its deadly and venomous fangs, the Basilisk has a murderous stare, and all who are fixed with the beam of its eye shall suffer instant death. Spiders flee before the Basilisk, for it is their mortal enemy, and the Basilisk flees only from the crowing of the rooster, which is fatal to it.

And beneath this, a single word had been written, in a hand Harry recognised as Hermione's. *Pipes*.

It was as though somebody had just flicked a light on in his brain.

'Ron,' he breathed, 'this is it. This is the answer. The monster in the Chamber's a *Basilisk* – a giant serpent! *That's* why I've been hearing that voice all over the place, and nobody else has heard it. It's because I understand Parseltongue …'

Harry looked up at the beds around him.

'The Basilisk kills people by looking at them. But no one's died – because no one looked it straight in the eye. Colin saw it through his camera. The Basilisk burned up all the film inside it, but Colin just got Petrified. Justin … Justin must've seen the Basilisk through Nearly Headless Nick! Nick got the full blast of it, but he couldn't die *again* … and Hermione and that Ravenclaw Prefect were found with a mirror next to them. Hermione had just realised the monster was a Basilisk. I bet you anything she warned the first person she met to look round corners with a mirror first! And that girl pulled out her mirror – and –'

Ron's jaw had dropped.

'And Mrs Norris?' he whispered eagerly.

Harry thought hard, picturing the scene on the night of Hallowe'en.

'The water …' he said slowly, 'the flood from Moaning Myrtle's bathroom. I bet you Mrs Norris only saw the reflection …'

He scanned the page in his hand eagerly. The more he looked at it, the more it made sense.

'The Basilisk flees only from the crowing of the rooster, which is fatal to

it!' he read aloud. 'Hagrid's roosters were killed! The heir of Slytherin didn't want one anywhere near the castle once the Chamber was opened! *Spiders flee before the Basilisk!* It all fits!'

'But how's the Basilisk been getting around the place?' said Ron. 'A dirty great snake … Someone would've seen …'

Harry, however, pointed at the word Hermione had scribbled at the foot of the page.

'Pipes,' he said. 'Pipes … Ron, it's been using the plumbing. I've been hearing that voice inside the walls …'

Ron suddenly grabbed Harry's arm.

'The entrance to the Chamber of Secrets!' he said hoarsely. 'What if it's a bathroom? What if it's in –'

'*– Moaning Myrtle's bathroom,*' said Harry.

They sat there, excitement coursing through them, hardly able to believe it.

'This means,' said Harry, 'I can't be the only Parselmouth in the school. The heir of Slytherin's one, too. That's how they've been controlling the Basilisk.'

'What're we going to do?' said Ron, whose eyes were flashing. 'Shall we go straight to McGonagall?'

'Let's go to the staff room,' said Harry, jumping up. 'She'll be there in ten minutes, it's nearly break.'

They ran downstairs. Not wanting to be discovered hanging around in another corridor, they went straight into the deserted staff room. It was a large, panelled room full of dark wooden chairs. Harry and Ron paced around it, too excited to sit down.

But the bell to signal break never came.

Instead, echoing through the corridors came Professor McGonagall's voice, magically magnified.

'All students to return to their house dormitories at once. All teachers return to the staff room. Immediately, please.'

Harry wheeled around to stare at Ron.

'Not another attack? Not now?'

'What'll we do?' said Ron, aghast. 'Go back to the dormitory?'

'No,' said Harry, glancing around. There was an ugly sort of wardrobe to his left, full of the teachers' cloaks. 'In here. Let's hear what it's all about. Then we can tell them what we've found out.'

They hid themselves inside it, listening to the rumbling of hundreds of people moving overhead, and the staff-room door banging open. From between the musty folds of the cloaks, they watched the teachers filtering into the room. Some of them were looking puzzled, others downright scared. Then Professor McGonagall arrived.

'It has happened,' she told the silent staff room. 'A student has been taken by the monster. Right into the Chamber itself.'

Professor Flitwick let out a squeal. Professor Sprout clapped her hands over her mouth. Snape gripped the back of a chair very hard and said, 'How can you be sure?'

'The heir of Slytherin,' said Professor McGonagall, who was very white, 'left another message. Right underneath the first one. *Her skeleton will lie in the Chamber for ever.*'

Professor Flitwick burst into tears.

'Who is it?' said Madam Hooch, who had sunk, weak-kneed into a chair. 'Which student?'

'Ginny Weasley,' said Professor McGonagall.

Harry felt Ron slide silently down onto the wardrobe floor beside him.

'We shall have to send all the students home tomorrow,' said Professor McGonagall. 'This is the end of Hogwarts. Dumbledore always said …'

The staff-room door banged open again. For one wild moment, Harry was sure it would be Dumbledore. But it was Lockhart, and he was beaming.

'So sorry – dozed off – what have I missed?'

He didn't seem to notice that the other teachers were looking at him with something remarkably like hatred. Snape stepped forward.

'Just the man,' he said. 'The very man. A girl has been snatched by the monster, Lockhart. Taken into the Chamber of Secrets itself. Your moment has come at last.'

Lockhart blanched.

'That's right, Gilderoy,' chipped in Professor Sprout. 'Weren't you saying just last night that you've known all along where the entrance to the Chamber of Secrets is?'

'I – well, I –' spluttered Lockhart.

'Yes, didn't you tell me you were sure you knew what was inside it?' piped up Professor Flitwick.

'D-did I? I don't recall …'

'I certainly remember you saying you were sorry you hadn't had a crack at the monster before Hagrid was arrested,' said Snape. 'Didn't you say that the whole affair had been bungled, and that you should have been given a free rein from the first?'

Lockhart stared around at his stony-faced colleagues.

'I … I really never … You may have misunderstood …'

'We'll leave it to you, then, Gilderoy,' said Professor McGonagall. 'Tonight will be an excellent time to do it. We'll make sure everyone's out of your way. You'll be able to tackle the monster all by yourself. A free rein at last.'

Lockhart gazed desperately around him, but nobody came to the rescue. He didn't look remotely handsome any more. His lip was trembling, and in the absence of his usually toothy grin he looked weak-chinned and weedy.

'V-very well,' he said. 'I'll – I'll be in my office, getting – getting ready.'

And he left the room.

'Right,' said Professor McGonagall, whose nostrils were flared, 'that's got *him* out from under our feet. The Heads of Houses should go and inform their students what has happened. Tell them the Hogwarts Express will take them home first thing tomorrow. Will the rest of you please make sure no students have been left outside their dormitories.'

The teachers rose, and left one by one.

It was probably the worst day of Harry's entire life. He, Ron, Fred and George sat together in a corner of the Gryffindor common room, unable to say anything to each other. Percy wasn't there. He had gone to send an owl to Mr and Mrs Weasley, then shut himself up in his dormitory.

No afternoon ever lasted as long as that one, nor had Gryffindor Tower ever been so crowded, yet so quiet. Near sunset, Fred and George went up to bed, unable to sit there any longer.

'She knew something, Harry,' said Ron, speaking for the first time since they had entered the wardrobe in the staff room. 'That's why she was taken. It wasn't some stupid thing about Percy at all. She'd found out something about the Chamber of Secrets. That must be why she was –' Ron rubbed his eyes frantically. 'I mean, she was a pure-blood. There can't be any other reason.'

Harry could see the sun sinking, blood red, below the skyline. This was the worst he had ever felt. If only there was something they could do. Anything.

'Harry,' said Ron, 'd'you think there's any chance at all she's not – you know –'

Harry didn't know what to say. He couldn't see how Ginny could still be alive.

'D'you know what?' said Ron, 'I think we should go and see Lockhart. Tell him what we know. He's going to try and get into the Chamber. We can tell him where we think it is, and tell him it's a Basilisk in there.'

Because Harry couldn't think of anything else to do, and because he wanted to be doing something, he agreed. The Gryffindors around them were so miserable, and felt so sorry for the Weasleys, that nobody tried to stop them as they got up, crossed the room, and left through the portrait hole.

Darkness was falling as they walked down to Lockhart's office. There seemed to be a lot of activity going on inside it.

They could hear scraping, thumps and hurried footsteps.

Harry knocked and there was a sudden silence from inside. Then the door opened the tiniest crack and they saw one of Lockhart's eyes peering through it.

'Oh … Mr Potter … Mr Weasley …' he said, opening the door a mite wider. 'I'm rather busy at the moment. If you would be quick …'

'Professor, we've got some information for you,' said Harry. 'We think it'll help you.'

'Er – well – it's not terribly –' The side of Lockhart's face that they could see looked very uncomfortable. 'I mean – well – all right.'

He opened the door and they entered.

His office had been almost completely stripped. Two large trunks stood open on the floor. Robes, jade green, lilac, midnight blue, had been hastily folded into one of them; books were jumbled untidily into the other. The photographs that had covered the walls were now crammed into boxes on the desk.

'Are you going somewhere?' said Harry.

'Er, well, yes,' said Lockhart, ripping a life-size poster of himself from the back of the door as he spoke, and starting to roll it up. 'Urgent call … unavoidable … got to go …'

'What about my sister?' said Ron jerkily.

'Well, as to that – most unfortunate,' said Lockhart, avoiding their eyes as he wrenched open a drawer and started emptying the contents into a bag. 'No one regrets more than I –'

'You're the Defence Against the Dark Arts teacher!' said

Harry. 'You can't go now! Not with all the dark stuff going on here!'

'Well, I must say … when I took the job …' Lockhart muttered, now piling socks on top of his robes, 'nothing in the job description … didn't expect …'

'You mean you're *running away*?' said Harry disbelievingly. 'After all that stuff you did in your books?'

'Books can be misleading,' said Lockhart delicately.

'You wrote them!' Harry shouted.

'My dear boy,' said Lockhart, straightening up and frowning at Harry. 'Do use your common sense. My books wouldn't have sold half as well if people didn't think *I'd* done all those things. No one wants to read about some ugly old Armenian warlock, even if he did save a village from werewolves. He'd look dreadful on the front cover. No dress sense at all. And the witch who banished the Bandon Banshee had a hairy chin. I mean, come on …'

'So you've just been taking credit for what a load of other people have done?' said Harry incredulously.

'Harry, Harry,' said Lockhart, shaking his head impatiently, 'it's not nearly as simple as that. There was work involved. I had to track these people down. Ask them exactly how they managed to do what they did. Then I had to put a Memory Charm on them so they wouldn't remember doing it. If there's one thing I pride myself on, it's my Memory Charms. No, it's been a lot of work, Harry. It's not all book-signings and publicity photos, you know. You want fame, you have to be prepared for a long hard slog.'

He banged the lids of his trunks shut and locked them.

'Let's see,' he said. 'I think that's everything. Yes. Only one thing left.'

He pulled out his wand and turned to them.

'Awfully sorry, boys, but I'll have to put a Memory Charm on you now. Can't have you blabbing my secrets all over the place. I'd never sell another book ...'

Harry reached his wand just in time. Lockhart had barely raised his, when Harry bellowed, *'Expelliarmus!'*

Lockhart was blasted backwards, falling over his trunk. His wand flew high into the air; Ron caught it, and flung it out of the open window.

'Shouldn't have let Professor Snape teach us that one,' said Harry furiously, kicking Lockhart's trunk aside. Lockhart was looking up at him, weedy once more. Harry was still pointing his wand at him.

'What d'you want me to do?' said Lockhart weakly. 'I don't know where the Chamber of Secrets is. There's nothing I can do.'

'You're in luck,' said Harry, forcing Lockhart to his feet at wandpoint. 'We think *we* know where it is. *And* what's inside it. Let's go.'

They marched Lockhart out of his office and down the nearest stairs, along the dark corridor where the messages shone on the wall, to the door of Moaning Myrtle's bathroom.

They sent Lockhart in first. Harry was pleased to see that he was shaking.

Moaning Myrtle was sitting on the cistern of the end toilet.

'Oh, it's you,' she said, when she saw Harry. 'What do you want this time?'

'To ask you how you died,' said Harry.

Myrtle's whole aspect changed at once. She looked as though she had never been asked such a flattering question.

'Ooooh, it was dreadful,' she said with relish. 'It happened right in here. I died in this very cubicle. I remember it so well. I'd hidden because Olive Hornby was teasing me about my glasses. The door was locked, and I was crying, and then I heard somebody come in. They said something funny. A different language, I think it must have been. Anyway, what really got me was that it was a *boy* speaking. So I unlocked the door, to tell him to go and use his own toilet, and then –' Myrtle swelled importantly, her face shining, 'I *died*.'

'How?' said Harry.

'No idea,' said Myrtle in hushed tones. 'I just remember seeing a pair of great big yellow eyes. My whole body sort of seized up, and then I was floating away …' She looked dreamily at Harry. 'And then I came back again. I was determined to haunt Olive Hornby, you see. Oh, she was sorry she'd ever laughed at my glasses.'

'Where exactly did you see the eyes?' said Harry.

'Somewhere there,' said Myrtle, pointing vaguely towards the sink in front of her toilet.

Harry and Ron hurried over to it. Lockhart was standing well back, a look of utter terror on his face.

It looked like an ordinary sink. They examined every inch of it, inside and out, including the pipes below. And then

Harry saw it: scratched on the side of one of the copper taps was a tiny snake.

'That tap's never worked,' said Myrtle brightly, as he tried to turn it.

'Harry,' said Ron, 'say something. Something in Parseltongue.'

'But –' Harry thought hard. The only times he'd ever managed to speak Parseltongue were when he'd been faced with a real snake. He stared hard at the tiny engraving, trying to imagine it was real.

'Open up,' he said.

He looked at Ron, who shook his head.

'English,' he said.

Harry looked back at the snake, willing himself to believe it was alive. If he moved his head, the candlelight made it look as though it was moving.

'Open up,' he said.

Except that the words weren't what he heard; a strange hissing had escaped him, and at once the tap glowed with a brilliant white light and began to spin. Next second, the sink began to move. The sink, in fact, sank, right out of sight, leaving a large pipe exposed, a pipe wide enough for a man to slide into.

Harry heard Ron gasp and looked up again. He had made up his mind what he was going to do.

'I'm going down there,' he said.

He couldn't not go, not now they had found the entrance to the Chamber, not if there was even the faintest, slimmest, wildest chance that Ginny might be alive.

'Me too,' said Ron.

There was a pause.

'Well, you hardly seem to need me,' said Lockhart, with a shadow of his old smile. 'I'll just –'

He put his hand on the door knob, but Ron and Harry both pointed their wands at him.

'You can go first,' Ron snarled.

White-faced and wandless, Lockhart approached the opening.

'Boys,' he said, his voice feeble, 'boys, what good will it do?'

Harry jabbed him in the back with his wand. Lockhart slid his legs into the pipe.

'I really don't think –' he started to say, but Ron gave him a push, and he slid out of sight. Harry followed quickly. He lowered himself slowly into the pipe, then let go.

It was like rushing down an endless, slimy, dark slide. He could see more pipes branching off in all directions, but none as large as theirs, which twisted and turned, sloping steeply downwards, and he knew that he was falling deeper below the school than even the dungeons. Behind him he could hear Ron, thudding slightly at the curves.

And then, just as he had begun to worry about what would happen when he hit the ground, the pipe levelled out, and he shot out of the end with a wet thud, landing on the damp floor of a dark stone tunnel, large enough to stand in. Lockhart was getting to his feet a little way away, covered in slime and white as a ghost. Harry stood aside as Ron came whizzing out of the pipe, too.

'We must be miles under the school,' said Harry, his voice echoing in the black tunnel.

'Under the lake, probably,' said Ron, squinting around at the dark, slimy walls.

All three of them turned to stare into the darkness ahead.

'Lumos!' Harry muttered to his wand and it lit again. 'C'mon,' he said to Ron and Lockhart, and off they went, their footsteps slapping loudly on the wet floor.

The tunnel was so dark that they could only see a little distance ahead. Their shadows on the wet walls looked monstrous in the wandlight.

'Remember,' Harry said quietly, as they walked cautiously forward, 'any sign of movement, close your eyes straight away …'

But the tunnel was quiet as the grave, and the first unexpected sound they heard was a loud *crunch* as Ron stepped on what turned out to be a rat's skull. Harry lowered his wand to look at the floor and saw that it was littered with small animal bones. Trying very hard not to imagine what Ginny might look like if they found her, Harry led the way forward, round a dark bend in the tunnel.

'Harry, there's something up there …' said Ron hoarsely, grabbing Harry's shoulder.

They froze, watching. Harry could just see the outline of something huge and curved, lying right across the tunnel. It wasn't moving.

'Maybe it's asleep,' he breathed, glancing back at the other two. Lockhart's hands were pressed over his eyes. Harry turned back to look at the thing, his heart beating so fast it hurt.

Very slowly, his eyes as narrow as he could make them and still see, Harry edged forward, his wand held high.

The light slid over a gigantic snake skin, of a vivid, poisonous green, lying curled and empty across the tunnel floor. The creature that had shed it must have been twenty feet long at least.

'Blimey,' said Ron weakly.

There was a sudden movement behind them. Gilderoy Lockhart's knees had given way.

'Get up,' said Ron sharply, pointing his wand at Lockhart.

Lockhart got to his feet – then he dived at Ron, knocking him to the ground.

Harry jumped forward, but too late. Lockhart was straightening up, panting, Ron's wand in his hand and a gleaming smile back on his face.

'The adventure ends here, boys!' he said. 'I shall take a bit of this skin back up to the school, tell them I was too late to save the girl, and that you two *tragically* lost your minds at the sight of her mangled body. Say goodbye to your memories!'

He raised Ron's Spellotaped wand high over his head and yelled, *'Obliviate!'*

The wand exploded with the force of a small bomb. Harry flung his arms over his head and ran, slipping over the coils of snake skin, out of the way of great chunks of tunnel ceiling which were thundering to the floor. Next moment, he was standing alone, gazing at a solid wall of broken rock.

'Ron!' he shouted. 'Are you OK? Ron!'

'I'm here!' came Ron's muffled voice from behind the rockfall. 'I'm OK. This git's not, though – he got blasted by the wand.'

There was a dull thud and a loud 'ow!'. It sounded as though Ron had just kicked Lockhart in the shins.

'What now?' Ron's voice said, sounding desperate. 'We can't get through. It'll take ages …'

Harry looked up at the tunnel ceiling. Huge cracks had appeared in it. He had never tried to break apart anything as large as these rocks by magic, and now didn't seem a good moment to try – what if the whole tunnel caved in?

There was another thud and another 'ow!' from behind the rocks. They were wasting time. Ginny had already been in the Chamber of Secrets for hours. Harry knew there was only one thing to do.

'Wait there,' he called to Ron. 'Wait with Lockhart. I'll go on. If I'm not back in an hour …'

There was a very pregnant pause.

'I'll try and shift some of this rock,' said Ron, who seemed to be trying to keep his voice steady. 'So you can – can get back through. And, Harry –'

'See you in a bit,' said Harry, trying to inject some confidence into his shaking voice.

And he set off alone past the giant snake skin.

Soon the distant noise of Ron straining to shift the rocks was gone. The tunnel turned and turned again. Every nerve in

Harry's body was tingling unpleasantly. He wanted the tunnel to end, yet dreaded what he'd find when it did. And then, at last, as he crept around yet another bend, he saw a solid wall ahead on which two entwined serpents were carved, their eyes set with great, glinting emeralds.

Harry approached, his throat very dry. There was no need to pretend these stone snakes were real, their eyes looked strangely alive.

He could guess what he had to do. He cleared his throat, and the emerald eyes seemed to flicker.

'*Open,*' said Harry, in a low, faint hiss.

The serpents parted as the wall cracked open, the halves slid smoothly out of sight, and Harry, shaking from head to foot, walked inside.

CHAPTER SEVENTEEN

The Heir of Slytherin

He was standing at the end of a very long, dimly lit chamber. Towering stone pillars entwined with more carved serpents rose to support a ceiling lost in darkness, casting long black shadows through the odd, greenish gloom that filled the place.

His heart beating very fast, Harry stood listening to the chill silence. Could the Basilisk be lurking in a shadowy corner, behind a pillar? And where was Ginny?

He pulled out his wand and moved forward between the serpentine columns. Every careful footstep echoed loudly off the shadowy walls. He kept his eyes narrowed, ready to clamp them shut at the smallest sign of movement. The hollow eye sockets of the stone snakes seemed to be following him. More than once, with a jolt of the stomach, he thought he saw one stir.

Then, as he drew level with the last pair of pillars, a statue high as the Chamber itself loomed into view, standing against the back wall.

Harry had to crane his neck to look up into the giant face above: it was ancient and monkey-like, with a long thin beard that fell almost to the bottom of the wizard's sweeping stone robes, where two enormous grey feet stood on the smooth chamber floor. And between the feet, face down, lay a small, black-robed figure with flaming red hair.

'Ginny!' Harry muttered, sprinting to her and dropping to his knees. 'Ginny! Don't be dead! Please don't be dead!' He flung his wand aside, grabbed Ginny's shoulders and turned her over. Her face was white as marble, and as cold, yet her eyes were closed, so she wasn't Petrified. But then she must be …

'Ginny, please wake up,' Harry muttered desperately, shaking her. Ginny's head lolled hopelessly from side to side.

'She won't wake,' said a soft voice.

Harry jumped and spun around on his knees.

A tall, black-haired boy was leaning against the nearest pillar, watching. He was strangely blurred around the edges, as though Harry was looking at him through a misted window. But there was no mistaking him.

'Tom – *Tom Riddle?*'

Riddle nodded, not taking his eyes off Harry's face.

'What d'you mean, she won't wake?' Harry said desperately. 'She's not – she's not –?'

'She's still alive,' said Riddle. 'But only just.'

Harry stared at him. Tom Riddle had been at Hogwarts fifty years ago, yet here he stood, a weird, misty light shining about him, not a day older than sixteen.

'Are you a ghost?' Harry said uncertainly.

'A memory,' said Riddle quietly. 'Preserved in a diary for fifty years.'

He pointed towards the floor near the statue's giant toes. Lying open there was the little black diary Harry had found in Moaning Myrtle's bathroom. For a second, Harry wondered how it had got there – but there were more pressing matters to deal with.

'You've got to help me, Tom,' Harry said, raising Ginny's head again. 'We've got to get her out of here. There's a Basilisk ... I don't know where it is, but it could be along any moment. Please, help me ...'

Riddle didn't move. Harry, sweating, managed to hoist Ginny half off the floor, and bent to pick up his wand again.

But his wand had gone.

'Did you see –?'

He looked up. Riddle was still watching him – twirling Harry's wand between his long fingers.

'Thanks,' said Harry, stretching out his hand for it.

A smile curled the corners of Riddle's mouth. He continued to stare at Harry, twirling the wand idly.

'Listen,' said Harry urgently, his knees sagging with Ginny's dead weight, *'we've got to go!* If the Basilisk comes ...'

'It won't come until it is called,' said Riddle calmly.

Harry lowered Ginny back onto the floor, unable to hold her up any longer.

'What d'you mean?' he said. 'Look, give me my wand, I might need it.'

Riddle's smile broadened.

'You won't be needing it,' he said.

Harry stared at him.

'What d'you mean, I won't be –?'

'I've waited a long time for this, Harry Potter,' said Riddle. 'For the chance to see you. To speak to you.'

'Look,' said Harry, losing patience, 'I don't think you get it. We're in the *Chamber of Secrets*. We can talk later.'

'We're going to talk now,' said Riddle, still smiling broadly, and he pocketed Harry's wand.

Harry stared at him. There was something very funny going on here.

'How did Ginny get like this?' he asked slowly.

'Well, that's an interesting question,' said Riddle pleasantly. 'And quite a long story. I suppose the real reason Ginny Weasley's like this is because she opened her heart and spilled all her secrets to an invisible stranger.'

'What are you talking about?' said Harry.

'The diary,' said Riddle. '*My* diary. Little Ginny's been writing in it for months and months, telling me all her pitiful worries and woes: how her brothers *tease* her, how she had to come to school with second-hand robes and books, how –' Riddle's eyes glinted '– how she didn't think famous, good, great Harry Potter would *ever* like her …'

All the time he spoke, Riddle's eyes never left Harry's face. There was an almost hungry look in them.

'It's very *boring*, having to listen to the silly little troubles of an eleven-year-old girl,' he went on. 'But I was patient. I wrote back, I was sympathetic, I was kind. Ginny simply *loved* me. *No one's ever understood me like you, Tom … I'm so glad I've got this diary to confide in … It's like having a friend I can carry round in my pocket …*'

Riddle laughed, a high, cold laugh that didn't suit him. It made the hairs stand up on the back of Harry's neck.

'If I say it myself, Harry, I've always been able to charm the people I needed. So Ginny poured out her soul to me, and her soul happened to be exactly what I wanted. I grew stronger and stronger on a diet of her deepest fears, her darkest secrets. I grew powerful, far more powerful than little Miss Weasley. Powerful enough to start feeding Miss Weasley a few of *my* secrets, to start pouring a little of *my* soul back into *her* …'

'What d'you mean?' said Harry, whose mouth had gone very dry.

'Haven't you guessed yet, Harry Potter?' said Riddle softly. 'Ginny Weasley opened the Chamber of Secrets. She strangled the school roosters and daubed threatening messages on the walls. She set the serpent of Slytherin on four Mudbloods, and the Squib's cat.'

'No,' Harry whispered.

'Yes,' said Riddle, calmly. 'Of course, she didn't *know* what she was doing at first. It was very amusing. I wish you could have seen her new diary entries … Far more interesting, they became … *Dear Tom,*' he recited, watching Harry's horrified face, '*I think I'm losing my memory. There are rooster feathers all over my robes and I don't know how they got there. Dear Tom, I can't remember what I did on the night of Hallowe'en, but a cat was attacked and I've got paint all down my front. Dear Tom, Percy keeps telling me I'm pale and I'm not myself. I think he suspects me … There was another attack today and I don't know where I was. Tom, what am I going to do? I think I'm going mad … I think I'm the one attacking everyone, Tom!'*

Harry's fists were clenched, the nails digging deep into his palms.

'It took a very long time for stupid little Ginny to stop trusting her diary,' said Riddle. 'But she finally became suspicious and tried to dispose of it. And that's where *you* came in, Harry. You found it, and I couldn't have been more delighted. Of all the people who could have picked it up, it was *you*, the very person I was most anxious to meet …'

'And why did you want to meet me?' said Harry. Anger was coursing through him and it was an effort to keep his voice steady.

'Well, you see, Ginny told me all about you, Harry,' said Riddle. 'Your whole *fascinating* history.' His eyes roved over the lightning scar on Harry's forehead, and his expression grew hungrier. 'I knew I must find out more about you, talk to you, meet you if I could. So I decided to show you my famous capture of that great oaf, Hagrid, to gain your trust.'

'Hagrid's my friend,' said Harry, his voice now shaking. 'And you framed him, didn't you? I thought you made a mistake, but –'

Riddle laughed his high laugh again.

'It was my word against Hagrid's, Harry. Well, you can imagine how it looked to old Armando Dippet. On the one hand, Tom Riddle, poor but brilliant, parentless but so *brave*, school Prefect, model student; on the other hand, big, blundering Hagrid, in trouble every other week, trying to raise werewolf cubs under his bed, sneaking off to the Forbidden Forest to wrestle trolls. But I admit, even *I* was surprised how well the plan worked. I thought *someone* must realise that Hagrid couldn't possibly be the heir of Slytherin. It had taken *me* five whole years to find out everything I could about the Chamber of Secrets and discover the secret entrance … as though Hagrid had the brains, or the power!

'Only the Transfiguration teacher, Dumbledore, seemed to think Hagrid was innocent. He persuaded Dippet to keep Hagrid and train him as gamekeeper. Yes, I think Dumbledore might have guessed. Dumbledore never seemed to like me as much as the other teachers did …'

'I bet Dumbledore saw right through you,' said Harry, his teeth gritted.

'Well, he certainly kept an annoyingly close watch on me after Hagrid was expelled,' said Riddle carelessly. 'I knew it wouldn't be safe to open the Chamber again while I was still at school. But I wasn't going to waste those long years I'd spent searching for it. I decided to leave behind a diary, preserving my sixteen-year-old self in its pages, so that one day, with luck, I would be able to lead another in my footsteps, and finish Salazar Slytherin's noble work.'

'Well, you haven't finished it,' said Harry triumphantly. 'No one's died this time, not even the cat. In a few hours the Mandrake Draught will be ready and everyone who was Petrified will be all right again.'

'Haven't I already told you,' said Riddle quietly, 'that killing Mudbloods doesn't matter to me any more? For many months now, my new target has been – *you.*'

Harry stared at him.

'Imagine how angry I was when the next time my diary was opened, it was Ginny who was writing to me, not you. She saw you with the diary, you see, and panicked. What if you found out how to work it, and I repeated all her secrets to you? What if, even worse, I told you who'd been strangling roosters? So the foolish little brat waited until your dormitory was deserted and stole it back. But I knew what I must do. It was clear to me that you were on the trail of Slytherin's heir. From everything Ginny had told me about you, I knew you would go to any lengths to solve the mystery – particularly if one of your best friends was attacked. And Ginny had told me the whole school was buzzing because you could speak Parseltongue …

'So I made Ginny write her own farewell on the wall and come down here to wait. She struggled and cried and became *very* boring. But there isn't much life left in her: she put too much into the diary, into me. Enough to let me leave its pages at last. I have been waiting for you to appear since we arrived here. I knew you'd come. I have many questions for you, Harry Potter.'

'Like what?' Harry spat, fists still clenched.

'Well,' said Riddle, smiling pleasantly, 'how is it that a baby with no extraordinary magical talent managed to defeat the greatest wizard of all time? How did *you* escape with nothing but a scar, while Lord Voldemort's powers were destroyed?'

There was an odd red gleam in his hungry eyes now.

'Why do you care how I escaped?' said Harry slowly. 'Voldemort was after your time.'

'Voldemort,' said Riddle softly, 'is my past, present and future, Harry Potter …'

He pulled Harry's wand from his pocket and began to trace it through the air, writing three shimmering words:

TOM MARVOLO RIDDLE

Then he waved the wand once, and the letters of his name rearranged themselves:

I AM LORD VOLDEMORT

'You see?' he whispered. 'It was a name I was already using at Hogwarts, to my most intimate friends only, of course. You think I was going to use my filthy Muggle father's name for ever? I, in whose veins runs the blood of Salazar Slytherin himself, through my mother's side? I, keep the name of a foul, common Muggle, who abandoned me even before I was born, just because he found out his wife was a witch? No, Harry. I fashioned myself a new name, a name I knew wizards everywhere would one day fear to speak, when I had become the greatest sorcerer in the world!'

Harry's brain seemed to have jammed. He stared numbly at Riddle, at the orphaned boy who had grown up to murder Harry's own parents, and so many others … At last he forced himself to speak.

'You're not,' he said, his quiet voice full of hatred.

'Not what?' snapped Riddle.

'Not the greatest sorcerer in the world,' said Harry, breathing fast. 'Sorry to disappoint you, and all that, but the greatest wizard in the world is Albus Dumbledore. Everyone says so. Even when you were strong, you didn't dare try and take over at Hogwarts. Dumbledore saw through you when you were at school and he still frightens you now, wherever you're hiding these days.'

The smile had gone from Riddle's face, to be replaced by a very ugly look.

'Dumbledore's been driven out of this castle by the mere *memory* of me!' he hissed.

'He's not as gone as you might think!' Harry retorted. He was speaking at random, wanting to scare Riddle, wishing rather than believing it to be true.

Riddle opened his mouth, but froze.

Music was coming from somewhere. Riddle whirled around to stare down the empty chamber. The music was growing louder. It was eerie, spine-tingling, unearthly; it lifted the hair on Harry's scalp and made his heart feel as though it was swelling to twice its normal size. Then, as the music reached such a pitch that Harry felt it vibrating inside his own ribs, flames erupted at the top of the nearest pillar.

A crimson bird the size of a swan had appeared, piping its weird music to the vaulted ceiling. It had a glittering golden tail as long as a peacock's and gleaming golden talons, which were gripping a ragged bundle.

A second later, the bird was flying straight at Harry. It dropped the ragged thing it was carrying at his feet, then landed heavily on his shoulder. As it folded its great wings, Harry looked up and saw it had a long, sharp golden beak and beady black eyes.

The bird stopped singing. It sat still and warm next to Harry's cheek, gazing steadily at Riddle.

'That's a phoenix ...' said Riddle, staring shrewdly back at it.

'Fawkes?' Harry breathed, and he felt the bird's golden claws squeeze his shoulder gently.

'And *that* –' said Riddle, now eyeing the ragged thing that Fawkes had dropped, 'that's the old school Sorting Hat.'

So it was. Patched, frayed and dirty, the Hat lay motionless at Harry's feet.

Riddle began to laugh again. He laughed so hard that the dark chamber rang with it, as though ten Riddles were laughing at once.

'This is what Dumbledore sends his defender! A songbird and an old hat! Do you feel brave, Harry Potter? Do you feel safe now?'

Harry didn't answer. He might not see what use Fawkes or the Sorting Hat were, but he was no longer alone, and he waited with mounting courage for Riddle to stop laughing.

'To business, Harry,' said Riddle, still smiling broadly. 'Twice – in *your* past, in *my* future – we have met. And twice I failed to kill you. *How did you survive?* Tell me everything. The longer you talk,' he added softly, 'the longer you stay alive.'

Harry was thinking fast, weighing his chances. Riddle had the wand. He, Harry, had Fawkes and the Sorting Hat, neither of which would be much good in a duel. It looked bad, all right. But the longer Riddle stood there, the more life was dwindling out of Ginny … and in the meantime, Harry noticed suddenly, Riddle's outline was becoming clearer, more solid. If it had to be a fight between him and Riddle, better sooner than later.

'No one knows why you lost your powers when you attacked me,' said Harry abruptly. 'I don't know myself. But I know why you couldn't *kill* me. Because my mother died to save me. My common *Muggle-born* mother,' he added, shaking with suppressed rage. 'She stopped you killing me. And I've seen the real you, I saw you last year. You're a wreck. You're barely alive. That's where all your power got you. You're in hiding. You're ugly, you're foul!'

Riddle's face contorted. Then he forced it into an awful smile.

'So. Your mother died to save you. Yes, that's a powerful counter-charm. I can see now – there is nothing special about you, after all. I wondered, you see. Because there are strange likenesses between us, Harry Potter. Even you must have noticed. Both half-bloods, orphans, raised by Muggles. Probably the only two Parselmouths to come to Hogwarts since the great Slytherin himself. We even *look* something alike … But after all, it was merely a lucky chance that saved you from me. That's all I wanted to know.'

Harry stood, tense, waiting for Riddle to raise his wand. But Riddle's twisted smile was widening again.

'Now, Harry, I'm going to teach you a little lesson. Let's match the powers of Lord Voldemort, heir of Salazar Slytherin, against famous Harry Potter, and the best weapons Dumbledore can give him.'

He cast an amused eye over Fawkes and the Sorting Hat, then walked away. Harry, fear spreading up his numb legs, watched Riddle stop between the high pillars and look up into the stone face of Slytherin, high above him in the half-darkness. Riddle opened his mouth wide and hissed – but Harry understood what he was saying.

'Speak to me, Slytherin, greatest of the Hogwarts Four.'

Harry wheeled around to look up at the statue, Fawkes swaying on his shoulder.

Slytherin's gigantic stone face was moving. Horror-struck, Harry saw his mouth opening, wider and wider, to make a huge black hole.

And something was stirring inside the statue's mouth. Something was slithering up from its depths.

Harry backed away until he hit the dark Chamber wall, and as he shut his eyes tight he felt Fawkes's wing sweep his cheek as he took flight. Harry wanted to shout, 'Don't leave me!' but what chance did a phoenix have against the king of serpents?

Something huge hit the stone floor of the chamber, Harry felt it shudder. He knew what was happening, he could sense it, could almost see the giant serpent uncoiling itself from Slytherin's mouth. Then he heard Riddle's hissing voice: *'Kill him.'*

The Basilisk was moving towards Harry, he could hear its heavy body slithering ponderously across the dusty floor. Eyes still tightly shut, Harry began to run blindly sideways, his hands outstretched, feeling his way. Riddle was laughing …

Harry tripped. He fell hard onto the stone and tasted blood. The serpent was barely feet from him, he could hear it coming.

There was a loud, explosive spitting sound right above him and then something heavy hit Harry so hard that he was smashed against the wall. Waiting for fangs to sink through his body he heard more mad hissing, something thrashing wildly off the pillars.

He couldn't help it. He opened his eyes wide enough to squint at what was going on.

The enormous serpent, bright, poisonous green, thick as an oak trunk, had raised itself high in the air and its great blunt head was weaving drunkenly between the pillars. As Harry trembled, ready to close his eyes if it turned, he saw what had distracted the snake.

Fawkes was soaring around its head, and the Basilisk was snapping furiously at him with fangs long and thin as sabres.

Fawkes dived. His long golden beak sank out of sight and a sudden shower of dark blood spattered the floor. The snake's tail thrashed, narrowly missing Harry, and before Harry could shut his eyes, it turned. Harry looked straight into its face, and saw that its eyes, both its great bulbous yellow eyes, had been punctured by the phoenix; blood was streaming to the floor and the snake was spitting in agony.

'No!' Harry heard Riddle screaming. *'Leave the bird! Leave the bird! The boy is behind you! You can still smell him! Kill him!'*

The blinded serpent swayed, confused, still deadly. Fawkes was circling its head, piping his eerie song, jabbing here and there at the Basilisk's scaly nose as the blood poured from its ruined eyes.

'Help me, help me,' Harry muttered wildly, 'someone, anyone!'

The snake's tail whipped across the floor again. Harry ducked. Something soft hit his face.

The Basilisk had swept the Sorting Hat into Harry's arms. Harry seized it. It was all he had left, his only chance. He rammed it onto his head and threw himself flat onto the floor as the Basilisk's tail swung over him again.

'Help me … help me …' Harry thought, his eyes screwed tight under the Hat. *'Please help me!'*

There was no answering voice. Instead, the Hat contracted, as though an invisible hand was squeezing it very tightly.

Something very hard and heavy thudded onto the top of Harry's head, almost knocking him out. Stars winking in front of his eyes, he grabbed the top of the Hat to pull it off and felt something long and hard beneath it.

A gleaming silver sword had appeared inside the Hat, its handle glittering with rubies the size of eggs.

'Kill the boy! Leave the bird! The boy is behind you! Sniff – smell him!'

Harry was on his feet, ready. The Basilisk's head was falling, its body coiling around, hitting pillars as it twisted to face him. He could see the vast, bloody eye sockets, see the mouth stretching wide, wide enough to swallow him whole, lined with fangs long as his sword, thin, glittering, venomous …

It lunged blindly. Harry dodged and it hit the Chamber wall. It lunged again, and its forked tongue lashed Harry's side. He raised the sword in both his hands.

The Basilisk lunged again, and this time its aim was true. Harry threw his whole weight behind the sword and drove it to the hilt into the roof of the serpent's mouth.

But as warm blood drenched Harry's arms, he felt a searing pain just above his elbow. One long, poisonous fang was sinking deeper and deeper into his arm and it splintered as the Basilisk keeled over sideways and fell, twitching, to the floor.

Harry slid down the wall. He gripped the fang that was spreading poison through his body and wrenched it out of his arm. But he knew it was too late. White-hot pain was spreading slowly and steadily from the wound. Even as he dropped the fang and watched his own blood soaking his robes, his vision went foggy. The Chamber was dissolving in a whirl of dull colour.

A patch of scarlet swam past and Harry heard a soft clatter of claws beside him.

'Fawkes,' said Harry thickly. 'You were brilliant, Fawkes …' He felt the bird lay its beautiful head on the spot where the serpent's fang had pierced him.

He could hear echoing footsteps and then a dark shadow moved in front of him.

'You're dead, Harry Potter,' said Riddle's voice above him. 'Dead. Even Dumbledore's bird knows it. Do you see what he's doing, Potter? He's crying.'

Harry blinked. Fawkes's head slid in and out of focus. Thick, pearly tears were trickling down the glossy feathers.

'I'm going to sit here and watch you die, Harry Potter. Take your time. I'm in no hurry.'

Harry felt drowsy. Everything around him seemed to be spinning.

'So ends the famous Harry Potter,' said Riddle's distant voice. 'Alone in the Chamber of Secrets, forsaken by his friends, defeated at last by the Dark Lord he so unwisely challenged. You'll be back with your dear Mudblood mother soon, Harry … She bought you twelve years of borrowed time … but Lord Voldemort got you in the end, as you knew he must.'

'If this is dying,' thought Harry, 'it's not so bad.' Even the pain was leaving him …

But was this dying? Instead of going black, the Chamber seemed to be coming back into focus. Harry gave his head a little shake and there was Fawkes, still resting his head on Harry's arm. A pearly patch of tears was shining all around the wound – except that there *was* no wound.

'Get away, bird,' said Riddle's voice suddenly. 'Get away from him. I said, *get away*!'

Harry raised his head. Riddle was pointing Harry's wand at Fawkes; there was a bang like a gun and Fawkes took flight again in a whirl of gold and scarlet.

'Phoenix tears …' said Riddle quietly, staring at Harry's arm. 'Of course … healing powers … I forgot …'

He looked into Harry's face. 'But it makes no difference. In fact, I prefer it this way. Just you and me, Harry Potter … you and me …'

He raised the wand.

Then, in a rush of wings, Fawkes soared back overhead and something fell into Harry's lap – *the diary*.

For a split second, both Harry and Riddle, wand still raised, stared at it. Then, without thinking, without considering, as though he had meant to do it all along, Harry seized the Basilisk fang on the floor next to him and plunged it straight into the heart of the book.

There was a long, dreadful, piercing scream. Ink spurted out of the diary in torrents, streaming over Harry's hands, flooding the floor. Riddle was writhing and twisting, screaming and flailing and then …

He had gone. Harry's wand fell to the floor with a clatter and there was silence. Silence except for the steady *drip drip* of ink still oozing from the diary. The Basilisk venom had burned a sizzling hole right through it.

Shaking all over, Harry pulled himself up. His head was spinning as though he'd just travelled miles by Floo powder. Slowly, he gathered together his wand and the Sorting Hat, and, with a huge tug, retrieved the glittering sword from the roof of the Basilisk's mouth.

Then came a faint moan from the end of the Chamber. Ginny was stirring. As Harry hurried towards her, she sat up.

Her bemused eyes travelled from the huge form of the dead Basilisk, over Harry, in his blood-soaked robes, then to the diary in his hand. She drew a great, shuddering gasp and tears began to pour down her face.

'Harry – oh, Harry – I tried to tell you at b-breakfast, but I c-*couldn't* say it in front of Percy. It was *me*, Harry – but I – I s-swear I d-didn't mean to – R-Riddle made me, he t-took me over – and – *how* did you kill that – that thing? W-where's Riddle? The last thing I r-remember is him coming out of the diary –'

'It's all right,' said Harry, holding up the diary, and showing Ginny the fang hole, 'Riddle's finished. Look! Him *and* the Basilisk. C'mon, Ginny, let's get out of here –'

'I'm going to be expelled!' Ginny wept, as Harry helped her awkwardly to her feet. 'I've looked forward to coming to Hogwarts ever since B-Bill came and n-now I'll have to leave and – *w-what'll Mum and Dad say?*'

Fawkes was waiting for them, hovering in the Chamber entrance. Harry urged Ginny forward; they stepped over the motionless coils of the dead Basilisk, through the echoing gloom and back into the tunnel. Harry heard the stone doors close behind them with a soft hiss.

After a few minutes' progress up the dark tunnel, a distant sound of slowly shifting rock reached Harry's ears.

'Ron!' Harry yelled, speeding up. 'Ginny's OK! I've got her!'

He heard Ron give a strangled cheer and they turned the next bend to see his eager face staring through the sizeable gap he had managed to make in the rock fall.

'*Ginny!*' Ron thrust an arm through the gap in the rock to pull her through first. 'You're alive! I don't believe it! What happened?'

He tried to hug her but Ginny held him off, sobbing.

'But you're OK, Ginny,' said Ron, beaming at her. 'It's over now, it's – where did that bird come from?'

Fawkes had swooped through the gap after Ginny.

'He's Dumbledore's,' said Harry, squeezing through himself.

'And how come you've got a *sword*?' said Ron, gaping at the glittering weapon in Harry's hand.

'I'll explain when we get out of here,' said Harry, with a sideways glance at Ginny.

'But –'

'Later,' Harry said quickly. He didn't think it was a good idea to tell Ron yet who'd been opening the Chamber, not in front of Ginny, anyway. 'Where's Lockhart?'

'Back there,' said Ron, grinning and jerking his head up the tunnel towards the pipe. 'He's in a bad way. Come and see.'

Led by Fawkes, whose wide scarlet wings emitted a soft golden glow in the darkness, they walked all the way back to the mouth of the pipe. Gilderoy Lockhart was sitting there, humming placidly to himself.

'His memory's gone,' said Ron. 'The Memory Charm backfired. Hit him instead of us. Hasn't got a clue who he is, or where he is, or who we are. I told him to come and wait here. He's a danger to himself.'

Lockhart peered good-naturedly up at them all.

'Hello,' he said. 'Odd sort of place, this, isn't it? Do you live here?'

'No,' said Ron, raising his eyebrows at Harry.

Harry bent down and looked up the long, dark pipe.

'Have you thought how we're going to get back up this?' he said to Ron.

Ron shook his head, but Fawkes the phoenix had swooped past Harry and was now fluttering in front of him, his beady eyes bright in the dark. He was waving his long golden tail feathers. Harry looked uncertainly at him.

'He looks like he wants you to grab hold ...' said Ron, looking perplexed. 'But you're much too heavy for a bird to pull up there.'

'Fawkes,' said Harry, 'isn't an ordinary bird.' He turned quickly to the others. 'We've got to hold on to each other. Ginny, grab Ron's hand. Professor Lockhart –'

'He means you,' said Ron sharply to Lockhart.

'You hold Ginny's other hand.'

Harry tucked the sword and the Sorting Hat into his belt, Ron took hold of the back of Harry's robes, and Harry reached out and took hold of Fawkes's strangely hot tail feathers.

An extraordinary lightness seemed to spread through his whole body, and next second, with a whoosh, they were flying upwards through the pipe. Harry could hear Lockhart dangling below him, saying, 'Amazing! Amazing! This is just like magic!' The chill air was whipping through Harry's hair, and before he'd stopped enjoying the ride, it was over – all four of them were hitting the wet floor of Moaning Myrtle's bathroom, and as Lockhart straightened his hat, the sink that hid the pipe was sliding back into place.

Myrtle goggled at them.

'You're alive,' she said blankly to Harry.

'There's no need to sound so disappointed,' he said grimly, wiping flecks of blood and slime off his glasses.

'Oh, well … I'd just been thinking. If you had died, you'd have been welcome to share my toilet,' said Myrtle, blushing silver.

'Urgh!' said Ron, as they left the bathroom for the dark, deserted corridor outside. 'Harry! I think Myrtle's got *fond* of you! You've got competition, Ginny!'

But tears were still flooding silently down Ginny's face.

'Where now?' said Ron, with an anxious look at Ginny. Harry pointed.

Fawkes was leading the way, glowing gold along the corridor. They strode after him, and moments later, found themselves outside Professor McGonagall's office.

Harry knocked and pushed the door open.

CHAPTER EIGHTEEN

Dobby's Reward

For a moment, there was silence as Harry, Ron, Ginny and Lockhart stood in the doorway, covered in muck and slime and (in Harry's case) blood. Then there was a scream.

'Ginny!'

It was Mrs Weasley, who had been sitting crying in front of the fire. She leapt to her feet, closely followed by Mr Weasley, and both of them flung themselves on their daughter.

Harry, however, was looking past them. Professor Dumbledore was standing by the mantelpiece, beaming, next to Professor McGonagall, who was taking great, steadying gasps, clutching her chest. Fawkes went whooshing past Harry's ear and settled on Dumbledore's shoulder, just as Harry found himself and Ron being swept into Mrs Weasley's tight embrace.

'You saved her! You saved her! *How* did you do it?'

'I think we'd all like to know that,' said Professor McGonagall weakly.

Mrs Weasley let go of Harry, who hesitated for a moment, then walked over to the desk and laid upon it the Sorting Hat, the ruby-encrusted sword and what remained of Riddle's diary.

Then he started telling them everything. For nearly a quarter of an hour he spoke into the rapt silence: he told them about hearing the disembodied voice, how Hermione had finally realised that he was hearing a Basilisk in the pipes; how he and Ron had followed the spiders into the Forest, that Aragog had told them where the last victim of the Basilisk had died; how he had guessed that Moaning Myrtle had been the victim, and that the entrance to the Chamber of Secrets might be in her bathroom …

'Very well,' Professor McGonagall prompted him, as he paused, 'so you found out where the entrance was – breaking a hundred school rules into pieces along the way, I might add – but how on *earth* did you all get out of there alive, Potter?'

So Harry, his voice now growing hoarse from all this talking, told them about Fawkes's timely arrival and about the Sorting Hat giving him the sword. But then he faltered. He had so far avoided mentioning Riddle's diary – or Ginny. She was standing with her head against Mrs Weasley's shoulder, and tears were still coursing silently down her cheeks. What if they expelled her? Harry thought in panic. Riddle's diary didn't work any more … How could they prove it had been he who'd made her do it all?

Instinctively, Harry looked at Dumbledore, who smiled faintly, the firelight glancing off his half-moon spectacles.

'What interests *me* most,' said Dumbledore gently, 'is how Lord Voldemort managed to enchant Ginny, when my sources tell me he is currently in hiding in the forests of Albania.'

Relief – warm, sweeping, glorious relief – swept over Harry.

'W-what's that?' said Mr Weasley in a stunned voice. '*You-Know-Who*? En-enchant *Ginny*? But Ginny's not … Ginny hasn't been … has she?'

'It was this diary,' said Harry quickly, picking it up and showing it to Dumbledore. 'Riddle wrote it when he was sixteen.'

Dumbledore took the diary from Harry and peered keenly down his long, crooked nose at its burnt and soggy pages.

'Brilliant,' he said softly. 'Of course, he was probably the most brilliant student Hogwarts has ever seen.' He turned around to the Weasleys, who were looking utterly bewildered.

'Very few people know that Lord Voldemort was once called Tom Riddle. I taught him myself, fifty years ago, at Hogwarts. He disappeared after leaving the school … travelled far and wide … sank so deeply into the Dark Arts, consorted with the very worst of our kind, underwent so many dangerous, magical transformations, that when he resurfaced as Lord Voldemort, he was barely recognisable. Hardly anyone connected Lord Voldemort with the clever, handsome boy who was once Head Boy here.'

'But Ginny,' said Mrs Weasley, 'what's our Ginny got to do with – with – *him*?'

'His d-diary!' Ginny sobbed. 'I've b-been writing in it, and he's been wr-writing back all year –'

'*Ginny!*' said Mr Weasley, flabbergasted. 'Haven't I taught you *anything*? What have I always told you? Never trust anything that can think for itself *if you can't see where it keeps its brain*. Why didn't you show the diary to me, or your mother? A suspicious object like that, it was *clearly* full of Dark Magic!'

'I d-didn't know,' sobbed Ginny. 'I found it inside one of the books Mum got me. I th-thought someone had just left it in there and forgotten about it ...'

'Miss Weasley should go up to the hospital wing straight away,' Dumbledore interrupted in a firm voice. 'This has been a terrible ordeal for her. There will be no punishment. Older and wiser wizards than she have been hoodwinked by Lord Voldemort.' He strode over to the door and opened it. 'Bed rest and perhaps a large, steaming mug of hot chocolate. I always find that cheers me up,' he added, twinkling kindly down at her. 'You will find that Madam Pomfrey is still awake. She's just giving out Mandrake juice – I dare say the Basilisk's victims will be waking up any moment.'

'So Hermione's OK!' said Ron brightly.

'There has been no lasting harm done,' said Dumbledore.

Mrs Weasley led Ginny out, and Mr Weasley followed, still looking deeply shaken.

'You know, Minerva,' Professor Dumbledore said thoughtfully to Professor McGonagall, 'I think all this merits a good *feast*. Might I ask you to go and alert the kitchens?'

'Right,' said Professor McGonagall crisply, also moving to the door. 'I'll leave you to deal with Potter and Weasley, shall I?'

'Certainly,' said Dumbledore.

She left, and Harry and Ron gazed uncertainly at Dumbledore. What exactly had Professor McGonagall meant, *deal* with them? Surely – *surely* – they weren't about to be punished?

'I seem to remember telling you both that I would have to expel you if you broke any more school rules,' said Dumbledore.

Ron opened his mouth in horror.

'Which goes to show that the best of us must sometimes eat our words,' Dumbledore went on, smiling. 'You will both receive Special Awards for Services to the School and – let me see – yes, I think two hundred points apiece for Gryffindor.'

Ron went as brightly pink as Lockhart's Valentine flowers and closed his mouth again.

'But one of us seems to be keeping mightily quiet about his part in this dangerous adventure,' Dumbledore added. 'Why so modest, Gilderoy?'

Harry gave a start. He had completely forgotten about Lockhart. He turned and saw that Lockhart was standing in a corner of the room, still wearing his vague smile. When Dumbledore addressed him, Lockhart looked over his shoulder to see who he was talking to.

'Professor Dumbledore,' Ron said quickly, 'there was an accident down in the Chamber of Secrets. Professor Lockhart –'

'Am I a Professor?' said Lockhart in mild surprise. 'Goodness. I expect I was hopeless, was I?'

'He tried to do a Memory Charm and the wand backfired,' Ron explained quietly to Dumbledore.

'Dear me,' said Dumbledore, shaking his head, his long silver moustache quivering. 'Impaled upon your own sword, Gilderoy!'

'Sword?' said Lockhart dimly. 'Haven't got a sword. That boy has, though.' He pointed at Harry. 'He'll lend you one.'

'Would you mind taking Professor Lockhart up to the hospital wing, too?' Dumbledore said to Ron. 'I'd like a few more words with Harry …'

Lockhart ambled out. Ron cast a curious look back at Dumbledore and Harry as he closed the door.

Dumbledore crossed to one of the chairs by the fire.

'Sit down, Harry,' he said, and Harry sat, feeling unaccountably nervous.

'First of all, Harry, I want to thank you,' said Dumbledore, eyes twinkling again. 'You must have shown me real loyalty down in the Chamber. Nothing but that could have called Fawkes to you.'

He stroked the phoenix, which had fluttered down onto his knee. Harry grinned awkwardly as Dumbledore watched him.

'And so you met Tom Riddle,' said Dumbledore thoughtfully. 'I imagine he was *most* interested in you …'

Suddenly, something that was nagging at Harry came tumbling out of his mouth.

'Professor Dumbledore … Riddle said I'm like him. Strange likenesses, he said …'

'*Did* he, now?' said Dumbledore, looking thoughtfully under his thick silver eyebrows at Harry. 'And what do you think, Harry?'

'I don't think I'm like him!' said Harry, more loudly than he'd intended. 'I mean, I'm – I'm in *Gryffindor*, I'm ...'

But he fell silent, a lurking doubt resurfacing in his mind.

'Professor,' he started again after a moment, 'the Sorting Hat told me I'd – I'd have done well in Slytherin. Everyone thought I was Slytherin's heir for a while ... because I can speak Parseltongue ...'

'You can speak Parseltongue, Harry,' said Dumbledore calmly, 'because Lord Voldemort – who is the last remaining descendant of Salazar Slytherin – can speak Parseltongue. Unless I'm much mistaken, he transferred some of his own powers to you the night he gave you that scar. Not something he intended to do, I'm sure ...'

'Voldemort put a bit of himself in *me*?' Harry said, thunderstruck.

'It certainly seems so.'

'So I *should* be in Slytherin,' Harry said, looking desperately into Dumbledore's face. 'The Sorting Hat could see Slytherin's power in me, and it –'

'Put you in Gryffindor,' said Dumbledore calmly. 'Listen to me, Harry. You happen to have many qualities Salazar Slytherin prized in his hand-picked students. His own very rare gift, Parseltongue ... resourcefulness ... determination ... a certain disregard for rules,' he added, his moustache quivering again. 'Yet the Sorting Hat placed you in Gryffindor. You know why that was. Think.'

'It only put me in Gryffindor,' said Harry in a defeated voice, 'because I asked not to go in Slytherin ...'

'Exactly,' said Dumbledore, beaming once more. 'Which makes you very *different* from Tom Riddle. It is our choices, Harry, that show what we truly are, far more than our abilities.' Harry sat motionless in his chair, stunned. 'If you want proof, Harry, that you belong in Gryffindor, I suggest you look more closely at *this*.'

Dumbledore reached across to Professor McGonagall's desk, picked up the blood-stained silver sword and handed it to Harry. Dully, Harry turned it over, the rubies blazing in the firelight. And then he saw the name engraved just below the hilt.

GODRIC GRYFFINDOR

'Only a true Gryffindor could have pulled that out of the Hat, Harry,' said Dumbledore simply.

For a minute, neither of them spoke. Then Dumbledore pulled open one of the drawers in Professor McGonagall's desk, and took out a quill and a bottle of ink.

'What you need, Harry, is some food and sleep. I suggest you go down to the feast, while I write to Azkaban – we need our gamekeeper back. And I must draft an advertisement for the *Daily Prophet*, too,' he added thoughtfully. 'We'll be needing a new Defence Against the Dark Arts teacher. Dear me, we do seem to run through them, don't we?'

Harry got up and crossed to the door. He had just reached for the handle, however, when the door burst open so violently that it bounced back off the wall.

Lucius Malfoy stood there, fury in his face. And cowering under his arm, heavily wrapped in bandages, was *Dobby*.

'Good evening, Lucius,' said Dumbledore pleasantly.

Mr Malfoy almost knocked Harry over as he swept into the room. Dobby went scurrying in after him, crouching at the hem of his cloak, a look of abject terror on his face.

'So!' said Lucius Malfoy, his cold eyes fixed on Dumbledore. 'You've come back. The governors suspended you, but you still saw fit to return to Hogwarts.'

'Well, you see, Lucius,' said Dumbledore, smiling serenely, 'the other eleven governors contacted me today. It was something like being caught in a hailstorm of owls, to tell the truth. They'd heard that Arthur Weasley's daughter had been killed and wanted me back here at once. They seemed to think I was the best man for the job after all. Very strange tales they told me, too. Several of them seemed to think that you had threatened to curse their families if they didn't agree to suspend me in the first place.'

Mr Malfoy went even paler than usual, but his eyes were still slits of fury.

'So – have you stopped the attacks yet?' he sneered. 'Have you caught the culprit?'

'We have,' said Dumbledore, with a smile.

'*Well?*' said Mr Malfoy sharply. 'Who is it?'

'The same person as last time, Lucius,' said Dumbledore. 'But this time, Lord Voldemort was acting through somebody else. By means of this diary.'

He held up the small black book with the large hole through the centre, watching Mr Malfoy closely. Harry, however, was watching Dobby.

The elf was doing something very odd. His great eyes fixed meaningfully on Harry, he kept pointing at the diary, then at Mr Malfoy, and then hitting himself hard on the head with his fist.

'I see …' said Mr Malfoy slowly to Dumbledore.

'A clever plan,' said Dumbledore in a level voice, still staring Mr Malfoy straight in the eye. 'Because if Harry here –' Mr Malfoy shot Harry a swift, sharp look, 'and his friend Ron hadn't discovered this book, why – Ginny Weasley might have taken all the blame. No one would ever have been able to prove she hadn't acted of her own free will …'

Mr Malfoy said nothing. His face was suddenly mask-like.

'And imagine,' Dumbledore went on, 'what might have happened then … The Weasleys are one of our most prominent pure-blood families. Imagine the effect on Arthur Weasley and his Muggle Protection Act, if his own daughter was discovered attacking and killing Muggle-borns. Very fortunate the diary was discovered, and Riddle's memories wiped from it. Who knows what the consequences might have been otherwise …'

Mr Malfoy forced himself to speak.

'Very fortunate,' he said stiffly.

And still, behind his back, Dobby was pointing, first to the diary, then to Lucius Malfoy, then punching himself in the head.

And Harry suddenly understood. He nodded at Dobby, and Dobby backed into a corner, now twisting his ears in punishment.

'Don't you want to know how Ginny got hold of that diary, Mr Malfoy?' said Harry.

Lucius Malfoy rounded on him.

'How should I know how the stupid little girl got hold of it?' he said.

'Because you gave it to her,' said Harry. 'In Flourish and Blotts. You picked up her old Transfiguration book, and slipped the diary inside it, didn't you?'

He saw Mr Malfoy's white hands clench and unclench.

'Prove it,' he hissed.

'Oh, no one will be able to do that,' said Dumbledore, smiling at Harry. 'Not now Riddle has vanished from the book. On the other hand, I would advise you, Lucius, not to go giving out any more of Lord Voldemort's old school things. If any more of them find their way into innocent hands, I think Arthur Weasley, for one, will make sure they are traced back to you ...'

Lucius Malfoy stood for a moment, and Harry distinctly saw his right hand twitch as though he was longing to reach for his wand. Instead, he turned to his house-elf.

'We're going, Dobby!'

He wrenched open the door, and as the elf came hurrying up to him, he kicked him right through it. They could hear Dobby squealing with pain all the way along the corridor. Harry stood for a moment, thinking hard. Then it came to him.

'Professor Dumbledore,' he said hurriedly, 'can I give that diary *back* to Mr Malfoy, please?'

'Certainly, Harry,' said Dumbledore calmly. 'But hurry. The feast, remember.'

Harry grabbed the diary and dashed out of the office. He could hear Dobby's squeals of pain receding around the corner. Quickly, wondering if this plan could possibly work, Harry took off one of his shoes, pulled off his slimy, filthy sock, and stuffed the diary into it. Then he ran down the dark corridor.

He caught up with them at the top of the stairs.

'Mr Malfoy,' he gasped, skidding to a halt, 'I've got something for you.'

And he forced the smelly sock into Lucius Malfoy's hand.

'What the –?'

Mr Malfoy ripped the sock off the diary, threw it aside, then looked furiously from the ruined book to Harry.

'You'll meet the same sticky end as your parents one of these days, Harry Potter,' he said softly. 'They were meddlesome fools, too.'

He turned to go.

'Come, Dobby. I said, *Come*!'

But Dobby didn't move. He was holding up Harry's disgusting, slimy sock, and looking at it as though it were a priceless treasure.

'Master has given Dobby a sock,' said the elf in wonderment. 'Master gave it to Dobby.'

'What's that?' spat Mr Malfoy. 'What did you say?'

'Dobby has got a sock,' said Dobby in disbelief. 'Master threw it, and Dobby caught it, and Dobby – Dobby is *free*.'

Lucius Malfoy stood frozen, staring at the elf. Then he lunged at Harry.

'You've lost me my servant, boy!'

But Dobby shouted, 'You shall not harm Harry Potter!'

There was a loud bang, and Mr Malfoy was thrown backwards. He crashed down the stairs, three at a time, landing in a crumpled heap on the landing below. He got up, his face livid, and pulled out his wand, but Dobby raised a long threatening finger.

'You shall go now,' he said fiercely, pointing down at Mr Malfoy. 'You shall not touch Harry Potter. You shall go now.'

Lucius Malfoy had no choice. With a last, incensed stare at the pair of them, he swung his cloak around him and hurried out of sight.

'Harry Potter freed Dobby!' said the elf shrilly, gazing up at Harry, moonlight from the nearest window reflected in his orb-like eyes. 'Harry Potter set Dobby free!'

'Least I could do, Dobby,' said Harry, grinning. 'Just promise never to try and save my life again.'

The elf's ugly brown face split suddenly into a wide, toothy smile.

'I've just got one question, Dobby,' said Harry, as Dobby pulled on Harry's sock with shaking hands. 'You told me all this had nothing to do with He Who Must Not Be Named, remember? Well –'

'It was a clue, sir,' said Dobby, his eyes widening, as though this was obvious. 'Dobby was giving you a clue. The Dark Lord, before he changed his name, could be freely named, you see?'

'Right,' said Harry weakly. 'Well, I'd better go. There's a feast, and my friend Hermione should be awake by now ...'

Dobby threw his arms around Harry's middle and hugged him.

'Harry Potter is greater by far than Dobby knew!' he sobbed. 'Farewell, Harry Potter!'

And with a final loud crack, Dobby disappeared.

Harry had been to several Hogwarts feasts, but never one quite like this. Everybody was in their pyjamas, and the celebrations lasted all night. Harry didn't know whether the best bit was Hermione running towards him, screaming, 'You solved it! You solved it!' or Justin hurrying over from the Hufflepuff table to wring his hand and apologise endlessly for suspecting him, or Hagrid turning up at half past three, cuffing Harry and Ron so hard on the shoulders that they were knocked into their plates of trifle, or his and Ron's four hundred points securing Gryffindor the House Cup for the second year running, or Professor McGonagall standing up to tell them all that the exams had been cancelled as a school treat ('Oh, *no*!' said Hermione), or Dumbledore announcing that, unfortunately, Professor Lockhart would be unable to return next year, owing to the fact that he needed to go away and get his memory back. Quite a few of the teachers joined in the cheering that greeted this news.

'Shame,' said Ron, helping himself to a jam doughnut. 'He was starting to grow on me.'

The rest of the summer term passed in a haze of blazing sunshine. Hogwarts was back to normal, with only a few, small differences: Defence Against the Dark Arts classes were cancelled ('but we've had plenty of practice at that anyway,' Ron told a disgruntled Hermione) and Lucius Malfoy had been sacked as a school governor. Draco was no longer strutting around the school as though he owned the place. On the contrary, he looked resentful and sulky. On the other hand, Ginny Weasley was perfectly happy again.

Too soon, it was time for the journey home on the Hogwarts Express. Harry, Ron, Hermione, Fred, George and Ginny got a compartment to themselves. They made the most of the last few hours in which they were allowed to do magic before the holidays. They played Exploding Snap, set off the very last of Fred and George's Filibuster Fireworks, and practised disarming each other by magic. Harry was getting very good at it.

They were almost at King's Cross when Harry remembered something.

'Ginny – what did you see Percy doing, that he didn't want you to tell anyone?'

'Oh, that,' said Ginny, giggling. 'Well – Percy's got a *girlfriend*.'

Fred dropped a stack of books on George's head.

'What?'

'It's that Ravenclaw Prefect, Penelope Clearwater,' said Ginny. 'That's who he was writing to all last summer. He's been meeting her all over the school in secret. I walked in on them kissing in an empty classroom one day. He was so upset when she was – you know – attacked. You won't tease him, will you?' she added anxiously.

'Wouldn't dream of it,' said Fred, who was looking as if his birthday had come early.

'Definitely not,' said George, sniggering.

The Hogwarts Express slowed and finally stopped.

Harry pulled out his quill and a bit of parchment and turned to Ron and Hermione.

'This is called a telephone number,' he told Ron, scribbling it twice, tearing the parchment in two and handing it to them. 'I told your dad how to use a telephone last summer, he'll know. Call me at the Dursleys, OK? I can't stand another two months with only Dudley to talk to ...'

'Your aunt and uncle will be proud, though, won't they?' said Hermione, as they got off the train and joined the crowd thronging towards the enchanted barrier. 'When they hear what you did this year?'

'Proud?' said Harry. 'Are you mad? All those times I could've died, and I didn't manage it? They'll be furious ...'

And together they walked back through the gateway to the Muggle world.

GRYFFINDOR

THE HOUSE-ELVES OF HOGWARTS

♦ GRYFFINDOR ♦

TOILING AWAY in the kitchens of Hogwarts, keeping the fires burning and whipping up delicious meals and end-of-term feasts for the students, is an army of rarely seen house-elves. Gifted with their own powerful magic that allows them to Apparate and Disapparate in and out of Hogwarts, where wizards are unable, they are also adept at Hover Charms and other enchantments, as Harry finds out when Dobby first appears in Privet Drive and charms Aunt Petunia's cream pudding.

These curious magical beings live lives of servitude, performing for their masters the kind of menial and tedious tasks, such as cleaning and cooking and fetching and carrying, that wizards and Muggles alike often prefer to leave to someone else.

The history of house-elves goes back to the very early years of Hogwarts. Helga Hufflepuff, founder of Hufflepuff house, gave house-elves work and good living conditions in an era where they suffered widespread abuse. This tradition of offering shelter is one that Dumbledore follows, taking in

Dobby, Winky and Kreacher during Harry's time at Hogwarts.

Few modern wizarding families have house-elves. They are most often connected to ancient wizarding families, who have been known to stuff and mount their heads after their deaths. They keep the family's secrets and uphold their honour, and are supposed to use their magic only with their masters' permission. The house-elf's highest law is his or her masters' bidding, and only exceptional house-elves will use their powers behind their masters' backs, as Dobby does.

Kreacher

A wily house-elf may, though, use their masters' orders against them. This was the case for Sirius Black. Having served the Black family loyally for decades, their ancient house-elf Kreacher is disgusted when Gryffindor Sirius returns to Grimmauld Place as master of the house. Kreacher regards Sirius – one of the only Blacks not to have been Sorted into Slytherin – as a traitor and spends his time retrieving Black family heirlooms which Sirius has thrown out, devotedly squirrelling them away in the boiler cupboard where he sleeps. When Sirius shouts the order 'OUT!', intending him to leave the kitchen, Kreacher uses the opportunity to leave the house and visit Narcissa Malfoy, ultimately leading to Sirius's demise.

The treatment of house-elves reveals an underbelly of exploitation and prejudice in the wizarding world. It is no surprise then that Hermione Granger takes up their cause in the year of the Triwizard Tournament, founding S.P.E.W. – the Society for the Promotion of Elfish Welfare. As house-elves can only be freed from their master or mistress if they are presented with clothes, Hermione makes it her mission to liberate them by leaving out woolly hats for them to take. Hermione begins her post-Hogwarts career at the Department for the Regulation and Control of Magical Creatures, where she is instrumental in greatly improving life for house-elves and their ilk.

THE ALUMNI OF HOGWARTS

♦ A QUIZ ♦

MANY GENERATIONS of witches and wizards have spent their formative years at Hogwarts. Some have gone on to illustrious careers at the Ministry of Magic, some have made groundbreaking magical discoveries, and a few have gained great notoriety. Take this quiz to test your knowledge of notable alumni who whiled away happy hours in their houses at Hogwarts completing their Potions assignments, playing wizard chess, and toasting crumpets in their common rooms.

1. **Which three members of Hufflepuff house went on to hold the post of Minister for Magic?**
   a. Grogan Stump, Eglantine Puffett and Janus Thickey
   b. Grogan Stump, Artemisia Lufkin and Dugald McPhail
   c. Grogan Stump, Adalbert Waffling and Vindictus Viridian

2. **Ravenclaw Professor Trelawney is the great-great-granddaughter of a celebrated Seer named:**
   a. Cassandra
   b. Inigo
   c. Araminta

Gryffindor
Common Room

3. The great wizard Merlin was a member of which house?

a. Ravenclaw

b. Gryffindor

c. Slytherin

4. The inventor of Floo powder, Ignatia Wildsmith, belonged to which house?

a. Hufflepuff

b. Ravenclaw

c. Gryffindor

5. Which of Sirius's Slytherin relations proposed a Ministry Bill to make Muggle-hunting legal?

a. Araminta Meliflua Black

b. Elladora Black

c. Phineas Nigellus Black

6. The wizarding village of Hogsmeade frequented by Hogwarts students was founded by which of the following wizards?

a. Gryffindor Sir Nicholas de Mimsy-Porpington

b. Ravenclaw Lorcan McLaird

c. Hufflepuff Hengist of Woodcroft

7. **Alice and Frank Longbottom were tortured to insanity by which notorious members of Slytherin house?**
   a. Mulciber and Avery
   b. Rodolphus and Bellatrix Lestrange
   c. Rosier and Wilkes

8. **Hufflepuff was the house of which famous Arithmancer?**
   a. Bridget Wenlock
   b. Bowman Wright
   c. Gulliver Pokeby

9. **Gryffindor Celestina Warbeck became a popular singing sorceress. Which of these songs was not one of her hits?**
   a. 'You Stole My Cauldron But You Can't Have My Wand'
   b. 'A Cauldron Full of Hot, Strong Love'
   c. 'You Charmed the Heart Right Out of Me'

10. **Upon graduation from Hogwarts, Gryffindor Oliver Wood was signed to the reserve team of which UK Quidditch team?**
    a. Chudley Cannons
    b. Puddlemere United
    c. Wigtown Wanderers

Turn to the final page of this book
to find the correct answers.

GRYFFINDOR HOUSE

♦ SYMBOLS AND INSPIRATION ♦

AWARD-WINNING illustrator Levi Pinfold talked to Bloomsbury about the inspiration behind the Hogwarts house crests.

1. **How did you feel about being asked to draw the Hogwarts house crests?**
   Life was a surreal wonderland for an hour or two, then I realised I had to actually do the work! Harry Potter means a lot to so many people, so it comes with a responsibility.

2. **Where did you take your inspiration from?**
   The crests are based upon the symbolism of medieval heraldry, so there's foliage in there, and animals and weird hands, all sorts of strange symbolism that they used to use back in the Middle Ages.

3. **Which house crest was the most fun to draw?**
   Slytherin – I enjoyed it because I've always wanted to draw a cockatrice and I had never had the opportunity!

4. **Which image was the most difficult to create?**
   Gryffindor. It took about 20 different versions until it looked right.

5. **What Hogwarts house do you think you would be in?**
   Pottermore tells me I'm a Ravenclaw, but deep down I think Hufflepuff is where it's at.

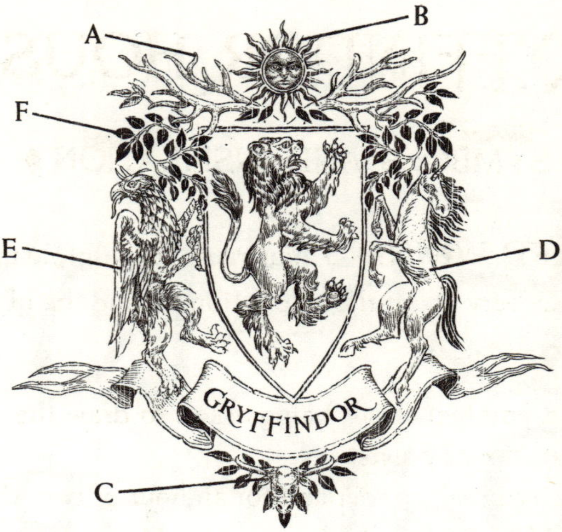

A	Antlers denote strength and fortitude
B	Sun – symbol of glory and splendour
C	Ox head denotes valour
D	Unicorn – symbol of extreme courage, virtue and strength
E	Griffin represents valour, death-defying bravery and vigilance
F	Aspen leaves represent determination and overcoming fears

LEVI PINFOLD has been drawing from imagination for as long as he can remember. His published picture books are *The Django*, *Black Dog* and *Greenling*. *Black Dog* won the prestigious CILIP Kate Greenaway Medal in 2013. Born in the Forest of Dean, he has somehow found himself living in northern NSW, Australia. He likes paintings, books, music, and some cats.

The Alumni of Hogwarts Quiz Answers:

1. b, 2. a, 3. c, 4. b, 5. a, 6. c, 7. b, 8. a, 9. a, 10. b